The Collected Stories of Sean O'Faolain

Volume I

By the same author

Novels

A Nest of Simple Folk
Bird Alone
Come Back to Erin
And Again?

Biography

Constance Markievicz
King of the Beggars
The Great O'Neill
Newman's Way

Autobiography

Vive Moi!

Travel

An Irish Journey
A Summer in Italy
An Autumn in Italy

Miscellaneous

The Short Story
The Vanishing Hero
She Had to Do Something
The Silver Branch
The Irish

The Collected Stories of Sean O'Faolain

Volume I

Constable London

First published in Great Britain 1980
10 Orange Street, London WC2H 7EG

Set in 10 on 12pt Linotype Pilgrim
Printed in Great Britain by The Anchor Press Ltd
and bound by Wm Brendon & Son Ltd
both of Tiptree, Essex

British Library cataloguing in publication data
O'Faolain, Sean
The collected stories of
Sean O'Faolain Vol 1
823'.9'1FS PR6029.F3A15

ISBN 0 09 463920 5

Contents

Midsummer Night Madness

I

For a second I looked back into the city, down through the smoke at the clustered chimney-pots and roofs on whose purples and greens and blues the summer night was falling as gently as dust, falling too on the thousand tiny beacons winking and blinking beneath me to their starry counterparts above. It was just the curfew hour and the last few laggard couples went hurrying past me, their love-making ended abruptly for the night, lest the Tans in their roaring Lancia patrol-cars should find them conspicuous on the empty white streets of the city. Then I turned to the open fields and drew in a long draught of their sweetness, their May-month sweetness, as only a man could who had been cooped up for months past under one of those tiny roofs, seeing the life of men and women only through a peep-hole in a window-blind, seeing these green fields only in the far distance from an attic skylight. Mounting my bicycle I left the last gas-lamp behind, and the pavement end, and rode on happily into the open country.

Yet, though the countryside was very sweet to me after all those months among the backyards, worried and watchful lest I should run into a chance patrol or raiding-party, I kept listening, not to the chorus of the birds, not to the little wind in the bushes by the way, but nervously to every distant, tiny sound – the chuckle of a wakeful goose or hen in a near-by farmyard, or the fall of water coming suddenly within earshot, or some animal starting away from the hedge where I surprised its drowsing heavy head, and once I halted dead, my grip tight on the brakes when a donkey brayed suddenly and loudly as if he were laughing at the intense quietness of the night. Fallen hawthorn blossoms splashed with their lime the dust of the road, and so narrow were the boreens in places that the lilac and the dog-rose, hung with wisps of hay, reached down as if to be plucked, and under the overhanging trees I could smell the pungent smell of the laurel sweating in the damp night-air. And all about me the dead silence of the coming night, unless a little stream trickled over the road and my wheels made a great double splash as they crossed it; then once again the heavy silence, drowsy with the odours of the night-flowers and the cut meadows.

I was on my way to the townlands of Farrane and Kilcrea, to see why to all appearances the local battalion had been completely inactive for the last three or four months. That portion of my task I did not relish for I had known and been friendly with Stevey Long, the commandant, ever since the chances of revolution threw us together. Still I should be free of the open fields for a few days, and there was enough romance left in the revolution for me to be excited at the thought that I was to stay at a house I had known and wondered at since childhood; I might even see and meet, if he were still alive, its strange mad owner whom as children we thought more terrifying than any of the ogres in the fairy-books – Old Henn of Henn Hall.

But I could hardly credit that he was still alive, for even when we were very young my mother always spoke of him as 'that old devil' or 'that old cripple' of a Henn. And an old devil he was, living up there all alone, in what she used to call his 'rooky-rawky' of a house, never married but always in a state of marriage with some woman or other. He began, I could well believe, with women of his own class, officers' wives from the barracks at B——, or Cork, or perhaps with what we used to call 'horsy women' from some neighbouring English hunt. But, judging by his later life, he cannot have been over-particular at any time in his choice of women, and many a tinted London beauty must have walked his fields, looking in utter boredom at the gulls flying after the plough or the rain hanging in the bare trees, until finally, like all her predecessors and successors of many years, she in her turn cursed Henn and his Hall, and Ireland and all belonging to it, and went back gladly to the flickering city-lights and the back streets, and the familiar loved smells of gas-lit theatres and stuffy hansom-cabs. Clearly, a man who lived by the things of the body – women, wine, hunting, fishing, shooting. My mother often told us how as she and a crowd of schoolgirl friends were returning from their first Communion one cold autumn afternoon they entered his fields to take a short way by the river to their homes, removing their new shoes and stockings as they always did when they left the high road, and they came on Henn – and he was a grown man then – standing in his pelt by the river, ready for a swim. She used shudder as she told how he chased them, and they ran from him, screaming with fear, throwing away the new shoes and stockings as they ran, their legs all torn on the withered rushes of the bog and the furzed hedge-tops, not daring to look back to see if the naked 'madman' were catching up with them, until, as she said, they had left his fields 'forty miles behind' and panting and exhausted they ran into their homes. Henn must have been delighted with his frolic, and I can see him, running back for his swim, his long legs and his long neck, that gave him the nickname of 'Henn's Neck,' cutting through the air as he ran. And he must have been especially delighted when in the late evening the fathers and brothers of the children came looking here and there timidly for the little blue or red socks and the black shoes. It was only one of many such escapades that my mother knew, all spreading the name and legend of madness that clung to him through his life. We needed few such warnings to avoid him and his estate, but we used to say to each other, some-body's warning half-understood, that if Henn caught a little girl 'he'd salt her', and we went in mortal terror of him and his salting for years. No wonder we used say that he had wires hidden under his fields and if you crossed even one of his ditches bells would ring up in the Hall and he would come galloping on a white horse with his hungry hounds to salt you.

It was a wonderful old house to look at, and often we looked at it from far off, sitting up on its own high hill, its two gable chim-neys like two cocked ears and all its empty windows gazing wide-eyed down the river-valley – very tall, with a wide door whose steps curled down and around like moustaches. The place was a pale rain-faded pink at the end, but it was often called the Red House, and if it was ever really the *Red* House it must have been visible for miles to anyone driving westward to Crookstown along the valley, following the little river and its dark line of woods. Yet, as I tried to recall it now, only one impression remained, for we came into the city when I was quite young and there I soon forgot the Hall; but at least two or three times afterwards my father took me on an unusually long walk in that direction, and each time when he returned he said to my mother – 'We could just see the Red House up the valley beyond Kilnaglory'. And each time she said

'Glory be to God, I wonder is that old devil Henn alive yet?' and told us all over again how he chased them in his pelt when they were little children. One of these walks was on a soft wintry day with packed clouds threatening to drop rain every minute, and the Lee and the Bride in flood, and the tall bare beeches with the rooks' nests in their tip-tops swayed and swung in the hard wind. The roads were muddy in places and there were many pot-holes full of rain or liquid dung and they were all wrinkled in the breeze and the flooded river ran frothing and brown and storm-blown by the very edge of the road. Off up the sodden valley, high on its rounded hill sat Henn's house, and it was really more red than pink that day because of the rain, and as we looked at it one solitary window showed a light. At the same time the cold, yellow sky behind it was turning to a most marvellous red as of blood, and the scarlet light blackened every leafless twig and already rain-black and rain-green tree-trunk that stood against it and every ditch and scooped riverbank, and lastly the road and the very sky itself became swarthy, and there was light only in the waves curling the river and the potholes of the road. When the solitary window shone my father said, 'That's old Henn,' and I pictured him as an old man with a beard and long claw-hands half into the glowing ashes, so that I said, 'I think, father, it's going to be thunder and lightning,' and he looked back and said 'it might,' and to my joy we turned our backs on Henn and his house and faced for the lights and the crowds and the shop-windows of the city.

Really, I am sure, that was not Henn; he would certainly have been down at the bridge-head with his rods and his basket and his gillie. But when those same winter rains streamed down the curtainless windows now, would he not have to stand watching it, backbent – if indeed he still lived – shivering in the bay, and return to crouch sadly – not so far removed from my childish picture of him – over his perpetual summer-to-summer fire?

You may pity him as I tell you of him, but I, riding along the darkling lanes that night, had nothing in my heart for him but hate. He was one of the class that had battened for too long on our poor people, and I was quite pleased to think that if he lived he lived only in name; that if he had any charm at all left he would need it all now to attract even the coarsest woman. For no London light-o'-love would be attracted to his ruin of a house now for other reasons.

Perhaps he was beyond all that, and if he was not, he would be like Juan in old age, for the farmers' daughters for miles around would shun him as they would the plague, and for such a man as Henn to descend to the women of the passing tinkers for whom alone his house would appear even yet a big house, was out of the question. And yet not even his maids who came from a distance would be in the house a day without hearing all about him from the neighbours. Perhaps, after all, the tinkers would have to suffice? But, thinking of the big Red House, with its terraced lawns, and its cypresses and its yews, and its great five-mile estate wall, all built by the first Henn, the founder not only of his line but of an industry – glass-making, and long since disappeared from Ireland – I could not believe that even such a house would fall so low.

2

As I came to a crossways where my road dropped swiftly downhill the tenting chestnuts filled the lanes with darkness as of pitchy night, and under my wheels the lain dust was soft as velvet. Before I took this last turn on my way I looked back the road I had come and saw upthrown behind the hill that distant glow of the city's lights, a furnace-glow that made me realize how near and how far I was to the roofs and chimneys I had left. But as I looked I saw, too, how the clouds were gathering like pale flowers over the inky sky and even as I dropped silently downhill the first drops beat the fronded layers above. On my left, high as two men, rose the estate walls that had once kept the whole countryside at bay but could not now (gapped and crumbling as they were) keep a fox out or a chicken in. I passed two great entrance-gates sunken in the weeds. Then the pale ghostlike pillars of the third gate came in view across a gap in the tunnel where the rain was beating down the dust, gradually changing its pattering blows for the hissing sound of a real downpour. Head bowed I raced across the unsheltered patch and edged my bicycle through the creaking gate and was just abreast of the little Gothic door of the lodge when it swung open and a woman stepped suddenly through the laurels and caught my arm, saying roughly and passionately as she did so:

'Stevey, why did you go away? Henn was down again tonight. Stevey, I . . .'

Astonished, I made no sound. The rain beat down on us, blotting out stars and moon alike.

'Stevey,' she went on, 'I can't help it. . . .'

Then she saw her mistake, and dropped my hand.

'I'm sorry,' she said. 'I thought . . .'

I laughed to put her at her ease.

'You thought I was Stevey Long.'

She turned and went back to the door and seeing me from there look after her she cried out roughly:

'Go on!'

And because I was slow in moving for all the falling rain, she cried again:

'Go on about your business. Go on!'

'What a rough, passionate creature!' I was saying to myself; only by degrees recovering from my surprise as I began to wheel my bicycle up the avenue, when I heard her steps behind me and felt her grip on my arm once more. She beckoned and drew me back into the shadow of one of the sheltering trees beside the little house and with the only grace she was capable of leant insinuatingly close to me, fingering my lapel, and said in her hollow mannish voice:

'You know Stevey Long?'

'Yes, of course, I do.'

'Are you the boy he was bringing to the Hall to stay?'

'Yes.'

'He told me about you. You know him well, don't you?'

'I know Stevey for a long time.'

'He told me you were in jail with him once.'

'Did he tell you that? I was. Oh yes! Stevey and I had many a bout together.'

She paused. Then in a low trembling voice she said, 'Do you know his girl?'

'His girl?'

'Yes. He told me all about her. He said you know her too. Tell me . . . where is she?'

Her voice was strained against the leash, become passionately intent in spite of her. I did not want to be caught by her country trickery, and I looked into her face by the light of the little window, as one always looks into the face of a person one doubts, from eye to eye searching for the truth. Seeing me hesitate she caught my arm the more fiercely.

'Tell me!'

'Why, I suppose you are Stevey's girl,' I bantered.

'Tell me, boy! She sent him letters to jail, didn't she? Oh, for Christ's sake, go on and tell me!'

She had me by the two arms now, her full bosom almost touching mine, so close to me that I could see the pouches under her eyes, her mouth dragged down wet and sensual, the little angry furrow between her eyebrows. The wind shook the heavy leaves of the chestnuts and as they scattered benediction on us the light from the little Gothic window shone on their wet leaves, and on her bosom and chest and knees. For a second I thought her blue apron drooped over her too rich, too wide hips. But when I would not speak she shook me like a dog and growled at me so fiercely that I could not refuse to reply.

'I don't know,' I said. 'She just sent letters to us, to Stevey of course, and cigarettes and fruit and things – that's all. I don't know!'

She threw me away so that I all but stumbled over my bike.

'I knew it was true,' she moaned. 'I knew it was true when they said it.'

'But anyone might write him a letter. . . .'

'He denied it. He denied he ever got a letter from her.'

In open country it is surprising how the voice sometimes echoes. Under those trees her voice resounded so that I feared she would be heard up at the Hall or down in the village.

'The liar. He's going to marry that wan. That's the wan he wants. The shcut! And look what he's going to do now.'

Her great bosom rose and fell in rage.

'Do?' I asked. 'What is he going to do?'

'Who'd mind Henn? I ought to know. But Stevey. But Stevey, with his grand talk. He said *he'd* never harm me. But I won't marry him. I won't marry him. I won't. I won't!'

And she turned and ran in to the lodge, leaving me with the feeling that this Hall and estate and countryside had an unpleasant, real life of its own, a life that would spoil for me the few days of quietness that I had been dreaming of this last hour as I cycled between the hedgerows. I scarcely noticed that the sudden summer shower had ceased as I made slowly up the mossed drive, dark with unpruned trees and black laurel. Everything here too seeming to send up its sweetness into the soft wet air, even the weeds bursting through the gravel, and when I came to the front of the house the great dark cypresses might in the wet failing light have been plumes of billowy smoke that rose against the sky. I was now on the terrace before the Hall, and as I looked down into the valley to where the sound of the waters of the Bride rose murmuring through the air purified by the shower, I almost expected to see the old libertine come floating up like a spectre or a long-legged ogre through the hills.

I found my way, as I had been instructed to do, to the rear of the house and in by the servants' quarters to the great kitchen. The pale still light of a candle on the table filled the room, and at the foot of the table beneath it was a basin of dusty milk, and before the embers an old sheep-dog yawned and stretched his legs. I sat down by the fire and, glad of the rest, began to try to understand what it was that so troubled the girl at the lodge, with her passionate raging outburst against Stevey, her cry 'I won't marry him, I won't marry him.' But almost on my heels I heard the sound of feet mashing the gravel outside and she came in to the kitchen.

'Put on some turf, boy,' she said at once. 'And blow up the fire.'

As I laid on the brown peat and sat by the side of the machine turning its handle she began to lay the table for my supper. Then we heard somebody else approach outside, and with a sudden shake of her fist to me by way of warning, she opened the door to Stevey. To her he gave a mere 'Hullo, Gypsy.'

To me he gave a cordial, 'Here we are again,' and he shook my hand several times and told me how glad he was to see me safe and sound. Sullenly the girl broke in on us with :

'Put the kettle on, Stevey, for the boy's supper,' and sent me out to the rain-barrel for some water. I rose and went, and as I passed the window, there she was struggling out of his arms like a wild animal. But when I returned she was again by the table, and he was bending down over the fire, swinging the great iron kettle forward on its crane to be filled. I lay back in the old basket chair and watched him move silently about the kitchen, finding everything where he expected to find it, his fair flock of curls all about his neck and brow like a mountainy sheep, his knees flinging apart at every step as they always did, and his hangdog head and his rounded shoulders more slouched than ever.

Since they would not speak to one another I began to ask random questions; the name of this or that townland; whether this or that family were still alive, and they answered civilly enough but would never talk a word to one another.

A nice companionable house I have come to! I was grumbling to myself; and a nice pair of quarrelsome suspicious lovers! And I was wondering if I should really have come to this house at all, or if I was to have any pleasure in my few days of freedom, when suddenly Gypsy broke silence to say that a lorry-load of Tans had gone past two hours ago on the valley road, 'roaring,' she said, 'with the great venom and the drink,' shooting over the thatch of the houses in the village; they had, she even heard, killed a child and gone on without a thought, laughing at the terror of the villagers. At that Stevey burst into a terrible profane rage, but he caught my eye and fell silent. He knew my thought – if he had not been so inactive for the past four months the Tans would not be roaring their way so daringly through his territory now. 'Did anyone come to warn me?' he asked.

'Aye. The girl of the Mullinses.' And she added, 'The boys are wild tonight.'

I wished Stevey would turn to see me sneering at him. I had something to go on already I thought, and I was looking forward to my talk with him, when the girl would leave us to ourselves. But his mind began to wander from the Tans and he began to hum moodily to himself like a man with something gnawing at his brain, until, at last, unable to keep silent any longer he came out with a very casual,

'Was, eh, was Henn down tonight, Gyp?'

I could see her turn towards me as she answered with a brazen 'No.'

Then she said under her breath to him:

'He knows what he'd get if he came.'

At once everything changed. Stevey burst suddenly into a wild roar of song, his old favourite 'Night of Stars and Night of Love,' the barcarolle from *Hoffman* – and he echoed it through the empty house so that even Gypsy gave me a wry smile as she bade me sit up to supper.

'By God, John,' he cried at me, 'we'll give those bastards of Tans something to think about. Won't we, girl?'

And he caught her up whirling her into a corner of the room so that she screamed with sudden delight and in mock fear of his rough hands. Stevey drew a long comical face at his stupidity and she smoothed herself down and said she was all right, and so they sat in a corner of the huge fireplace while I, with my back to them, ate my salted rashers and my country bread and butter.

'Ate up, there, John,' he said; and then I heard them kissing secretly.

'I am tired,' I said.

'That's the man,' said Stevey, and they kissed again and she giggled to herself, and turning I found her tousling his already wild mop because he was making too free of her where she sat on his knee.

'She has great titties, John,' said Stevey coarsely, and she slapped his face for that, and as I went on with my supper I heard him kiss her in return. So they made their love in the dark corner, shamelessly, until I was almost finished and ready for Stevey, and then they rose suddenly and left me, to walk, as they said, down to the village now that it was so fine in the heel of the day. Stevey waved me aside when I wanted to detain him, saying the night was long and tomorrow was good too. So I was alone in the Hall, listening to the corncrake at his last dim rattle in the meadows and the doves fluting long and slow in the deep woods through the fallen dark.

As I lit my pipe and smoked under the shadow of the fireplace I began to feel that I should not have come to this house at all. True it was safe because it was the home of one of the 'garrison' people, one of those thousand unofficial blockhouses of the English on Irish soil, the last place to be suspected of harbouring a rebel. But with Stevey's girl – or rather, knowing him as I did – one of his girls in the same house, this was not a suitable place for the investigator of Stevey's shortcomings. But, as when I came along the road, the quietness and the peace gradually drove all other thoughts out of my head. The city, I thought, would by now be as empty as if it had been deserted, the Lancias booming along the naked streets, their searchlights shooting down the dark lanes and the side alleys, and the funereal tramp-tramp, tramp-tramp of the patrols taking with them from every door they passed its heavy sigh of suspended fear. All this Stevey had escaped. Not for him as for us, for months on end, the sight of a rusted roof in a city back-yard, the stale odour of airless bedrooms. Strange to think that one could work better in that sort of a room than where the walls were deep in lush grass and the springtime rain green-dripping from the trees into the water-butts and the cupped flowers.

The great front door banged, its echoes thundering, and steps clanked in the front hall. Another door opened and was closed again. The night had settled down about the Hall, seeped into the woods, calming the doves, and only the old tireless croaker kept up his ceaseless cry. A door opened again and steps shuffled along the passage and halted; then an old man's voice coughed and called wheedlingly.

'Gypsy?'

I was silent and again the old voice wheedled, now almost at the kitchen door:

'Is he gone, Gypsy? Are you there, my pretty?'

And as I said nothing the shuffling came nearer and the stick-tapping and coughing, and Mad Henn stood peering at me around the candle-flame. I knew him at once by his long collarless neck and his stork's legs and his madman's face beaked and narrow like a hen.

Even here indoors he wore a little faded bowler-hat cocked airily on one side of his head, and over his shoulders and draping his body a rug. He had the face of a bird, mottled and bead-eyed, and his hair, tawny in streaks with the glister of oil, had one lock at the back that stood out like a cock's comb. As he looked at me for a moment he pulled the loose flesh of his throat or scraped with one finger the tawny scum about his lips as if he were trying to remember whether he might not have asked me to come there or had some business with me that he had forgotten. I stood up awkwardly.

'Gypsy is gone for a walk with Stevey, Mister Henn,' I said.

'And who might you be, young man, if I might ask a polite question?' his eyebrows working up and down with irritation and the strain of having to speak.

'I . . . I'm a friend of Mr Long's.'

He sniffed so that a drop fell from his beaked nose.

'Mister Long,' he muttered in scorn. 'So you're another one of 'em are you? Eh? Are you?'

'I don't quite understand,' I said, and mentally cursed Stevey for not having arranged things better than this for me. For the old fellow began to pound with his heel on the floor and his legs and hands twitched for rage so that I expected him every second to turn me out of his house at the point of his stick.

'I suppose, I say,' he piped sardonically again, 'I suppose you're another one of our new patriots? Eh? Eh? I suppose you think you can walk into any man's house and sit on his armchair and drink his liquor, eh? And threaten him if he protests against you for a cad and a bully, eh? You're another of those, are you?'

He held a decanter in his right hand, and it was filled with dancing liquor. I thought it best to humour him.

'I beg your pardon, indeed, Mister Henn,' I said as humbly as I knew how, for I did not want a quarrel with the old devil. 'I'm sorry if I have intruded. But I didn't mean to. I think I have made a mistake – and I'll try if I can find the servant, or . . . find Stevey, that is . . . wherever they are . . . just now'

It was a very undignified speech, but it seemed to strike the old man with astonishment.

'Ho!' he said. 'This is a new one. Quite polite in fact. You're not very long on the road, young man,' he added with an air of bitter experience.

'That's all right,' I said, as I turned sullenly to go.

He halted me as I laid my hand on the door-latch – where I was going to I didn't know.

'Here! It is all right. Your apology is perfectly all right. Don't go, boy. Don't you go.'

At the word 'here' I noticed how tenderly he said his r's – *here*, and *your*, and *perfectly*. It was the last bit of blazonry he preserved, making him off for all his degradation as one of the conquering race.

'Did you call me?' I asked.

'Yes,' he said.

We looked at one another silently; then, in quite another tone, as coolly and politely as if he were speaking across his decanter in a club:

'Will you have a drink?'

I looked at him in surprise.

'Come along. I should like to talk to you. You are the first of your kind that I have met who seems to have any bit of education. I'd like to talk to you for that reason. We'll have a whisky and soda. Will you join me?'

I returned, no doubt a little flattered, but largely because I did not know what else to do; and our feet went clanking on the hall-flags as if the whole house were a vault, and indeed there was everywhere a musty smell of rooms long abandoned or never tended. His drawing-room was just as I expected, a good room but battered and unkempt like a tramp. At the farther end was a great superfluous fire and standing by it he poured me out a jorum of whisky in a glass whose crevices were brown with the encrustations of years, all the time peering at me around the side of a pink-bowled oil-lamp whose crude unshaded light made everything look even more drab and dirty – the bare uncarpeted floor, the fine marble fireplaces mottled and cracked, the china cabinets with broken glass and no china in them; and I remembered the look of the yards with their rusted churns and staveless barrels, and everywhere and on everything the fur of mildew and green damp.

'Here! Drink that,' he said, pouring himself another glass and throwing it off at a gulp, raw.

'That's the way to take your liquor. I suppose you'll empty the siphon in yours, eh? Hum! If you didn't have a revolver stuck in your back pockets what would you young fellows have over us? Oh, you're stronger – but have you more grit? Let me look at you.'

I stood up for the drink, and he peered at me.

'Ah!' he wailed. 'There's only one thing I regret, one thing I've lost and that's clear eyes. The whole year is all like foggy autumn to me. I see the trees and the woods as if they were clouded in mist. It's a great blessing. I go out on a fine evening like this evening and it's like an evening in winter to me when the light fails at four o'clock in the afternoon and every hill is a valley and every tree is twice as far away as it really is.'

His streaming eyes strayed to the caverns of the fire, but the flames shone dully in the milky cataracts of the old fading pink-shot pupils.

'Why are you in this business, tell me?' he asked of a sudden.

'I . . . I believe in it,' I said awkwardly.

He threw up his hand in disgust.

'I believed in things once,' he said. 'I had ideas about the people, the people on my land. I thought I'd get them to do things with their land – I was ready to help them with loans and advice. I'd tell them how to drain it, how to grow more variety of vegetables, and how to make money out of their gardens selling the produce in the city, and how to make better butter and keep their eggs clean . . .'

He sniffed a long sneer at himself and pulled his throat and looked absently into the fire.

'Look at them, today. As dirty as ever, as poor as ever, as backward as ever, and I suppose they blame people like us for it all. If they had my land they'd know how to farm it, they think. But why haven't they done anything with their own? Why? Why?'

He was a hot-tempered old fellow, flying into a temper at a second's warning.

'But you're a city boy, you know nothing of the people. It's people like us who know Ireland. We belong to it – we who've grown up on the land and know it and the people on it.'

'Your people were merchants,' I said rather timidly.

'They made their money on bottles,' he said reaching for the whisky. 'And I've spent their money on bottles,' he added with the air of a man who has often made the same joke and grown serious over it. For as he began to pour the liquor out tremblingly he turned savagely on me.

'And who makes glass in Ireland, now?' he wheezed.

'When we stopped, why didn't somebody else take it up? They could make lovely glass in Ireland at one time. It might have become a great, distinctive national industry, and everywhere you'd see the men blowing the glass into lovely shapes. People would be coming from abroad to see them. I've seen them as a lad. Pouf! And there you had a globe of glass, shining, coloured, glowing. Oh, no, Oh, no! What do we see in the shop-windows, now?' he cried, leaning forward and baring his rotting, easily-moved teeth. 'Cobblers! Yah! A race of cobblers. That's what we are – a race of cobblers! They hadn't it in them. They hadn't it in them!'

I saw for the first time how deep the hate on his side could be, as deep as the hate on ours, as deep and as terrible, and although he angered me there was so much contempt in his face and voice that I could scarcely muster up the courage to meet his eyes. His whisky was rising in my head.

'Oh, that was all begun two centuries ago,' I cried back at him. 'It was the Union with England that ruined us and our industries. Can't you see that? It ruined you. It ruined your glass-business. Aren't you part of Ireland as much as us?'

'Ach! It's always the same. This ruined us, and that ruined us, and the other ruined us. I tell you I'm ashamed to be called an Irishman, and in fact I'm not an Irishman. I'm a colonist – a planter – whatever you like, one of those that tried to come and do something with you people. Why didn't the people fight for their rights when they had a parliament?'

I tried to answer but he wouldn't let me, spilling his liquor all over the hearth in his rage.

'I know what you'll say. But look at the Welsh, and look at the Scotch. They haven't a parliament and they have prospered. What's to stop us from making our linens and our woven silks, from weaving patterns into them like the Indians and the Slavs? Where are our crafts? What can we show? What have we ever done? Except dig patches and plough fields? Why haven't we stuffs, yes, stuffs, stuffs, stuffs, of our own – stuffs (how he spat it out!) that any woman would love to fold around her body, stuffs she'd love to feel against her flesh? Coloured, brilliant, delicate stuffs?'

And he began to rub his little hands down his thighs.

'Oh, fantastic!' I said, and leaned back from him smiling.

'Ah, there's your revolver man talking. But it could be done. Or why don't we export bulbs or cut-flowers like the Dutch and the French and the Channel Islanders?'

'It's impossible – the climate.'

'Pah! It's on our side. The Gulf Stream would do.'

'The Gulf Stream?'

Mad Henn!

'Yes! It warms our southern shores. You can grow acacias in Kerry in the open air in mid-winter. (A rush of delicate r's here.) I've picked London pride on the mountains in early March. Jasmine, lilacs, fuchsias. . . .'

'Fuchsia isn't a cut flower,' I taunted. 'Nor a bulb!'

He twitched in every limb, dashed his glass in the fire and banged the hearth with his stick, and stuttered all the rest he had to say to me.

'It grows, it grows, I tell you it grows wild in mid-winter. In the open air. You're a damned obstinate young fellow. And wallflower, lily of the valley, freesia, gardenia, arbutus, mignonette. And all sorts of delicate ferns. A marvellous but a lost opportunity. These things will bring them in more money than potatoes. But they tread on them. It's so silly, really, because it's just like treading on gold.'

'But the people are farmers.'

'What are the Germans, the Dutch, the Belgians? Ah! (It was a long-drawn-out Ah! of sweet memories.) I know the people. You city fellows don't know them.'

Then his voice fell.

'I know their women,' he said.

He rubbed his little hands again and tapped me on the knee.

'I know every sort of woman: English women, French women, Italians, I've even known a Russian woman. The Russians are like the Irish, you know. But too stubborn and too obstinate and too proud. Prouder even than the Irish. And not one of them all can equal the Irish woman – of the right sort. But they're airy. You have to bind them down with a brutal religion or they'd fly over the fields from you. Don't you feel that too, eh?'

And he cocked his hat even still further over on one ear and laughed a little elfish laugh of delight and his loose lock behind almost curled like a drake's tail. He poked the embers with his stick. He filled my glass in spite of me – delighted like all old bachelors whose club-days and dancing-days are done to have anyone at all who will talk with them.

'Ah! Yes,' he sighed as he poured my whisky, 'the women are all right. So lovely and plump. Muscular from the fields. Arms . . . right! (He moulded them with the bottle in his hand.) Breasts like tulips. Lovely! Lovely! But you don't know. You only know the city. The city! Puh! I wouldn't give that much for a city woman.'

I threw off his whisky neat.

'Why shouldn't I know the country?' I cried. 'By damn but I do. As well as you, better than you. I know their women. Many a mouse I moused with their women. What's more than that, I was born in the country and born right here in this townland. My mother was born and is buried and my grandmother and all her people before her down there in Kilcrea churchyard. I lived in the townland of Farrane myself, as a child and my father lived there before me.'

I thought he shrank into himself at that, pulling down his long neck like a snail or a tortoise at the approach of danger.

'What's your name?' he asked quietly.

I told him.

'I remember your mother well,' he said. 'She held land from me. And I remember your father. He was stationed at Kilcrea. I met him first at an eviction on my land. They shoved a red-hot poker through the door at him and he caught it; and by God he pulled it from them, so he did. A fine man.'

'I remember that,' I said, quiet myself, too, now.

'No, boy, no,' he said sadly. 'That was a long time ago.'

'Oh, but, I do well,' I cried. 'I remember the bandage on his hand.'

'Not at all,' and he smacked the stick on the side of the marble fireplace. 'This was a long time ago. Forty years or more. Forty years or more' – and as he said it his eyes strayed, rheum wet, from me to the fire and back again as if he were trying to see my father in me and those dead years that were gone from him for ever.

'Where is he now?' he asked.

'He's dead,' I said.

'Ah, and is he dead?'

'Yes.'

'And your mother?'

'She is dead,' I answered quietly.

'Ah!'

He looked into the embers and they seemed to glow but faintly on his all but sightless balls – a quietness more than the night fallen on him secretly and unexpectedly. Just then a step resounded on the hall-flags and the door opened and in came the dark, muscular Gypsy, behind her Stevey, slouching as ever. He did not see me at first, and he approached the old man with a low 'Good-night' and I thought the long neck drew into itself again. Henn did not reply, but he raised a feeble hand and took the girl's fingers in his palm. His was as tiny as hers – and the fire shone pink between his bony fingers, ridged with the veins and threaded with the thousand wrinkles of age. As their eyes met the swan's neck curved up to her lovingly.

'Have you had a nice walk, pretty?'

'Yes, down to the bridge at the pub.'

Before him how delicately her lips said, *down*, with a voluptuous upward curve at the corners of her mouth so that they swept into her cheek as the curved initials on his ring swept into the gold. Her sullen eyes were soft and in this light she almost looked beautiful. His hand wandered over her arm as he asked the next question – a question as familiar as Sunday. She smiled as she replied.

'Was there anything rising?' he asked.

'Down be the bridge they're leppin,' she said.

'It's the breeze. There's always a breeze fluting down that side of the valley.'

Stevey laughed loudly at them both, and his voice was rough and coarse beside the rich voice of the girl and the cultured voice of the old man.

'Leppin'? Rise? Rise, how are you! That was me spittin' when she wasn't looking.'

'Oh, then, there was a rise,' she cried. 'I saw their silver bellies shining as they leaped.'

'Ooh!' mocked Stevey. 'Bellies! Naughty word! Ooh!'

Henn gripped his stick until it trembled and his knuckles strained the skin white. He stamped at Stevey.

'If the girl says there was a rise, there was. Aren't you enough of a gentleman not to contradict her?'

But his voice trembled as if he were half afraid of his own daring. Well he might. In a second Stevey was in one of his violent passions, almost raising his fist over the old bowler-hatted head.

'I don't want any English pimp to tell me what to do or not do with the girl – or any girl. Mind that!'

Henn's hand shook, and all his legs as he pulled himself up on his stick, taller when he stood than any of us, his bent back straightened, made gigantic by the great shadow that climbed the wall behind him. I could see what a man he was in his heyday, what a figure on a horse, wielding the rod from the top of a rock, a wiry, bony giant. There was almost majesty in him as he pointed his trembling stick to the door and faced down to Stevey with;

'Leave my house, sir. I'll not be bullied any longer by you – not an hour.'

'And I'll leave it,' cried Stevey, 'when and only when I choose. I'll not be ordered by *you*. Who the hell do you think you are ordering? Do you think you can order *me*? Ho, and but let me tell you, Mister Alexander Henn, I'm *staying* here.'

I could see he had taken drink while down at the pub, and the devil was in his eyes: he skipped across the hearth by the side of Henn and flopped mockingly into the chair the old man had just left. Then he stretched out his hand for Henn's glass on the mantelpiece, and wiping the side of it on his coat-sleeve raised it in mockery of the old man. There was silence for a second and then Gypsy laughed, and the laugh cut through Henn. He raised his stick and lashed at the hand that held the empty glass in the air, and as the splinters fell I leapt, Henn thrusting his face across my arm into Stevey's face, Gypsy barely holding back Stevey's fist before it crashed into the old rheumy, half-blind eyes. Henn was all but weeping for vanity, for that laughter of the girl at his age and infirmity. All he could say between his sobs was 'You young ruffian. You ruffian. You ruffian. . . .'

I thrust Stevey back. Henn turned to me.

'This young woman. If anything should happen to her, which God forbid . . .'

'Oh, you hypocrite,' cried Stevey, turning to the empty air for somebody to appeal to. 'Oh, listen to that, God! God forbid! Oh, the hypocrisy of it!'

'Yes, yes, yes,' I appealed and implored Gypsy to take him away and pushed him from us, and the girl dragged him, and pushed him, and persuaded him out of the room. She was strangely cool as if abuse and quarrelling and coarse talk were nothing to her. I put the old man in his chair and filled a glass for him and left him and found Stevey sullenly akimbo on the top of the steps. He was ashamed, I felt, to have played his heroics opposite me and I thought he might not have quarrelled with old Henn if he knew I was there. So I stood beside him without speaking until he said he was sorry he had broken out like that since it would ruin my chances of staying at the Hall. I could not tell of what else he was thinking, but I was thinking to myself: Where shall I go now? For I could neither remain in the Hall nor go with Stevey. My hopes of a quiet, serene night were already vanished, and I felt to Stevey as one feels towards some hooligan who breaks in on lovely music with his loud shouting and laughter. We stood in silence and looked down into the night. A frightened bird fluttered in the woods; a star fell in a graceful, fatal swoop, vanishing in mid-air as if a mighty hand had scratched the sky with light.

Biting his nails, Stevey said, 'Tell Gypsy I want her.'

I went back to the drawing-room where the girl and the old man stood by the window.

'Stevey wishes to speak to you,' I said; and when she went tramping wearily, heavily, from the room I looked at Henn and he looked back at me and neither of us spoke. As I looked away again through the shining window I could see the old man's eyes fixed on me. At last I buttoned my coat about me and turned to him.

'I suppose I'd better be going,' I said.

'Going? Where are you going?'

'I don't know really, but . . .'

'Hum! You were to stay here, I take it, eh?'

After a long hesitation I answered, 'Yes – I was. I was. I may even stay in your hay-barn yet, for all you know. Good-night,' I concluded, 'I'm glad to have met you.'

'No, boy. I won't say good-night. And you won't stay in my hay-barn, because I have none. Stay where you intended to stay. Even though you didn't choose to ask me, stay. If not for your own sake, for your father's and mother's sake.'

He rose and went slowly and feebly to the door, his half-emptied bottle in his hand.

'Could I stop you,' he said, 'if you wanted to stay here a month? Stay! And be damned to ye!'

'I won't,' I said.

He turned to me at the door.

'Please do stay,' he pleaded, nodding his head many times to encourage me. 'Stay, stay, stay.'

He was maudlin with the excitement and the liquor.

'Will you stay?' he asked again.

I looked out into the dark.

Stay! I thought to myself it must be near to eleven or midnight.

'Thanks very much,' I said; and being satisfied he waved his bony hand, slipping his bottle into the great pocket of his swallow-tailed coat; then he turned and went, his little hat perched on one side of his head and his rug trailing after him on the uncarpeted floor.

I sat by the table and looked about me again: at the table-cloth like a gypsy's shawl, at the threadbare carpet on the floor, at the dusty lace curtains dragged to the ends of their poles, and everything my eyes fell on mocked him and his desires. Lovely woven silks, he had said, and woven linens, and stuffs such as women might love to feel? And such strange flowers and bulbs as the Dutch and the Channel Islanders grew, as freesia, gardenia, mignonette? What a liar, I thought; and bitterly I was pleased to end the triad, calling him (as the farming folk had called him for fifty years) a lunatic; and he would not deny he was a libertine as well.

Gypsy returned, and I told her I was staying in the house, and once more she went and returned. We heard Stevey's steps vanish down the drive, and then silently she took a candle and lit me upstairs to bed. As we went I asked her what her name was, and she said:

'My name is Gammle.'

'Indeed,' I said, thoughtlessly.

'Why *indeed?*' she asked, halting in her step and looking at me.

'Nothing,' I said. 'It's just a strange name.'

But I did not tell her I was thinking that the name was well known in North Cork for a tinker tribe, in Charleville and Doneraile and the borders of Limerick and up into Clare, a name few decent men or women ever bore.

'Good night,' she said, and left me in a great empty musty room, the bed all tousled and the bed-clothes soiled, and yellow. I lay down as I stood, and to the sound of the branches of the trees tapping on the bare window I dozed and slept.

3

I awoke, wide-eyed of a sudden insomnia, to the rusted, wailing drone of an old phonograph in the room below me. By the light of the moon I looked at my watch, it was past twelve o'clock, an hour when cities begin to live and the fields are fast asleep. How many times had I not lain awake for hours listening to the quietness of the city, or to late parties singing their way homeward, before the war and curfew sent us all to our beds, I would be awake now almost until the dawn broke. Rising peevishly I went to the door, opening it in time to hear a new record begin its nasal introductory speech – This is an Edison Bell recawrd; number one seven nine nine; songs from the Awpera of Dawn Giovanni by Mozart. And then through the hollow-sounding house the stifled music of one of the loveliest of operas; and humming with the singer, or rather behind the singer, came old blear-eyed maudlin Henn's cracked and drunken voice:

'Batti; batti . . .'

I bade sleep good-night, and dragging on my pants sat on the edge of the bed, my coat about my shoulders, smoking a cigarette. Or watched the branches beating on the panes, or the laurels shivering and shining in the tangled garden beneath my window, or the Bride rain-laden far below glinted between its ancient gall-black alders under the starry sky.

> *'Questo é il fin di chi fa mal,*
> *E de' perfidi la morte, alla vita è sempre ugual!'*

The pair and their song died slowly, and when silence fell Henn kicked his enamel chamber-pot until it rang. Croaking and humming the love-song he shuffled out on his landing. From my door I watched him almost stumble headlong down the stairs, out of the house, on to the gravelled drive and out of sight into the dark.

One by one I began to hear them – those innumerable, inexplicable sounds that are to be heard at night in a house when all the casual day-sounds are still; timbers that stretch and contract, little insects that make a great creaking noise. And feeling that I had rather be in the open air than alone in this empty house I pulled on my boots and went down to the open door and out on the avenue and down towards the cottage in the track of Henn. Here a chill wind was blowing last year's leaves high in the air, but near the lodge where the drive fell sharply down to the gates between the trees on their high ditches the dust lay in soft whispering drifts – soft and white as snow under the moon, so soft that as I stood by the little deserted lodge peering curiously in through one of the windows I might have been a rabbit or a fox for all the warning

I gave anyone who might have been inside. Only a shaft of wavering light lay thrown across the tiny hallway from another room. Moving cautiously to the other window I peered in again. There they were, Gypsy and Henn: she with her skirt drawn above her knees, an old coat over the warm skin of her bare shoulders, toasting her shins to a little flickering fire – Henn, as he did the first time I saw them together, holding her fingers in his palm and leaning forward over her round knee to see into her eyes.

Strange to watch the unequal pair looking at one another so long, so silently, seeming not to say one word to each other, her dark head bowed sidelong to his lips, her fallen lashes on her cheeks, her parted lips that never moved, he, with a smile, foolish yet tender, sagging his quivering mouth apart, his old hat cocked forward on eyes that streamed their water to his cheeks; and yet, though Henn was old and decaying, and she warm-fleshed, white to her teeth, full of the pride of youth, and – Henn, was right – her breasts like tulips fully blown, if anything too magnificently full, too Jewess soft, yet he could for all that, raise his hand now with so much languid grace to feel their roundness, hold the precious globe for one moment, so lightly, so fondly on his fingers before his withered hand fell as if in despair into her lap, that finer woman than Gypsy might well have smiled, even as she smiled now, with head turning slow from that flattering gesture of the epicure, with long slow-drawn sighs at the uselessness of such praise from him. To which of these men, I wondered, had this girl given herself? For now with her hair dragged on the ridge of her chair and her head falling lower and lower on her bosom until her eyes caught in the embers of the fire, she permitted him to move aside her skirt, ever so little, from her bare knee, and caress it with his withered hand as softly as if it were swans-down, caress it even after the glow of the fire shone on her eyes drowned in tears, caress it while she sat rigid with misery, her moans breaking out in trembling waves to the whispering night outside. And yet not a stir or word from Henn, but as if hoping that his old hand could quiet her childlike sobs, he caressed and caressed and looked and looked dog-like into her face. Alas! each exhausted sigh was but the prelude to a new shuddering burst of tears like waves that are silent for a while and then burst suddenly and inevitably on the shore.

I could not bear those dog-like eyes of the old libertine, nor those sighs and sobs of the young girl; and stumbling away from the light of the little window and out of the creaking gate I found myself walking on and on under the tenting chestnuts in the windy dust-blown lane, up and along the highway I had come that evening, too moved to return and sit alone in my unkempt bedroom in the Hall. For somehow country and freedom seemed a small thing under this austere darkness with that pair, heavy with one another's sorrow, down in the weather-streaked decaying cottage; and with the memory of those drooping mother's breasts and that large mother's belly on the young girl, and the look of pity on the old libertine's face I find myself walking aimlessly on and on.

But suddenly across the black valley there rises a leaping yellow flame, and through the night air on the night wind comes the crackle of the burning timber, joists moist with the damp of years, burning the vermin in their cracks and the resinous veins.

The flames through the trees flickered like a huge bonfire and running down the lanes toward Henn Hall I could see from time to time as I ran the outline of windows, of a gable-end, of a chimney silhouetted against the glowing air about it. At the lodge the little light was still shining in the window but without looking through I knocked and knocked until bare padding feet came along the floor and the girl's voice said:

'Who is it? Who's there?'

'A fire,' I cried. 'What can we do? Across the valley, a big house.' And in my excitement I cried out, 'Where's Mad Henn?'

She answered through the door.

'He's not here. Isn't he at the Hall?'

I was, I admit, a fool that night.

'I don't know,' I shouted back to her.

'You don't know?'

She opened an inch or two of the door and looked out at me with frightened eyes.

'Whose house is it?' she asked.

'I don't know. It's straight over the river – straight across there.'

Holding her clothes about her body she stepped to the corner of the lodge and looked across at the blazing house.

'It's Blake's,' she said. 'We can't do anything. They may come over here. Where's Henn?' she asked then, suddenly terrified.

'I thought he was here.'

She stared at me, astonished, yet full of cunning that was mingled with fright for Henn.

'Isn't he at the Hall?' she insisted nervously.

'Maybe,' I stuttered, 'yes – perhaps he is – I suppose he *is* at the Hall.'

'Did you try?'

'I was out walking,' I said.

'Walking!'

There was a pause.

'What time is it?' she asked.

As I peered at my watch, saying, 'It's well after one o'clock,' I could see her eyes looking at me with fear and suspicion, and having spied on her I was ashamed to look up. But slowly I understood why she was watching me in that way, she thought that my coming there that night, a man 'on the run,' had something to do with this burning house, that I had caused it, as a reprisal, an act of revenge, and that in some way Henn too would suffer by it, and that Stevey, probably, had been the man who carried it out. How stupid I had been – but such reprisals were as yet rare in the country and it had never occurred to me that this was one until in her eyes I saw fear and distrust and hate.

'A nice time for walking,' she said shortly, and raced down the slope of the ditch and up to the Hall and there she knocked on the heavy hen's-head knocker until the countryside resounded and even a dog, somewhere across the fields, began to bark-bark at our knock-knock-knock on the echoing door. I tried to explain myself.

' 'Tis why I came to the country – to sleep. I get insomnia. So I got up and came out.'

'How did you get out? Henn keeps the key in his room.'

'The door was open.'

But I was now concealing something from her and she would not believe me.

'My God,' she moaned, 'what's happened him?'

Then in her fear and rage and suspicion she turned on me, a tigress robbed of her mate – and even in that instant I remember saying to myself, Oho! So it's Henn, is it?

'Where is he?' she cried. 'What did ye do with him? Christ blast ye all, ye set of ——s. What did ye do to him?'

Her voice was echoed by the stony face of the house, thrown

back into the fields and echoed there again and again by the barking dog.

'I know nothing about him,' I said angrily. 'He's probably dead drunk. Knock him up.'

And I clouted the hen's head until my hand ached. Not a sound replied but the dog over the fields, now thoroughly aroused, and the crackling of the flames across the valley, and, within, the old sheep-dog, who stirred and howled mournfully.

The girl caught my arm in fear.

'Oh, it's the dog crying before somebody dies.'

'Sssh! Is that a window?'

'Is it the I.R.A that burnt it?' she asked, looking up and then over her shoulder.

'I know nothing about it. How can we get in?'

'It's for the child the Tans killed. Oh! Ye've done something to Henn. Ye've surely done something to Henn.'

We found a little scullery window open and through it I clambered and let her in at the front door. Up we climbed the dark stairs, the dog flopping along behind, and up to his room, and into it. We found him there in his bed, snoring on his stomach with the weight of drink, his night-shirt crumpled above his bare knees, and on his head a fluff-laden night-cap of scarlet wool. Ashamed of the sight of him with his dirty toes and the engrimed creases across the base of his neck and half-way up his skull, Gypsy shook him madly into a gasping wakefulness; and seeing me, in the faint glow that filled the room, smile at his comically stupid look she straightened his cap on his head as if he were a child, and covered his shoulders as he sat up in bed looking about him at the angry waving light – like a picture of Juan in hell.

'Are you all right?' she asked.

'I – yes – oh, I'm all right. But . . .'

'Look.' She pointed, and he looked.

'My God!' he cried. 'Totty Blake's.'

His eyes bulged as he looked, and trying to master himself he shambled across the floor to stoop in the open window in his shirt.

'Oh! My God! My God!' was all he could say, and then, 'Do you hear them? Do you hear the noise?'

'The flames?' I said.

'No! The rooks. They'll never nest there again. They're ruined with the heat.'

And he began to tousle his cap and sank on his knees crying like a child. Gypsy stood over him where he knelt.

'The Blakes will be likely coming here for the night.'

He stood up at once like a hardened toper, and turned to us.

'Go down,' he said, 'and lay the table for them, and set the fire going. And you, boy, go, like a good fellow, and give her a hand.'

Gypsy went but I thought he was unable to look after himself and tried to coax him from the window.

'I'll stay here,' I whispered. 'It's cold, you know. You must dress, now. I'll help you. Come on.'

But when I tried to lead him back to the bed he flung my arm aside, peevishly.

'Am I a child?' he cried.

So I left him in a palsy of trembling, dragging his nightshirt over his head, rump-naked, fumbling for his clothes by the pale light of the candle and the fluttering light of the burning house.

In silence we set about blowing the seed of fire on the hearth into flame, and I dipped the kettle in the dark water of the butt and the crane swung it slowly over the fire. The false dawn of the fire and the distant rooks cawing with fright had awakened the doves and all the birds on this side of the valley and the night was sweet with their music. From time to time as we passed from kitchen to parlour with ware or food we halted to look at the fire that sometimes seemed to have died away and sometimes flared up more madly than ever before. There Henn joined me and we waited there, wondering if the Blakes would come or if we should go back to bed and try to sleep out the end of the night. At last he drew me into the room and filled out a drink for himself, while I yawned, dry-eyed for lack of sleep.

'I don't know where else the Blakes can go,' he said. 'Though if there was another house within three miles of them they'd rather die than come under my roof. I'm sorry for his two tits of sisters, though.'

'Only two women?' I asked wearily.

'Philamena and Agatha. Two sour tits. And the Captain, their father. That's all that's there. Oh, but Philamena *is* a sour creature. I chalked that very word on the door of the church about her when

I was six – got whipped for it too. And she never spoke a word to me after. And I gave Agatha a penny at the age of eight if she'd let me swing her so high that I could see her drawers. They would never let her see me after that. I once went,' he said, throwing back his liquor, 'I once went to church to a Handel service, and I had to run out of it when I saw the two virgins singing away "*To us a child is born; to us a son is given.*" But, ah!' he snarled, 'they're sour titties. Vinegar for milk they have. Sour and old and virginal.'

He was getting angry with them, I could see.

'They'd just raise their hands in horror at a girl like . . . at a girl that would, that would . . .'

I stood in the corner of the window watching the sparks rising and falling endlessly like fireflies, silenced as one is always silenced by a raging fire, to think of calamity on one's doorstep.

'Gypsy,' says Henn, suddenly rising and going to another window, 'Gypsy was sick tonight.'

'Bad?' I asked sleepily.

'Bad? Oh, no! Not yet.'

'Not yet?'

'That's what I said. Didn't you hear me?'

'Yes.'

He came shuffling over to me on his stick.

'The girl is ruined,' he said, peering into my eyes that filled with shame as he looked at them.

'What do you mean by that?'

'Gypsy is going to be a mother next month or after.'

I answered his stare.

'Who do you think is to blame?' he asked.

For answer I looked angrily over the valley at the house. What did it matter to him what I thought? What would all the country think when they heard it? Another servant of Henn's – it was an old story – about to bear a child.

'I'll not be blamed,' he cried and his tubes were hoarse with passion. 'I am not to be blamed.'

'What does the girl say?'

'How does she know?'

And he went back to his glass and his fire.

And then up the avenue in a shadowy mass, singing and shouting, came the incendiaries, Stevey at their head, ready for anything, drunk with whisky and triumph. Had it been six months later, he could safely have burnt half the houses in the district and we should not have dared, nor cared, nor had the time, nor even wished in the heat of passion – for things grew very hot by then – to question any such act of his. But tonight I ran to the door determined to thwart him. He faced up the steps and shouted for Henn, Henn the whore, Henn the cock, the Henn's neck, and all about him shouted with him out of the dark in their rough, country accents:

'Henn! Henn! Come out, you whore. Henn! Come out, Henn!'

There was a glint of a revolver in one man's hand as I ran down the steps and faced up to Stevey.

'What rotten sort of soldier are you?' I shouted at him.

'What do you mean?' he cried.

'Is that what you call soldiering?' I shouted into his face, pointing across the valley at the burning ruin. For an instant he looked at it, and then to his men and at me.

'Ah,' he shouted. 'We burnt the bastards out; didn't we, boys? And damn right well they deserved it.'

They shouted it back to him, their memories full of the days when their people died of starvation by the roadsides and the big houses looked on in portly indifference. Again and again they echoed it back to him.

'And we'll burn Henn out,' cried Stevey, and made a dive for the steps. I caught him and swung him about while Henn hung over the iron railings and croaked down at us:

'If I had a gun. Oh, if I only had a gun.'

'Shut up,' I shouted at him. The crowd was nasty enough without this.

'Oh, for a gun,' he persisted. 'Just for one minute . . .'

'Go in, blast you,' I shouted at him while Gypsy tried to drag him from the steps.

'You're fine fellows. Oh, you're great fellows,' I taunted them. 'You haven't, between the lot of you, fired a single shot in all this district for four months. Unless you shot a sitting hare or a tame fox. It's what you'd do by the look of you. And now you go and burn a couple of women out in the middle of the night. Oh, you're grand soldiers entirely. You cowardly mob!'

'You keep your tongue quiet'; from Stevey. He was a head higher than me.

'I'm here to talk to you,' I said, 'and I'll give you and your men my talk now, if you want it. Let me tell you you have the reputation of being the tamest commandant. . . .'

He flew into a passion at once and drew his revolver at me. At once the country fellows skipped aside – they didn't at all like this business of drawing a gun on one of their own, and they began to mutter and pluck at Stevey, and to signal me to hold my peace; but I knew my man.

'Now, now, Long,' they muttered. 'Be aisy now, Long.'

'You won't bully me,' I said. 'Why don't you use your gun on the Tans?'

He turned to them.

'Are you going to be stopped by a city caffler?'

And to me:

'We know what Henn is.'

'What am I?' croaked Henn who was still grasping the railings, with Gypsy trying to persuade him to come in.

'What did Henn ever do to *you?*' I asked.

'Aye, what did I ever do to you?' gasped Henn, hoarse with excitement, sweeping his little hat off his head and leaning down over the railings like a man giving a speech. 'What did I do to you? What did I ever to do you or yours?'

'Ah,' shouted Stevey up to him. 'Ah, you whore-master' – and I thought he'd blow the old man's brains out. 'What do you know what's mine or yours? You blasted father of thousands.'

Utterly beyond himself he pointed with his gun at Gypsy, and shook his fist in the old man's eyes.

'Look at that girl. What did you do to her? Answer that or you'll not have a house by morning.'

Then quite without warning the rest of them turned and raced over the lawn into the surrounding night. Only one waited to pluck Stevey by the arm and whisper:

'It's the Blakes. They're coming. Come away out of this. They'll know us.'

'I don't care about the Blakes,' said Stevey, too intent on having his way with Henn that night to care about anything else. 'Ask him,' he said to me, 'Ask him what did he do to that girl? Ask him that?'

'Stevey, Stevey,' implored the girl as she tried still to induce Henn to move.

I drew Stevey to one side as Henn, who had also seen the Blakes come up the drive swaying with the weight of the bundles they bore, stood down on the steps to meet them, his hat in his hand like an ambassador or a prince receiving his guests, his head like a gander's head, jigging up and down as he bowed them in; and as the two old maids came timidly up to him, peering here and there in their fear, and the portly captain, their father, brought up the rear, peeping over their shoulders because he was almost as blind as Henn, they all looked more like frightened ganders and geese than human beings able to look to themselves. They clustered together on their way up the steps, Henn wheezing about not being 'quite up to the tip-top of readiness,' and saying, 'You have me at a disadvantage, Miss Blake. But come in. A cup of hot tea, now. A shot of Martell's, captain? Most regrettable! Terrible! This way, now. Allow me. This way. That's right – there we are. . . .' And so into the hall with his visitors.

When they were gone the dark figures gathered about us again, like wolves, or tormenting flies that had been driven aside for the moment.

'I'll make that man marry the girl,' said Stevey under his breath to me, 'or I'll burn this house to the very ground.'

'We'll burn him out,' they growled, the lust for destruction in their blood.

'He'll marry the girl, or he'll have no house over his head by morning.'

'But the man is eighty if he's a day,' I implored, 'and the girl is a mere slip of a girl. Is she twenty itself?'

'Well, he ruined her,' said Stevey up to my mouth as if he would force the words into it.

'I do not believe it,' I said.

Another shower had begun to fall by now, growing heavier drop by drop, dimming the starlight and shimmering dark about the distant fire. Stevey waved his hand to his fellows.

'The city fellows are a lot of help to us,' he said. 'But I'll show you. I'm not going to stand here all night in the rain talking with you.'

He rushed past me up the steps and into the house with his

mob after him. I managed to stop him at the door of the drawing-room and we parleyed there for a while, whispering as we peeped through the cracked door. There, where fifty years ago he had leant across the shining walnut to his perfumed lights-o'-love, smiling quizzically down on them from his swan's neck, approving the painted lips, the tilted eyebrows, always gracious to them, however cynical, perpetually on the smile, only leaning back from his scandalous whispering when the butler laid a new course or refilled his glass – there, now, he offered his smoke-tainted tea, with the airs of fifty years ago, though they creaked and stuttered a little from lack of use, to the two silent, miserable old maids.

'Oh, yes, do drink a cup of tea, Miss Blake,' and he puffs out his cheeks to encourage her. 'Just one?'

'Thank you. I don't believe I really want one, Mr Henn.'

'Oh just one cup. Just one.'

But they sat very straight-backed and unbending, trying hard not to keep looking over the valley at their ruined home. They looked instead at the soiled table-cloth, the unequal ware, the tarnished silver, or at one another, or at the old captain, their father, who sat sucking his brandy, heavy jowled and heavy bodied, by Henn's fire. Or they looked at Gypsy, who, careless of her ungainly, ungirlish shape, danced superfluous attendance on them, full of pity for their misfortune, glad to be in the presence of real ladies even for an hour.

So they were sitting when Stevey burst in on them, calling on Henn so loudly that they almost screamed.

'Henn,' he said. 'We want you.'

'Don't go, Henn,' said the captain at once, as if he felt as much for his own sake as for Henn's that it was better they should all cling together now.

'What do you want, now?' stuttered Henn.

'I want you to come too, Gipsy,' said Stevey.

'Oh, Stevey, Stevey,' said the girl, utterly ashamed before the company.

'Come on, Henn,' bullied Stevey. 'Or will I tell my business here?'

'Out with it,' says the captain.

'One minute now,' pleaded Henn.

I thought it best to get the matter over, and went up to the old man and whispered that it would be best to come – I could not keep those fellows in hand for him any longer.

'Don't go Henn,' said the captain again.

'No, no,' said the old maids, with the same thought as their father in their minds that even Henn was better than nothing in their extremity, homeless as they were at this hour of the morning.

But he rose and went into the kitchen and Stevey and Gypsy and I after him. There he turned and faced us, looking down over us all, even over Stevey himself. And Stevey alone returned his glare, for the girl sat with her head in her hands by the fire and I looked at the rain spitting on the dark window. When Stevey had finished, all Henn could say was, 'You liar, you liar!' And all the girl could do was weep and say, 'My misfortune. My misfortune. My misfortune.' Even when I went to her and put my hand on her shoulder she only burst away from me and cried to let her alone, let her alone in her misfortune; for God's sake to let her alone in her misfortune, and sate at the table hiding her face in her hands, shaken with tears.

'You liar!' muttered Henn.

'I'm no liar,' cried Stevey.

As the girl wept with renewed shame that no man would own now that he ever loved her, Henn looked at her and said very gently to me:

'Supposing I won't marry her?'

'No harm will come to your person,' I said, and faced Stevey on that.

'Your house will go the way of Blake's,' said Stevey and faced me on that, 'If not tonight, tomorrow night, and if not then the night after. But if I have to wait a year to do it, up it will go.'

I shook the wretched girl by the shoulder.

'Do you want to marry this old man?' I cried into her ear.

She gave no reply.

'Speak up, Gypsy,' said Stevey. 'You will marry him, won't you? You said you would.'

She said not a word now.

'I'll not marry her,' said Henn.

Stevey had cunning enough to play his last card.

'Then tell your Blake friends to get out of this house, if they have sense. Or, you needn't – I'll do it.'

Henn stopped him at the door.

'Stop. Don't! Don't!'

And thereupon he sank into a chair with a sudden dizziness, and I had to hold him up from falling sidelong to the floor.

'Gypsy,' I said. 'Get a sup of whisky.'

'Alec!' she said, going to him, and he took her hand, her little hand in his when she stood by his side and said his name. 'Alec! Will I get a sup of brandy?'

There was silence for a few minutes, with only the noise of the rain cat-pattering against the window and the three of us over Henn. At last he began to whisper through his fingers, and I leaned down to hear him.

'Will she marry me?' he was whispering while the spittle dropped like a cow's spittle between his fingers to the flagged floor.

'Now!' cried Stevey triumphantly. 'Gypsy! Will you have him?'

In her deep man's voice she replied:

'And who else would have me now? Since others won't – others that have their own life and their own plans and plots?'

And seeing that the old man was not in need of help she went out of the kitchen, holding her stomach in her little palms, murmuring as she went,

'I will, if he will.'

I pushed Stevey before me from the kitchen and leaving Henn to himself we drove the rest of the herd before us from the hall, into the darkness, so rain-arrowy and cold. From the great front door I watched them go tramping down the avenue and as I, too, turned to go upstairs to my bed I heard Henn, back in the drawing-room, trying once more to play the host, after his fifty years' interval, with his smoky tea and his patched ware. I wondered as I tramped upstairs if he was thinking that, with this young wife, he might begin life again.

From my bed I heard the summer downpour drip about the house and occasionally spit down the chimney on the damp papers stuffed in the grate, tainting all the room with their sooty reek. Not until late noon did I hear another sound, and then it was the birds singing and the croaking corncrake and the doves in the high woods, and when I rose the whole house was radiant with sunshine reflected from the fields and the trees. There was nobody about the house but Gypsy. The Blakes had gone since early morning and Henn did not leave his bed for several days. Stevey I could find nowhere and the local men said he was gone into Kerry, swearing he would only return to make Henn keep to his promise. Two days I waited for him and searched about for news of him, and then I called a meeting of his battalion and replaced him by a new commandant.

One evening I left Henn Hall as I had come, but before I went I visited Henn in his room to say good-bye and I found him sitting over his fire, drinking punch and reading an *Anglers' Annual* of thirty years ago.

'Be careful of yourself, boy,' he warned as I turned to leave him.

'Oh, yes,' I said. 'I'll be careful.'

'Do you believe Long's story?' he said, then, leaning forward to me.

'I have no cause,' I parried, 'to believe or disbelieve anybody.'

He leaned back and stared at the fire.

'Anyway,' he said after a while, 'I'm going to marry her. She's as good as the next, and better than some, even though she *is* only a tinker's daughter. Besides,' he added proudly, 'if it's a boy 'twill keep the name alive.'

As if he were a Hapsburg or a Bourbon!

One night two months or so later we heard in our back-yard bedroom that a strange pair left Cork for Dublin that afternoon on the Mail Express, all their dozen or so of trunks and bags labelled forward to an address in Paris. The woman, in a massive hat with a scarlet feather, had flaunted her way to her carriage – the old man, her husband, hobbling and shuffling along yards behind her. His travelling coat almost completely hid him, its tail touching the ground, its coat-collar up about his ears, and so weak did his eyes appear to be that even in the dim filtered light of the station he had cocked his hat forward over his eyebrows and shaded his eyes with his withered hand as he walked. But I find it too painful to think of him, there in Paris, with his scraps of governess-French, guiding his tinker wife through the boulevards, the cafés, the theatres – seeing once more the lovely women and the men gay in their hour. Life is too pitiful in these recapturings of the *temps perdu*, these brief intervals of reality.

Lilliput

On those nights when curfew came at ten o'clock and people were hastening within doors, locking doors, bolting doors, chaining doors at a full quarter to the hour, the poor alone were leisurely. Shandon had therefore struck ten before the last of the apple-sellers began to drag her basket after her into the lanes, but once she was gone the bridge was as empty as a plain.

There had been a fragrance in the air as long as the apples lay there exposed but the smell of the river was about to conquer again. A light fog had crept up the valley of the Lee from the harbour mouth and the lamps on the bridges had gathered from it a rich and reddish hue, while their dagger-like reflections trembled but slightly in the cold and glassy river-water. Farther down the quays the lovers were parting in the darker nooks, the men with one eye raised for the coming of the patrols, the women drawing their shawls closer around their lovers for the last embrace. Where the nets were drying there hung an odour of tar, and where they wash the sheep-skins the slips and pavement smelt in the night air. Already in the side-streets where there lie stables and storehouses and an occasional dwelling-house it might have been the first hours of the morning. But in one of these streets which lead from the quaysides to the centre of the city through a middle-class quarter, there stood, and had stood all the day long, a cart surmounted by a black box-like erection – a sort of miserable caravan without windows, without chimney and without an animal to support the slanting shafts. It might remind you of the little cart of the Poor Shepherd Nuns, or of a small-scale fever-cart intended to carry away the infected clothes from a condemned house. Inside were three children fast asleep. Clothes and cloths and mere rags filled this box of a house. Straw, a bucket, a board, chains – these with some huge stones at the wheels were scattered around it on the street. The cart carried no lamp. The open doorway facing the shafts was curtained by an old yellow coat, but at this hour the whole was a black mass inviting collision from the last-minute jarvey-cars careering past with their drunken passengers clinging to the seat.

It was now several minutes past the forbidden hour, and any moment the first lorries would be heard tearing along the quays and through the principal streets. None the less you could hear in the square near-by a war of words and distinguish them if you chose to listen. A woman was answering two or three male voices, young and soft in spite of their jeering tones, and as they parted farther and farther from one another, and the steps of the woman came nearer, and the voices of the others more shrill in the distance you might have heard every swear.

'Aha! The Kerry porther is the best porther, I can tell ye.'

They answered with a crying call such as a savage might use in battle.

'Go home to yeer mothers,' she responded, and followed with a cry as wild as theirs.

Just then the lorries began to whir in the distance and the boyish feet scampered for safety. Indifferent to them she sang herself back to her cart, sometimes muttering between the lines about her husband, and the police, and her donkey-ass. She sang out,

'O-o-oh!
Will anybody tell me where the Blarney roses grow?
Is it over in Kilmurry South, or yonder in Cloghroe?'

and tumbled into her cart, and sank at once into a profound sleep. The people of the quarter, however, sate up in their beds for an hour waiting for the patrols to come and take her, and when she was still there in the morning, they said such ungenerous things as 'The devil always looks after his own'; or, 'Look how a good person wouldn't have been so fortunate'; and went by to church with disapproving eyes.

At the first Angelus the haze still hung over the city, but the morning broke in sunshine shortly before the second bell rang in the noon. From that onwards there were ding-dongs all over the city at intervals of hours or half-hours. Finally when all the children were returning from their usual Sunday Mass she was arisen and had made some slops of tea. The city children gathered around her in wonderment as she washed the little girls' faces in the water she had borrowed near-by. Unperturbed, she combed their hair, peering at the scalp.

She was a sturdy woman with fresh colour in her cheeks, but her dun-coloured hair hung around her in contrast to the neat little figures that watched her and her cart in wonder. She saw this herself and eventually sate down on the sloping shaft to examine their spotless muslin frocks, their white shoes, their frilly lace, and sky-blue ribbons. She began to tell them disconsolately of her husband who was in Moore's Hotel – they knew Moore's Hotel was a jail – and she spoke pityingly of her three children and of the donkey-ass whom 'Cruelty' had led away when her husband was taken. So, all the day long she sate there, only rising at intervals. Once she picked and plucked at the three children, and went off with them to the jail. But she soon returned like a huge liner with three small tenders on her flanks, and began speaking of their father to some women that had gathered around her. The 'polis' had taken him for beating the donkey-ass 'till he brayed and died.' It was a tree fell on the donkey-ass, she said. They asked her had she come far, and she said from Headford. They said she was a pity, and one of the poorest came to her with a pot of soup and vegetables and potatoes. But her eldest child knocked it over by accident, and her mother called her a jade, and sate down for a spell.

All day long there was a changing little crowd around her. Patiently she told again and again of the donkey-ass and *their* father, and Moore's Hotel. She had once lived in Blarney Street and was four years on the road. Or she had lived in Barrackah and was ten years on the road. Or she had been born on the road and didn't know what a roof-tree meant. She told all her stories with her cheek on her fist, occasionally cocking her eye at her listeners but with a bored air. Each one of her listeners said she and her three children were a pity. She told them of the blackguards who called her low names last night, and they promised to keep guard for her, even to go to the sessions with her, and she answered she must rely on the help of God and her neighbours in all things. Some of the women did not like her and asked her questions that she refused to answer, but the other women said that these things were her own business.

At tea-hour the crowd did not slacken. The children from the streets all around became more noisy and familiar and had to be hunted away by the women. She borrowed water again, and a passing man bought her the last two loaves from the nearest huckster's shop. She gave tea to her three little girls within the cart, she herself eating from the roadway like a photographer behind the curtaining yellow coat, just as if her cart were a huge black camera.

At dusk and dark the people of the district became very nervous, and wondered why the police did not come to move her away, and complained that the whole country was in a shocking state, and feared above all, saying so to one another from door to door and window to window, that she would attract the attention of the Tans and the patrols to their quiet street and they would have no wink of sleep at all that night. At last the police came, but they had no mind to argue with her, and they merely told her to take her cart to hell out of that street even as she brought it in, and then because they knew she would begin to ask how was she to do that, they went away at once so that they should have the last word.

Then the children around began to enjoy themselves in earnest. They laid themselves under the shafts, and, shouting, began to strain and pull, or they heaved the huge stones from beneath the wheels and cried out for orders from the woman. The hoydens from the lane-ways told her to wheel her cart to this place or that, and the children chimed in that Harper's Lane was not at all like this street, but was a small narrow lane, down below there. The women gathered around her again and again, or sank on their haunches before her children and returning, told the mother that they were chatting away to themselves. Amid cries the cart began to move, and the loose chains to swing and ring in the dark as the children dragged it from the kerb. But the woman hailed them, and they ordered one another to wheel it back again, and there it stayed yet another night. She lit a candle and put the little girls to bed and its light shone brightly from the interior of the cart until she drew the yellow coat across it.

It was now almost ten o'clock and the women began to scatter, talking among themselves and asking her if she would be all right there. She walked away with a few of them and the wind blew the candle out and the night moulded the cart into the blackness of the street, and the street became as quiet as early dawn. A man who asked the children who owned the cart, and where she was now, had to chase them because they pelted him with stones and called out ribald answers. Then the street settled down to the night again. But a priest walked down the street from the riverside, showing like a statue in jet under the lamps above him. Three girls clasping one another's waists cried out that he was coming and retired to a corner of the square. He looked around when he reached the cart, and down the street ahead of him, and tapped politely at the side of the cart, and looked to the right and then went home tapping his silver-headed stick on the flags. The girls ran another way to watch him and all was still again until the lorries began to whir in the distance as Shandon struck the hour and the girls raced for their homes.

The woman returned shortly after and crept into the cart on her knees. An old woman shuffled along and asked her if she were there last night also, and asked why was the poor man taken, and prayed God to help us all. The woman within spoke out to her to go away for Virgin Mary's sake and let her sleep – which the old woman did, looking back several times as she padded away on her bare feet, the woman within snoring out loud snores that might be heard by a passer-by long before he distinguished the cart from the darkness around it.

Towards midnight a patrol of military tramped slowly down the street while the wakeful householders held their breath. The patrol halted at the cart, and the officer flashed his torch into the interior. Then he murmured something to his sergeant and the sergeant ordered his men to move on.

'Blimey!' whispered the sergeant to the corporal, and he passed on the word to the men. 'Blimey, if it isn't a woman.'

'Oo is it?' asked a stupid private.

'Mary Mac and the Holy Trinity,' said the corporal, who was an atheist; and sniggering they all tramped away – quietly and slowly as if they would not disturb her sleep.

Fugue

The clouds lifted slowly from the ridge of the mountains and the dawn-rim appeared. As I stooped low to peer over the frame of the little attic-window I whispered to Rory that it was pitch-dark; and indeed it was far darker than the night before when we had the full moon in the sky. Rory leaned up on one elbow in bed, and asked me if I could hear anything from behind the river.

The damp of the dawn was everywhere that I might look. It softened the lime gable of the out-house beneath me, it hung over the sodden hay in the barn and, like the fog and mist last night under the blazing moon, it floated over the rumbling river to my right. I could imagine the flow taking strange courses in its flood, swishing in this neither dawn nor day nor dark, through all the alders and the reeds and the rushes and, doubtless, covering the stepping-stones that we hoped would give us an escape to the mountains beyond.

So I whispered to Rory that I could only hear the water falling in the weirs, and tumbling out of his bed he called a curse from Christ on the whore of a river that was holding us here to be plugged by the Tans for a pair of Irish bitches.

As I peered, standing in bare feet on the timber floor, I recalled last night with a shudder. We were retreating from Inchigeela by the back-roads and we two had lost ourselves in the barren and rocky place they call the Rough, a difficult place by day and almost impassable by night. We had tramped up and down and up and down until I felt my eyes closing as I stumbled along, and scarcely had the energy to push back my bandolier when it came sliding around my elbows. Rory, a country fellow, seemed tireless, but my shirt clung to my back with cold sweat. The fog lay like a white quilt under the moon, covering the countryside, and black shadows miles long and miles wide stretched across the land. Up and down we went, the fog growing thicker as we stumbled into boggy valleys, our feet squelching in the sodden turf, and fear hovering round our hearts. Earlier in the evening before the night fell, I had heard a noise before us in the lag, and had clicked a bullet in my rifle-breech and fallen flat, but Rory swore at me and asked me in amazement if I meant to fight them? After that I had no guts for anything but to get away from the danger of an encounter, to get across the river and the main road before the dawn, and up to the higher mountain on Ballyvourney beyond. So we trudged on and every natural night sound terrified us, a bird's cry, a barking dog with his double note, bark-bark, and then silence, bark-bark, and like that now and again the whole night long from one mountain side or another. People say the most lonely thing of all is the bark of a dog at night, but to us the most lonely sight was the odd twinkle of a light, miles away, one dot of light and all the rest of the land in darkness, except for the moon in the sky. The little light meant friends, a fireside, words of advice, comfort – but for us only the squelching and the trudging that seemed never to end, and maybe a bullet in the head before the dawn.

Once only we rested when Rory lost all patience and flung caution to the wind to light a cigarette in the hollow of his palms. I stretched out on the sodden mass – God, how restful to sleep there for an hour or two – but Rory muttered to himself, and I tried to keep awake by watching the coming of the red glow in his palm every time he drew in a fresh puff. The moon was a few nights from full roundness, and I thought it looked like a jolly wench laughing at us both and the missing segment like a bonnety tam cocked on the side of her fat head. The devil would look after his own, Rory was saying, blast them, two again' twenty, we couldn't fight them. Rory pulled me up and we went on, and I cursed Rory for not knowing the lay of his own countryside and he cursed me for a city snot that had no business out here in the mountains. Then we heard the cattle plunging in the boggy hollow beneath us, and we plunged ahead ourselves down a sharp descent where the river must have cut its way centuries ago: down we went sliding and running until the heavenly sight of trees broke against the sky and the dark mass of a house against them. Rory knew it for Dan Jamesy's house and we hammered with our rifle butts on the door, anxious only for sleep, and food, and the sight of friends. From an upper window she called to us and Rory spoke his name. Used to this sort of thing, and pitying us, she came down; barefooted, her black hair around her, a black cloak on her shoulders not altogether drawn over her pale breast, a candle blown madly by the wind slanting in her hand.

Rory had dressed himself while I peered out at the wall of mountain before me, and slinging his equipment over one shoulder he went down to eat something before we faced the river and the road – both half a mile away now. I followed him in a moment and found the old woman of the house and a little boy seated on the settle, his eyes wide with interest, hers full of uneasiness at our being in her house, a danger to her sons and husband. The young woman who had opened the door the night before stood like a statue before the wide fireplace, her bright arm bare to the elbow, and – curious gesture – her hand on the crown of her head as if to keep in position the hair brushed and close-combed around her skull like a black velvet cap shining in the firelight. She smiled at me as I entered, but I was too anxious to reply with more than a wan smile. Rory asked her many questions about the encircling troops, and she replied, looking down at his ruddy earnest face, that some lorries had passed by an hour ago, and when he asked about the river she said that it had risen over the stones and could not be crossed. She stooped down to reach the teapot, keeping one hand on her hip as she poured the tea: before the hour was out I recollected how she looked at me while she poured me out a cupful, and at the recollection I felt just as when I saw the night before an odd, twinkling window-light heading a deserted valley full of moonlight and mist. Stooping again she replaced the pot and went to sit on the other side of the little boy, and laying one hand on his knee spoke to him.

'That fir Tom brought last night has no fire in it.'

'Tis a bad fire, God bless it.'

'Get a good log, now, Jamesy, will you? Will you?' The little fellow looked at us only, and said: 'I will,' but he did not stir. The old woman broke in irritably:

'Wisha, Jamesy couldn't.'

'Indeed, Jamesy is a great man, isn't he, Jamesy? Imagine Jamesy not to be able to carry a baulk of fir! Will you, Jamesy?'

But Jamesy sat with dangling legs watching us eat and she rose and with easy steps went out: the old woman stirred the wood fire; one of the sons handled my revolver with dull curiosity, and another fumbled in a rope-loft over Rory's head and replied that another lorry was gone by. We prepared for the river and the road, on our guard, not so afraid as when the night was all around. I went to the door to see if it rained, and stood looking into the dark archway of the stables and at the dark hollows under the thatch – nowhere else could I see the soft, silent fall. As I looked at the dark archway she appeared in it with an armful of logs and raised her head towards me and smiled once again and then approached pulling her blue apron over her head to protect her from the rain. I saw her smile and it tortured me. But Rory and the old man of the house came out and went towards the stables, arguing about a horse to carry us over the flood, and I followed them, and we came at last to where the river was tearing madly over the drowned stones.

As I sat behind the old fellow on his white mare clasping him firmly about the waist, and trying to keep my eyes from the swirling water that tore the gravel from the unsteady hoofs, I saw from the corners of my eyes the drops that splashed up and flashed in the sun as they fell again on the prancing knees and the brown water. I saw at the identical moment the young woman in the blowing wind of the night, and her looks at me twice, thrice that morning. I longed for an end to this vagabond life, longed for I dared not think what; but there was in it the scent and light of flowers and the scent of woman and her soft caresses. She had looked at me as if we had between us some secret love: not one woman in ten thousand will look so at one man in as many thousand, perhaps not one in all his life, never more than one I would have said a day ago, and now one such had looked at my eyes and I thought at once of the evening glow of the city streets when the sun has gone behind the tallest houses, when the end of the day is near, and the canyon-alleys are suffused with dusk and slow-moving lights: when men waken from the sleep of day and returning in upon themselves think of love, and the darkness where love is, and wander out from the city to the dark fields seeking a secret loneliness for their pain.

Rory had forgotten that he must not look down and he fell sidewise on the horse's back, and when he reached the opposite bank he began talking of his foolishness and never ceased reverting to it the whole day. He looked down, you see, he looked down into the flood, he forgot, man, he looked down, and, by God, if he hadn't looked, but he looked into the water, he knew he shouldn't, – wasn't it I myself was telling you not to look at the flood, but whatever happened I looked down. And Cripes! when I did. . . . To stay him and have peace for my own thought I told him that he had but little talk the night before: but he did not heed my jibes, and chattered on, glad of the morning and reckless about the last mile between us and the foothills. He was a little bellied fellow, his mouth like a crack across a potato, his cap distended by a cane hoop just like a plate on the top of his head. He had pinned a coloured minature of the Virgin to the front of his queer cap, and when in the mood, his talk bubbled from him in anything but a virginal flow. How he had sworn at me yesterday when he sighted the enemy troops, and I could not see at all the tiny khaki figures below us on the lower slopes!

'Do you see them?' he had cried with equal stress on each word after the manner of his dialect. 'Christ, can't you see them?' he had shouted in rage, saying it as if it were spelled in two syllables, Chi-rist. 'Will you look at them, Christ, will you look at them when I tell you?'

I used to wonder at his affection for me in spite of such failures as this. In better mood now he jabbered on while we made our way up against the sprung wind and a hilly place. At last we heard the incessant knocking of a threshing engine on the bald summit in front of us, and we made our way to it. Up here the wind was a storm, and it blew the chaff about the sky like yellow snow blown before the wind. First the blue slate-roof, then the white walls of the house, the yellow stack of corn, the stone-wall fences of the fields, and at last the little black engine jumping like a kettle on the hob, while all the time the men swung their arms to and fro in labour: soon we were amongst them telling one group after another of the night's and day's adventures. Rory gabbled between every pant after his climb, telling about the horse and how I could not see the little grey figures when they came around us the evening before. From where we stood, the Rough looked like a flat plain and the distant mountains like hunchbacks in a row. I watched the whole country change with the shadows of the flying clouds, listening to the engine, with its disyllabic knocking, ceaseless since the dawn, and the wind's cry, and Rory shouting above all.

'There was the bloody mare in the middle of the river, I'm not in the habit of horses, you know, a man that was used to horses wouldn't mind, but I wasn't in the habit of them and I never was, and what did I do and the bloody mare there in the middle of the river, what did I do, what did I do? The thing I did! What should I *do*, I ask you, but look down at the flood, so look down at the flood I did. I looked down and only for the lad got a grip of me I was down. Cripes, I was. I was! If I would only not look down at the flood, you see, but I looked down, and by Christ!'

Here Rory began to shake in his excitement, too moved to be articulate.

The chaff was always driving away before the wind, and now and again someone would look up and around at the sky and say to the man whose stack was being threshed in this communal fashion of the mountains:

'Maybe, it will hold dry.'

The other would look up and around and say:

'Maybe it will. It might then. It's a strong wind.'

Then they would set to work again, piking and tossing the broken sheaves and we moved down at last to the road.

The road twisted eastward behind the rocks, and nothing but the tops of the telegraph poles showed where it ran after that. It was bare and empty, so we ran for it, crossed it, and in another moment Rory was crying that a lorry was coming around the bend. Heart-leaping, we doubled our pace and fell upon our bellies in the moss, squirming around like legless things to face the road. In a moment more the shots began to whine away over our heads, and I saw two awkward figures firing at us as they ran: I fired wildly in reply until my bolt jammed, and then rolled away into a hollow that by the fortunes of war lay behind me: thereupon I ran through the rocky place, through the bracken and the bog, more madly than ever in my life before, and raced for such a lengthy spell that when at last I fell helpless upon the ground my breath pumped in and out painfully and my heart beat against my side like a thing trying to leave my body. I heard the shots still ringing and the bullets whining high up in the air, flying no doubt in a great parabola so that I fancied that I heard them thud when spent into the soft earth, a rainbow curve completed.

When at last they ceased and our hearts returned to a normal beat we were come to a little lowflung wood of birch and rowan, the silver bark peeling black stripes horizontally from the birch, the red berries of the rowan wind-blown on its delicate branches. Grey rocks covered the interstices of the trees and the sun fell sometimes on the rock to warm the cold colour: a stream twisted through the rough ground and its sound was soft and bass, and up on a sudden promontory silhouetted against the sky was a single figure who was working in a series of vigorous thrusts on a spade. We remained in the little wood for many hours, listening to the bass-viol of the falling water, to the wind pulling at the larchtops and shaking the tender rowan, and sometimes listening with attention to the drumming of a lorry as it passed in and out of earshot in the near distance.

Excited by danger, and by the beauty of this calm place, the falling stream beside me, the trees moving all around, I began to think again of the young woman in the black cloak who had become aware that I too lived just as much as anyone she had hitherto known at church or fair. I saw her always as she had come to us in the night, her black cloak hanging heavily against her skin as she led us to the quiet kitchen and the dead embers on the hearth. Surely life had a less miser purpose in this encounter than in the thousands of thousands of meetings when men cross and recross in towns and country places? Time and again they had appeared barren and futile, but rather than believe them fruitless, rather than feel as a spool revolving in a shuttle, I had lived instead in the unrest of a chessman fingered by a hesitant player. Now sloth of mind, as sometimes before, drew down my heart to the beauty of this life, and in this little birdless wood, I began to dream. When the stream had carved itself a majesty, passing barges and lights on the barges would ride the brown smoke of the evening air, each crossing the scurrying wake of waves from swifter hulls to disappear slowly through the dusk while men sat on each deck and smoked in content with life, and recalled all the dead among my acquaintances who have suffered too willingly the futility of life. There is an owl in the Celtic fable who had seen each rowan as a seed upon a tree, and its length seven times fallen to the earth and seven times over raised in leaf; it had seen the men whose bones were washed from these boulders when the rain was rounding them to pebbles from seven hundred times their height this dropping evening; it had seen the men for whom the promontory above me was a bottomless valley and the hollow place where Rory and I sat was a high mountain before the Flood. Such an owl called out of the dusk at me and its cry filled me with age and the peace that comes when we feel the wheels of the passing years turn so slowly it is almost complete rest. I dozed as I lay – life stopped for me while my eyes swayed and fell.

But Rory, his mind whirling, sang of passionate life. He sang of the old Newgate murderer, the song found scrawled upon his Newgate cell after they hanged him and buried him: how eerie to see him ghosting like this in Ireland, his disjointed spine rattling Rory, not aware that before the night had fallen death would have got him, too – his body plugged full of English lead – sang cheerily: –

My name is Samuel Hall, Samuel Hall,
My name is Samuel Hall, Samuel Hall,
My name is Samuel Hall,
And I've only got one ball,
Here's my curse upon you all,
God damn your eyes!

I killed a man 'tis said, so 'tis said,
I killed a man 'tis said, so 'tis said,
I hit him on the head,
With a bloody lump of lead,
And I laid the buggur dead,
God damn his eyes!

I did not heed the words, but the sense, entering my mind, broke my drowsy dream in part. Looking up I saw the West grow cold and saffron as if the threshers of the morn, reduplicated in valley after valley had blown a storm of corn-sheaves against the falling cape of night. A score of birds fulfilling their ancient ritual flew homeward in formation: as they passed into the blazing sun I dropped my eyes again to the stream, but while I had turned away it had changed to silver against the dark stones. Night was dropping upon us secretly and we must move onward to some house where we could sit before the flames and doze before a chimney-wall browned with soot and old invading rain and sleep quietly while the night passed by.

We tramped ahead, keeping to the backroads still, but quite without fear now that we were so many miles from the enemy, and at last, high up among the hills, walking in the reaches of the wind we came to the little roadside house that was shop and post office in one, and we sat there wearily by the fire.

The land was cold and windswept here, and the few elms that stood outside, landmark for many miles around, were torn by the wind and being blown to pieces like the clouds in the sky. Rory was to stay here for the night, but I must move farther on, and I sat by the fire waiting impatiently for the cart that was to carry me part of the last few miles to a supper and a safe bed. At the end of the kitchen the old carter was whispering across the little counter with the woman of the house; the young daughter of the house stood beside them lighting an oil-lamp that hung from a beam overhead, and presently the two grey pates were lit from above. The light fell in a warm glow on the unpainted counter, plain as when its planks first arrived from the town of Macroom twenty miles away and were flung on the kitchen floor for the admiration of the little fat woman with her little fat baby. The glow fell on the soiled and mutilated bank-notes, on the silver and copper coins and on the blue sugar-bags and the dun surfaces of the remainder of Saturday night's groceries. I waited while they talked in a secretive whisper, perhaps over the account, perhaps about their oldwives' gossip of the countryside. Perhaps they were wishing us wandering guerillas farther on and wishing the fighting at an end lest their barns be burnt over their hay or their thatch over their heads. Outside in the windy night the old horse was tethered to an elm, its head bent low and its eyes heavy with sleep like a Buddha's. Thinking of it I sat by the fire and raked in the ashes with the muzzle of my rifle. I felt it would rain heavily tonight though the wind was getting stronger, and once again I thought of the girl in the black cloak; but already she had slipped many miles into the things of the past, and in another day she would have slipped wholly from my mind not to be recalled unless in some odd place at some odd time when I would wonder about our strange encounter, and in sentimental mood wonder if she ever asked a comrade where I had gone, saying that I was a nice boy, perhaps more than that. She had been at such a door as this in her mother's arms and would as her mother had done stand there again in one, two, three years' time bidding farewell to the very last mocking couple of her bridal party, and looking at the sky with her young husband, see the coming of the rain and lock and latch the door upon it, and returning to the dying fire would hear the first drops fall on the warm core, and the rising howl strip the elms; he would draw her toward him and she, feeling her youth passed for ever, would weep softly and secretly in the dark and then smile for her first ungirdling. What sad weavings the old Weaver of life can think of, as if all will not fray away and moths rise from the eyes of his dears, and all his storms crumble at the end in dust.

I heard Rory chant some passage from a hedge-school memory, and turning I saw the young girl of the house watching him, ready for a burst of laughter at the end.

'This,' chanted Rory, 'is a man, the beauty of whose eloquence and the wisdom of whose conversation is balanced only by the impeccability of his character and the noble qualities of the mind wherewith God has endowed him, for it is abundantly clear to me,' continued the emperor in a graver tone, 'that wherever the original refulgence of the human mind is neither adumbrated in its infancy nor adulterated in its maturity, the unique powers of the will of man must inevitably produce in every individual, no matter in what clime he has been born, nor under what star he has first seen the light of day, if only he be true to what is right and turn from what is wrong, the genius of an Alexander, the oratory of a Cicero, the wisdom of a Solomon, or the sublime skill of a Leonardo da Vinci, as the case may befall.'

The little bellied fellow finished with a breathless rush, and turning to the girl clapped his hands and clapped her hands in applause at his own performance.

I found that this child was to accompany me a little way on the road and we snuggled into the back of the cart and sat shouting our farewells as it jolted away from the two yellow squares of light and from the figures crowding the open door. Then as we entered the spacious dark, silence fell on us three. I stretched back on the floor of the cart listening to the braggart storm. I felt young and wilful under its breath; I loved to hear its impotent whine: off behind the ridge of mountain through which a pass had been cut maybe five centuries ago by roadmakers rotted in the grave there came the great spreading light of the moon. We were following the direction of the racing clouds, they flying beyond us in the sky. My eyes were beginning to close with the rough swaying of the cart when suddenly the child clasping my hand said:

'Are you afraid of the pookas? I am!'

And fell upon my breast and laid her head by mine and I put an arm around her and we lay so, jolting along under the stars and the driving fleeces overhead. But as suddenly, when about a mile had passed she pressed nearer and swiftly kissed me. Then she rolled away from me to the other side of the cart, though still grasping my coat-sleeve in terror of the black night all around.

Presently I left them, and the old cart was soon out of earshot. Jogging on through the dark, my thoughts wandered at will. I pictured the bed where I would sleep – I had slept in so many hundreds that it might be any size or shape, but I chose from my set of images one bed most suitable to the stormy night. It was the marriage bed of the peasants, made of plain wood, closed on back, side and top, and but only the front left open, and that sometimes covered by a curtain on a string: it was like a beehive with a flat crown and sloping roofs, shallow at head and foot, so that a man could stand in comfort only in the middle of the bed. The storm might howl for all I cared, the rain might drench the stooks and fill the yards with pools of dung; the windows might rattle – I would sleep the night through and wake to find the skies clearing in the morning. I was hungry for food and sleep, and in this bed I would lie for a while thinking over the day's happenings, trying to find a scheme for things in the true dreamer's way, a scheme into which everyone would fit as by nature, the woman of the cloak, the little girl, myself, the dead husband, the carter, the crowds that meet and remeet, as it seemed aimlessly, blindly – and all these would jumble in my mind and quaint combinations occur and confuse me, and my reasoning fall under the sway of interweaving images and sleep come secretly with her hood.

At last the bright square of window-light slid into view, quartered by the crucifix framework, and I found the causeway to the door and groped my way to it after the window vanished in its own recess: I played blindman's buff with the door and at last with outstretched hands I stumbled against it and grasped the latch.

Fire-flames, a settle, and maybe a white cloth and something to eat other than dry bread and tea with goat's milk. I lifted the latch and looked in: a young woman stood with her back to me stiffened in a posture of surprise as when I first fumbled at the door, but relaxing and turning when I spoke, touched her soft hair and bade me enter: it was the young woman of the morning.

'Is there e'er a wake here?' I asked seeing the lone kitchen, my voice trembling as I spoke.

'Devil a wake then!' She was smiling at me again.

'Yeer very quiet then,' I said, looking around at the cleanswept kitchen, and then at her skin like a boy's under its first white down.

' 'Tis quiet, wisha,' she answered making way for me as I moved to the settle. I asked if there would be room for the night, and she said there would be and welcome.

'And a bit to eat for a hungry man?'

'Surely, if you don't mind waiting for just a moment or two.' I wanted to ask how she came before me to the hither side of the country twelve long miles away from her last night's hostel. I flung aside my bandolier and raincoat; I laid my rifle and pack and belt in a corner. She went to the end of the kitchen and I heard the splash of water and the paddling of hands, and when she returned to me by the fire, wiping her fingers, they were rosy when the apron fell. She half knelt before the fire to blow it with a hand-bellows, and as she worked her body formed a single curve, one breast on one knee, and her arms circling the knee while she worked lustily at the bellows. I could see the little wrinkles at each corner of her lips – laughter wrinkles, maybe?

'Are the old people in bed?' I asked.

'Yes.' Her voice trembled, I thought.

'And the rest? Where's the rest from you?'

'There's nobody else. Tom, my brother, is on the run in Kerry.' I leaned back on the settle and the flames crackled into life.

'Well, you must be very lonely here all alone.'

'I have got used to it,' she answered, patting her hair with the fingers of her hands: how soft it looked! Then she stood up and began to spread a white cloth on the white table, and then to lay a milk jug, a cup and saucer, a sugar basin, a pot of jam.

'Do you live here?'

'Yes.'

'But you're not always as desolate as this – surely?'

'Desolate, just as you say; this is a lonely district, you know.'

'Well it's not so bad at all now,' I said. 'I shouldn't mind if I lived here – the mountains and the valleys....'

She halted in her step and faced me: the little mouth was gathered into a hard white button of flesh.

'You would soon tire of these mountains! The city, though, that's where I'd like to live. There's company there, and sport and educated people, and a chance to live whatever life you choose!'

She had put two eggs into a little black pot of boiling water, and the water bubbled and leaped around them with a hissing. A blast of wind came down the chimney and drove a cloud of firesmoke into the kitchen. We sat silent and presently went to the table and she poured me red tea to drink and I cut the brown loaf and plastered it with butter and jam, and ate greedily. She sat before the fire, and I asked her why she did not like the district, but she only looked at me and said nothing. I asked again, pleading that I wished to know, really and truly. She answered:

'Because this farm is bare and high. The land is poor. And this townland has a Northern aspect.'

A heavy drop of rain fell on the fire – the storm was howling. I saw the sea of discontent and unrest that these words were born of, saw the drizzling rain and no sun shining on it, saw her looks steal round her to this farm and to that and back from them to her own home. Another gust of wind blew the smoke around her and she turned away from it and clasped my knee to prevent herself from falling from the low stool.

'You'll be choked,' said I, and her eyebrows stirred and she smiled at me. I laid my palm on her hand and thought of the whole livelong day I had spent, the rick that must be threshed before the wind fell, the carter jogging through the wet night, the sea of darkness outside the door. How many days could I live without a complete revolt! I spoke earnestly.

'It's a cruel country to have to live in.'

She spoke kindly to me then.

'I think you are honest,' she said.

'Do you think that?'

'I think you *are* honest. *Really* honest,' she said again.

Looking at her soft eyes, and at her soft hair my eyes wandered down to the first shadows of her breasts: she caught my glance and looked down at her warm bosom and then at me and she smiled. As I moved to her I saw the little broken corner of her tooth; I had no word to say; so I sat beside her before the leaping flames and put my arms around her and felt in the cup of my hollow palm the firm casque of her breast. Smiling at me as a sick woman might smile upon a doctor who brought her her ease from pain she slipped my hand beneath her blouse to where I felt the warmth of her skin and her warm protruding nipple, and I leaned to her for a kiss.

A rush of feet came to the door and the little girl from the roadside house flung it wide with a cry to me to run, to run; Rory was shot dead; they were coming West for me! I bundled up my equipment, ran in a flash through the open door into the dark night, and raced on and on – stumbling and falling and going I cared not where but away from the flashing lights to the North. When I fell into a panting walk I was like a man who has been listening to music the livelong day and after it his mind is full of strange chords, and ill-recollected they torture him with a sense of something lost. On my bare head the rain fell heavily and aslant, now and again it was blown into my face by the wind, and the clouds totally blotted out the moon. Full of terror for such a death as I knew Rory's was I filled every house with armed men, fierce men to whom killing was a little thing and torture but little more, and my imagination and the stories I had heard drove me blindly on through the sodden night. I trudged a way through the pathless bogs and tore through briery dikes: all that night I found no shelter from the lashing rain and I met not a single tree in leaf: long after midnight I saw a little glinting window leap suddenly out of the dark about a mile away, and as I thrust away from it, away to safety, into the rain, the memory of its light tortured me as the memory of cool winds must torture the damned of hell.

At last I came upon a lonely ruin upon the mountain, three walls, and I lay on the lee side of it while the rain dripped on me from the remnants of its eaves. When I awoke a dim radiance lit the falling haze, but whether it was the dawn or the sinking moon or any hour past three or before three I could not say. No sound was to be heard: no living thing moved: no bird stirred the wet air: the falling haze made no sound. I rose chattering and trembling, and my feet splashed through the wet earth and the drowned grass, and when I halted there was quiet. I crossed a little stone wall and one of the stones fell with a mighty sound. I might have been the last human creature to crawl to the last summit of the world waiting until the Deluge and the fortieth night of rain would strain him upwards on his toes while the water licked his stretched neck. Yet everywhere they slept sound abed, my dark woman curling her warm body beneath the bed-clothes, the warmer for the wet fall without, thinking if she turned and heard the dripping eaves – that the winter was at last come.

Cold till doom!
The storm has spread.
A river is each furrow on the slope,
Each ford is a full pool.

Each lake is a great tidal sea,
Each pool is a great lake,
Horses cannot cross the ford,
Nor two feet.

The fish of Ireland are wandering,
There is no strand upon which the waves
  do not pound.
Not a town is in the land,
Not a bell, not a crane's whining cry.

The wolves in the wood of Cuan cannot rest,
They cannot sleep in their lair:
Even the little wren cannot shelter
In her tiny nest on the side of Lon.

Keen wind and cold ice
Have burst upon the little world of birds.
The blackbird cannot shelter its side
In the wood of Cuan.

Cosy was our pot upon the nook,
In the crazy hut on the slope of Lon:
The snow has crushed the wood,
And toilsome is the climb to Ben-bo.

The ancient bird of Glenn Rye
Is grieved by the cold wind:
Her misery and her pain are great,
The ice will get into her throat.

From flock and from down to rise
Were folly for thee! Take it to heart.
Ice heaped on every ford,
Wherefore I say 'cold till doom.'

Down below me in the valley I heard an early cart; the morning wind, light and bitter, sang occasionally in the key of the flooded streams. The dawn moved along the rim of the mountains and as I went down the hill felt the new day come up around me and felt life begin once more its ancient, ceaseless gyre.

The Small Lady

I

Three days after the disappearance of Mrs Sydney Browne this scandalous ballad – I dare not give it in full – was being sung in every market town in Munster. The groups that listened to it in the side-lanes listened with averted faces as if they feared to be interrupted before the end, and when it was finished there would be a scramble for copies of the song and everyone would then move quickly away, the women hiding the green sheet of the ballad between their breasts, the men stuffing it into their clasped purses among the silver and the dirty notes:

ON THE SIX SINN FEIN BOYS SHOT IN CORK
BARRACKS BY DRUM HEAD COURT MARTIAL

(*Air*: Canada-io!)

Come all ye brave Sinn Feiners
And listen to my song,
How six brave Irish rebel boys
Were murdered in the wrong.
An English woman that sold them,
A servant of the crown,
And the name of the cursed she-spy
'Twas Mrs Sydney Browne.

She drove to Aughameelinn
And told the English Tans
To come and take these brave young boys
With all their armed bands.
They came and took them by surprise

And caught them where they lay
And shot them by drum head court martial
In Cork at the dawn of day.

The name she had was the Small Lady,
Five foot in her scarlet gown;
God's curse may light upon her
And fall from heaven down,
For she sold our boys to England's Tans
So they fell without a blow
Face to face with a firing squad
All standing in a row.

But now the Tans are searching wide
For our Mrs Sydney Browne
In Cork and Kerry and Tipperary
And up to Dublin town.
The Small Lady is hard to find;
And why do you think 'tis so?
They've searched the whole of Irish soil
But they haven't searched below.

Dig five by two by two foot five
For yeer scarlet hat and gown,
But ye will never find her alive –
The servant of the crown.
She's in bed with her fancy serving man
Where the pissabeds do grow . . .
So, dig down and down and down, me boys,
Dig down and down and down,
And the Tans will never find her
Till they meet her in Hell below.

She heard a version of it, her death-song, the night they took her from her home and drove her into the mountains in the car they stole from a nearby garage, singing as they tore through the village into the night. How the car ever carried its load nobody ever knew, for it had stood under the rains by the side of the road ever since old Lord Bandon had made a jesting gift of it to the garage proprietor winters ago. Its roof and upholstery were torn and tattered, and fouled by roosting hens; it had four flat tyres and all its parts were loose; but they filled it with petrol and pushed it until it started and so it screamed out of the village with its load of singing guerillas, and the little red-coated woman sitting at the back, beside her butler, almost buried under the trench-coated riflemen clinging to every aery perch they could find on roof and wing. Of course after a mile the first tyre whirled off but when the driver halted to replace it the captain would have no delays and ordered him to drive on. When the second tyre bounded into the ditch the driver looked enquiringly at the captain, but the captain only grinned and jerked his thumb forward. So that at the loss of the third and the last tyre, and mile by mile of the other loose parts, the toolbox here, the bonnet there, a window, then another window, the crowd only roared with delight, interrupting their ribaldry for the moment, and even the butler grinned feebly. But to the woman, who loved cars as she loved her dogs and her horses, it was almost terrifying to hear this skinned thing screaming up through the silent hills in its cloud of boiling steam and burning oil, and when it halted finally, a bearing burnt clean through, throbbing and choking like a winded hack, she was gone white – even the little red spots under her eyes were pale and you could see through the rouge the blue of her lips. But her rage did not last long; it vanished as she stepped from the car. The well-known valley stretched beneath her eyes.

The sun was setting not beyond one but several horizons that reached to the ultimate haze where sky and land swam together. In the valley the sun was set and the river shone there like silver, and a tree-crowned islet floated in it like a black ship. Down there was her house and her dogs yapping for their supper and her servants, forgetful of them, talking of her before the red glow of the kitchen fire. If the yards were cold and silent and wet underfoot, there was, too, the pleasant drip-drop into the hollow waterbutts, and by the river's edge the willows dragging their tender buds of March in the milk-smooth tide. A mist was coming up the hills like an advancing army, and she pulled off her hat and bared her throat to the breasts for the fall of the gentle pricking rain, slipping insensibly into what her friends used call 'her O Goddam mood,' indifferent to, even contemning anything that could happen her. She had loved this day of clouds moving low in the sky, of soft showers streaming down the air, a day of aqueous light that seemed to have nothing to do with sun but came and went like cold waves, a radiance rather than a light, as if the white clouds were luminous by nature and carried their pale glow within them as they moved. She had made love to it since morning when she plunged naked into the icy river, racing back barefooted in her scarlet dressing-gown over the soaked lawn. She would not care now if they made her spend the night wandering over the mountains – she even laughed quietly to herself to think of the game rising against the moon, the little fishes darting out of their sleep – she would not care if they sate the night out watching the embers dying in some farmer's kitchen, not even care if they then shot her in the dawn for 'a cursed English spy.' Only she must have a few more hours of beautiful and passionate life, and then, 'O Goddam all, good-bye green fields, blue sky; off I pop into the great Has-been!' Yet when the gentle fall began to trickle across her lips and down the channel of her breasts she shivered: it was cold up here even where the sun still shone, cold with the coldness of the sweating earth, and when she turned to look at her captors she thought they looked like homeless animals clustered in a storm. They broke up even as she looked at them, and the young fellow set off as her special guard motioned her with them into the woods. In here the pine-needles clung to their boots and every leaf bore a bright drop, and though there was light in the sky above, the evening star shone like a lantern through the swaying tops of the pines. When the car had stopped they had hurled it with shouts of glee over the edge of the road, but she had noticed that they fell at once into a gloomy silence when the quiet murmur of the stream rose again, uninterrupted out of the dusk. Now again she noticed how they moved in complete silence, their rifles at the ready, looking nervously left and right into the dark alleys of the wood. She knew that there was no likelihood of meeting anybody here, miles away from anywhere, in the heart of the hills, but as they went up and on in this furtive manner, the branches caressing their faces, swishing back after they had passed, she began to feel less confident. When some bird or a bat squeaked past her face she even caught her guard's hand for a second in terror, and soon the damp smell of rotting leafmould and dead-wood that made this place heavy like a tomb sucked her last drop of courage from her and left her, like them, glancing to and fro into the dim shadows. A branch crackled and they stopped dead as if every man were turned to a statue; whereupon as they listened the silence became ponderous and rang in their ears. A bird fluttered but gave no cry. Then through the darkness a bell tolled with long pauses after each deep stroke, and as they quickened their paces the trees rolled away and there was the darkening blue of the sky and the first bright stars.

In the monastery it was not so much a fine soft day in spring as Friday, a day of hard Lenten fare. In the refectory there was only one guest, a drunkard, one of those wretches whom the city sends periodically to the monastery to be cured of sights and mad visions. The monks receive the poor creatures with a kind of sardonic pity, feeding them with ever-dwindling drams of the whisky that has maddened them until they can be finally weaned of their lust for it and turned loose on the healthy food and drink of the monastery farms. Then there is no escape from penance, the realization of sin, the promise of reformation. In the refectory, watching this shivering wretch pick sadly at his dry bread and sip sadly from his mug of black tea, was also Brother John the guestmaster, his temples deep-hollowed, his cheeks scooped, his beard white and scanty, his lips thin and bloodless from a life of penance and hard living. Absolved as guestmaster from the rule of silence he gabbled so incessantly to the drunkard at the table-head that he might have been making up for time lost when as a young fellow in brown cloth he tamed his lusty blood with silence and fasting and praying and the flagellations of his cincture on his rump as he sang in the choir-loft at his Hours,

. . . de coelo praestiti eis,

and a blow,

. . . delectamentum habentem.

Often he washed the blood from his thighs before he lay to rest, and could not sleep. *He* could tell topers how to tame the heat of the flesh: if they only would, he often told them, lower their breeches nightly for twenty or thirty years to the knots of a stout rope they would, presently, become different men.

The drunkard was still on his diet of whisky though the allowance was down to a glass every morning and night now, but Brother John thought it great fun to watch him nibble his Lenten fare. It was good March fare for any Christian man, and Brother John had himself eaten little more during the whole day and he had not tasted meat for many weeks, even on Sundays when he might.

'Aha, me boyo,' said Brother John, stroking his white whiskers upwards and outwards with back of his bony hand, 'if we had you here a twelvemonth we'd soon make a monk of yeh.'

'It's poor fare for any man,' whispered the toper. 'It's the poorest bloody fare I ever ate.'

'No "bloodys" now. No bad words in the monastery. Do you want to destroy all the virtue of your fast? God can withhold his grace even as he can give it.'

'Excuse the language, father....'

'Brother. Just plain Brother John,' said the monk, fearful of the sin of vanity at his elbow.

To the drunkard every frocked man was a priest – his was not a mind to distinguish half-ways and go-betweens, it must be with him a feast or a famine, the highest throne in heaven or the lowest pit in hell. So he was by turns either a total abstainer or a hopeless bib.

'Yes, father; I mean – yes, brother. I do forget.'

He sighed deeply and sucked his black tea.

'I dunno how we'll ever get to heaven, brother. When I sees all the monks do in here I gives up all hope of ever attaining salvation.'

'That's despair,' warned the guestmaster with a bony finger. 'It's a sin to say the like. Even to think the like is a sin, one of the greatest sins that may be committed. It's one of the seven deadly sins. It's almost a sin against the Holy Ghost, and the sin against the Holy Ghost will never find forgiveness. Beware of the sin of despair. God is infinitely merciful to us all. One sinner returned to the fold who enters heaven rejoices Him more than the ninety-nine blessed. Let me never hear you say the like again,' he concluded, easily slipping his palms between his belt and his empty stomach.

'It is a sin, father, I mean brother. Sure God is good and He will forgive us all.'

'He will forgive us all,' said Brother John, with a gentle mockery in his voice at the drunkard's lapse now into the contrary sin of presumption. 'He will if we do penance and seek the means of salvation. If we do penance, I say. Do you hear me? How do you find the bread now?'

'Ah, it's bloody dry, father. I mean it's a dry mouthful.'

'Did I hear you say "bloody?" Do you want to be without your little glass of John Jameson, tonight?'

'It's dry, father, it's dry. Sure God knows it's dry. I mean no harm in the world, father; sure you can see for yourself I'm as gentle as a lamb. Only for the wan failing I mean no harm in the world. I beg your pardon, father. I mean the bread is dry.'

'Ahadee, but you were the unlucky man, I think,' said Brother John, pausing to look out of the black glass of the window at shining Hesperus, 'the unlucky man, that is to say, to come to Mount Melleray for a cure in the month of March.'

The drunkard forgot himself so utterly at the bitter truth of this that he banged his fist on the table and cried out in earnest blasphemy:

'Jasus, wasn't I though!'

At the profanity Brother John flew into a sudden rage and his white eyebrows gathered into a knot above his weak, dimmed eyes and his beard rose as his lips tightened. The drunkard had realized the transgression of his oath even as he made it, and he raised his hand cringingly like a dog expecting a whiplash. He glanced in fright right and left of the old pink-cheeked brown-cassock, down at his skirts, at his hairy ankles, into the dark corners of the room, anywhere but at the hard fur-rimmed eyes that glared down at him in silent contempt. But just then feet began to crunch on the gravel walk outside and the window frames shook under a blast of mountain wind and splashes of sudden rain broke against the windowpanes like the crackling of empty sea-shells. The guest-master's bell rang in the kitchen and Brother John swished around from the drunkard so that his beads rattled and his personal odour scented the air, and he walked off into the gloomy shadows of the hall where on each side of the door two blue side windows cut in the darkness graded lengths of a somewhat lesser gloom. As he undid the bars and put the door on its chain the drunkard peeping out after him saw through one of the side windows a very bright star and lowered his head slowly, so slowly that it might have been the hour-hand of a clock, for at his heels he had suddenly seen a gleam of light on the pitch-pine leg of the hall-stool and behind it he could hear a real rat gnawing in the dark. When the bell rang loudly again he jumped with terror, and his heavy lower lip began to dribble. Then the door opened gratingly, and he was staring beyond the flame of the monk's guttering candle into the rain and dark at the wet glitter of arms and the crowding faces of hunted men. He did not see the guestmaster's stern face soften in welcome, but the next minute the hall seemed full of dripping figures whispering and clustering about the old monk and his blowing candle. The drunkard smiled too, for he always declared he was a fierce-minded man and he hoped that one or other of these 'shinners would have a half a pint of whisky in a bottle in his pocket to wet a fellow-patriot's whistle.' But as he was lost in rumination of the golden liquor and its labelled bottle they pushed past him into the fire where he followed, to hover disconsolately about them, giving his pipe to one, his matches to another, his tobacco to a third, but getting no smell of the whisky he craved so much. Now that they were safe and sheltered they showed by their sudden relaxing into careless comfortable positions, on the floor, on the chairs, by the walls, that they had been through a great deal in the past few days; they dried their knees wearily before the little fire, smoked with the heavy pulls of men long denied a smoke, and ate and drank ravenously of the poor leavings of the supper-table. The toper left them in a bad humour and went off, peeping into the hall again, where besides Brother John and the captain he found only another young fellow and a ladylike sort of little woman in a red coat bending over an old hatless man collapsed on a hall-bench. But he slid away when the old monk looked at him and, though he returned now and again to peep at the woman in the red coat and even once whispered to her timidly to ask what was 'up with the old four-eyes,' he never remained, and at length, unnerved by his own caution and the dread of the monk's eyes, he disappeared by a back door and was seen in the refectory no more that night.

The rain dripped outside and the wind blew in under the door and chilled Brother John's bare ankles, and the wet feet and the thighs of the woman. She had left the old butler, for she could not bear his apologies, and she stood in the centre of the hall looking at the monk picking at the candle until his fingers became engrimed, and at the captain picking at the monk's vest in his eagerness to convince him that there was no harm in housing her there for a night. But the old monk argued the rule *contra mulieribus* and scratched his poll with his grease-covered nails and the captain blew his nose between his fingers in exasperation. In disgust she turned to the boy at the door and seeing his face clearly for the first time she was delighted to find herself looking at the eager uplifted face of a boy of the cities. She let her eyes wander over his long tapering hands that clasped his rifle, his waist like a colt or a greyhound, back to his eyes that looked at her with a frank and open look, and at once she felt she could speak to this boy: she felt the same thrill she had often felt as a young woman in Africa or India when she saw the pale cheeks of a European traveller or tourist in a boma or bazaar, a thrill that used set her thinking sadly of England and home, her parents and her sisters, loved bits of town and country and all that home meant to a young girl exiled on her marriage-day. So she looked at him now, with what her male friends had dubbed her 'please-please eyes,' and before he could gather his wits against hers he had smiled back at her, and in a minute he was promising to get her something for her butler and later on, if he could manage it, a cup of tea for herself if they remained there the night. She was much older than he, but her hair was still flaxen and wavy and the pink spots under her cheeks had returned, and he could not refuse those appealing looks and her slightly whimpering voice. But she could get no farther just then for Brother John tapped her on the shoulder and beckoned her to follow him, and she had to go after the bony heels down a long whitewashed corridor into the monastery. As she passed the refectory door she saw the merciless eyes watching her, and (as a painter might realize the drabness of life by seeing in passing a face in a photographer's showcase) she realized her position for the first time when one face among those that looked at her grinned cruelly to see her go: he was a black-faced fellow with a row of jet curls low across his forehead, a black-eyed brute that looked up at her like a bull ready to charge, and, as she passed down under the Gothic arches of the corridor, that face remained in her mind with her other pictures of the dirty hands and head of the monk, his dirty underclothing showing at the neck, the stain of spilt tea on the cloth in the refectory, the cold emptiness of the hall, so that as she entered the guests' corridor, now deserted, she felt that everything here was stale and dirty, that her footsteps left circles of dust on the long brown carpet, that every cranny was filled with spiders' webs and dead flies, and she hated the feeling that ugliness had descended on her and that she might die surrounded by it. Then the monk ushered her into a high musty room and, leaving her the dirty wick, locked the door after him and padded away out of earshot. The silence of the night enveloped her and her ears began to ring with it again until by degrees she began to distinguish the dripping of the rain on the sill outside the window, and the occasional whisper of the light wind in the trees beneath it. Wearily she moved to the window and lifted the heavy frame to let in the night air. The rain had ceased, and she leaned her elbows on the wet sill and looked over the dark countryside and up at the blowing clouds. There she remained a long time, perhaps an hour, listening to the distant fall of waters, and watching the come and go of the moon edge the saw-toothed pine-forests. Then for sheer weariness and hunger she lay on the great damp bed to rest and because she was afraid of the dark she did not blow out the smelly wick. She found herself reading over and over again the typed script tacked to the timbered wall beside her head. Clearly it was intended to be the last thing one saw before falling asleep, the first on waking. It said:

You

are alive tonight. *You* may not see another night. Before the next night has passed you may be dead.

ETERNITY, ETERNITY, ETERNITY!

Every idle thought, word, deed and omission will be judged against you. By the result of that judgment *you* will either be in heaven with God or in Hell with the devils for all

ETERNITY, ETERNITY, ETERNITY!

Will *you* barter a few short years in this Vale of Tears against all ETERNITY? Life is short, but the joys and the terrible pains of Eternity go on

For ever and for ever and for ever.

ETERNITY, ETERNITY, ETERNITY!

Will *you* barter the brief lusts and passing pleasures of the few moments of this life to be in the flames of Hell for all

ETERNITY, ETERNITY, ETERNITY?

Burning without cease, without a second's rest, without one single moment's pause, in torment, taunted and tortured by demons, aching and suffering, writhing with the pain of loss and the pain of the flesh, through

ETERNITY, ETERNITY, ETERNITY!

As she read the dead quiet began to smother her and she would cough or swallow loud spittle to break the silence. She waited for the regular fall of the drops outside, but when she moved her feet they made a terrifying rustle at the dark end of the bed. She tried to sleep, but sleep would not come, and so she read and reread the hateful script until she felt that they were already stealing her life from her before it was time. She sat up in bed to see the great monastery stretching away in black straggling masses; with its daily round it had killed the years one by one which she in the valley had sucked as one sucks an orange dry, flirting, smoking, drinking, hunting, playing bridge for high stakes, one long empty round of pleasure. In spite of herself she thought of the old guest-master, walking down the corridor, his candle throwing wavering shadows on the white arches of the ceiling as he swished along; he and all of them would be there tomorrow and after, year after year at their changeless routine, and she lying dead. She feared them because their sureness was snatching from her the only world she had ever known, and as she thought of them, staring out at the monastery buildings, she could almost feel it falling away from her as a field falls away from a soaring bird. The drops fell incessantly from the roof; the cold wind stole along her body. Words from the script seemed to jump out to her as the dying flame leaped and fell. 'You are alive tonight . . .' Sinking in the ooze of a bog, the rain would fall on her as she lay, but not for her; the sun would set over the waves of the horizons, but she would not know it. Others would see the willows swishing their pale hanging leaves in the rain-high tide and love them the more for knowing that *they* lived in their time, whoever else might be dead; and she remembered how on days when the sun glittered in the middle of the blue air she used think of the most passionate people she knew, of Baudelaire and Toulouse-Lautrec and the harlots he used to paint, of La Goulue and Mimi *patte en l'air* and of Yvette Guilbert, and how she used rejoice to think that they were dead and she lived. But now no more? An end to her too? To live no more? In a passion she jumped to the floor and began to undo her frock and smock, and tearing aside all her silks and soft clothes, some falling pale on the dusty carpet as the candle died and blackness folded her she stood and faced the night and the open fields and the straggling buildings, as white then, naked to her breasts, as the moon that came swimming out of a cloud to look at her.

Somebody was tapping at the door for admittance. She ran to it, heard the key being turned, felt the door opening, saw by the light from the sky the boy she had spoken to in the hall. He was carrying a tray of food, and he came in holding it out before him awkwardly.

'You are in the dark,' he said.

'Is that you?' she whispered.

'Have you a match?' he said.

'No.'

'Do you mind taking this tray while I get a candle?'

'We don't want a candle.'

When sitting in the window she had thought of him too, of his long pale hands, of his boyish gestures when he spoke, of the down just curling on his lip, and above all, of his inexperience that seemed to her so infinitely charming. Coming now behind him she found his shoulders and laid her arms about his neck while he stood non-plussed holding out his tin tray.

'What have you for me, dear?'

She wondered if she were being too daring.

'Some cocoa and dry toast. It's all I could get. A fast day.'

Whereupon she tousled her hair with one hand and laughed at him, and because it amused her to think of him standing there with his tray she refused to let him go until he promised he would stay and talk a little: she said she was frightened of the dark, and he believed her, and unaware of what she had done, laid down the tray and came to the window to answer a question about one of the buildings across from her room. It was the chapel, and she spoke of the dim light shining in its ugly red and blue windows and asked if that meant a special service for the Sunday, but he reminded her that it was Friday and explained that it was the sanctuary lamp that never dies before the high altar and the host. Looking sideways where she pointed a white arm in the starlight he touched her soft bosom with his elbow, and to his nostrils rose the scent of her breasts and looking at her he saw her white body. He was only a boy yet, and she who had known many men and travelled far, seeing in his eyes the old troubled look thought he was fallen into her net. But instead, with an extraordinary gentleness and tenderness, he said to her that she must put on her clothes. And this, all unwrought by the experiences of the past few hours, she did with trembling hands and lips, finally beginning to weep silently in pity of herself like a very tired child. Then in a voice more gentle than she had ever heard since her husband courted her so long ago with whispered words, he said to her:

'Won't you eat your cocoa and toast?'

Again she did what she was bidden, and felt again like a child overcome with some small misery, but in her tears she hated the lukewarm cocoa, and could see ahead of her the return of her gloomy mood and tried to keep him by her with little talk. She could not swallow the coarse grains of the cocoa, made without any milk because of the double fast; she asked him to try for a cup of tea or a little glass of wine and some meat after midnight when the fast would cease, and he promised to try. She found him very boyish, and they spoke a little longer of this and that, trifles like the size of the monastery and the guestmaster's name and the drunkard's. His own name was Denis. Hers was Bella. Since he left college he had been fully a year tramping around the mountains with the rebels, and he said he often spent the livelong night walking up and down, up and down under the moon, or watching the rain-pitted mountain lakes, rather than go down to comfort in the dangerous valleys where the roads were. Their talk was like the talk of children telling one another of different worlds. She would have wished him to talk on and on but there was not time and he was extremely shy and became more awkward still when she would speak of her own life. The countryside was very dear to him too, and for so long wandering about in it his body and mind had become as it were soaked and bathed in its beauty, and all physical desires dropped away leaving behind only a calm, placid, thoughtless mind. She believed him completely, even when he spoke to her of the most extraordinary things, just as she used believe her children coming to her without any thought of deceit with their childish tales, and she flooded up with a love for this inexperienced youth such as she had not felt for any male thing since she had her first son; and when he spoke to her of his virginity she believed him and would have loved to take his head on her breasts and weep over her own lost youth. Tears were very near her as she sat in the dim silence with him, but she knew he would go away if he saw her weep, and her throat heavy with their surge, and the corners of her mouth trembling from the effort, she forced them back and tried to talk a little longer of indifferent things. She would have loved to talk of young love and late love, but she only said that she hoped he would come back again before the night ended, and that she would try to be a good woman and not tempt him. But to hear herself say these foolish words was too much for her, and she began to cry to herself, hoping he would not notice. The thought of the irrevocable years overcame her: the thought that all was now gone, marriage and motherhood. Even her friends, her last link with life, were drifting away from her like the dropping leaves. He rose and began to move away, carrying his tray, and she did not know how to keep him before he would have gone, maybe (like so much she had known) never to return.

'Denis, I am not really a sensual woman. But my life – one makes these, so many compromises, one bargains with life to be let live. I suppose I was like you when I was your age. O God, you just don't know it all.'

But he, not even yet begun to live, knowing as yet no great unhappiness or misfortune, thought that these tears of hers were unwomanly, sentimental; he even thought of them with secret contempt as Sassenach tears; and ignorant of the heart-weariness of the woman holding his hand in hers he edged out in silence and, awkward, shut to the door.

She left her door unlatched hoping he might return, and lay on the bed listening. Shortly before Lauds she was awakened from a drowsy sleep by a knocking on the outer door but her heart fell to see the drunkard grinning at her across a tray of tea and cold ham. She asked him to wait for the tray, and to hear him gabble she nibbled at the food. Sitting on the bedkerb he told her in confidence, his breath coming in odorous waves, how with the help of her 'old four-eyes' next door he had stolen a bottle of whisky from Brother John's tallboy. As he spoke, his pig's eyes bulged out till they were like great red-speckled gooseberries, and when he told of the white china handle on the monk's door, creaking as they turned it stealthily, he gripped her arm tightly, and his eyes threatened to burst as he told her of the little red lamp always burning before the altar in the monk's room, and his mouth dribbled on the edge of her tray as he drank again in imagination the hot golden liquor. As he described how they stole away down the corridor in their stockinged feet he lifted his feet in turn, and then he laughed loudly at it all, rubbing his hair up the back of his poll so that it stood on his head like upturned whiskers. She drew him on to talk of Denis.

'Yoy! It was all thanks to the chiseller that kep old Johnny talking Irish to him. Ould Johnny 'ull be looney. Ould Johnny is a bloody ould sham – God forgive me for saying it. He don't know is it on his head or his feet he is, with the column in on him and he keeping it quiet from the abbot. You know Johnny is a great Irishian. And he's a learned man too. He was a lawyer, don't you know, up in Dublin and they say he was a divil entirely for his drop. And it was all over his mother dying he came into the monks. God betune us and all harm, didn't she come to him in her graveclothes and he on a batt. He got a terrible turn. And no wonder! He was in the D.T.s for a month after it. Sure me heart goes out to him. But anyway he came here to the monastery for a cure, and if he didn't make up his mind to go for a priest. So bedad he was for years going for a priest. But sure God didn't call him, and he left the priests and he went back to Dublin and of course, I needn't tell you, he met his ould cronies and he was sousing for a month after, and back he kem to the monastery and weights on his hands and legs for fear he'd tear his gullet out with the desire for it....'

Patiently she drew him back to Denis. He told her how Brother John was even then talking to the boy, delighted to have a listener for his endless Irish verses and riddles and proverbs.

'Oh, but Johnny has great Irish, don't you know. And as vain as you like about it. With his "ahoo, eminent min have complimented me on my facility in the tongue of my fathers." '

And the drunkard put on a very refined accent to imitate the old man.

'And his, "ahoo, I have a remarkable gift of extemporizing on a given theme." Not but that he haven't clever sayings, in Irish and

English. He'd say to you, and you trying to get away from him – ahoo, let me gather me wits now for a specimen. " 'Twas fate they say – ahoo, 'twas fate they say, 'twas wayward fate our web of discord wove, and whilst our inimies jined in hate we never jined in love. Is not that apposite," he says. And now he says, "I wish to give the same thought in an entirely diferent manner. 'Twas fate they say, a wayward fate, that wove our web of discord, and whilst our inimies jined in hate – we never jined in concord. . . ." The bloody ould sham. God forgive me for saying it, but that's all he is. . . .'

She got tired of the wandering gabble of the drunkard and sent him away without the tray, and when he had gone sniggering and jerking his shoulders with a hiccuping delight in his own humour, she sat thinking of the old monk – vain, cocksure, glad to have heard about him since he helped her to think that all there were like him, cocksure and vain. But her thoughts wandered off to Denis, bored by the old monk, and she sniggered to think of his annoyance, and then she wished he would return and talk about it all with her.

When at last Denis broke away from the old monk, under the plea that he must see if his prisoner were safe, it gave him great pleasure to think that he and the guestmaster were the only people awake in all that great monastery among the mountains, and it elated him to think that he alone was enjoying the loneliness of the late hour. He wandered down the guests' corridor as if he were in a deserted building, opening doors at random, and finding every room empty would halt and look through its dark and through the window opposite at the windy, starry sky, and rejoice again that he had the night to himself and that none but he and the wind were awake. When he came to a foxy photograph on the wall, a group of pilgrims taken somewhere in the nineties, he might have been a *revenant* coming looking at the relics of his past world. Pensively, then, listening to the falling rhythms of the wind, like waves falling on a shore, he opened another door and found himself looking at Bella, sleeping on the bed, but as he stood watching her, the night breeze rushed through the room and she opened her eyes wide and with a curved arm drew him down to kiss her. Then the door banged to in the breeze and they were alone in the dark, listening where, through the open window, a dull singing of voices rose up from outside. By the radiance on the ceiling she knew the chapel was lighted up and these the monks chanting their Lauds. She drew him down beside her and though she could not speak for the choking of delight not a shadow of desire entered her; yet, when they heard a short, heavy breathing pause outside their door like a dog about to scratch for entry and Denis moved as if to leap to his feet – her arm held him firmly, until the breathing passed away.

'Who is it?' she whispered.

'It must be Brother John going to Lauds,' he said, and his voice trembled.

'How long will he be away?'

'An hour at least.'

'My darling boy!' and she kissed him and began to murmur love-talk to him.

But it was not Brother John who had crept past the door: it was the drunkard, his thirst grown frenzied now as the pleasure of the stolen liquor evaporated, stealing along the corridor like a tiger, his eyes on the china handle of the guest-master's door.

She lay smiling beside her boy, murmuring such words as no young girl had ever murmured to him, calling him gently by his name as if he were her son, and kissed him again and again with brimming happiness, wishful only that the night should never end. But in him desire moved like a slow serpent, and when she stirred and the musk of her body came to him it circled in his brain like a drunken vapour. His hands grew passionate and she did not resist – rather, gently, almost humbly she permitted his love, never so moved as when she felt his body tremble at the meeting (terrible to him as she knew) of their limbs.

They remained in one another's arms for so long that she lost all feeling of time, and it was at last a wild cry that broke the charm, rising time after time in the corridor outside where the drunkard ran howling past, beating with his fists on their door and every door, crying out in the horrors of drink, 'O Lord God have mercy on me a sinner, Lord God! Lord God! For all Eternity, for all Eternity, for all Eternity!' and so he cried until somebody dragged him away by main force, perhaps some of the guerrillas in their shirt-tails, and there was silence again but for the dull murmurs of the choir below and their own breathing in the dark, except when stopping his mouth with hers, she kissed him long and slow, and even then the choir was silent, until they breathed again. He told her that when she kissed he could only hear a singing within him, and she said it was the eternal singing of the sirens that sit upon the seven turning spheres and whose song we hear only when we make silent love. But she regretted having said this: she had said it too often before to other men, and she genuinely loved her boy.

They parted before the praying had finished below, and that he might not by any chance be suspected she sent him down to the chapel. He hated to enter it, and shy and ashamed he crossed to his pew under the eyes of all the monks, kneeling to the host as he passed over the wide, empty spaces of the nave, a sinner before God and man. When he was kneeling in his place he found he was the only layman in the chapel, and as he looked about him he felt a reproach in everything he saw. The monks of the choir were pale and worn and they sang in brittle passionless voices. The bare planks of the church, every nail hammered by the dead, were as the boards of a coffin, and the altar, bare because of the Lenten time of any flower or ornament except the brown candles shrouded in the purple of sorrow, was as a bier of death. Everywhere he looked was the sign of adoration of the Ender of life. This chapel was the temple of the bodiless, and as the monks sang on and on, he felt more and more the grossness of his own body, and that he, foul flesh, was cursed in the presence of his God. A very tall monk came before the great altar – one of the tallest men he had ever seen, drawing the high scarlet curtains. His long brown sleeves, long and wide as they were, did not cover his red wrists, and as he bowed his head abjectly before the Host his long neck above and his calves below showed as thin as reeds. When he turned and showed his temples, broad and bony and skin-drawn, and his eyes sunken in them, a death's-head. Denis could not bear to look at him or to think of what his life in that monastery was and had been, and bowing his head in his hands allowed himself to sink into the dark ocean of despair as a doomed swimmer will at last abandon hope, and sink into the depths. If he could have wept he would have, or run into the darkness of the woods to bury his unhappiness, but the tears would not come, and even the thought of the moaning trees outside filled him with fear. When all had filed out he, too, rose and passed from transept to transept with averted head. Brother John was waiting for him outside eager to recite another quatrain, but he saw that the boy was tired, or worried, and mercifully he did not approach him and allowed him to pass to his room where he lay awake almost until the dawn came, alone with his despairing heart.

2

So in the morning, when he was sent to bring his prisoner to breakfast, he was silent and shamefaced, and she, seeing him so, went down gloomily after him. She was given breakfast in a little locked room where there was dried spittle and unswept cigarette-ash in the grate, and the cloth wrinkled by many elbows and ring-marked by many a dribbling cup of tea. The early morning had risen in mist and hoar but she could see over the edge of her thick-lipped mug through the window of the breakfast-room little patches of blue, and she heard Brother John say to the captain that it would be a fine day after all; and sure enough as they descended the farther side of the mountain the blue and white patches were chasing one another and the bog-cotton at her feet blew slantwise. But beside her Denis walked in complete silence and as her eyes roved from one to other of his companions the immanence of her fate began to oppress her. Once she saw through a bare, black thorn-tree the wrinkled surface of a mountain-tarn blown yellow with froth by the night, and she so ached that she could not point it out to him that a feeling of loneliness settled heavily on her, a smother about her heart. When she nudged his arm and smiled, he looked sullenly where she nodded her head and then without pleasure to the valley beyond, and moved aside from her so that she should not accost him again. They were now walking on the edge of a shut-in valley or coom and to try him again she spoke, saying it did not seem to her that men and women could live in so desolate a place, but he made no reply and she fell into a sad silence herself. It was a stretch where there was not a tree, not even hardy shrubs like holly or haw, to be seen for miles around, and the only living thing they saw was an occasional stare or snipe rising suddenly from the coarse grass beneath their feet, and once a flock of sheep in the distance that made echoing moan through the valley as they tumbled like grey maggots down the opposite mountain-side. About an hour later, almost perpendicularly beneath them they saw a dirty white cabin all but buried in a bit of sandy level – a household clutching its patch of earth that the streamlets had in the course of the centuries brought down grain by grain from the high slopes. She looked down at it and thought it was more suitable as a tomb than a dwelling-house, and glancing all about the deserted country that circled this hidden coom shuddered at it. Several hours later they had clambered down the monster heap of sodden moss and sweating rocks that lay behind this farm-house and they confined her under its high thatch in a loft with one cobweb-covered pane that faced the valley-end, where, all day long, wherever else there was blue, low clouds trailed slowly past and were followed by more that had endless more in train. So that as the early dusk began to fall, and she was permitted to walk abroad for an hour, she was utterly surprised to find the western air fall sharp and clear about every rock and fence and pool and every stream that ran tinkling over the drowned stones. Down the valley some holly clustered under the grey rocks, and even a rowan drooped, and even a beech or two, though small and weakling here, stood motionless as if there were no air, and farther on, edging a broad loch, were flags that stood by the blue water as if they were part of the mountain that hung ponderous above them in the clear air. It was not at all like an evening in spring: it was one of those evenings that defy the order of the seasons, for though the road and all things – trees, rocks, walls, and bushes – were heavy and wet the sky seemed as if it held, suspended aloft blowing through the upper regions of the air, a light-as-feather fall of early October snow. Denis accompanied her but was so evidently unwilling to speak that she tried to lose herself in the beauty of the fading light and the purity of the air, until seeing across the lake a fire or two and twin pillars of dove-grey smoke, she asked who these were, and he replied in a low, tired voice that these must be travelling tinkers going to Nantenan beyond the hills where there was a pattern on the following day. She stood watching the flickering fires with a passionate envy welling in her. The voices resounded across the lake, a cart-wheel jolted, a laugh echoed among the hills, and as if delighting in the replication of their voices, they laughed and laughed or cried long haloos. Then because the darkness was gathering about them they had to return. Denis told her that her case would be decided that night – the adjutant and quartermaster were come – but he said it all without pity or interest in his voice as if it were a message he had been told to give her, and as he spoke he looked away beyond the edges of the coom so that her eyes should not look into his. She did not try; and when they were returned to the cabin and she climbed to her loft and he called after her as if wishing to speak to her, 'Can I do anything for you, Mrs Browne?' only her heavy footsteps replied. And when the wee girl of the house came to her with her evening meal she was lying on her bed, her shoulders gathered up about her as if she would cloak her head with them, gazing through the little dirty window to watch the darkness come down from the heights, covering in the valley and the great rocks until all had become blacker than the night itself. Before the light failed completely she felt rustling in her pocket a crumpled ball of paper and pulling it out read on it a portion of a letter she had been writing to her husband the morning before when they took her suddenly from her house. She read those thoughts of yesterday as one might read an old diary, her mind again shaping those memories first called up there, of how, unlike this winter, other winters had been empty and lonely and pitiless, with wild winds that rushed wave-like through the sponge-heavy trees, nights when the moon was almost always obscured by mist and haze; mornings when, as she lay thinking enviously of Indian or African sunshine, she used hear from her bedroom an occasional creeper leaf stealing like a thief along the gravel in the little winds that blew before the light came. And yet, this night drew her back into the mood of those old winters, and what her letter said seemed false and a pretence. 'My God! The Malabar coast for you in April? You poor dear Jack! And the heat coming! I can see the heat-haze shimmering along the red mountain-tracks, the roses and acacias and petunias drooping in the midday sun, the greasy gum-trees dripping in the grizzling sun. But here! Oh, Jack! The lashing rains of March and the rivers in flood, our willows hanging their hair in the curling tide. You know me? I went out last night on the balcony and stood absolutely naked in the downpour until I was soaked. It was godly. I shall do it again.'

Below a door opened and shut, and a shaft of light streamed out and was gone. It was dark night and she could read no more, but other sentences came back to her as she gazed into the black valley-head. 'All the winter there has scarcely been a day when there has not been on the road before our gate, two or three, once there were even six powerful Lancia motor-cars.' Or, another bit. 'They are my boys, these fine, black-bonneted, tight-breeched, khaki-coated, pipe-smoking, six-shooter men. It has been a different Ireland with them. The old lonely winters are dead. I am in love with three of them at once. You don't mind, dear?'

She could see the chinks of light through the timbers of the floor and hear an occasional dull sound from the kitchen beneath. She lay on her bed where all was dark and quiet, and only the wind outside roaring in the streams.

Denis wandered back along the dark lake-side where the wind was gathering the brown spume about the rushes and heavy with the night-scent of the bog-myrtle.

Farther on was a little lime-washed, green-streaked church among the rocks and farther still the pink house of the curate, its bright window staring at him through the dark. For a long time he walked by the edge of the water listening to its rippling waves and whispering flags. At first the far-off mountain was dark and the sky was dark and only the near waters gleamed when they fell in ripples with a light that came from nowhere, but after a while he sat on a rock by the edge of the loch and the mountain slowly outlined its dark head. He looked often at the brightly lighted window but he dared not go into the bright room face to face with the priest. He longed to go into the little chapel and lay his head on the lap of his Christ and weep out his sin and be comforted, but only the rustling and the lapping answered him, and across the loch the impenetrable yawning darkness of the mountain and the wind roaring down the coom filled him with a terror at his own littleness. Moving a foot he felt the shell of a snail crackling under his boot and he removed his foot hurriedly with the fear of a greater One than himself to Whom he was no more than the dead creeper. The pinprick glow of a cigarette and a man's steps approached along the shore; he was smoking fitfully himself and knowing he was discovered he did not stir. It was the priest taking the night air before he turned in. The voice came through the dark – a young man's voice.

'Any luck tonight, Paddy?'

'Goodnight, father.'

'Oh, who's that?'

'One of the boys.'

'I didn't know any of ye were around.'

'We're moving in the morning.'

'Have ye cigarettes? Can I give ye anything?'

Denis did not hear the question – he was glad of the dark. The priest stood beside him and they both looked silently across the water.

'What about confession, father?' he murmured.

'Any time ye like,' said the priest willingly. 'Come up to the house.'

'I . . . I'd like to make a confession, father,' said the boy flinging his cigarette end into the water where it hissed in the foam between the reeds.

'Come up to the house, my child,' said the priest, falling into his professional voice.

'No. It doesn't matter.' He felt his chance of happiness slipping from him. There was silence for a minute, and he noticed that the priest had stopped smoking, and he rose as if to go. The priest stepped forward and caught him by the arm.

'Will you promise to wait here while I go and get my stole? Will you?'

'Yes, father.'

The priest's footsteps crunched rapidly away. Now he must tell his secret. How could he say it? The mountain wind came down the valley in one of its sudden gusts – the faery wind they called it among the mountains when it came like that without warning churning the lakes into storm before it passed on. 'Father, I was with a woman.' The very thought of anything so coarse and ugly made him step rapidly away into the dark. Then he halted. 'Father, I have sinned with one of the opposite sex.' At that he shuddered and turned and ran into the dark away from the priest's house and the chapel followed by a voice shouting: 'Where are you?' He halted and came slowly back, ashamed, and knelt silently on the pebbly shore. He could see the purple ribbon of the stole falling in an arc about the priest's shoulders. Then it was: 'Well, my child, tell me your sins,' and with the cold faery wind circling his head he murmured out his dark secret, in what words he could never remember, but they were an old formula worn into an easy smoothness like a coin long in use. As he walked back in the teeth of the mountain wind he felt like a colt turned loose from a stable; he almost choked with happiness; he actually laughed out at the crying wind, and the night and the mountains were clothed in beauty without end.

At the point where the carcase of the abandoned car lay damming the murmuring mountain stream the headlights of a Lancia motor-car shone along the rising road and into the pinewoods where the road turned. The engines were silent and the black-bonneted occupants sat with rifles at the ready listening tensely to every sound borne on the wind. On the dark road behind the car an officer conversed with his guide, an old grey-pated constable who whispered out all he knew of the roads and by-paths leading to the monastery. When they had finished half of the party went with the old man up through the woods where the night before Bella and Denis had clambered along on their way to the guest-house door; the other half, with lights dimmed and engines racing, cut through the wind to the gates of the monastery avenue, and up between the swaying elms towards the outer gates of the guest-house. The old constable scarcely needed to look right or left, he knew the way as the palm of his hand. He tramped on staring before him into the dark between the trees, finding his way by sheer memory, his present thoughts turning unhappily on the ungrateful task they had set him, making of him a spy on his own people – on the monks who had been so good to him, whom he loved so much. It was only last July he had come down that path, enjoying the cool shade of the trees, the nutmeg scent of the crushed leaves, the soft carpet to rest on when weary. It was harvest time, and he loved to walk down after breakfast among the fields where the monks were at work, and lying under a cock of hay draw out his brown beads or his prayer-book and in the presence of the beauty of the coloured country stretched before him praise the good and great God who made all. He had never been so happy as during those two weeks of retreat, and he grew to love and be loved by the monks working silently day after day in the fields, and to whom he would talk without expecting a reply and tell the latest news from the world outside without ever a question. Smiling he would take up his position in the silent row that bound the grain after the clanking reaper and work with them, halting and straightening his back when he remembered a piece of news he had not told them before. He might say:

'There was a terrible earthquake in Japan and there's thousands homeless. A terrible business entirely. I believe houses fell on all sides of one Catholic church and the church wasn't touched at all.'

Or,

'There's terrible work in Morocco and the Spaniards have great trouble there with a fellow called – oh, some queer name – that they can't catch like the English with Kruger in South Africa – Ah, yes! Abdul Krim!'

Or,

'There's to be an election in Cavan and the Irish Party have stood down for the Sinn Feiners. I believe the Government intend to interfere with it in some shape or form.'

Or he might tell some innocent joke about the latest cure at the monastery and the monks would all raise a silent laugh and go on with their binding and stacking, but keeping an eye open for any attempt of his to begin again, when they would straighten and listen with eager faces. But he would soon have no more to recount, and then he would sidle up to one of the older monks and say to him shyly:

'Father, I have a son, Denis; he's a bit of a wild boy. He's up and down with them Sinn Feiners, and his poor mother is worried to death over him and it is his last year at the University. Won't you say a prayer for his success for God's sake, for I've done all I can for him now? God bless you, father.'

Whereupon he would smile over them all a silent good-bye and taking his coat in his arm – a fine well-built man he always was – stride off down the valley to where a little tarn stood edged by a few whispering reeds, and a bent thorn-tree, and walk on around it, his chin lifted as if the whole countryside were a flag and he marching past, his mouth sometimes opening to drink in great draughts of air. Often a well would lie in his way and he would drink deeply of its precious wine and if his way lay by an outlying ploughland of the monastery he would always stop to examine the work. And so back at evening time to the simple fare in the filled refectory – life for a couple of weeks in her quietest mood, every moment of those regular days a new delight, the praying, the eating, the long walks, the snoring sleep under trees or in bed when the last bell tolled over the pines for all the community to come to rest. Thinking of it all he tramped up the well-known path, sucking in his white moustaches and chewing their ends in his bitter unhappiness at his present task. It was a fresh bitterness to see – even in that darkness – such little changes as a tree cut here and there to widen the way, or at one sharp point a few rough steps made with flat stones and driven stakes. But the familiar was even worse – the sudden slow tolling of the distant bell going through him like a spear, the rolling away of the trees at the summit of the wood and the sight of the distant buildings dark on the hill-top against the sky.

In the monastery the drunkard sat in the guest-house refectory, shuddering at the roaring wind that shook the avenue elms and all the trees about the house. His hands were in a continual tremble and his pig's eyes winked and blinked without stop as if he were semaphoring with them across the room to something in the gloom beyond. For a long time there had been silence in the room and when Brother John began to speak suddenly the toper put his cup of black tea into the slops of the saucer so roughly that they flowed over on the cloth in a circular wave and dyed the edge of his dry bread a pale beer-brown.

'Even Saint Pether,' continued the guestmaster sternly, as he stroked his empty stomach by way of assuring himself that his remarks had no personal application, 'Saint Pether did penance for his sin in betraying our Lord. He wept for it until the tears made furrows in his two cheeks. Yes, and Saint Mary Magdalene, the holy fathers say, never stopped weeping from the day Christ died until she died herself.'

'Well, well, well,' muttered the drunkard, as if these remarks had no personal application to him either.

'And yet,' continued Brother John, his pitiless eyes on the wretch blinking away beneath him at the imaginary semaphorist in the opposite corner, 'and yet do you know what some of the fathers hold? They say she is even to this very moment burning in Purgatory, and will continue to burn there until the last trumpet releases her, for all the terrible sins committed before she was converted.'

' 'Tis hard on the poor woman,' murmured the toper miserably.

'What hard?' grumbled the old monk. 'The woman was nearly damned for all Eternity but for the great goodness of God.'

'Yes,' whispered the toper, completely cowed.

'Ah, penance! Penance is the only cure for sin. Forgiveness washes away the guilt of sin, but not the temporal punishment due to it. Do you hear that? Not the temporal punishment due to it.'

He paused as the wind blew past in a violent gust.

'Do you hear that,' he asked so suddenly that the toper all but leaped with terror and shouted out that he did, indeed.

'They say,' murmured the old monk quietly, 'that the wind is the crying of lost souls.'

'God help us all,' said the toper fervently.

'May God help each and every one of us then,' said the monk.

Another pause followed. The coals fell suddenly in the grate and the blind flapped and Brother John sucked at his teeth and gazed down at the dark ebb of tea in the drunkard's cup. Then he came up out of his deep meditation with –

'I wonder, may a man (and he paused) eat between his collations (pause) the food that sticks between his teeth . . . since the last meal? We had an orange for supper,' he explained in conclusion.

'Damn little sticks in my teeth, then,' said the drunkard angrily.

'Huh!' said the monk and began to laugh quietly at the joke.

Silence fell on them again, even more profound since the wind had fallen into a momentary calm, then beginning again to tap at the blinds and ripple the window blinds into a cat-like patter. Then it seemed to scream up the avenue towards the guest-house and a second later, there was indeed a thundering on the door that made the old monk whirl off the candle to the hall with a benediction of grease on the table-cloth as he went, fearful that this noise would awaken the whole community from their beds. In a second torches were flashing into the hall and armed men behind these bayonets of light rushed into the refectory. Black-bonneted devils out of the deepest pit of hell they seemed to the drunkard so that he choked when he would speak.

'I – ah – uh – you – gentlemen – ah – ah pathriots! Always was a pathriot! Genl'men, one of yeerselves. Don't shoot don' wan' to die. Not ready. Haven't made confession. Stole a bottle of Johnny Jameson. Holy Father, Mary mother of God! Genl'men, we're all wan!'

'Who's all one?' said a great elongated officer, jabbing the wretch's swollen stomach with the long nose of his black Webley revolver. 'Who do ye think we are, eh?'

The toper, utterly confounded, semaphored madly and shook like a scarecrow in the wind. The old constable, whispering like a man in a church, intervened mildly.

'That's Jerry Kane of Cork. He's in the D.T.'s. He's a simple man and there's no harm in him.'

'What's that,' growled the officer. 'Speak up man. Do you know him? What's he doing here? Is this a hospital?'

'He's on a cure. He's in charge of him,' said the old constable, pointing almost shyly at the guestmaster, an El Greco figure in brown watching them intently over the heads and fists and murderous faces and whirling torches of the black-bonnets moving around him. The officer glanced at the monk, and looked back at the toper who, almost sobered with fear stared up at him from under his knotted eyebrows with the intent stare of a frightened cat or bird. With his revolver the officer motioned the constable to one side.

'Take that fellow away,' he said, 'upstairs or somewhere and lock him in until I come.'

With bitter, disdainful eyes Brother John watched the pair go, the old constable and the drunkard. He knew that whatever the drunkard knew he would tell, and when the abbot came and, on hearing the officer's angry explanation of the raid, ordered the old monk to his cell for the night, he did not close an eye or rest for one second, pacing up and down thinking of the danger to the rebels sleeping unsuspectingly in the coom. He imagined them surprised, surrounded, shot to pieces in that valley-trap and he kept moving to the window to listen for the sound of starting motors, hoping the storm would continue, wishing for a night fog, downcast when the clouds parted and every field showed almost as bright as day, pleased when a dark cloud swam across the sky and the great fields filled with shadows and heavy drops fell. He was kneeling red-eyed and weary at the open window when the first pale ring of dawn circled the horizon, and he only slept on his arms in the window recess, when the moon sank and the stars waned and the little birds began to chirp in tune. By then the cars had not yet left the monastery courtyard.

What did happen in the end he never knew, for in the morning the abbot sent him back to silence among the cloistered brothers, and there he remained for so many years that with time he forgot it all, and nothing remained in the end but one meaningless picture of a heavy-coated policeman leading one of the drunks down the guest's corridor. It might be ten years after that he and the drunkard met again, the aged monk again guestmaster, the old toper still a toper, and they talked of that night that both had all but completely forgotten. The toper could only remember scraps of their conversation.

'He was a dacent man, God rest his soul. But that boy of his – I could tell you a thing or two about him. Somehow I haven't it clear at all now. But there was that woman they killed – what was her name? Wasn't I watching the two of them. God forgive me I was mad for the drop you had in your room. There he was tryin' room after room for her and he got it at last; and did he come out? Good-bye to you, says I, you're all right for the night and I seein' him shut the door after him. . . .'

But the monk had forgotten the boy and only gathered roughly that the toper was telling him of some indecency and would not listen, bidding him sternly to speak no evil in that room if he didn't wish to be without his little glass of John Jameson for the night. So they ended their talk of that night so many years ago, the toper murmuring apologetically that 'he was only sayin' how he was tellin' the constable, God rest him, about the goings-on of his boy.' He might have remembered more if he had seen the constable stealing out after Lauds, bent under his heavy coat and helmet, into the empty chapel to pray. The high red curtains were closed before the high altar and for light only the little tongue of flame in the red sanctuary lamp that cast its leaping shadows into the dark and moted well and womb of the empty nave, and threw no beam at all – unlike the occasional moo[illegible] - into the choir stalls where the old man knelt, his bald pate bent and all his body with it fallen in utter despair into the shelter of his crooked arms. He remained there muttering so fervently that he might have been talking to some real person through the gloom.

'O immense passion! O profound wounds! O sweetness above all sweetness,' came his heartbroken litany, 'O most bitter Death, grant him mercy. May the most sacred and loving heart of the good, kind Jesus, the good, kind, loving Jesus, grant us all and especially poor Denis Thy mercy. I beseech Thee, O good Jesus, O good, sweet, kind, and loving Jesus. . . .'

Until he fell asleep there, and he too awoke chill and stiff in the dawn to hear the little fluttering birds chirping outside in the branches of the trees.

3

In the coom at dawn a chill wind came over the edge of the mountains and Bella was wakened by it in time to see the cold light spreading southward in the sky. She stood in her bare feet under the thatch and rubbed the damp pane with her hand. Like magic a waterfall appeared high up in a crook of the mountains and the golden morning star above it in the sky and below it in a pool on the floor of the glen. As she stood listening to the silence and watching the dark sky grow grey she heard faintly the distant sound of the falling waters, and from a distant cock there came echoing through the valley a long forlorn crow. As she leant her forehead on the cold pane the inevitable repetition came trailing and wavering as if the morning mist choked it. Everything looked bedraggled and shaggy after the storm but indifferent and timeless as the stones of the hills, indifferent, deathless, going on and on without end. The cock shrilled again, but its cry wavered and was lost in the silence. Even the cock, she thought – red-eyed, red-combed, bedraggled – was indifferent to everything but the rhythmical return of the dawn and the ritual of welcome. When she heard the little girl of the house tramping up the stairs she smiled to hear the feet halt on every step, but when the child entered the room and she looked at its wide frightened eyes, wide like a deer or pet cat, fear surged up around her beating heart. At the same moment the melancholy bird outside called again, as if to say to her, 'Here's-to the-end-of you, oh, here's-to-the-end-of you-u-u!'

The child laid her breakfast on the window ledge and almost crying from fear turned to go, but with a sudden motherly impulse she caught at the little trembling shoulders and kissed the white face and plucked the pink frock into shape. Then she found her gold compact and dabbing a bit of powder on her cheeks and glancing for the last time at her hair she snapped the case to and pressed it into the tiny fist.

'To go with your frock,' she said, trying to smile gaily.

'It's me new dress,' said the mite shyly.

'Oh?'

'I have it on for to go to Mass in it.'

'To Mass?'

Footsteps passed by behind the house, resounded for a moment and were out of earshot. Far up the opposite mountain-side a group of people were moving down to the valley. The child, fingering the gold toy, had forgotten its fears, but it remembered a message and said of a sudden, pointing to the food on the tray.

'If you want more of that stuff you can have it and welcome.'

It was a big tumbler of whisky.

'What is it for?' she asked in a low voice.

'It's the min have it below in the kitchen. They're dhrinkin' it since the morning....

All but sickened she faced the window. There she spoke to the child without turning.

'I want paper and a pen. I must write a letter.'

The little steps went from the room, halting on each knee of the stairs as they clambered down. She tried to grip herself, summoning up her thoughts in order: Dearest Jack, or Darling Jack, or just plain Jack: To say good-bye. I thought it would be easy but it's hateful. I thought I'd just go. I can't. But I shouldn't complain. Life has been good while it lasted. Dot and Billie are happy. We have done our duty. Say good-bye to them for me. They are good girls. I'd love to see you again. But it isn't to be, is it? I have had my time. Yes, she could go through with all that – it was easy to say good-bye to him – he would understand, and if there was an after he would follow in his time. Don't worry about these people, they will meet their end too. It isn't worth while. It has been good fun while it lasted. My time, I mean. You, too, make it spin. It soon goes. So cheerio. Oh, it would be very easy to write a cheerful letter just like that, to him. But there were other things, things that would not hear, and would not follow after, the ancient eternal things she loved, that morning star, the sinking moon, the hours of change between night and day, the lovely, lovely light, the beautiful, beautiful dark, the various hours, so lovely, all so cruel, come and go, come and go, for ever, as if she had not so much as been. Heavier steps tramped up the little stairs and there was a knock at the door and turning she saw Denis. He came in and with shame-heavy eyes laid a penny bottle of ink and a sheet of notepaper and a child's pink-handled steel pen on the table.

'Have you been drinking?' she said bitterly.

'No. I am going to Mass.'

'Mass?'

'To Communion.'

'Come and go, come and go.'

'I will pray for you.'

'You can go to hell!'

'I'm sorry.'

'Oh, all right.'

'I am sorry about all this. I could do nothing. Headquarters were against it, are against it. But there's the six boys. They are all drunk.'

'Go to Communion.'

'Can I take a letter?'

'Will you?'

'I promise.'

'Though I shall know nothing about that.'

'I promise. Write another and give me the one you want to go.'

'You mean, write two?'

'Yes.'

'You mean two letters.'

'Yes.'

'I hope you will be very happy, boy.'

'I am happy.'

'You will be very happy, I think. I liked you. Lead your life, child, while it lasts.'

'You'd better write.'

He felt a prig as she turned and knelt by the window and wrote. But he had laid out his course and he must follow it. The church-bell began to ring up the valley and he hoped he would not be late for the Communion. They would ask him below-stairs what she said but they were too drunk to notice if he told an awkward lie. He was glad he was going to Mass and they had let him out of the whole hateful business. Afterwards he would leave the column for a few weeks and go home to the city to see his father and mother. God had been very good to him so far. He must keep good always now. Always and always, for ever and ever, without a single lapse. It would take a long time to forget that night in the monastery but he must not think of it again, and he was glad the priest had forbade him to go back over it. He must just take it for a lesson. He must remember that life was a hard struggle but with the help of God he would spend the remainder of it as pure as he was at that moment. She handed him her letter and he put it in his pocket. Then he said good-bye and went down to Mass.

As he entered the little weather-beaten church the bell ceased its insistent ringing. He gave his rifle to a boy among the crowd kneeling outside the door and took his place farther in; yet from where he knelt he could see over his shoulder, through the great open door that filled the entire rear wall of the church, the sharp rise of the mountain, dark green save where the shaggy clouds swept their lower edges along its slopes. These bare mountains were infinitely beautiful to him, and as he waited for the Mass to begin he pictured how the church would appear from their summits, set by a bowl of lead in the mountains. It was a place where old hermits were said to have lived in complete silence while the storm howled down about their huts and stirred up the lake to an angry sea. They, too, weathered by the rains would have looked like rocks or withered bushes or old worn statues – the church itself would seem from the hills as if carved out of the tumbled stones, even down to the worshippers clustered shoulder to shoulder outside the door, the peasants in their green-black frieze, all on one knee, facing forward to the altar as their forefathers must have before the altar-rock of Christ or Crom.

The Mass went through all its phases to the Communion time and Denis, following each movement of the ceremony of adoration, and preparation and final miracle, with eyes closed and his head and all his body bowed forward into his hands felt as he had never before the great calm of harbourage, the peace of the anchor-hold in from the surge of the sea. But far up the coom there reverberated through the echoing hills a volley of rifle-fire. As the echoes vanished so did the peace within him, and his heart was once again in storm. Not so easily, not so quietly was life to be left behind. O Immense Passion, O profound wounds, O sweetness above all sweetness, grant her eternal rest. Then the boy to whom he had given his rifle was pulling at his shoulder and all the little congregation were looking with frightened eyes up along the dark-green slopes where a scattered line of troops was moving slowly down out of the shaggy fog. In a second he had his rifle in his hand and was out of the chapel and was racing under the shelter of the graveyard below the mountain out towards his comrades in the coom. It was a long way and there were innumerable turf-cuttings and dikes hewn out of the bog and he splashed in and out of brown bog-water and sank to his knees many times in the spongy mould as he ran his way. The shoulder of the mountain now hid the advancing figures and he could not see how widely they were deployed or how near they came as he ran. When he passed the cabin not a soul was to be seen but as he entered the shadows of the coom he could see far up the glen the cluster of men coming and going with little steps as about some special task. His voice as he shouted made but little noise in the wide, ravine-high place, for his throat and palate were dry and his heart beating madly against his side and his gasping breath robbed it of all energy. But soon they saw him stumbling toward them and he waved his hand behind him and made for the nearest stream to clamber up its course out of the trap of the coom. They understood at once and scattered up the slopes and for a long while he saw nobody, climbing up hand over hand, resting as long as he dared like a hunted stag in the trickling water, drinking it up as he lay. After a while, less than an hour, he caught sight of a group of his fellows struggling upwards to the head of the coom and he changed his course to meet them but before they could come together he saw from his higher position a scattered group of khaki figures top the coom-head not more than five hundred yards away, and open fierce bursts of fire down the slopes. Up here he was better sheltered than the others, and as he climbed he fired; it was not his first fight and he was not frightened, and he was full of the knowledge that he was never in his life so prepared to die.

More conspicuous than the other figures at the coom-head was one tall officer, long-legged against the sky as he directed his men. Denis chose him for his target and repeatedly he fired at him. He emptied his clip and shoved in another and emptied that. Finding a good position behind a rock he loaded his breech once again, and first looking behind him and above him to make sure that he was not in danger from these quarters took long, careful aim and fired in rapid succession. Long-legs was not aware of him and now stood up to change his position and at the same moment there was a sudden lull in the volleying so that even the echoes had time to die away. Once more the boy aimed, and his shot rang out alone. This time the tall figure stumbled and with one hand flung high fell prone.

Just then the clouds, as they often do in these high mountains, sank down slowly like white fleecy curtains on the whole valley, and (enveloped in the driving fog) the boy clambered away to the north, elated at his success, and drove on until he found the ground levelling under his feet. He was on the edge of the plateau above the coom, and to the south the cabin and farther west the little leaden lake and the tiny chapel at its white edge were still occasionally visible. What looked from below like white clouds was here wet flying mist, and here it was the rocks not the bog-water pools that were the contrast with the wraiths flying heedlessly past him. The pools were as mirrors breathed on, the rocks were storm-polished to ebony. He could see in his mind's eye this region as it appeared on the maps – marked only by the trailing ends of tributary streams and petered mountain paths or by the ultimate peak-circles of the contour lines, or such homeless words as Stone Circle or the long Irish names of the mountains, a pathless waste; and knowing the danger to be gone – yet taking no chances – he struck away northwards to the heart of it, sure that before the night ended he would reach the next valley-stop and find rest and shelter by some peasant's turf-fire or in the odorous warmth of a farmer's winter hay.

And as he tramped on, straight as an arrow for fear of losing his sense of direction, through every little obstacle, pool or clustered tuft, his thoughts slowly gathered and he let them gather at their will for they were, he had often found, the best protection against rough weather and long marches – thoughts of the city, thoughts of home, other thoughts not so welcome that made him drive faster on as if he would leave something that hurried with him behind, until unexpectedly there loomed out of the mist another figure which, before he had time to be startled he recognized as one of his comrades – the black-browed, black-eyed fellow they called Rory, and Rory was singing a song that he barely interrupted for a greeting, a song that he would for no pleadings of Denis cease to sing, adding verses to it as he sang, each new verse more hateful than the one before.

> Will anybody tell me where is Inchigeela's shore
> For there's a bed new-made down there for somebody
>   we know,
> The blanket is of Irish green, the quilt it is of red,
> But she that's lying underneath is dead, me boys, is
>   dead . . .
> Her coat was red and her blanket's red . . .

And so they tramped on through the driving fog, quiet only until a new verse broke the profound silence, tramped until the sun gleamed silver through the lightening mist, very low because it was sinking, and then as the new night came to turn the world from light to dark they both were walking on in utter silence. Their feet squelched over the pebbly places and the withered gorse rustled dry in the wind, slanted perpetually away from the prevalent blasts. A little light in a window miles away glinted out of a sudden and Rory spoke.

'That was a narrow shave, Dinny. We left it go too long.'

'What?'

'That bloody she-spy. Do you know where we are?'

'No.'

'That's Knockane down there, I know a domn fine girrl down there will give us a warm bed for the night. By God the shtars is out.'

'Hesperus.'

'What?'

'The evening star,' said Denis.

'I know a pome about the wreck of that wan.'

'That was a ship. But it was called after the star.'

'It's very bright, by God.'

'Aye,' said Denis, 'it will be a lovely night.'

'Do you know, Old Johnny sent a message while you were at Mass?'

'Why didn't ye tell me?'

'We left it go too long. We were nearly caught ourselves.'

'I plugged the Tan that led them,' said Denis.

'Are you sure?'

'I saw him drop.'
'The son of a bitch.'
'He nearly finished us. He'll talk no more.'

In this valley it was another world. The sky was cleared and the stars winked and shone firmly one by one – a lovely, lovely night.

'Chi-rist,' said Rory, 'I'm domn tired.'

'It's my back,' said Denis, moving his shoulder-blades.

'We'll have a good sleep *tonight*,' said Rory.

'Aye. We need it,' said Denis. 'I need it sorely.'

Talking like that they dropped into the valley with all its lights, and by the time they were at the door of the 'domn fine girrl' they were in a gay mood, rejoicing in the loveliness of the night, and their own youth, and the promise of infinite days yet to come.

The Bombshop

At first it was easy to work steadily in the Bombshop, all day long and into the night too. They found all the pleasure they needed in making the bombs and there was a special malicious pleasure in knowing that while they made them there were the markets, so fussy, so noisy, beneath their windows, too busily engaged selling their fish to suspect anything. The three would chuckle when they thought of it and say to one another with a wink: 'If they only knew!' and return with vigour to their deadly tasks. There was never any question, then, of going out into the streets, not even after dark or in the early dawn, or if they thought of it they were ashamed to mention it. Even when the work began to pall on them, when they began to halt in the middle of it to lounge and smoke in the front room, or to peep through the drawn blinds at the streets, they returned shamefaced with a joke about the Freedom of the City that would one day be conferred on them. And when they did at last confess to one another that they would like to go out into the streets it was a long time before they talked of it as something that might possibly be done. When they did they found that only two things prevented them – the danger to themselves and the danger to the Bombshop; they might easily be recognized by a spy and arrested, or, worse still and more likely, they might not be arrested at once but watched as they went back to their lair. So they abandoned the idea, only to return to it again, and abandon it again, and return to it and abandon it, until the very thought of the streets tormented them. In this way they discovered something that nobody else could have taught them – that it is easy to do anything at first, no matter how difficult or dangerous, but the inevitable desires of the heart swell and burst in the end like a well gathering beneath the surface of the earth.

They came to fear special hours of the day, and the nights tormented them. They feared especially the early cock-crow when the market-life began and their sleep ended, the dark hours of the morning when the carts went rumbling in beneath their windows from the fields and the seashore. Leo, the youngest of the three and who should have slept better than any of them, was the first to admit that he often rose on his elbow to watch the loads go by, the cabbage glistening, the fish crates brown, the domes of hay darkened by the rain falling on them so heavily from the great leaking sieve of a sky that the fish almost swam in their boxes and the cabbage-heads cupped the water and splashed it on the fishwives who unloaded them from their places in the carts. Once he saw a drenched carter look enviously up at his window and angrily flick his horse's glistening rump with his whiplash. 'If he only knew!' said the boy, with a bitter self-pity, and leaned back wearily in his bed wishing he could sleep again. Their work would not begin until the angelus bells began to chime, here, there, everywhere, over the city, and from that on the roar of the spirit-lamps and the rattle of the pestle in the mortar, and the hiss of sifters kept the city sounds at bay, except alone the cries of the fishwomen outside that they could not stifle – the 'Here's the herrings, here's the herrings, here's the herrings' in a torrent of words, or the wail of 'Fine cod a' hake, oh, fine cod a' hake'; but at lunch-hour the lamps would fall silent and all the city enter through the windows, and from that on they toiled as best they might through the long afternoon. Then the markets would gradually be dissipated and the dark fall, and they too cease work, and old memories and old habits recur.

On wet nights – almost every night that is for the two months since they came – they sat before their fire in the sitting-room while the rain dripped musically on the tin roof in the yard, and Shandon tower struck out the hours from the wet dark above their heads. They could see it through the window in the landing if they chose to look, a tapering mass, dark against the wet luminous sky, its golden weather-fish swimming endlessly through the aqueous air. They sat there, almost always in silence, playing chess, or reading, or writing long letters until Norah – their courier and housekeeper – returned with dispatches, and the dispatches almost always taunted them to hurry, to get finished, saying that everything and everybody was ready for the attack but the Bombshop. Or if there were no dispatches, one of them wishing to be alone would go to his room till the following morning (as Leo did more often than any of them) or another down into the yard to sit on the ash-bin, to smoke and look up at their square of sky, returning with his hair wet with points of mist like dew.

On the few fine nights there were, they could see, by peeping carefully through the front windows, the lane-children racing and shouting under the lit lamps, or hear a group of girls circling arm in arm about the markets, singing as they went the mournful harmony of old sentimental numbers – those songs from the Edwardian music-halls that are remembered in the provinces long after they are forgotten elsewhere.

> Come over the garden wall,
> Little girl to me.
> I've been lonely a long, long time,
> And the wall isn't hard to climb.
> Just jump up and then jump down,
> I won't let you fall.
> We'll play at sweethearts
> And then we'll be married, so,
> Come over the garden wall.

Or they would sing something from the *Prince of Pilsen* or *Florodora*; and Sean, with his great awkward body, would leap up and imitate the girls of the chorus with their fleshy, pink-tighted thighs that popped in and popped out like the mechanical men on circus roundabouts, and the others would laugh at him and at them. But hearing the voices come from the distance and vanish into it as the girls went round and round the squares the three bomb-makers would hum in turn after them.

> 'I've been lonely a long, long time,
> Little girl of mine. . . .'

Or they would read the evening paper over and over again, sharing it between them until it became a wrinkled ball. Then Norah would come and draw the tiny envelopes from her bosom and they receive them still warm from her flesh – and, reading them, forget her.

Sometimes, indeed, they were merry, if there were many dispatches from Norah. Or if she brought much news they would gossip for hours on end. Or they would be coaxed from their silence on the rare nights when they were visited by Mother Dale. She was the owner of the house, the only other woman who knew of the Bombshop; she kept the old-clothes shop beneath them, and lived between them and it.

She rarely troubled them – as if she knew that they did not want her old woman's talk, but now and again of nights the door would open and there she would stand under the lintel, tall in the gloom like a slender statue from a Middle Ages porch, a spear carved into woman-shape. She was a wonderful old woman; even Sean and Caesar, rough fellows as they were, could find no other word for her but that, and as she peered down at them, with child-soft eyes and inclined brow, unbuttoning her little mouth, that was wrinkled like cloth, into a smooth gentle smile they would wink at her or smile foolishly, not knowing whether to believe those open mother's eyes or her torture-tightened lips.

One wet night she came, early in the night, not going out that one night of all her nights to pray in the chapels for them, and as they looked up at her wet spangled bonnet, Norah ran and gently removed it from the lowered pate before her, pretending to be exasperated that she should have been out in such weather. But she only removed her wet cloak, and smiling at them said:

'Sure the best night of all to be out is the wet night when there's nobody to follow me. If it was a fine night I'd be rounding the markets for an hour before I'd come to my own door-bell, and all for fear of a fellow that warn't watching me at all, but only out for a drink after hours. But a night like this there's none abroad but the lost cats and the night police. And how is Leo?' turning to the boy amongst them.

He grinned back at her.

'I went out to pray for ye,' she continued, 'and to pray for the good work, but I got a pain in my side and I came home. And what need is there to pray for ye or the work when God is always on the watch for the boys of Ireland. Look what I brought ye, Sean.'

It was a bottle of invalid's wine. Out went his great hand, and back she snatched it in her bony one.

'Oh,' he wailed in mock despair, 'and I that haven't been in a pub for two months.'

'Ye'll get none of this then.'

'Oh, oh,' from Sean as if he were the most crestfallen man in the world.

'Not a drop! If I was to let you put your big mouth to it the bottle would be empty in a flash.'

Then she laughed at him.

'Ah, no. Sure no? I don't mean that at all. Take it, Norah. It's for all of ye. I pray for yeer souls and I bring wine for yeer bodies. Norah understands me, doesn't she? Norah?'

'Yes I do, Mother Dale,' from Norah, her prominent teeth bared, her soft lips spread.

'Mind yeerselves though, boys,' she said, as she rose and turned to go. 'They say the city is full of spies.'

She laid an envelope of new records on the table for Sean's gramophone.

'I nearly forgot them. Good night, Sean.'

He raised his big paw.

'Good night, mother.'

'Caesar?'

'Good night, mother.'

'Leo?'

'Good night, mother.'

'Good night, Norah.'

'Cheerio, mother,' said Norah, who always had a special 'good night' to herself, the last of all. The old woman had to stoop her lofty head to leave the room. Down she went to her own room below, and they opened the wine and sipped the weak juice in a returning silence while Norah went out quietly for her nightly batch of messages. Even as she closed the hall-door behind her she could hear the opening bars of the 'Turkish Patrol' ('As played by the band of the Highland Light Infantry') come blaring from the great brass-horned gramophone. She was glad that Sean had something to occupy him for the night, but as she thought again of the great maw of the gramophone, pasted all over inside and out with postage stamps, and of the rusted needles, and the cracked sound-box, she strode gladly away, into the drizzling rain, crunching savagely over cabbage stumps and the heads of decapitated fish. But the wind over the bridges blew her umbrella inside out and the rain seeped into her shoes and her body became chilled in the cold womb of the chapel, where she exchanged dispatches with the

Headquarters courier, and on her way back she felt so miserable that she almost thought of the Bombshop as 'home.' Once inside the door, however, there was the 'Turkish Patrol' still blaring away as if they had all gone out and forgotten to shut off the record and it had ever since been repeating and repeating itself while the needle wore to a stump. She raced up the stairs in a rage and found Caesar hanging over a chess problem and Leo staring mournfully and without interest at the gramophone. By this a new record had been set in the machine and as she entered the room Sean caught her up in his great hands and set her down right before it – he had the hands and body of a navvy and the concave profile of a prize-fighter, and as she glared at him he laughed at her, and winked behind Caesar's back. Before she could speak a nasal whine of song scraped and whined in the horn.

'It's just one line,' roared Sean, 'one line we can't make out. It's called – "Where the old horse died."

'In the lag behind the hollow.
Where the grath ith golden red,'

cried a deep basso from the depth of the gramophone.

'Now,' cried Sean.

'And the coopoo gooloo moonoo nuroon,' said the basso.

'What do you make of it?' roared Sean, the gramophone whining on and on.

'There we sometimes hear the churchbells,' roared the basso.

'There no more we hear them now.
In the place where the old horse died.'

'Well?' repeated Sean.

'Not a word of it,' said Norah, wearily removing her hat and damp coat, while the chess-player groaned and Leo shook his head and sighed.

'Slowly now this time,' said Sean, and as for a moment he held the needle from the record to adjust the regulator they could hear the rain drip before the wind on the tin roof outside and Shandon booming out the quarter. Then the rite began once more.

'In the lag behind the hollow,
Where the grath ith golden red.'

sang the basso for the hundredth time in the house that night, now with the slowness of a dead-march.

'Now,' roared Sean towering over her.

'And the coopoo gooloo moonoo nuroon,' said the basso once again.

'No,' said Norah, and she shook her head.

'We think,' he said, 'that it's either "and the grey grass blooms upon the lawn," or "and the church-bells bloom through the dawn." But wait. Twice as slow this time.'

The silent chess-player looked up and in a low voice of bitterness he said:

'Stop it!'

Caesar was quite different from the prize-fighter – a long slim figure with the eyes of an ascetic or a fanatic, one of them slightly askew so that he always had an impenetrable look; but it was his pendulous nose and his hollowed cheeks and his elongated neck that had christened him.

'Ah! Caesar!' mocked Sean at him. 'One more little bouteen now. One more now. All listen with the utmost attention and devotion, and in all moments of temptation danger and affliction' – he quoted blasphemously from the Catechism as the rite began again and the chess-player leaped to his feet and thrust out his hand to the machine.

At once broken-nose grew dark-faced and stood up to him.

'For God's sake give it a rest,' said Caesar.

'Why should I?' cried Sean. 'What else have we here to occupy our minds?'

'Sean!' implored the girl, while Leo sat still and looked gloomily at the three of them. This was what life had been like in the Bombshop for a month now.

'Let it alone!' cried Sean.

'In-the-lag-behind-the-hollow,' wailed the dying basso.

'Stop it or I'll smash it,' said Caesar, and with his fist he smashed the whirling black circle, and the rain dripped audibly on the corrugated roof. The prize-fighter was furious. He thrust his fist into his hip-pocket and the nickel of a revolver flashed. Norah was between them in a second but as they struggled two deafening shots rang and the air was hot-flavoured with the smell of powder. At once they all grew quiet, looking at one another to see if anyone was hurt, and then they returned to their places. Caesar fingered his chessmen; by the fire Sean ejected the empty shells, and dropped the broken record bit by bit into the fire, frowning as each morsel melted in acrid flame. Secretly we were all listening for some sign that the shots had been heard in the street. Norah removed her shoes and felt her damp feet, and to fill the uneasy silence she turned to the boy.

'Not a single dispatch tonight,' she said. 'But I met Frank Boland.'

'Where has he been?'

'He's been in the mountains, and in Dublin and Kildare, too.'

'My home counties,' said Leo. 'Where was he? Clane or Sallins or Celbridge? Has he any news?'

'He said it was very wet weather there.'

'Yet the beech would be out by now,' said Leo.

'He said something was out. He watches things like that.'

'He does.'

'Maybe it was the beech, he mentioned,' she said. 'But he preferred the mountains for all that they were cold and harsh. He said every road there is a bog and the torrents pouring down the mountain-cliffs like snow.'

They could see that Caesar was listening, and Sean held a piece of broken record poised on his fingers.

'Out there,' said Leo wistfully, 'every pool is a big lake.'

'And every pub,' said Sean, 'is a filled room.'

He was thinking of the frieze-coated peasants, with their pints before them and the smell of the bogs and the byres from their clothes and their twisted bits of ash-plants scraping the spittle into shapes on the sawdust floor. Leo turned to him.

'Wouldn't you scoff a frothy pint now, Sean?' he mocked timidly.

'It's not the pint I want,' he said, and he rose and went to bed.

When he was gone they looked at one another as people might who have heard a strange sound and wonder if their companions can explain it. And as none of them had anything to say Norah leaped up and went down to Mother Dale. They knew she would be wondering what had happened, frightened by those sudden shots.

The two heard Norah's steps go down the stairs, the old woman's door open, and then a brief silence.

'I was once in Sallins,' Caesar was saying, when they heard scream after scream ring through the silent house. They heard Norah pounding up the stairs and when she stood panting before them her face was as pale as her bosom. She pointed through the floor and as they looked stupidly down at it they saw two neat little holes drilled there by the passage of Sean's bullets.

They found the old woman seated as if asleep in her armchair, not a rib of hair askew, her arms lying on the arm-rests, her body as erect as a Caryatid supporting a great weight on its head, but as Leo laid his hand on the back of her neck his fingers grew wet and sticky with blood, and her blood was warm still though the flesh was already rough with the chill of death. There they left her, for all that Norah could say, with tears of pity and rage, half-mad with both, protesting against Caesar's orders that he gave through his tight fanatic's lips. Not a priest nor a doctor would he have; she was dead, cold as a stone already; priests and doctors could do her no good. He stood and looked coldly while Norah applied a mirror to her lips to see if there was any life at all, and then as the glass came away untarnished he looked at the girl and shrugged his shoulders as if to say, 'I told you so.'

'Let us kneel and pray for her,' he said, perhaps with some thought of easing the girl's pain, perhaps to think quietly while we prayed. But at any rate he could not lead our prayers but stumbled and stuttered at them, and Norah rose and pleaded again.

'The work must go on at all costs,' said Caesar. 'Unless she can be removed secretly she stays where she is. Lead the Rosary for her, Norah.'

But Norah cursed him and all of us for a pack of cowards, while Caesar placed a crucifix between the dead woman's fingers and laid a cloth over her face, and as they went up to bed Norah followed them step by step taunting them as she went.

All night long Leo heard her turning uneasily on her pallet and in the morning she was heavy-lidded and her hands trembled. That day they were so long in beginning work that before the lamps began to boom the country carts were long trundled away and the parallelograms of sunlight disappeared from the tiles of the kitchen floor. Then Sean discovered that a jar of his acid was cracked behind its straw and had leaked empty and there was nothing for him to do but fall idle for the day.

Those idle hours finished him. He wandered aimlessly about the house, and they even heard him enter the dead woman's room. He came to Norah where she sat in the kitchen cutting the cotton-wool in long strips for the incendiaries and tried to gossip with her about his children, and when she would not he went poking in the old disused front room. When she followed, after listening for a long time for any sound from him, she found him at the window watching the children playing in the sun; there, she at one side of the window, he at the other, they stood watching them, delighted, until the musty air began to choke her and she fled to her work. It was an old lumber-room, crowded to the door with boxes, trunks, and packing-cases, in which and on which every kind of useless but cherished household god was living – or rather dying, malodorously. To her, too young to care about anybody's past, these sea-shells stuck on velvet, those rows of cracked decanters, the fox under the glass dome (with a special hole cut for his long tail), all those long-cherished useless things commemorated the breaking one by one of the heart-strings of the dead woman. Mother Dale, she knew, had kept them – and all women keep them – because they hope that as long as they look at them their past is not yet dead, their lives not yet spent. During the long ennui of those empty days passed in hiding in whatever house opened its 'front drawing-room' to her, she had become artful, and hated herself for being so artful, in smelling out the faintest musk of those private and particular gods of her woman friends – the chinaware shoe (from Youghal), the filigree plate (from the Royal Oriental Exhibition), the tarnished silver teapot presented at marriage or retirement, the specially-bound prize book (from Sister Joanna to dear May), the *Cabinet of Literature* never cut, the *History of all Time* never read, memories all, mortuaries of the dead past. When she would be older, she well knew, she too would have her monuments and love them as old men love antiquity that is musty like their hearts and she would look fondly at them and carefully preserve the photograph of her marriage-day and the marble clock with the tarnished brass-plate commemorating the first step in the ending of her youth.

'Sean,' she called into him, 'come out of that bloody charnel-house.'

But he had found a red velvet-covered, brass-bound, gilt-latched photograph album, with a musical-box buried in it so that as one looked at the pictures of one's antecedents it ping-ponged out its sad meowing tune:

'Oh, there's, no, place, like, home; oh, no, place, like, home.' Guffawing at it, he opened it again and again, and would not come to her.

As if to mock her and tempt him the sun burst on the city at noon, and the damp of three months rose in curling exhalations from the pavements. Feeling the sun she returned to peep into the streets and found them filled with points of light that leaped from the scales of the mackerel, the white bosoms of the women, their arms diving among the flat fish and the sprats and the slender plaice. She looked up and the seagulls turned their white breasts to her and the vegetables below shone like polished ware; she looked up into the sky where the clouds were lifted slowly up through the blue air like flock for gods to lie on, and below the onion-girls and the lane-children were crying louder than ever, screaming as they ran, the one for customers, the others as for pure joy in the sudden parturition of the year. Even the wail of 'Fine cod a' hake' became faster and more joyous, and even this dim blind-drawn room filled with warmth and light, the great sun glowing through it like fiery bronze. But in the gloom of one corner behind her the musical-box iterated its dozen notes, and Sean, in his fine baritone voice, sang the same few notes over and over again:

> 'Mid pleasures and palaces,
> No matter where we roam,
> Be it ever so humble,
> There's no place like home.'

She turned and swore at him. 'For Christ's sake, stop it, Sean.'

He only laughed at her, and the others, hearing them, left their work to join in the fun. Before them Sean donned a bonnet and a wrap.

'But I haven't the wasp waist,' he roared at them, 'nor the puffed shoulders. If I had the waist it would only be after a month of pulling and hauling on the laces with the maid cocking her leg on the side of the bed for leverage.'

'No, you haven't the waist,' said Leo, imitating his capers.

'The corset wasn't made that would circle your belly,' said Caesar more coarsely than he had even before spoken in that house.

'To be sure women have narrower waists than men,' said Leo, and then he blushed; he saw Norah bite her soft big lips with her prominent teeth, and look at up him through her hair that had fallen forward over her bowed head. In his confusion he spoke foolishly.

'Who do you think, now,' he said, 'wore them things last?'

They broke up at that, silently, like men parting in a church or at a funeral – one going one way, another that, overcome by the thought of the passing away of something they had loved.

The sun moved downward so slowly and so brightly that they noticed without difficulty the lengthening of the day. They talked of the spring while they worked, Leo speaking often of the beech-woods of Kildare, Norah of the smell of the furze and the bracken hot and damp in the mountains. When the dusk fell Sean was still in the old lumber-room watching the scattering of the markets, and when the dark came he packed his bag and despite Caesar's furious taunts he left the house. Norah accompanied him, hoping it might be safer for him, and Caesar and Leo spent the night examining their secret dump under the stairs to see how little they had yet done. There was yet not a third of the amount required, and Caesar, rather than receive another taunting note from the quarter-master when Norah should return, went in despair to his room and Leo sat alone before the empty grate, watching vacantly where a yellow slug, tempted by the sudden heat, drew his silver trail inch by inch to the open window.

It was not the market-people who awoke them the following morning but the milkman thundering on the door. After he had made the whole street resound they saw him stand back from the door and survey the house and then whip up his pony in wonderment, looking back many times as he went. For the first time they realized the risks they were taking. The old woman had few friends, but one of the few might come at any time to visit her, and be astonished at the shutters on the shop-windows and the closed door. At once Caesar went rummaging in the dead-room for a specimen of the old woman's script – finally breaking open a tin safe where she kept her money and her private papers. He winked at Leo with his impenetrable eye and smiled at his own cunning as he copied her hand in a notice for the shop-door: *Gone to the country for a fortnight, May Dale*. If they could now get a man to replace Sean, get a new jar of acid, and arrange to remove the body of the old woman they might bring their work to a successful end. But there was no longer any excuse now for bringing a packing-case or a trunk to the shop as they formerly did whenever they needed raw material, and headquarters complained that it would be even more difficult to get a new man for them than to get a case in or a coffin out. But Caesar threw their taunts back at them in a long dispatch that Norah carried out that night, and he made extreme plans and preparations like a successful general who has received an unexpected defeat. Norah was not to leave now until quite late at night; he would have the Scouts extinguish the lamps near him in the markets so as to give additional darkness; they would rise earlier and finish later. He over-flowed with a rash self-confidence and he always said afterwards that he would have won through if the unexpected had not happened. For his plans did not get very far. Norah actually went out the following night quite late, and the Boy Scouts extinguished every light in the markets – that was Thursday, the third night after her death – by shooting every bulb to pieces with their revolvers; they thereby attracted the attention of the patrols for the first time to the markets and attracted to themselves Caesar's rage, for he sent their Master a long profane dispatch pleading for a 'less spectacular method of hastening the gentle night.' He need not have been so sarcastic with the boys. Even while they were making cock-shots of the market-lights there occurred, at the very gateway of the police headquarters over the river, an ambush in which three Tans and two soldiers were killed, and as a punishment an instant curfew was imposed to the very boundaries of the city, and every man and woman was ordered to be within doors from five o'clock in the afternoon until five o'clock on the following morning, and so nightly 'until further notice.' *Until further notice* read to Caesar like – *For Ever*.

The first afternoon of curfew the foot-patrols were doubled and armoured-cars roared through the deserted streets, leaving as they went from earshot a silence as of death in their wake. In the Bombshop they feared to continue working after the silence of Curfew fell and they peeped through the blinds at the bare markets where the only live thing was a cat quietly washing its face in the warm sun, and a dog crunching a fish-head. Beyond the end of the square a section of main street stood empty as if it were early dawn instead of an hour before sundown, and the naked tram rails in the distance and the closed warehouses made it appear as if every clock in the city had stopped and all Cork had forgotten to rise.

Then night came and there was no moon, and in the markets not a lamp was lit; everything was impenetrable shadow out to the farthest end of the distant street and the cold light of a street-lamp. Once towards ten o'clock a lorry roared into the square and a searchlight flooded the place with a sudden blaze as of protracted lightning. The cats stood still and glared into the light, the cabbage-stumps and the fish-crates leaped out of their black shadows as if they were alive. Then the light swooped and the lorry moved slowly to another street. As they returned to sit by the empty grate they thought to themselves that it would be like that now for weeks to come. They looked at Caesar questioningly, and Caesar shrugged his shoulders and returned to peep again out of the lumber-room; in their hearts they felt defeat gradually approaching. As they listened to the strange quietness they felt themselves islanded in an empty sea.

It was plain to Caesar that he was in the position of an outpost whose communications had been cut, and so, at eleven, promising to return if the luck were with him, he gave his revolver to Leo, put a battered hat on his head – it was his only disguise – slipped a half-filled whisky bottle in his pocket, first taking a dram to fume his breath. Then he stole quietly out of the house and the door was closed to behind him. When he and Leo met again, months afterwards, in the mountains he merely said that immediately he sat down that night in his own house, unnerved by the danger of the journey, he saw at once 'how impossible it all was.' Leo asked him if he attempted to return, but he shook his head and looked at Leo out of his impenetrable eye, and Leo nodded, and they spoke of other things.

But that night in the Bombshop they waited patiently, certain that Caesar would return. Shandon tower alone struck, and struck the hope from their hearts. It was their first night sitting awake in that house and as the hours came and went into eternity they remembered that another besides themselves was sitting, waiting also, below them. To distract the girl, Leo talked and talked of the beauty of the driving clouds and said that it was many a month and more, it seemed like many a year, since he had the peace of mind to look up at the sky at night and marvel at its beauty, while she said passionately that he seemed not to care whether Caesar returned, and called them cowards again, and wished Ireland were better served than by such soldiers.

'Caesar will return in a few hours,' said Leo, almost glad to see her angry because it kept her mind free of thinking on other things. Oh, yes, Caesar would come back, he was a fine fellow, he was sure to return if it could possibly be done. Last night when there was a moon he wished they had been alone. There were four squares of moonlight under the lobby window and they were good to look at, better to stand on, he in one square, she in another.

'There must be beauty in a thing to make it worth fighting for,' he said trying to make her argue. 'A man won't die for a mere abstraction. Keats said Truth was Beauty. I say Freedom is Beauty. Christ was not really the Son of the God of Love, he was the Son of the God of Freedom. He freed men because He knew that in Freedom all beauty has its source. Shelley was wiser than Keats, more human, more true. If Keats had not been a poet, a sensuous youth, he would have been an abstract rationalist. With his "truth is beauty"! A Manichean, a bloody Manichean he'd have been, like all abstract thinkers – like Augustine. *Gaudium de veritate*, your eye-brow! I say *Gaudium de libertate*. The whole Irish church is on the Augustine tack. They herd us in, they circumscribe us, they herd us up the gangway to Heaven, they take us by the scruff of the neck and shove us into Heaven whether we like it or not. They always did it, so overcome by the fear of Hell-fire that they have no time for the love of the Christlight. Scholastics without the scholastic brains, medievalists without the medievalists' sense of beauty. If man could only be free, truly free, if he could only be as God made him. . . .'

But Norah could have hit him in the face. And she left him because she could not hold her temper in, going upstairs, with that strange attractive waddle she had, to lean recklessly with arms akimbo on the moonlit window-sill, thinking that the dead woman sitting below was happiest of all, wishing to the dead Christ – she swore in her rage and despair – that she was lying on her hands and face on the green fields she could see across the city in the light of the rising moon. As she leaned there the quarters and the halves struck, and she listened to them with a sinking heart, thinking of the men on the hills, seeing the quartermaster trudging through the boglands to his dumps, marking up his smudgy note-book by the light of a farm-house fire – so few incendiary bombs, so few cartridges for the grenades and cursing them and everyone else that they could do no better with the lives of men depending on their efforts, and the success of a great cause in the balance. She went wearily to bed, feeling so lonely as she lay, that before she slept she sobbed at the darkness and the emptiness of the house like a little child.

It was only by pure will-power that she rose from bed that Sunday morning. On looking at her watch she found it was only half-past five, and suddenly hearing the first chapel-bell toll faintly across the streets she decided she must go out to mass. The dawn was so dark that she had to light a candle and it reminded her of Christmas time when one lights the lights over the Christmas dinner, even in the daytime. She stole down past Leo's door, and as she glanced at it she noticed that it was open. Peeping through the slit of the hinges she saw the bed was empty and she could hear no breathing. She opened the door cautiously and found the room deserted. She tried every other room – she even opened the dead woman's door and peeped through. There in the dim light of the curtained room sat the corpse, still and statuesque as they left it. Fright overcame her and she fled thundering down the stairs and out into the markets, and not daring to think of her or of Leo or of anything, she hurried across the intervening streets to the monks' chapel. It lay at the end of a great sweep of grazing land; on the grass a soft mist like frost, and through the morning dusk the little Gothic windows of the chapel glowed yellow like the windows of a toy house. When she reached it a stream of people was passing in from the Incurables hospital across the road, the blind, the crippled, the stumbling, the maimed – people whose disease was hidden from the eye. Nobody spoke as they hurried into mass – all cold and silent but for their feet on the damp gravel-path, around them the city lying quietly asleep. They were like a meeting of the dumb and sleepless ones of Cork hurrying to a gift of peace that sleep had denied them, hurrying as if to snatch that gift before the morning should come, for overhead the sky was still dark and the larger stars were shining and the night wind swept through the higher regions of the air.

The chapel was full when she entered, and as if Death were never to be avoided a coffin on trestles stood under a black and silver shroud in the centre of the flags. She sat on a bench that faced the pall, peeping nervously around, half afraid for having ventured out, beginning to wonder where she should go when mass had finished. Two young people attracted her for a long time, a young man and a young woman who prayed so seriously, for their youthful looks, that she wondered at them in her heart. They seemed as if they had only recently been married, or not married for very long, but they were here at the earliest mass in Cork, on a cold April morning, kneeling shoulder to shoulder and praying to what Leo once called a problematical God with an earnestness that frightened her. It was not beautiful to see in the body such young people so fanatically pious – it made her fear God. Meanwhile the ceremony went on, the priest genuflecting as he passed the tabernacle, the acolyte tapping the low-booming bell at the consecration of the Host. Then there was a general scurry as people rose to approach the altar rails. There, as she looked at them, she saw among the crowd the youthful face of Leo; he knelt, he waited for the priest to come with the Host, he raised his head, and the age-old ceremony was fulfilled. Christ the God, the God of Love or the God of Freedom – which she thought was Leo thinking of? – descended on earth to lie on the boy's tongue. She hid her face as he passed back and the next thing she heard was the organ playing tremulously and the priest saying: 'Your prayers are requested for the repose of the soul of Brother Senan who has died at the age of twenty-one.' The congregation murmured pityingly in reply: 'May God have mercy on his soul and the souls of all the faithful departed, Amen.' She rose and slipped out, and when she stepped on the gravel path the sky was bright and the east was red and all the stars were gone. She hurried back to the Bombshop, looking over her shoulder many times, to see if Leo were in sight, and then to her room where she lay on her bed fully dressed, listening for his return, listening to the city wakening by degrees from its night's slumber, to the bells of the city churches, to the occasional footsteps returning from or going to the early Mass.

At last he came, and when she descended he was already at work, and as she fried the rashers for their breakfast the tang of the potassium rose in the air. She entered the workshop smilingly to call him to breakfast, but immediately she looked at him she noticed a change. The Mass that had filled her heart with peace, a serene and happy peace, had filled his with far other feelings. He would not talk to her; and when she ventured a question or two – as whether the incendiaries would be finished in time – he replied with a short No.

'Why not?' she asked.

How could they? Anyway, why should he care? What a small business they were engaged in! A dirty business. Bombs? Incendiaries? He would do the grenade cartridges. He would do that. Others would have to do the bombs. And when, because she did not understand what he was driving at (and woman-like seized the practical objection first), she protested that he had never done the grenade cartridges which were always Caesar's job, he flared up and his tongue loosened, and he became argumentative.

'Can't do them? I'll tell you how to do them. Empty the old Mausers first of all. Now listen!'

As he spoke he jabbed his greasy fork in the air, so that she had to draw back from his whirling hands. Afterwards when she realized that the well had merely burst through his clay also, she was sorry for him, but now as he argued that she had neither sympathy nor patience left.

'Weigh out the grains,' he cried, 'with the utmost care. I know what I'm talking about. Clean the old cartridges with dilute nitric, and when they're ready cut them down and file them down. Then the cardboard wads. And the cotton wads. Then after that you just coax the little grains carefully, one by one, a single one might make twenty yards of difference in the cast, and ram the wads tight, and the paper wads, and close the lot with your tweezers.'

'But, Leo, what is it all for? What do you want to change for?'

'Now, let me finish. I'll show you if I know.'

'But even if you do know, Leo?'

'Now, the cap. Shellac for that. And a trick to dry them is to put them on a hot plate over a Bunsen. Yes, well, now, the caps. The caps. Oh yes! They must be impressed. Tight. And that's not all. . . .'

She looked at him, and he saw she was looking at him as one looks at somebody one has known for a long time and trusted for a long time and suddenly begun to doubt or suspect. He fell silent, and returned her look in kind. There they sat, all about them the monuments of their hopes, the bags of chemicals, the roughly-fashioned ovens and heating trays, the books of instructions, the jars of acid. Beneath them the silent statue in her chair. Outside the awakening city and the climbing sun; there at least was peace, or the appearance of peace, with the shadows slanting from the houses, the bells falling into silence.

Knock, knock, knock-knock! Like cringing curs their tongues sank down in their throats and they swallowed hard with fear, staring at one another and listening for the next bold knocking on the door below. Knock! And after it a series of running knocks in the rhythm of the cry of 'Here's the herrings, here's the herrings, here's the herrings.' So they had come for her? Or was it a raid? If so this was the end. For some reason Norah wondered why the old woman did not rise up and go down to that insistent knocking and say 'Here I am, and long enough I waited for you.' A long silence was followed by a single knock. They stole on tiptoe to the lumber-room window and peeped out, half-expecting to see scattered figures in uniform thrown in a half circle before the house, rifles at the ready. All they saw was a man passing by on the opposite side of the square look across in the direction of the door. Nobody came forward to look up at the house, but after a while steps moved away from the door beneath them and they returned and sat as before. Then Leo jumped to his feet.

'This puts a finish to it,' he said.

'I don't see that,' persisted Norah, flinging her hair back from her brow.

'Are we to wait to be taken? Who was that at the door?'

'They're gone.'

'Do you think they won't return? Do you think she has no relations or friends who don't know she never went "to the country" like that before. Let's clear out. Come on quick.'

Panic had seized him. He caught up the sweeping brush with some wild notion of leaving the house tidy as they found it, the death below left unexplained.

'You are afraid,' she taunted.

'Sean and Caesar were right to leave you,' he retorted, 'with your bickering tongue.'

'How soft the men leave their posts! Wait till the story spreads on you. Leo, Leo! Aren't you thinking of the men on the hills waiting for the stuff? They must have something to fight with.'

'For God's sake....'

She laid her hand gently on his shoulder. He could not bear that – after all he was only a boy.

'Leo,' she pleaded, 'I know you dearly love Ireland....'

'Oh, vomit on Ireland,' he cried. 'Vomit on her.'

He began to sweep the workroom, the silver powder and the grey powder and the red, the curls of cotton-wool, the brass-filings, and she began to work on the incendiary cartridges at the bench by the window. But he followed her, packing away the things she needed, brushing the dust around her feet, he even knocked the brush-end deliberately against her ankles. He put the matches in his pocket, saying they were his, and when she went to the kitchen for more he snapped them up, saying he believed they were his also. When she changed her place over to the other window, he followed her and flung open the shutters and chanted some song out to the back-yards that had never heard a man's voice in that house as long as the oldest resident could remember. At that she turned on him in a rage, and he in a rage turned to face her. She gripped the shutter to close it; he held it to keep it wide. They could see a woman looking across at them in amazement from the window of a slum-house opposite. Tears came to the girl's eyes, and her flaxen hair fell around her shoulders so that the sun made an aureole of it about her trembling features, and looking at her the boy released his grasp and blushing with shame he left the room.

As she began to work on the little caps, dropping warm shellac one by one into each, she could hear in the distance a group of merry-makers leaving the city for the day in cars, the sound of the horses' hoofs and the sound of their concertina playing gaily, and those happy, indifferent sounds dispirited her. The room now grew warm, and she felt the sweat gather on her brow, and the sky darkened until presently her spirit lamp was throwing leaping shadows on the benches, and her hands as they moved were shadowed on the ceiling. Between the room and the murmurs of the city there seemed to hang a heavy curtain dulling all sound, and what light came through the chinks of the shutter was livid. One by one she filled the caps, arranging them when filled in a neat little row before her. Once the lamp threw a strange shadow high in front of her and she leaped around in terror to see who was in the room, and from that on she kept glancing right and left, listening to know where Sean was, looking over her shoulder at the door, looking down at the floor as if she thought she heard some noise below her. At last she seemed to hear something clearly, and she rose and faced the door; she had heard the heavy steps come slowly up the stairs, step by step, to each landing, to the last landing, to the very handle of the door.

'Les! Les!' she screamed. 'She's coming. She's coming!'

'What is it? What is it?' he cried and ran in to her.

'Look at her! Look! Look!'

A frightful rattle of thunder crashed over the room as if mighty billiard-balls were cannoning in the sky. He clasped her to him and she clung to him – she could see the fish-head eyes of the corpse staring at her through the linen cloth. Then the soft rain outside changed into a downpour so that they heard it on the iron roof in the yard. Leo flung open the shutters again so that they could see the sun shining through the falling water, and as she continued to tremble he kissed her right on the lips. She did not try to prevent him. She heard him whispering that this was the best end of all, and she did not try to deny it, for as he whispered she grew calmer and knew that an end there must be.

So they spent that morning cleaning the house, packing everything away in the secret dump, ready to be removed if the chance should offer. Last of all they unlocked her door and dusted and tidied her room, and they set a great fire going on front of her, and they poured fresh milk into her glass and put their own food in her cupboard. The last thing they did before they left was to remove the linen cloth from her face. Then they walked boldly out into the markets and the city streets just a little before curfew when everybody was hastening home. They spent the night in a country house on the hills that lay just outside the city to the south-west, sitting silently together as soon as they could be alone, hand in hand. Norah flung her shoes from off her feet, and to please Leo she let her hair down about her shoulders.

'I am afraid, darling,' she said to him, 'there are streaks of grey in it.'

'I cannot see them,' he said gallantly.

'I shan't search for them,' she said gaily, holding his hand tighter than ever.

If they wished to raise their eyes from under the glow of the old reading-lamp they could see through the open window the fire-flies of the city far below them, a thin row of footlights to the night, but where they could smell the country smells of budding-time they had no wish to look down into that dark hollow with its thousand blinking eyes. No city should they see if they looked, but a house in the centre of the markets, vegetable and fish refuse around it, dogs barking in the yards behind it, and the one occupant they left there seated before the warm fire, staring into its flames.

The Death of Stevey Long

Macroom Castle was built somewhere in the sixteenth century by the MacCarthys, a building of great height raised on a solitary outcrop of rock and with a moat and a demesne reaching down to the river-edge. As Macroom is the last town on the western road through the mountainy divide of Cork and Kerry the castle has always become a barracks in troubled times, the last outpost for the wild, disaffected country beyond. It has a long history: it suffered at least one siege, and passed through several hands. The O'Sullivans lost it in 1606 to the Earl of Cork and in 1675 the crown confiscated it and put troops in it to overawe the rebels to the West, that broken land impenetrable to everyone but tories and raparees. It had its dungeons and its secret passages, and in fact when the Tans took it over as a barracks, in their time, they thought it best to close up several doors that, it seemed to them, led nowhere. But it was not a suitable place to imprison anyone; the river bred too many rats and moles and beavers, and when the mountains sent their rain-water churning down the rocky valleys the floods rose so high that they overflowed into the basement, and from the later-built cells a little higher up a prisoner could see the trees and the hedges growing out of the water almost on a level with his eye.

In one of these cells, his elbows resting easily on the window-sill, stood Stevey Long gazing westward to where the faint blue of the mountains was barely discernible against a white sky. Beside him was a little man whose finger-tips barely clutched the stone edge on which Stevey leaned, and as he strained up to peep at the mountains Stevey looked down at him with amusement.

'They'll shoot you tonight, Fahy,' said Stevey suddenly.

'Ah, shtop that talk now, Long,' said the little man with an imploring upward glance.

'Oh, but I hear them saying it,' said Stevey. ' "Bring out that fat murderer of a teacher," they'll say. Or they'll say, "Bring up that assassin of a teacher, and we'll teach him".'

'Oh, suffering Heart!' wailed the teacher. 'Me nerves is all upsot. Shtop it now, Long. It's not fair.'

As Stevey gazed off contemptuously at the mountains the teacher defended himself.

'Anyway,' he said, 'I never let on to be a fightin' man. And it's all very well for you. You haven't a wife and seven children.'

'Seven children?' asked Stevey. 'Is that all you have, teacher? You ought to be ashamed of yourself.'

'Isn't it enough? You're mocking again, Long. Saying your prayers would befit you betther. That dirty tongue of yours will bring the wrath of God on us.'

'My tongue,' said Stevey vehemently, 'is our only hope.'

'Then why,' said the teacher peevishly, 'don't you get round that bastard of a jailer for us?'

'Oh! Oh! Bastard? Naughty word, teacher. Naughty word!'

'Go to hell,' said the little man in an agony of anger and fear, and he retired to a corner of the cell, by now almost in tears.

Stevey went to the iron door of the cell and listened for any sound in the passage-way. Then in one of his sudden rages he stooped over his companion.

'Haven't I told him enough lies to drown a cathedral? Said I was at Festubert? Said I had an English wife? Said I knew Camden Town and Highgate like the palm of me hand? Told him every dirty story I ever read or heard? And what have you done but sit there and cry?' – and he raised his hand as one might to a child – 'you long-faced lubber!'

Stevey returned to the window.

'And after all that,' he continued, 'all he says is, "Aow! How interesting!" God, how I despise the English!'

'It's no use, Stevey,' said the teacher. 'We can't get round him.'

The teacher would have been secretly pleased if Stevey would believe it. For two weeks he had had to sit in that unsanitary cell listening at all hours of the day and night to Stevey and the Tan who had been on cell-fatigue since they came, exchanging indecent stories. Stevey poured them out without an effort of memory: stories he had heard in the pubs and garages and lavatories of Cork, stories he had read in the *Decameron*, the *Heptameron*, French joke-books, Maupassant, the Bible – at first to the amazement, and gradually to the horror of the little teacher. He had read nothing since he left his Training College ten years before, and he still talked of Dickens on the strength of the one novel he was obliged to read there. What horrified him most of all was to find himself gradually inveigled into listening to these stories, and (with a start) he would find himself grinning with delight before he realized that the sewer-stream had been let loose once again. Stevey was a plumber by trade – he was always saying how proud his father was of 'the profession' – and he would begin to talk of red-lead or three-inch pipes, and proceed slowly via lavatory-traps, the sewers of Paris, chronic constipation, tablets for anaemia, or cures for impotency, to the brothels of the world or the famous courtesans of history – all with great seriousness and a show of modest indignation – and he would illustrate with a vast amount of inaccurate, and even for his subject, defamatory detail at which the teacher's eyes would swell and his fat head would shake with wonder and sudden enlightenment. Or he would spend a whole night hinting at his affairs with the loose girls of the city, returning quickly to the cess-pools or chloride-of-lime if the teacher showed disapproval, or to Margaret of Navarre or Boccaccio as if his life, too, were one long legend and romance. But he could pollute even the sweetest women of literature, and the teacher would find himself trapped again when Stevey would fling Madame Bovary or Boule de Suif or Tess into the same bawdy-box as Mata Hari or some creature out of the *Rat Bleu et Jaune* or some local beshawled laneway light-o'-love just previously removed to the city madhouse. To the Tan he was as the Shahrazade to her Persian king. The Englishman heard such stories from him as he had never heard in tap-room or barrack-square – even an old story would become fresh and vivid in Stevey's mouth, and weak with laughter he would scarcely have enough strength to turn the key in the door as he staggered off roaring with delight to retail what he had heard to his comrades upstairs. Then Stevey would, as now, return to the window muttering contemptuous curses under his breath and appeal to Fahy for something to add to his stock of bawdry. When Fahy would reply with an apologetic wail that, 'I was always on the althar, Stevey,' or , 'I was a great Confraternity man, Stevey,' the gunman would lose himself in gazing at the pale, far-off horizons, wave after wave of land, paling into the all-but-invisible peaks of the real hinterland fifty miles away. Since the days of the Earls of Cork a hundred rebelly Irishmen must have gazed just as longingly at those changeless mountain-tops, thinking first of the misfortune of their capture, then of wives or friends, then of the fate in store for them, but soon reduced, as they looked out on the unattainable freedom of the hills, to thinking of nothing at all, waiting only for the dusk and the dark and the forgetfulness of sleep. None can have spent his hours, as Stevey did, thinking to coax his English jailer with bawdry, but few, if any, can have been as cruel, and as cunning, and (it must be admitted) as fearless, as Stevey Long.

Suddenly steps clanked down the passage-way and the cell began to taint of gas – the jailer had turned on the tap outside the door, and the little blue flame leaped up on the shelf above the lintel, and the circle cut in the centre of the door was filled by an eye.

'Hey!' whispered the Tan.

'Yes,' said Stevey, at the door in a flash.

'You two blokes are to be moved.'

'Where?' asked Stevey while the little teacher crowded up against him to listen.

'Cork Male Prison,' said the Tan.

Stevey groaned. There was an end to his hopes of escape from the castle, and he knew Cork Jail well enough not to like it. The eye disappeared and was replaced by a pair of lips.

'But you ain't goin'!' they whispered cautiously.

'Why not?' asked Stevey, excited with hope.

'Cos' I 'ave other plans for you,' said the Tan, blinking a wink at them. 'I won't 'ave it. 'Ere's the order,' he said curtaining the circle for a moment with a buff paper. 'There's two deserters here from the Wiltshires, higher up than you, right upstairs, and I'm jolly well going to run them out on this order. They came in an hour ago and they're blind and blotto with Irish moonshine.'

'Oh,' said Stevey, 'but you can't....'

'See if I don't,' said the Tan, and he opened the door and entered the cell. He cornered Stevey by the window and prodded his chest with his finger as it were a revolver or a knife.

'Hark at me!' he said.

'Yes?' said Stevey and the little teacher put in his fat face to listen.

'Go away, you,' growled the Tan, and Fahy retired like a kicked dog. 'Go and stand by the door and hear if anybody's coming.'

He turned to Stevey.

'You know about my wife?'

Stevey did indeed know about the wife. She had been, he always knew it, his main hope. She was London-Irish and a Catholic, and it was she who made Stevey declare his wife was London-Irish and a Catholic too, by Heaven.

'Yes,' said Stevey.

'She keeps on nagging at me in her letters,' complained the Tan. 'She's delicate, and she has nerves, and she's a Catholic.' (This last seemed to be a great grievance with him.) 'I was proud of all that when I married her. It's so romantic, I thinks to myself, to have a delicate wife that's a Catholic into the bargain. But now! She says I'm earning blood-money. I told her about you, and she writes and says she weeps to think of you. But that's all right. She weeps to think of anything, she does. I don't mind that. But now she says such things about leaving the kids and going to live with her married sister that I don't trust her.'

'I wouldn't trust her,' says Stevey.

'How I 'ate married sisters,' said the Tan; and then, 'Why wouldn't you trust her?'

'She's all alone in London,' said Stevey in a gloomy voice.

'She's got her kids. She's got her married sister.'

'Ah,' said Stevey in a hollow voice, 'but where's her husband? From what we know of women,' he continued seriously, 'and especially married women,' he added with an air of sad wisdom, 'you can't trust a woman that's separated from a man that she thinks isn't fond of her.'

'Nor I don't trust her,' said the Tan. 'And I'm goin' home. That's where you come in.'

'Yes,' said Stevey like a shot. 'I could get you out of this country within ten hours, without anybody knowing it – if I were free.'

'You've said so. Dozens of men – deserting, if you like to put it that way.'

'It's my job,' said Stevey. 'City of Cork Steam Packet to Liverpool. Think you were travelling first-class. Easy as that.'

'I'll chance it,' said the Tan. 'Back to London I must get. To tell you the truth I'm sick of this bloody place.'

From inside his uniform he pulled a hacksaw and a length of stout rope. Stevey took them in a grab.

'After dark,' said the Tan. 'I'll bring supper as usual. Now get to work and quietly. If that blade cracks I can't get you another one.'

As he opened the door to go Stevey's mind flamed; as fast as a bullet it flew to the old coach road south-west of the castle where they would probably begin their trek west or east.

'Sst,' he called.

The Tan turned.

'Take a message for me to the village,' said Stevey.

'No,' said the Tan.

'You must,' said Stevey. With a stub of pencil he wrote on a sheet of paper from the Tan's pocket-book, and gave it to him. The Tan read it and winked back at Stevey.

'It's the little bicycle-shop just across the bridge,' said Stevey.

'You're a clever fellow,' said the Tan. 'Of course we must have bikes.'

When he was gone Stevey wound the rope round the belly of the teacher and put him with his back to the door so as to cover the spyhole and listen for approaching feet. Then he began, stealthily at first, to saw at the first of the three bars in the window.

'This scratching,' he said, 'will be heard all over the town of Macroom.'

'If we only had a bit of grease for it,' said the teacher like a fool.

'I once read about Casanova,' said Stevey, and then he stopped talking and hacked away.

'By God,' cried the teacher, 'I once heard a story about that fellow. . . .'

'Eat it,' said Stevey, working like a madman.

The evening was now falling, and as Stevey worked the interior of the cell grew dark. Away to the south-west the sun was sinking over the distant mountains and as she sank they grew first a rich, deep brown, and then purple, 'their very peaks became transparent,' and lastly they paled into an unreal mist. The last level rays threw Stevey's shadows on the iron door and the limed wall, and the little teacher's face was warmed to a ruddy glow. As the air grew cold and rarefied they heard all the sounds of the village life, the children that cried out in their play and the cart that lumbered over the cobbles of the bridge.

About half-past six o'clock the teacher, weary and stiff for so long standing in a fixed position, was almost glad to announce the approach of footsteps. By that time Stevey had cut to within a feather's breadth the top and bottom of two of the bars, filling with clay from the floor the shining track of the saw through the steel. The clanking steps came to the door – it was their friend the Tan. He laid their supper on the bench and bent his head to whisper.

'I'm going with you,' he said to Stevey. 'Mind you promise to get me out of it safe and sound.'

'I swear to Christ,' said Stevey like a shot.

The little teacher was like a kettle on the hob with excitement.

'Naow!' said the Tan. 'No swearing. Parole. Give me your parole, word of honour.'

'Word of honour,' said Stevey, without a thought.

'Oh, God, yes, word of honour,' said the teacher heatedly.

'Shut up, you,' said the Tan angrily, and the little fellow piped down miserably, fearing to be left behind if he angered either of them.

'The Tommies are gone to Cork,' said the Tan with a grin. 'There'll be hell to pay when they get in with the Shinners in Cork Jail. When will we go?'

'When is sundown?' asked Stevey. 'Is there a moon?'

The Tan consulted his diary.

'Six forty-six, sun sets. Full moon, eight-ten.'

'It'll be dark at eight,' said Stevey. 'We'll go then.'

'Is he coming?' said the Tan, pointing to the teacher.

'We'll bring him,' said Stevey.

The Tan looked at the teacher and then he went away without a word. They ate but little that night and Stevey kept going and coming in a corner of the cell.

'God,' he said nervously, 'I'm like a cistern tonight.'

'Will we go wesht?' asked the teacher, stuttering with terror.

'You'll go wesht if you're not careful,' said Stevey. 'Remember that bastard has a gun in his hind-pocket. And we have none.'

They kept watching for the faint moon but the reflected glow of the village and the fluttering light of the gas-jet confused them. All the country to the west was now wrapped in night and the mountains could no longer be seen. With the fall of darkness their ears became sharper and they could hear now the last cries of the children quite plainly and the murmur of the river far below. A mist spread itself over the land before their window, and a faint mooing of cattle occasionally came out of the darkness. As he peered into it Stevey made up his mind that he would not go west – he was sick of that wild, broken country where, as he used to say, 'they ploughed the land with their teeth,' sick of the poor food, the dry bread and jam, the boiled tea and salted bacon, sick of the rough country girls. He was pining for the lights and gaiety of the city and he decided he would do a little 'deserting' of his own. When the Englishman came down, sharp at eight, he had donned a civilian's coat over his green-black policeman's trousers and a wide-brimmed bowler hat that pressed his two ears out like railway signals.

'Ready?' he whispered.

Stevey nodded. From outside he extinguished the jet and plunged the cell in darkness. Stevey unwound the rope from the belly of the teacher, and the Tan pressed with all his might on the cut bars. They would not give. Stevey dropped the rope and threw his weight on them and still they held. The Tan swore, the teacher entangled himself in the rope, and Stevey searched in the dark for the saw. At last he found it and with a few sharp rasps the blade broke through the steel. It was easy then to bend the bars up on a level with the higher coping, and when the rope had been tied to the uncut bar and flung out into the dark they were ready.

'I'll go first,' said Stevey, 'and signal with one pull on the rope if everything is clear below. Send him after' – pointing to the teacher. 'And come last yourself.'

'Oh,' moaned the teacher, as he looked at the aperture, 'I'm too fat to get through that.' But they paid no heed to him.

Stevey wriggled out first, his feet scraping the wall as he was pushed behind by the other two.

'I'll never get through them bars,' wailed the teacher in a deep whisper to nobody in particular.

Stevey vanished downward, swaying as he went, hand over hand. He landed in a great bed of stinging nettles and resisting an impulse to turn and run for it he listened for a second. The little river gurgled noisily below him; he could distinctly hear the quiet munching of cattle just beyond the mound where he stood. He pulled the rope once and stood looking up. A faint white radiance was beginning to appear where the moon was rising on his left. Stevey saw the teacher's fat legs waving in the air and his fat bottom squirming skyward. But there he remained, not advancing an inch, and after a long pause he was pulled in again, and Stevey saw the bare shins of the Tan, then his black trousers dragged up to the knees, then his body following after. In a second he too was among the nettles.

'Where's Fahy?' asked Stevey in a whisper.

'Come on,' said the Tan fiercely.

The fat pale face of the teacher appeared at the window.

'I can't get out,' he wailed in a loud whisper.

'Use the saw,' said Stevey. 'We can't wait.' And he clambered down the mound, grinding his teeth as a pile of loose stones rumbled after him down the slope.

'Ssh!' said the Tan. 'The sentries will hear us.'

'Lie still,' said Stevey, and they dropped on the dew-wet grass. They heard a sentry's voice call to his mate, and the mate's reply. They heard the grounding of arms, and then the noisy river, and the wind in the willows above them shivering and whispering incessantly by the river's edge. After a while they rose and in a stooping posture they half-walked, half-ran along by the edge of the river through the grass, feeling the ground (when they left the river) rise steeper and steeper, and when they fell panting again on the ground, there below them was the black pile of the castle and the hundred eyes of the town.

'That bloody teacher nearly ruined us,' said the Tan.

'He'll never get out,' said Stevey.

But he soon forgot him, and he did not in fact live to know what happened him in the end. They were now standing on the soft dust of the old coach road, below them the next valley, and, as if it were standing on the tip of the distant ridge beyond, the great ruby moon. To Stevey it was all familiar and congenial, but to the Englishman it was cold and desolate.

'We're out of it,' said Stevey gaily, and he slapped the Englishman on the back.

'I'm in it,' said the Tan gloomily. 'Well, where are the bikes?'

At that Stevey squared his shoulders and clenched his fists. He looked up and down the narrow, shaded road, and then at the Tan.

He looked down at the far-off lights of the town and at the Tan again. Then he jerked his head onward.

'This way,' he said. 'They should be here.'

He went on ahead, peering right and left, whispering in a low voice as he went 'Jimmy? Jimmy?' When he passed a blasted oak a bicycle fell clattering on the road at his feet. He peered up and there was a gaitered leg and the tail of the inevitable trench-coat. Everything was happening just as he expected it.

'Here's one,' he shouted. 'Try is the other there,' and he pointed backwards to the opposite side of the lane. As the Tan groped in the far ditch Stevey whispered madly to the hidden figure.

'Have ye the skits?'

'Yes.'

'Get 'em ready.'

'How many are there?' said the voice.

'One.'

Then Stevey shouted back to the Tan.

'Have you got it?'

'No.'

'Here,' called Stevey. 'Hold this one.'

The unsuspecting man came forward to hold the bicycle, and as he took it Stevey passed behind his back. The bicycle crashed as Stevey leaped like a tiger at his neck, roaring at the same time to 'Jimmy' to give a hand. Two trench-coated figures leaped from the hedges at the cry and fell on the struggling shouting soldier, and in two minutes he was bound with Stevey's trousers belt and his kicking legs held and tied with a bit of cord. Finally his yelling mouth was stoppered by Stevey's handkerchief and then, except for their panting and an occasional squirm from the helpless man at their feet everything was deadly quiet again.

'Gimme his skit,' said Stevey.

The captive looked up with the light of terror glaring in his eyes. Stevey stood over him for a second with his finger wavering on the trigger.

'Here,' he said then to one of the two. 'You do it. I gave him my word I wouldn't.'

He made for the bike, dusting himself as he went, and threw his leg over the saddle. A horrible double sound of a revolver being discharged tore through the night.

'Gimme that,' said Stevey.

The revolver was handed to him, and he thrust it in his pocket.

'Are you sure he's finished?' he asked.

'Sure,' said the other.

'Good-bye boys,' said Stevey, and he pedalled swiftly along the dark lane.

Presently he freewheeled on to the lower road and came to a dimly-lighted pub. An old cart and a sleepy horse were tethered outside the door. This was the pub known as The Half-way House, and Stevey decided that he needed a free whisky. First peering through the glass door he entered. There was nobody inside but the bar-girl and an old farmer leaning in the corner of the counter and the wall; the girl said nothing, and the old farmer merely nodded. Those were tough times, and they had heard the double shot.

'Any Tans about?' said Stevey when he had ordered his drink.

The girl only shook her head silently and poured the drink, watching him as he swallowed it. The farmer lowered his eyes to sip his porter whenever Stevey looked at him, raising them slowly whenever he felt he was not being watched, nodding and smiling foolishly whenever Stevey's eyes caught him. A tiny clock among the whisky bottles ticked so loudly in the silence that Stevey looked up at it startled. It was nearly nine o'clock.

'By God, it's late,' he said.

The girl nodded and said nothing, and when Stevey looked at the farmer he was turning his glass round and round in its own wet circle, his eyes shooting side-glances towards Stevey all the while.

'Christ,' swore Stevey, 'you are a talkative pair!' And putting down his empty glass he strode out between the swinging doors and walked to his bicycle. Then it occurred to him to return on tip-toe and listen at the glass-doors. The old farmer was speaking:

'Aye,' he was saying, 'a bit o' money is a great thing.'

'Yes,' said the girl listlessly.

'Sons how are ye!' said the farmer.

'Aye,' responded the girl. There was a pause, and then:

'Money is betther than sons any day,' said the farmer.

'Yes sure,' said the girl with a sigh.

With a superior grin Stevey mounted and rode away.

Had Stevey kept his word with the Englishman he might be alive today. He would certainly have avoided Cork that night. But now, knowing nothing of what awaited him and with nobody to warn him, he covered, in less than four hours, the forty odd miles that separate Macroom from Cork. He had cycled along the winding roads among the bogs where the mountains come down to the plains, and when the mountains vanished from sight he pedalled over a bare, high plateau where he measured the distance not by prominent hills or valleys but by a tree here and a tree there, or a cross-road, a familiar house, or a school. At last he came to the valley of the city river and for miles he cycled above it, straight as a crow's flight to the edge of the city. It was about one o'clock when he stood looking down over all its sleeping roofs as over a vale of quietness, a slight drizzle of rain beginning to fall, a gentle wind blowing it in his eyes as he peered across to the uttermost farthest light that marked the remote side of the city to the north where his father lived. He might have made a long detour to reach Fair Hill, but why should he? Had he known the city was under curfew he would never have dared to do anything else, but his two weeks in Macroom Castle were two weeks cut off from the world, and now, flinging his bike into the ditch, he dropped downhill into the danger of the streets.

After his three long months in the mountains it was sweet to feel the ring of the pavements instead of the pad-pad of the mud roads, to see the walls and the gas-lamps all about him, so sheltering after the open darkness of the country nights. But as he went on the streets were so strangely empty, even for one o'clock in the morning – there was not even a wandering dog abroad – that Stevey became worried and ill at ease. As he approached the open business section of the city especially he began to realize what a grave risk he was taking in coming back into the city at all where he was well known for a gunman; but to come late at night, with no crowds to mingle with, and the police on the alert for late wanderers was doubly dangerous. Still, as the mist thickened, became heavier, finally changed into a wind-blown downpour, it did not occur to him that any reason other than bad weather was required to explain the strange emptiness of the streets, until suddenly, not more than a few blocks away, a dozen rifle-shots broke through the hiss of the falling rain, loud above the river purling in its narrow bed. Stevey halted in his stride. Then as there was no repetition of the sound he went on, down to the quays that shone under the arclights webbed with moisture.

The rain hissed into the river, cold and spearlike, and his calves were now wet, and his face and shoulders and he could feel his coat was sodden through. Then, in and out of the glow of the lamps on the pathway in front of him he saw a girl racing in his direction, calling as she ran to another girl to hurry, the other calling to her to wait. It was a relief to Stevey to meet somebody, but when the first girl, who ran against the rain with lowered head, rushed into his arms and then screamed and cowered away from him into the wall – he stood angry and astonished.

'Oh! Sir, sir!' she wailed. 'I'm goin' home.'

'Hello, hello!' said Stevey. 'What's up with you?'

'I'm goin' home, sir,' she said again, trying to cower past him. 'I am, honest.'

'Well, go home!' cried Stevey exasperated, and passed on. The other girl, he found, had turned and fled from him as from the devil.

Stevey now observed that the houses towering about him were almost pitchy black. All the erect oblongs of light had long since moved up nearer the roofs, wavered there for a while, and then vanished suddenly; the sitting-rooms had become bedrooms and then been blotted out, and now only red eyes of light showed bedroom walls where one could no longer see bedroom windows. Once a moving candle-flare showed the turn of a stairs, a landing, a high window. Bare boards, thought Stevey, under bare feet unheeding the silver of hammered nails in the white wood, long white neck-frilled night-dresses bending over the balustrade to call to a tiled hallway for surety of locked doors. A blind sank down, squares walking up its yellow ground. A pair of gold parallelograms disappeared, and then began to reappear and vanish, faint or defined, but never steady for a moment, and to Stevey's thought a woman curved over the flames, her fingers slipping her shoes from her feet, silken stockings falling after. All the while the rain lashed the shining pavement – a real mixture of March wind and April shower – and the spouts poured their overflow across the cement flags. Everyone was asleep in bed but he. He possessed the whole city, as if it had been made for him alone.

Again the rifle-shots rang out and this time they were followed by a rattle of machine-gun fire and a few isolated explosions. Again Stevey halted, drawing into a door and peering along the quays. He felt that after his fortnight in prison and his three months in the hills he was become a stranger to this city-world in which he had once moved so easily and safely, and he wished he had made a call in some friendly house before entering the city – it almost seemed to him as if something strange and unusual were occurring around him. He left the quays at this thought, and began to dodge among the side-lanes and the back-streets, but to cross the river he finally had to come into the open. As he crossed the railway bridge he saw on the opposite quay, spread across the street, a squad of soldiers whose accoutrements and arms glinted in the rain and the arclights, and seeing their weapons at the ready he drew back behind a girder and waited. They were approaching gradually and he knew that he would certainly be discovered if he remained there. He moved in quick bird-like leaps across the bridge, from the shelter of one girder to the shelter of another, peeping all the time at his enemy. Then he had to leave the bridge and cross the street. His heart beat faster; he breathed quickly. He heard a cry of 'Halt' and he took to his heels. Over his head, by his very ears it seemed to him, whistled the bullets. At once he took to the side-lanes, up and down and in and out until he had lost his pursuers and himself thoroughly, and exhausted he fell back into a doorway to think. It did not take him long to realize this time that it was Curfew, long threatened even while he was in the mountains, suddenly clapped on the city while he was in jail, and he had walked like a fool into the net. His hand stole to the revolver in his pocket. If he had been caught with that it would have meant anything. Now completely unnerved he left the door, halting at the slightest noise, looking around every lane-corner and down every passage-way before he dared pass them by. Gradually he began to recognize where he was – in the network of lanes between the river and the fish-markets, an isolated quarter to leave which would bring him into the open streets once more. A lecherous pair of cats made him leap for an arched alley-way. He laughed at himself the next minute but he realized that he could never hope to reach Fair Hill in this way, across the other bridge and along another set of naked quays. Over his head Shandon boomed out two o'clock – there would be at least three hours more of Curfew. He wiped the sweat of fear from his forehead and peeped cautiously out of his alley-way, thanking his good-fortune that he did so, for the next instant the heavens seemed to open with light and every cranny and crevice of the lane was flooded by a powerful searchlight. At the same moment he heard the soft whirring of a car and low voices. He was taut and trembling like a string that has been made vibrate by a blow. He thought he heard steps approaching and he slunk backwards down the alley, halting in doors and watching the flooded light of the lane, beyond the tunnel of the arch. He came to the alley-end and his feet crunched on the head of a dead fish, the guts oozing under his heels. He glanced about the great pitch-dark square – he was in the markets. In the limelight of the arch far down the alley he saw two khaki figures who turned towards him and entered the arch and faced the wall. It was enough for Stevey – he turned and crouched his way along the markets, slipping on the rotting vegetables and the slime of fishgut, resting in door after door with something of the feeling that he had walked into the wrong region, that here were troops of men, that in any other part of the city it would have been far different if not entirely safe. But he felt his last turn taken when a whirring lorry roared suddenly around the corner and its floodlight poured into the street, lighting the very pavement at his feet, where he stood with his back to a door; and as if to give him no possible chance he saw, and cursed as he saw, that the jambs and lintel and panels were pure white. With the instinct of the trapped man he crushed back against it and the nearer the car came the more he crushed. Slowly, as he pressed against it, the door swung open behind him. He passed in and closed it behind him and listened, not even breathing, while the car passed slowly by. Then he began to breathe tremblingly, and panting, and with his hand to his heart, he laughed quietly to himself. Trust Stevey, said he to himself, to get out of any corner.

The hallway was blackness unbroken, and with his two hands out, one grasping his revolver, a crucified gunman, he groped his way in. His feet struck the first knee of the stairs, and he began to climb. A window-sill and an empty pot – he passed it by. A lead-lined sink and a dripping tap – he moved on upwards. A door. Was this a man or a family, or a lone woman? Damn dangerous business this, thought Stevey to himself; but not half so dangerous as the streets. What should he do? Sleep in the hall? Clear out? Neither. Was it Stevey Long not to get himself a good doss for the night? As his father would say, he must think of 'the profession.' He moved up higher and came to a landing window. Through it he could see Shandon dark against the glowing sky of the city. Across in another house he could see a back-window all lit up, and framed in it two men, both in pants and shirts. He could hear their quarrel, see the bigger of the two crash his fist into the face of the other, see a ragged-haired lane-woman drag them apart. Then the light vanished as she moved away upstairs with the candle, and the small man wiping the blood from his cheeks stumbled downstairs out of sight. Looking up diagonally Stevey saw a landing; looking down, the dark well of the stairs; through the window a tin roof on which the chutes above dripped and dripped. He went up to the landing and here he noticed a streak of yellow light at the base of the door. He tapped softly, hardly knowing what he was doing. He knocked again and still there was no reply. He peeped through the keyhole and there before a warm fire he saw an old woman sitting bolt upright in her chair.

Even to Stevey the old woman was a touching sight, her corrugated hands clasping her crucifix, her mouth all wrinkled and folded, her eyes lost in the firelight. He was moved by the peace of this room high above the markets and the river, warm after the rain. How cosy she looked! – no, not cosy, but how calm, and yes, how holy! How holy! Stevey smiled and shook his head at her. He looked at her more closely. Then he entered, closing the door softly behind him. He laid his hand on her shoulder – on her face – on her left breast. She was dead.

He looked around him slowly, and slowly he removed his wet coat, hanging it on a chair before the glowing fire. Then he sat quietly warming his hands to the flames, stretching his long legs, and drying his face. He chuckled quietly to himself. Here was joy!

He awoke before dawn and thinking he felt a little cold he threw fresh coals on the fire. Feeling thirsty he drank half the milk in the glass beside him. Then he fell asleep again until a church bell tolling faintly in the distance gradually percolated through to his senses. For a full two minutes he stared sleepily and in wonder at the corpse seated beside him, and then, as the cries of the market-girls came to his ears his mind reverted to the city. He realized at once that he was back among his own people, as safe as a house.

He rose stretching his stiff shoulders and began to move through the house. As for the old lady, he did not trouble himself about her – heart disease no doubt or a sudden stroke, and he remembered the warm fire and the fresh glass of milk. One room was full of strange lumber, and as he peeped at the markets through the drawn blinds his hand fell idly on an old album. When he opened it and it began to ping-pong out its little tune he shut it with a fright and hoped nobody heard. The back-room was an ordinary sitting-room. He saw a chess-board and wondered cunningly who played chess in that seemingly empty house. Surely there must be a man somewhere he thought, and he felt certain of it when his eye fell on a great brass-horned gramophone, every inch of its dark maw pasted over with foreign postage stamps. He felt it best to get out of the house as soon as possible and hearing Shandon bells strike eight he decided that now was the best time – it was Monday morning and he could mingle with the crowds going to work; they would be too preoccupied to notice his wet, wrinkled clothes, his dirty boots, his unshaven face. First, however, he returned to the dead room to look for food. He found bread, and a pot of jam, and milk that was only just a little sour. He was raising the milk to his lips when his eye caught a black-japanned tin box by the window and the glint of silver in it. He strode across and looked down at the wad of notes and the loose pile of florins and shillings and half-crowns and little worn sixpenny pieces. The lock, he noticed, had been broken at some time previously. Without a thought he put his hand on the thick roll of notes and filled a fistful of silver into his pocket. Then, abandoning the food he had prepared for himself he turned and tramped down the stairs, opened the hall door and walked right into the arms of a raiding patrol as it alighted from a lorry. He looked right and left and made one step as if to attempt an escape, but in a second a dozen rifles were pointed at his heart. In another second he was seated high on the car with a crowd of market-people gathered wonderingly about him.

In a dream he found himself smoking one of a bundle of cigarettes handed him on all sides from the sympathetic fish-women. All they knew was that he was a 'Shinner' and they cheered him repeatedly for it. As he sat there in a daze one woman actually put a little tricolour rebel flag into his hand, and he waved it feebly from time to time, and the fish-wives and the onion-girls cheered him wildly as he was driven away. As they turned the corner of the markets one of the guards smiled grimly and said 'Good-bye-ee,' and Stevey smiled weakly in return and stuffed the flag into his pocket.

It was the last smile Stevey Long smiled on this earth. The search of the house discovered, hidden under the stairs, a conglomeration of explosives, bombs and grenades and incendiaries, finished and unfinished. It took the military an hour to remove them all, and to crown the amazement of the market-folk, they then brought up a coffin, carrying it in lightly, carrying it on four bending shoulders. At his court martial, which they held an hour later at drumhead – martial law was in force – question after question was fired at Stevey and he dodged and twisted like a hare, but he was a hare in a net. By degrees they wearied him, and finally cowed him.

'Where did he get that revolver?'

'I found it,' said Stevey.

'Where?'

'In the fields.'

'There were two bullets discharged?'

'Were there?' said Stevey innocently.

'When did you find it?'

'Last night.'

'Where did you come from last night?'

At that Stevey paused, feeling that these questions were leading back to Macroom Castle, realizing that he could not substantiate any statement he might make as to his whereabouts the evening before. The President repeated the question testily.

'Where did you come from?'

'East Cork.'

'Where in East Cork?'

'Midleton.'

'What were you doing in that house?'

To this Stevey replied truthfully, and though it was the only true thing he said that day, they did not believe him.

'Do you mean to say,' asked the president, 'that the people of Midleton didn't know a curfew order was in force in Cork?'

A few such questions drove Stevey to the wall, but it was when they told him that the woman was shot by a point four-five bullet, of the same calibre as the gun found on him, and charged him with the murder of the old lady that he paled and grew thoroughly confused and realized the danger in which he stood. His advocate did his best for him but it was no use, and when in the end Stevey was asked if he had anything to say he grew excited and began to talk foolishly, leaning forward and waving his hands, swearing that he would tell the whole truth this time, and contradicting almost everything he had previously said. His advocate tried again to save him but the president intervened; he had caught his man and now he would have a little sport with him.

'Let the prisoner speak,' he said, and leaned back in his chair and glanced at his colleagues. They, in turn, glanced back at him and drew their fingers over their mouths and looked down at the table – the old man, they thought, was in a good mood today.

The truth was, said Stevey, that he was coming from East Cork and he was ambushed by Sinn Feiners. He fired two shots at them....

'At your own people?' asked the colonel.

'Well they fired at me,' cried Stevey with an oath.

'Go on,' said the colonel politely.

'The bastards fired at me,' said Stevey in a towering rage at his imagined enemies.

'One moment,' said the president. 'Where did you really get this revolver? Do you admit possessing it?'

'Ain't I telling you?' said Stevey. 'It was a Tan that gave it to me.'

'Indeed?' said the colonel politely. 'Go on.'

'I fired at them, once, twice. And then, I'm sorry to say, I ran.'

'To Cork?' asked the colonel sarcastically.

'I got a bike,' said Stevey sullenly.

'Where?' asked the president, leaning forward. 'Can we substantiate that?'

'Well, to tell the truth,' said Stevey, 'I – I stole it.'

'Like this money we found on you? You admit you stole that, too?'

'Yes, I stole it, I took it,' admitted Stevey.

'Can we even confirm that you stole the bike?' asked the president. 'Where did you steal it? Where is it now?'

Stevey told six more lies in his efforts to avoid admitting the bicycle was in a ditch on the wrong side of the city. The old colonel lost his patience here.

'Where did you steal the bike?' he roared.

'It was in the dark I stole it,' muttered Stevey and the court rocked with laughter.

'It's true,' wailed Stevey.

'Remove the prisoner,' said the old colonel in disgust.

In order to disgrace him as well as punish him he was sentenced for murder and robbery under arms.

The Patriot

It was doubtless because of the inevitable desire of man to recapture the past that they went to Youghal for their honeymoon. Their friends expected them to go at least to Dublin, if not to London or Paris, but they both knew in their hearts that they had spent the gayest days of their lives in this little town, and so as if to crown all those early happinesses to Youghal they went, like true voluptuaries deliberately creating fresh memories that would torment them when they were old.

Across there on the little stone promenade, when they were as yet little more than girl and boy, they had met for the first time. She was on holiday with her sister; he had come with his aunt for the day. In the train they had met Edward Bradley, his former teacher, and Mister Bradley had walked about with him (in spite of his aunt) for a few hours, and given them tea. He had been flattered, he remembered, because old Bradley stayed with them so long, and afterwards he pretended to Norah that Mister Bradley was really a great friend of his. Off there at the end of the promenade they had sate, the three of them, because his aunt was too old to walk far without a rest and as they sate there Norah and her sister came and halted opposite them to lean on the wall. A liner was passing slowly, almost imperceptibly, along the horizon and everybody was looking at it, and his aunt was asking him to tell them – he was young, God bless him, and had the better sight – was it two funnels or three it had. He had stood up, pretending to look at the liner, but he was really trying to look at Norah's black hair and her jet-black eyes without being seen, growing irritated because he and she could not be there alone, and growing more irritated still because he saw that she too was trying to look at him without being observed, turning her back frequently on the sea to look, as it were, up over their heads at the crowds on the cliffs, curving herself backwards over the wall and standing on her toes as if to show herself off to him. In the end her sister drew her away as the ship became too faint to be seen and Bernard became so disconsolate and silent that his aunt plucked at him and said,

'What on earth's wrong with you, Bernie? Are you tired, or what is it?'

But Mister Bradley cocked his eye at him and winked without his aunt seeing. Old Bradley was a cute boyo, he had thought, and flushed because he felt he had been observed. After tea he and his aunt were alone again, and she who had been so sweet to their companion, was now abusing him roundly for a firebrand who was leading all the young men into wild politics. 'Some day,' Bernie defended, 'that man will be Lord Mayor of Cork and then you'll sing a different song,' but she would have none of it and as he just then caught sight again of his dark girl in the distance and wished to walk on and catch up with her he did not argue further. Alas! his aunt got tired once more, saying that tea was like a load on her stomach, and they had to sit on another bench. His dark vision passed out of his sight and he felt she had merely floated before him and he would never meet her again.

When he did meet her again it was several years after and she was again on holiday in Youghal, and it was only by degrees they realized they had seen each other before. On this occasion he was an Irregular guerilla – doubly a rebel – seated high up on a lorry, with his rifle across his back and his coat-collar turned up, and his cap thrown back and upwards from his forehead to let his curls free to the wind. Seven other lorries were roaring along behind him through the streets and as they tore their way under the old clock archway, there on the pavement, smiling up at them, and waving her green handkerchief to them, was the loveliest dark-haired girl he had ever seen. Their lorry halted just beyond the arch to wait for the troops marching in from the railway, and he alighted and by virtue of being a soldier was able to approach her on the pretence of wanting matches or cigarettes. By the time the troops came into the town they were in a little tea-shop, and he was flirting away with all the bravado in the world. As the men passed outside, four by four, they sang their rebelly songs, waking as he said to her, the ghosts of old Raleigh who had once lived there, and of the stiff Earl of Cork from his tomb in the Christ's Church, and the ghost of every Elizabethan sailorman who had cast a rope ashore by the crumbled quays they could see through the rear door of the shop, edging with their fallen stones the glittering blue of the bay.

There were descendants of those seadogs in that town still, she told him, for having come there year after year on her holidays since she was a little child she knew Youghal as if she had been born there. She chanted the names to him, the Merricks, the Gurneys, the Boyles, the Brisketts, and at each name he swaggered his cup on high to curse them, so that it was a profane litany that finished their tea.

'The Yardleys too,' she said, laughing at him.

'God damn them for ever!' he swashbuckled.

'Of course the Townshends are Cromwellians,' she smiled.

'God damn them for ever!' he cried again.

Her eyes wandered to the bay. A brown sailed yawl was floating past on the blue water as gracefully as a yacht.

'Isn't she lovely?' she cried, flushing with the delight of it.

'Not as lovely as you,' he bantered.

'Oh! Come and watch her,' she invited, and away they went.

When he found his way to the abandoned military barracks they had taken over, it was late night – discipline was a joke in those days – but he did not sleep for many hours, standing at the window of the great deserted mess-room watching where the moon poured down across the face of the shimmering ocean, into the little harbour. It lit up as if it were day the shouldering furze-bright hills, and the white edge of motionless surf at the base of the distant cliffs, and every sleeping roof in the town clustered beneath him.

It was curious that it was there in Youghal, too, that same summer, that Norah had first met Edward Bradley. There had been a public meeting in the market-place while the guerillas held the town and one of the chief speakers was Bradley. That day he had spoken with a terrible passion against England, and against the Irish traitors who had been cowed by her, and his passionate words caught and flared the temper of the people so that they cheered and cheered until their voices echoed across the smooth surface of the water into the woods beyond. Bernie had cheered like the rest where he stood beside Norah, proud to be that man's friend. After the meeting the three met, and the teacher, flushed with his success, walked between them along the tumbledown quays. He found that he knew

Norah's people quite well, though he had not seen them for many years.

'But I'll call on them often now,' he said, looking at Norah and he began to take her arm, and then he remembered Bernie and he took his arm – like a grandfather Bernie had said, jokingly, to him, and was angry with himself for saying it for a deeper blush crept over the face of the older man and halting he had said,

'Maybe I am too old to be walking with the like of ye,' and cocking his eye at the girl again he had laughed, half-bitterly as Bernie thought, and with a 'God bless ye, my children,' turned and walked away. Wasn't he a very nice man, Norah had said, and stood looking after the teacher so long that Bernie almost thought he was going to be jealous; but he had not thought long of it. It was a warm autumn day, and so clear that they could see across the channel where the hay garnered in for the winter had left white patches on the clovered meadows. Tempted by the fields beyond they had rowed slowly across the bay to spend the afternoon on the other side. The geese had cropped the grass of the foreshore until it was as close and clean as a golf-course, except where a few odd straws lost to the granary lay strewn about and with them, cast up by the tide, bits of reedy sea-wrack, and here and there the dark-grey droppings of the fowl. The air was so rarefied that as they crossed the low stone walls on their way into the oak woods the stones fell with a gurgling sound like water, and far away the ocean boomed deeply into the crannied rocks. They had gone deep into the woods to lie there while the misty darkness fell, bringing in the night wind a little rain, to lie there in their deep love as still as corpses, as still as fallen leaves. They returned late at night to the town whose yellow windows, bright across the channel, spoke to them of sanded floors in quayside pubs and the first fires before the winter warming the cold chimneys of summer.

But before that week was out the town was abandoned and Norah had to stand under the shelter of the old town-walls watching the great barracks smoking against the fading sky and the distant mountains, themselves so faint that in their greyness they blended and were lost in the darkness and the smoke.

It was the way of that guerilla life that for months on end a man never even thought of home or friends, and for months Bernard wandered among those grey mountains to the north of Youghal, as aimlessly, and he used to feel more uselessly, than a lost sheep. Once only did he use his rifle in those seven months of guerilla life and that was when sniping from fifteen hundred yards a village supposed to contain enemy troops. He slept in a different bed each night and never ate twice in succession from the same table so that most of his time was spent in going from place to place in search of food and rest. He did so less from a sense of danger than a sense of pity towards the farmers who had to feed and shelter him and his fellows, never thinking that as all his fellows did as he was doing, it saved nothing to the flour bin lying lightly on the loft, or the tea-caddy on the high mantel-shelf, emptied almost daily. The days scarcely existed for him and the weeks flew over his head as unnoticed as birds homing at night, until as a human being he almost ceased to be, enveloped by the countryside as if he were a twig, a stone, an ear of corn. And then, without the slightest warning, as suddenly as the breaking of a thunder-shower, he remembered how lovely Youghal had been, and how lovely Norah, and he hated to look up at the cold and naked mountains. It was late February with the rain falling as by the clock, and for a month they had been hunted through it, day and night. Thinking of that and thinking of the summer his memory began to work on him like a goad. All about him on the night he thought of her, sitting alone by the embers of a turf-fire after the family had gone to bed, the mountains lay black and silent, wet as if they had been dipped in the sea, and overhead a white path of stars more clear in the washed air than if there were a frost abroad. Out there, too, he felt was danger; he was listening so intently that he almost leaped when a little cricket chirruped in the dark warmth of the hearth, and yet he feared even to stir so great a noise did every movement make – almost as great, it seemed, as the resounding drop-drop of the leaking thatch beyond the door.

In his pocket-book he had her one letter, reminding him of that little wood where they had loved:

'I went specially to Youghal to see our wood again. The autumn is over it and over all the land. The days are shortening, farmers are threshing, thatching turf-ricks, digging potatoes, culling sheep from their flocks to barter in fair and market, fields are decaying with grief for the loss of their fruits, and grief is a brown and withered hag, nuts are ripening, black-berries are rotting, holly berries are reddening, leaves are dropping yellow. Mists cover the mountains like a hooded cloak, grey rocks ooze tears of desolation, green ferns on the hill-side are withering, and purple heather is turning grey. Birds are silent, winds rustling in denuded boughs. In Youghal tourists are departed – no more the hum of the motor, nor the flash of fashionable attire. In my little hotel Mrs M—— is resting and knitting, K—— turning over stacks of McCall's Journals and Home Gossips, the serving-girl is considering her return to her mother's home, P—— L—— wearing her shoes "going aisht and wesht," B—— twinkling with gestating jokes, and R—— counting the takings of the season. Norah is at the moment writing to Bernard; at other moments? – thinking, reading, peering into a dimly-lit future. . . .'

He smiled at that letter, so full of life as it was. Then he thought of the night outside and went to the door. He could hear the streams swirling down the dark *leaca* and as he listened their roar mingled terror with the desolation of the black silence, and he wished passionately to be away from so lonely and cruel a place. Three miles across the hills, in a little fishing hotel by a mountain lake, was the head-quarters of the Division. There, he hoped, he might get money – a few shillings would do – to help him on the road home, and maybe they would give him a clean shirt and collar, and a better hat and trousers than these guerilla's rags that, up to now, he had been flaunting as with a deliberate joy in their torn dirt. Above all he might meet Edward Bradley there, for he too had been hiding for several months in the mountains not daring to stay in the city for fear of arrest. He felt he wanted to talk to somebody like Bradley, someone who would persuade him that this struggle of theirs was not hopeless, that all their humiliation of poverty and hunger was not, as he had long since begun to feel, a useless and wasted offering. Quietly he unbolted the door and stole through the yard into the sodden starlit fields.

It was midnight when he saw the lake below him and to his surprise every window in the little hotel was lit. He approached warily, alert for a sentry's challenge, fearful of an ambushed enemy patrol – for he might, he knew, be shot as easily by either. But he continued to walk unaccosted past the sleeping farmhouses and the great strewn rocks until he came to the lake-side edge and the lighted windows, and all the way he did not meet a living soul.

Inside the steamed window the room was filled with armed men, smoking, drinking, arguing in groups. He recognized the faces of three or four officers. There was the adjutant with his eyes swollen with too much drink and too little sleep – it was common knowledge that he lived like that. By the fire was Boyle, a great black-faced commandant from Kerry; under the lamp in the largest group he recognized Tom Carroll from East Cork – clearly a meeting of the officers of the Division.

He entered unchallenged where a group of men were lounging in the dim candle-lit hall. Three officers strode out of the room – it was the dining-room – with empty glasses in each hand, returning gingerly when the glasses had been filled to the brim with black stout or porter. He saw the quartermaster coming out of the kitchen with a pair of black pint-glasses dripping their froth about his wrists, and he went over to tell him how dangerous it was to leave the back road unguarded. But the quartermaster only growled,

'Well, what are you doing here then? Go up yourself and sentrify it,' and passed on.

The column captain came out from the bar with a tray of divers-coloured glasses and to him also Bernie told how the North road was unprotected. But the captain flew into a rage and glared at him over the tray.

'I've told off six men, there, to go,' he said, jerking his head at the loungers in the hall.

One of them spoke back at him, a fellow with only two walrus teeth above and below in his gums.

'We won't go. Why should we go? Ye're all dhrinking. Why don't we get a dhrink?'

'Go into the kitchen and get it,' said the Captain.

'Where'll we get the money.'

'Ask the quartermaster.'

'Damn the quartermaster.'

'I want the quartermaster,' said Bernie. 'I want a couple of bob to get home.'

The loungers scoffed at him in a loud chorus, and Buckteeth called him Sweet Innocence. Two more joined them, swaggering in their belted and ragged raincoats, out from the glow of the dining-room into the dark hall. As they came they deliberately crushed against the captain's tray all but upsetting his yellow and purple argosy. With a curse at them he raced like a waiter balancing his tray into the dining-room, returning to grab Bernard and put him standing in the between-passage outside the dining-room door.

'Stand there, you,' he growled. 'And let nobody into this room unless he has business there.'

The loungers cheered.

'Will ye go up, for Christ's sake,' the captain implored them, 'to the North road and watch it or the whole Division will be caught?'

'Oh! It's always deh Division, aw!' piped up a little fair-haired sprat of a boy from the foot of the stairs. 'What about deh men, aw? Dere's never any talk about deh men?'

'For God's sake get us a drink, Jim,' appealed the man with the walrus teeth.

'Go on, Jim,' joined in three or four more. They seemed to have no sense of pride left.

With a sudden air of intimacy the captain stepped into the middle of them, bending his neck right and left among them like a pecking hen.

'Go in,' he said, 'and take it. Say the quartermaster will fix it up. They'll never know in the hotel.'

Buckteeth turned away in disgust.

'No! They feed us, and they sleep us,' he said, 'and we're not going to soak drink from them as well.'

'Well I have no money for you,' complained the captain.

'Deh quartermaster have buckets of it,' declared fair-hair.

'*Buckets* is deh word,' sneered a tall man in spectacles from his dark corner at the door.

They laughed at the word in spite of their anger: it measured the quartermaster's thirst.

'Well, I can do no more for ye,' said the captain in a temper, and left them.

Bernie stood where he had been placed by the dining-room door and everybody passed in and out without paying the slightest attention to him. The quartermaster, already flushed with drink, returned to fill his glasses once more, and timidly Bernie touched him on the shoulder.

'Well? Are you here still?' said the quartermaster.

Bernie had not the courage to face the refusal of a loan so he asked instead for cigarettes. The quartermaster thrust a package into his hand.

'Here,' he said. 'You fellows do nothing from morning to night but bum and soak for cigarettes. Why don't ye do something?'

As he passed by a piece of black and white paper fluttered gently to the ground in his wake. Bernie picked it up. It was a hundred pound note. For a moment he thought of rushing out to his fellows in the hall and waving it in the air before their eyes; for another moment he thought of using it himself to get home. Then he realized he could not steal money like that, and even if he did nobody would change so large a note for them or him. As the quartermaster returned he tapped his arm once again. A wave of whisky belched into his face as the fellow turned on him and stuck his potato nose into his face. Bernie held up the note, saw him look stupidly at it, without a word thrust it into his vest pocket and stride into the dining-room with his dripping glasses. What a hopeless sort of army they were, Bernie thought, and he made up his mind that he must at all costs go back into the city out of these bleak mountains where they did nothing for month after month but eat the substance of the people and lounge over their fires like sleepy dogs. Things were still happening occasionally in the city. If he could rest for a while and see Norah, he would become invigorated by her and be of some use again. Suddenly there was a great stirring in the room and the captain returned to tell him close and guard the outer door. Bernie did not have the energy to tell him that all this was so much utter foolery. Instead he begged a match from him and lit a cigarette and leaned into the corner of the passage to think. He had waited so long he could wait now another couple of hours until the dawn.

By the glow of the lamps in the room beyond the passage-way he read Norah's letter again, scarcely hearing the talking and arguing rising hotter and hotter at the meeting, though he faintly gathered as he read the letter by the dim light that they were considering the whole military situation in the south and that some were for laying down their arms at once, and others for fighting on. He was hardly interested. He was thinking only of the summer that was gone and of every little incident of his last meeting with Norah in the woods beyond the bay at Youghal. Gradually the discussion in the room changed to an argument about men and ammunition and money and as the voices fell his thoughts wandered freely to the brownsailed yawl they saw floating past the frame of the restaurant door, the sun shining on the blue and white sea in its wake and the curling foam at its bows. He remembered how he had whispered an old song to her as they lay among the leaves and to himself he hummed it over again:

> 'O beloved of my inmost heart
> come some night and soon,
> when my people are at rest,
> that we may talk together;
> my arms shall encircle you
> while I relate my sad tale
> that it was your pleasant soft voice
> that has stolen from me heaven.
>
> The fire is unraked,
> the light extinguished,
> the key is under the door.
> And do you softly draw it.
> My mother is asleep,
> but I am awake.
> My fortune is in my hand
> and I am ready.
> I will go with you....'

He heard Edward Bradley's voice addressing the meeting. Why he should be there he did not know, for he was not an army man. But afterwards he told Bernie that because he was older than anybody there and they wanted to hear what the politicians had to say they allowed him to speak. He was imploring them not to lay down their arms – far better to be defeated, at a blow or by degrees, though that would be slow and terrible for them all. As on that day at Youghal his passion carried the meeting with him and they cheered him loudly when he finished. When he came into the passage he was flushed and trembling, and when he saw Bernie he drew him with him out into the hall, and because the loungers were still there, out into the cool air by the side of the lake. A sedge of broken reeds had been washed ashore by the storms, reminding Bernie of the sedge of sea-wrack on the foreshore across Youghal bay, but across the lake the mountain-streams made a ceaseless desolate moaning as they fell, and a night mist was blowing in their faces so that they had to shelter in the pitchy darkness of a gable-wall. He told Bernie how terrible things were all over the country – so everybody at the meeting had said – and Bernie told him what he knew of the state of the men among those hills, all of them weak and scabby and sore, not a penny in their pockets, not a pipeful to smoke, nothing to do from one week to another but run when danger approached, never together, badly led, beaten all but in name.

'And in this hotel,' said Bradley, 'the officers taking their breakfast at six o'clock in the evening and drinking in the dawn.'

Suddenly Bradley said:

'Do you hear at all from that girl now?'

'What girl?'

'The girl in Youghal.'

'A long time ago. I got a letter.'

He hated to talk of Norah. It was as if she were a secret part of him and he would not bare it.

'She is a very intelligent girl,' said Bradley.

'Yes,' said Bernie as if he were not really interested, but he felt his breath come in heavy waves.

'Oh, yes!' said Bradley. 'I saw a good deal of her before I came out here. I stayed at her house for safety several times before I took to the hills. And she's a very nice girl.'

Bernie shivered, his blood turning over in his body, but it was not from the cold.

'Well I'm leaving in an hour or two,' said Bradley. 'This place won't be safe for twenty miles around after the news of this meeting gets to the military.'

In the hall the candle was guttering out but the loungers still remained. To say something to them as he passed in Bernie told them what Bradley had said of the conditions about the country and of the officers in the hotel.

'Puh!' taunted the tall bespectacled fellow. 'And what does he do himself but hang over a book in the comfort of the hotel fire from dawn to dark?'

Bernie returned to his position in the passage. He was sick of these tauntings and tale-bearings, and he wondered how a man like Bradley could remain out there where he must hear them and notice them day after day. And if Bradley chose he could go back to hide in the city any day – there would be many people glad to receive and shelter him, and Bernie wished he had asked for the loan of half a crown and a clean collar and tie. He must see Norah again, and the city, and his people, and friends. The quartermaster was talking now, in a thick but fierce voice.

' "No surrender" must be our cry,' he was saying. 'I'd rather be shot any day than surrender. Let those that are tired of the fight go into the city and surrender!'

He peeped in to the long room. One lamp was guttered low to a smoking circle of red wick. The other glowed like a yellow ball through the skeins of smoke woven in heavy layers from table to ceiling. Beer bottles and empty glasses were everywhere. The men were yawning and stretching themselves, some talking among themselves, paying no heed at all to the speaker, and the chairman was drawing idle circles with a pencil on the table before him.

Somebody silenced the quartermaster with a question and by degrees the talk fell again to a drone as they discussed men and money and ammunition. He leaned back into a corner of the passage and while he thought of the road home, of every wind and turn in it, of every side-road and back-road he could take, he fell into a doze where he stood. He awoke to hear Boyle from Kerry cry out in a fury at somebody:

'Let them that want to rat, do it. Myself and John Jo Sheehan will hold Kerry anyway. Won't we John Jo?'

The meeting seemed to be ending. Sheehan was standing huge against the window with his back to them all, in spite of the lamp, black-shouldered against the pale glimmer of the dawn hanging over the mists on the lake outside. In taunting and utter disbelief he cursed over his shoulder at Boyle.

'Hold Kerry, how are you? You and Kerry may go to hell!'

The meeting broke up in laughter, men standing and talking in little groups, edging around their Chief to discuss private questions of their own. It seemed as if they would never come out and Bernie sate on the ground to sleep. The first few officers leaving the room poked his stomach with their boots in mockery of their sleeping sentry. He made his way out to the kitchen where the loungers were strewn asleep on the settle, the table, on chairs or about the floor near the grey embers of the fire. He rolled a porter barrel in from the bar and sate on it and through the sounds of the departing officers, horses stamping, carts trundling out, searchings in the dark for last drinks, calls and farewells, he slept in the corner of the cooling hearth. When he awoke the morning had come and the loungers were like him shivering together over the grate where Buckteeth was blowing the seed of fire into a fresh sod of turf. Seeing him open his eyes they asked him:

'Well? What was deh end of deh meeting, aw? Are we to go home or stay here? Aw?'

'Fight on!' said Bernie.

They looked at him too tired to mock the phrase.

'Stay here, he means,' said Buckteeth. 'Stay bloody well here.'

Bernie shared his cigarettes about and they smoked in silence while the fowl awakened by the echoing crow of the cock began to clatter and suckle in the rain-water of the yard, for the rain was now darkening the window, pouring straight down into the dung-filled haggard. Looking out at it Bernie saw again the mist hanging in the woods of Youghal, and Norah running down the slip to the ferry, her black curls swinging as she ran. Their hunger began to stir in them, but they could not find a scrap of food in the house – it had all been eaten by the crowd just departed. In their search they found the quartermaster snoring on the sofa of the dining-room, a roll of bank-notes hanging from his pocket. At once they grabbed them, sharing out the smaller notes, leaving the twenty-fives and the fifties and the hundreds, but as they argued over the division the quartermaster awoke and in a fury he demanded the money. Buckteeth who held the fistful of notes showered them over the furious man's head, and while he clambered under the tables and the chairs to collect them they mocked at him. Beside himself with rage he cursed them for lazy, useless louts and rushing off to tackle his horse and side-car in the yard he left through the blowing rain while in a crowd they cheered him from the door. But money would not buy them food and they went about draining the ebb of porter in every glass, then wandering over the hotel from floor to attic to see what they could find. There was not a soul there but the people of the house sleeping heavily after the long hours of work the day before, and they returned to the kitchen to wait.

At last the girls of the house came down the ladder-like stairs, their legs thrust bare into their dung-covered boots. They sate on the settle by the fire, bowed over their knees until their mother followed.

'A bad morning, Mrs O——,' said Bernie to the mother.

She stood by the low window and looked sadly at the rain.

'Isn't it a bad morning, thanks be to God?' she sighed.

Not a word of reproach was said, or of enquiry about the meeting, or of complaint at their long labour. The girls sate looking at the fire or out at the rain. There was nothing for them to eat, and nothing to do on such a wet day. The mother set to scrape the bins and the bags for flour and when the boy of the house came in he milked the cows. The dough was dampened with spring-water and fresh milk. It was kneaded and shaped and put in to the bastable while they all looked on. Through the open door they could see the rain splashing the causeway outside and a duck poked his eye in by the jamb. Buckteeth spat at the cocked eye and the duck clattered out, but nobody laughed. The bastable was over the fire and they had all turned to it to watch it whilst it baked. While they waited six other men came to the house, sodden with rain, arm and thigh and chest, searching for a breakfast and news of the meeting, but when they found the others before them they moved on patiently to the next farmhouse a mile off. They said they must be in Mill-street, twenty miles away, before night. Then they would walk on into Limerick along the Feale. For Limerick, they declared, bare and open though it was, was safer now than Cork. One of them, a Kerry lad, had no socks and his feet were torn by the bare leather of his boots. He had no overcoat, his very shirt clung to his back with wet, and he coughed ceaselessly. The woman of the house took pity on him and asked him to stay, and when he heard the others argue that Limerick was a far more dangerous place than Cork he sate down wearily by the fire and began to cry, telling his companions between his tears that he was afraid to go on with them and would hide here among the mountains. All the while Buck-teeth and the others looked awkwardly at him. They offered him cigarettes and tried to cheer him by assuring him that that place was as safe as a house, and while he and they drank the scalding tea and the soft hot cake the girls searched him out a pair of socks and a dry, if torn, shirt. But while they ate they were less sure about the safety of the glens and they argued and argued as to what they should do next. The Kerry lad could say nothing but 'We must hide. We must hide in the holes of the mountains,' and the little fair-haired city gamin kept whining plaintively 'But where are our officers? Where are our officers from us now? Aw?' At intervals the boy of the house assured them again and again that it was madness to stay there another day with the valleys filled, as he said, with 'people taking the heels from one another with the news of the meeting to the military in the next village.' So when the rain lightened they scattered, some going to the north, one declaring that the safest thing was to skirt the village to the east, and Bernie found he had lost courage to attempt the journey home. Tomorrow he would go, he thought, and with Buckteeth and Kerry, as they christened him, he went up among the cliffs in search of a cave to hide in. The boy of the house, though he kept assuring them it was madness to stay there, showed them a dump that had been made in a cleft between the rocks, a grave-like place dug out of the earth and covered with a sheet of corrugated tin and hidden by stones and withered brushwood. There was barely room for the three to lie in this dark, damp tomb, but as Kerry implored them to go into it at once, they lay down there, shoulder to shoulder, peering up and out all day long at the grey spears of the falling rain.

At dark, in spite of their hunger and the cold they slept, and so tired were they, they slept past the following dawn, past the rising of the sun and past the late morning, and all the while it rained and the whistling of the rain seemed to lull and keep them asleep in spite of encircling danger. They were awakened by the shattering echoes of machine-gun fire and the impact of hundreds of bullets tearing at the rock above their heads. When the first volley ceased the echoes carried its rat-a-tat-tat across the cliff-top to where another echoing air seized upon it and its thunder was reduplicated fainter and fainter into the heart of the mountains before it finally died into silence. There was such a long interval that it seemed as if everybody were listening to that last faint replication so high up and so far away. Then they heard the shouts below them:

'Come out! Come out, ye snipes! Come out or we'll bomb ye out. Come out!'

Those cries were echoed, and then a brief silence followed. The next minute the gun seemed to tear the tin roof from over their heads where they crouched helpless, their faces to the clay. They had placed their boots to dry, the night before, on the ledge before their dump and these now shot in on their foreheads torn to pieces by bullets. Again the echoes were reduplicated to the farthest uttermost glen and again the shouts came, mingling with those echoes and their own that followed after.

'Yeer last chance! Ye whores! Come out!'

The Kerry boy began to weep again.

'O God!' he shouted. 'Leave us out. Leave us out.'

'Throw down yeer guns,' cried the echoing voices below.

They did so, and Buckteeth tearing a sleeve from his shirt raised it before him as he crawled out into the rain. Below them was a score of sturdy green-clad riflemen and in a minute the three were among them, shivering with fear and excitement – broken, timid as children.

They passed through Youghal as prisoners, standing high on a lorry, conspicuous in their rags, and as it roared its way under the old clock archway, there across the windblown bay Bernie glimpsed his woods shrouded in mist, growing, as it seemed, out of the grey-green bay. Never did anything seem so definitely past to him as his summer flirting under those trees. It might have happened to him in another life, it might have been something he read of in a novel, so distant did it seem.

They drove him to Cork that night and there he remained in prison until the winter was passed and another winter had come again. Norah wrote to him many times while he was in jail – at first briefly but kindly, sending him gifts as she might to any other prisoner, later on long letters at greater length, as to a special friend. After a while she brought herself to reproach him for his long silence of that lonely winter, a winter in which she had tried hard, and vainly, to be as he had been forgetful of the sweetness of their early summer and autumn love. It was Christmas when he received a letter from her confessing how miserable and unhappy those months had been, and he was glad of the confession though it was a torment to him to be reminded, in the place where he was, of his foolishness when he had been free. And when she wrote that Edward Bradley often stayed with them, and spoke kindly of him, it was a double torment – that worst torment of all prisoners – to think what lovely things life could have given him, too, had he been out in the world and part of it. When he was freed he was very ill and weak and the doctor ordered him to the sea and he went, as a matter of course, to Youghal. It was February again, just a year since he had passed through it as a prisoner, and the woods and the bay were again shrouded in haze, but because Norah came to see him, and walked with him there, and showed him the rain in the cob-webs among the branches, and – it was so mild there by the sea – an early celandine hiding under a root, he thought those woods even more beautiful than they had been almost two years before when they watched the red globe of the autumn sun sinking behind its black branches.

Small wonder then that they should come back years after to this little seaside town for their honeymoon, the consummation of their love. It was Easter and so late in the spring – the fifteenth of April had been Easter Sunday – that the catkins' furry paws were already raised to the sun, and the long tails and the tiny wet noses of the lambs protruded from the red and blue creels rumbling in to the lamb-fair. The yellow furze was ranged high against the blue sky along the slopes of the hills, and over the surface of the sea beneath there was a cold layer of air that made the waves break with a brittle noise such as one never hears in the soft, dead heat of summer. They went about that first day, their wedding day, noticing everything with new delight – the spears of green grass shooting through the dead fields, the primroses and the violets clustered near the grey stones in the ditches, the beech-buds swollen red, the patches of hawthorn green lighting the withered hedges. The long country lanes were empty; they had the ocean to themselves. The summer visitors had not yet even thought of coming and all the length of the old stone promenade was bare. They even felt a delight in the shuttered windows and the bathing-boxes nailed up since last autumn. On the sands stretching for miles in front of them, lost in the end in the spume of the incoming waves far off in the distance, they saw only a sandpiper or two strutting by the skirts of the spreading sea, or peewits in their swoop turning as if to command on their white bellies, turning again their dark wings low over the thunderous sea. When they lay under an early blossoming blackthorn high above that singing sea and in the long silences of deep love gazed over the empty horizon, or back at the clustered smoking chimneys on the farther shore, Bernard felt, and knew that his young wife felt, that if another gull should wheel through the blue air, another distant lamb call out to its dam, their cups of ecstasy must overflow and roll upon the ground. They crossed back then, as of old, to the points of light that marked the town through an early sea-haze and sought out that little restaurant where so long ago they had cursed the Elizabethans and the Cromwellians, and there they had their tea, watching back through the open door at the rear of the shop the channel darkening with the fall of night. As they ate they suddenly saw beside them a little green poster bearing that day's name and date. They read it with interest:

SINN FEIN ABU
A
Public Meeting
will be
addressed in
the Town Hall
at 7 p.m. by
EDWARD BRADLEY. . . .

'Shall we go?' asked Bernard.

It was almost the hour as they made their way down the wandering sidelanes that lead to wharves and the Town Hall. There, hidden deep in the crowd they stood by an open window through which they could see the ever-present channel and the waters of the bay. The gas-lights in the hall hummed like flies, huge green luminous flies that had floated in from the half-night outside, so blue and lovely where it sank down, darker and darker over the masts and the brown sails of the fishing smacks in the harbour, and far in the distance the peaked mountains that Bernard knew so well. It was so lovely to watch the hollow night fall outside, and through it now and again a green light climbing up a mast, and to turn from it to the pale pink-washed green-lit room within, that they paid but little heed to the speakers until their friend the teacher rose. The years between that night and the day in the market-square had not dulled his eloquence, and though his temples were gone quite white now – premature for his years – the terrible passion of the man blazed like the fire of burning youth. Yet as he talked the lovers did not join in the cheers of the audience. The night had fallen now and nothing showed beyond but the eyes of green or red on mast and poop. The mountains had vanished. The far woods were gone. They barely heard the lapping of the bay. As by one thought they moved quietly out through the cheering crowd into the darkness. But, shyly, they did not go back directly to their hotel. Wrapped in their own silence and the silence of the night they wandered about the quays or in and out among the lanes as if prolonging the night to the very last moment. The meeting was over before they returned to their hotel, and the lights of the houses in that street, and doubtless of every street in the town, were gone up to the second storey. When they entered their room they saw that the pale light of the gas lamp outside the window fell on the high old-fashioned ceiling and from there glimmered down on the wide, carved bridal-bed, and needing no other light they used none. Across the street was another row of sleeping houses, and beyond that the bay, widening to the ocean, and when they stood without stirring they could hear the low boom of the waves on the cliffs and across the bar. As they undressed the faint hum of a motor rose in the distance and approached along the street.

'Bernard,' she whispered.

Over his shoulder he could see her pale form in the dim light, but where he stood by the window with one hand raised to the blind his eyes fell on the passing car. He saw the white hair of their orator-friend, the old bachelor, the patriot, driving out of the town into the country and the dark night. The hedges would race past him; the rabbits skip before his headlights on the road; the moths in the cool wind would fly round his flushed face and his trembling hands. But that wind would not for many miles cool the passion in him to which he had given his life.

'Bernard,' she whispered again, and her voice trembled a little.

He drew the blind down slowly, the lamp shadowing the framework of the window on it, and slowly he turned to her where she smiled to him in the dark.

A Broken World

I

'That's a lonely place!' said the priest suddenly. He was rubbing the carriage-window with his little finger. He pointed with the stem of his pipe through the window, and the flutter of snow and the blown steam of the engine, at the mountainy farm to his right. He might have been talking to himself, for he did not stir his head or remove his elbow from its rest. He was a skeleton of a man, and the veins of his temples bulged out like nerves. Peering I could barely see, below the pine-forest of 'The Department,' through the fog of the storm, a lone chapel and a farm-house, now a tangle of black and white. Although it was the middle of the day a light shone yellow in a byre. Then the buildings swivelled and were left behind. The land was blinding.

'Aye!' I said. 'It is lonely. But,' I said easily, 'sure every parish is a world in itself.'

He grunted and pulled at his cherrywood pipe and kept looking out the window at the whirling dots of white.

Then, without looking at me – looking down at the flap of my trousers, instead – he leaned forward, one bony hand gripping his left knee, and his elbow resting on the other knee so that he might still hold and smoke his pipe in comfort. I could see that he spoke less for the sake of conversation than from a desire to instruct me, for he seemed to get no other pleasure out of his talk.

'That used to be a credo with me, too,' he said, 'that every parish is a world in itself. But where there is no moral unity there is no life.'

'Moral unity?'

There were ten notes in the wind, boom and whistle and groan and sigh. Listening to them I hardly heard him. The snow had stopped.

'Yes.' He was cock-assuredly positive. 'Life is a moral unity with a common thought. The *compositum* of one's being, emerging from the Divine Essence, which is harmony itself, cannot, unless it abdicates its own intelligence and lives in chaos, that is to say, in sin, be in disunity with itself. Since society, however, is an entity composed of many members, life becomes a moral unity with a common thought. You can see that?'

'Yes.'

He went on, while I wondered if he was a professor in some seminary trying out something he had been studying. He enunciated his ideas with indrawn lips. That gave him a hellish, pedagogic look. The glare outside turned him into marble.

'In places like that – you have a broken world, and there is no unity.'

In spite of this abstract way of talk the next thing he said showed me that he was not a professor.

'Let me give you an example of what life is like in those isolated places,' jerking his head. 'When I was ordained my first parish was a lonely parish in the County Wicklow. From my presbytery window I could see the entire coast, a long straight beach, miles to the north, miles to the south, with a headland at each end stuck out into the sea. By the sea it is marsh. Then comes the first wave of high land around villages like Newtownmountkennedy. The land isn't bad on those hills, though it isn't what you would call really good land. They grow good turnips and potatoes and mangolds; the greens are not bad; but they cannot grow wheat. You need a good marl bottom for wheat. I was a young man then, and keen, so I studied these questions.'

(Whatever else you were, I said to myself, you must have been a bloody bore.)

'Look!' he said, pointing through the opposite window.

A vast, white plain, level as a sea, mapped with black hedgerows, all diminishing in size, spread away and away, maybe twenty miles, to a much lower range of mountains.

'My parish was in the same relation to that good land as these mountains here (nodding over his shoulder) in relation to that plain. That is to say, it was mountain bog, reclaimed by much labour, but always badly drained. Last of all, beyond me, was the utterly, miserably,' – his voice was almost oratorical here – 'wretched moor. Miles and miles of it on the plateau of the mountain-tops. The native tribes lived as freebooters up there as late as the end of the eighteenth century. It was wooded then, and untouched by any road. Then, in Ninety-eight, two so-called Military Roads cut it across and across like a scissors. They were fifty miles long, and straight as rulers. By the way,' he asked suddenly, catching me looking idly out through the window, 'were you ever in County Wicklow?'

'Oh, no, father,' I replied, as suddenly. I forced myself to attend. Just then my eyes caught the eye of an old farmer seated opposite me in the carriage; he was midway on the same seat as the priest, and, so, near enough to hear everything. A pool of water had gathered around each boot. Spits starred the dry patch between. Seeing me look at him he took from his mouth, with his entire fist, a bit of a cigarette he was smoking, and winked at me. Then he put back the cigarette and contemplated the priest's face with an air of childlike wonderment. At that wink I began to listen more carefully. Evidently my priest was a local 'character.'

'They are remarkable roads,' went on the priest. 'Well, the people of my parish were all poor. The interesting thing about them is that there were two sets of names – either the old tribal names, like O'Toole or O'Byrne or Doyle, or foreign names like Ryder, Nash, Greene, Pugh, Spink, Empie, Gascon, Latour.'

A little smile took the corners of his mouth as he said those names; but he never raised his eyes.

'The Greenes and Ryders and Pughs, and the rest of them, were soldiers who long ago trickled down into the houses of the poor, intermarried there, and became poor themselves as a result. However, they brought the people respect for law and order. Or; if you like, they knocked the last bit of rebel spirit out of them.'

'Interesting!' I said, politely. I was beginning to enjoy the joke, for I could see the old farmer getting cross, and at the end of that last bit he had spat out his butt-end of cigarette.

'But the middle land, the good land, remained in the possession of the big people who never intermarried. When I went there to take over my duties I looked up the history of those wealthy people in *Debrett* and *Who's Who*, and *Burke's Landed Gentry*.'

His palm became an imaginary book, and with his pipe-stem he followed the lines and pretended to read:

' "Lord Blank, family name of Baron Blank. Fifth baron. Created in eighteen hundred and one. Lieutenant of the Seventeenth Hussars.

Married Dorothy, oldest daughter of, let's say something like James Whipple Teaman of Grange House, Dilworth, Dorsetshire, you know the kind of thing. Succeeded his father in nineteen-eighteen. Educated at Eton and Sandhurst. Address, Grosvenor Square, London. Club – Travellers' or Brooks's. Recreations? Oh, as usual, hunting, shooting, fishing, racquets, riding." '

Again the thin smile. The farmer was gob-open.

'My parishioners were their stable--boys, gate-lodge keepers, woodmen, beaters, farmhands, lady's-maids, etcetera. *They* were always intermarrying. *Their* bits of farms, reclaimed from the furze, were always being divided. I've seen people live on a bit of land about twice the size of this carriage.'

The farmer leaned forward, listening now with great interest. Our three heads nodded with the jolt of the train.

'Then there was emigration. In the five years I spent there I had one solitary marriage. I had sixty schoolchildren on roll when I went there. I had thirty-five when I left. Last year I heard they were reduced to eleven, and five of those were all one family. No wonder the county is full of ruins. You come on them in scores on scores, with, maybe, a tree growing out of the hearth, and the marks of the ridges they ploughed, still there, now smooth with grass.'

'Begobs, then, they're here too, father,' said the old farmer. The priest nodded sideways to him and proceeded:

'I liked the people. They were clean; hard-working; respectful. Too respectful – tipping their hats to everybody. They were always making what we call "the poor mouth" – a mendicant habit of centuries, I suppose. They gave me no trouble, except for two things. They had a habit of writing anonymous letters, and I couldn't stop it. They were at it all the time. They wrote them to one another.'

He paused. I prompted him. The farmer leaned closer and closer.

'The other thing?' I asked.

'The other thing?' he said irritably to his pipe-bowl. 'In every one of these cabins they earned money by taking in boarded-out children – children unwanted by poor parents, or simply illegitimates. There was hardly a cottage without one, two, or three of these stranger children. They were well looked after, and the people often grew so fond of them they wouldn't part with them; and, I suppose, that was a nice trait too. But the point is that the only fresh blood coming into the county was . . . Well . . . a curious county, as you can see, and the morals were a bit curious too. However, that's enough about them.'

And he had at least enough sense to go no further with that.

'Well, there you are. That was my parish, and you can't say it was a world in itself. It was too incomplete. Too many things left out. The human dignity of men is always impaired when, like that, they're depending on other people who can make or break them. They weren't men. They were servants. That's the whole of it.'

'But did that make their lives lonely? You said they were lonely?'

For the first time he looked up at me. The veins on his temples, swollen from holding his head down, throbbed with relief.

'I didn't say *they* were lonely.'

His eyes wavered sideways to the farmer. I easily followed him over the hiatus when he jumped to –

'One day, after three years without stepping out of the parish, I decided to see if the neighbouring parish was any better.' (When I heard the personal note come into his voice I wished the farmer was not there; as it was he kept to his cold, factual description.)

'Do you know, the contrast was amazing! When I climbed down to the valley and the good land! And it was the trees that made me realize it. Beeches instead of pines. Great, old beeches with roots like claws on the double ditches. The farm-houses, too. They were large and prosperous with everything you might expect to find in a sturdy English farm – barns, ducks in the pond, thick-packed granaries, airy lofts, a pigeon-croft, a seat under an arbour, fruit-gardens.

'All that was good. But it was those beeches that really impressed me. They were so clean and old, not like the quick-growing pines of the mountains – dirty trees that scatter their needles into the shoots of the houses and block them up three times every winter.'

'Oh, they're buggurs, father!' agreed the farmer earnestly.

'I climbed lower still and came to the gates of the houses where the gentry used to live.'

'Used to?'

'Used to. I should have expected it, but somehow it hadn't occurred to me. It's funny how we all forget how time passes. But there they were – the gate-posts falling. The lodges boarded up.

Notices, *For Sale*. Fifteen years of grass on the avenues. You see? "Owns ten thousand acres in Ireland. Address, Grosvenor Square, London." '

The pipe-stem travelled across the palm.

'I met an old man who took me down one of those avenues to see the ruins of a big house burned out during the troubled times. It was a lovely spring evening. The sky was like milk. The rooks were cawing about the roofless chimneys just like the flakes of soot come to life again. I spotted a queer little building at the end of a cypress avenue. The old man called it "the oftaphone." He meant octagon. It was a kind of peristyle. He said, "The Lord" – just like that, "The Lord used to have tea-parties and dances there long ago." I went into it and it had a magnificent view, a powerful view, across the valley over at my mountainy parish, yes, and beyond it to the ridges of the mountains, and even beyond that again to the very moors behind with their last little flecks and drifts of snow. They could have sat there and drunk their tea and seen my people – the poor Ryders, and Greenes, and O'Tooles, making little brown lines in the far-off fields in the ploughing time.'

'They could! Oh, begobs, father, so they could!' – and a mighty spit.

'Or at night, of summer evenings, they could have sipped their brandy and coffee and seen the little yellow lights of our cabin windows, and said, "How pretty it is!" '

'Begobs, yes! That's true!'

If anyone entered the carriage then he would have taken us for three friends, we were huddled together so eagerly. The priest went on:

' "They must have had good times here, once?" I said to the man who was with me. "The best, father!" says he. "Oh, the best out. The best while they lasted. And there were never any times like the old times. But they're scattered now, father," says he, "to the four winds. And they'll never come back." "Who owns the land, now?" I asked him. "They own it always, but who wants it?" says he. "The people here don't want it. They'd rather live in the towns and cities and work for wages." '

'That's right,' said the farmer, as if we were really discussing his own county. 'Begobs, you're talking sense now, father!'

' "The land was kept from them too long," says he. "And now

they have lost the knack of it. I have two grown sons of my own," says he, "and they're after joining the British Army." '

'Begobs, yes!' said the farmer, leaning to catch every word; but the priest stopped and leaned back.

The white, cold fields were singing by us. The cabins so still they might be rocks clung to the earth. The priest was looking at them and we were all looking at them, and at the flooded and frozen pools of water divided by the hedgerows. By his talk he had evoked a most powerful sense of comradeship in that carriage, whether he meant to or not: we felt one. Then, as quickly, he proceeded to break it.

'Well!' I asked eagerly. 'Well?'

'Why, that's all!' said the priest. 'I came back from my voyage of exploration, much refreshed. Much improved in spirits. You see, I had extended the pattern of life of my own poor parish. I saw how, how – I mean, how the whole thing had worked, hung together, made up a real unity. It was like putting two halves of a broken plate together. As I walked up another one of those hill-roads on my way home I passed more prosperous houses – smaller houses this time, what you would call private houses. They had neat, green curtains with fine, polished brassware inside on the polished mahogany. And through another window three aluminium hot-water bottles shining on a dark hall-table, signs of comfort as you might say . . . Yes! I had completed the pattern. That parish and my parish made up a world, as neither did by itself, rich and poor, culture and . . .'

'But,' I cried angrily, 'where's your moral unity? Your common thought? It's absurd.'

'Oh, yes! I realized that even before I got home. I just tell you the thing as it happened. But they in their octagon and we in our lighted cabins, I mean to say, it was two halves of a world . . .'

The farmer was looking at us both with dull, stupid eyes. He had lost the thread of the talk.

'Yes, I suppose so,' I agreed, just as lightly. 'But now that the gentry are gone, won't the people, the mountainy people, and so on, begin to make a complete world of their own?'

He shook his head. The farmer listened again.

'I refuse to believe they won't,' I said.

He shrugged his shoulders.

'And is there no possible solution, then?' I asked him.

He was looking out of the window, his poll to the farmer. He rolled up his eyes under his brows – a warning look, and faintly indicated the man behind him. Then he actually began to laugh, a cold, cackling laugh, an extraordinary, inhuman, kind of laugh that ended in a noise like a little groan.

The train slowed up, and we were in a station, and he was gathering his bags. He got out without even saying 'Good day' to us, and his face was coldly composed. A manservant, touching his cap, took the bags. The station-master touched his cap to him. The porter receiving the tickets touched his cap to him. The jarvey, who was waiting for him, bowed as he received the bags from the manservant. Black, tall, thin, and straight as a lamp-post, he left the lit, snow-bright station with every down-looking lounger there bowing and hat-touching as he passed. When I turned away the train was moving out, and the old farmer, in his own place, had lit another cigarette.

2

'Do you know his reverence?' I asked – as irritated as somebody from whom a book has been snatched before the end of the tale.

'Oh, aye!' said the old man, and he added, without interest: 'He's silenced.'

There was a touch of dread in that word, 'silenced.'

'What did they silence him for?'

'Politics.'

'Oh? He was too extreme?'

'Aye!' Still without interest.

'A clever man?'

No answer. His mind had gone to sleep. I looked at him in annoyance.

'What kind of ideas had he? I mean, what did he want?'

'Begobs, I dunno.'

Then he added, as if it was a matter of no importance –

'He wanted the people to have the land.'

'What land?'

'The land. The gentry's land.'

I leaned to him eagerly –

'But isn't that what ye want? Isn't that what the whole trouble is? Isn't that what the Government wants?'

'Aye. I suppose it is, you know? But he wanted it to be a sudden business.'

'They didn't silence him for that?'

'Maybe they didn't. Ach, he's odd. Sure, he took ten or twenty foolish young lads and, one night, he thrun down the walls of Lord Milltown's estate. He started some sort of a League, too. He's odd. God help him.'

'What did he want to do with this League of his?'

'I dunno. It was some kind of faddy business. He wanted halls . . . and . . . some kind of halls he wanted. Halls. I dunno what he wanted 'em for. Ah, he's a decent poor man.'

I tried another line.

'I suppose it's true for his reverence – ye have a hard time of it up here on the poor land?'

Puffing at his ease he was looking idly at the passing fields. A woman and two small boys, crushed into the doorway of a cabin, waved to us. He looked, and when they were gone his eyes were still fixed, seeing whatever passed beneath them with equal interest – or disinterest?

He tilted his head, but he said nothing. I made one last effort to shake him from his lethargic mood – possibly, most likely indeed, the mood in which he spent the greater part of his life.

'You know,' I said, warmly, 'I think I'd die in this lonely place. That priest is right!'

He looked at it, and scratched his ear, and said:

'Aye!' And then, suddenly, he added a second 'Aye!' – and then, when I thought he was finished, he actually added – 'I suppose 'tis quiet,' and relapsed into indifference.

Angrily I burst out at him –

'But damn it all, don't you mind, or is it that ye don't want to stir, ye're too damn lazy to stir?'

He took the butt-end from his mouth, and he looked at me, and by the way he looked up and down at me, I was hoping he would say something bitter and strong. But his stare was childish, and the eyes wavered, as if he was very tired. He just dropped one last, vast spit on the wet floor, snuggled into his corner, and went to sleep under his hat.

In his sleep he was as motionless as a rock; but you could not say he was 'like a rock' because he was like nothing on earth but himself, everything about him was so personal to him. Unless, because he was so much a random accumulation of work and season and all that belongs to the first human that was ever made, I chose to say, as I glared at him snoring in his corner, that time and nature had engendered something no more human than a rock. So I thought, as the dusk drew down, and the wind moaned in many keys, and the snow blew horizontally and stuck to the edges of the window. It was as if we two might have been jolting into a blank beyond either sleep or night, and I wanted to get up and kick him. I felt that if I did he would only moo.

We halted at several stations, with their one or two silent white-shouldered figures. He slept on. I was just wondering if I should wake him when suddenly, at a station, identical with every other station, as if some animal magnetism in the place stirred him, he rose and stumbled out. He did not speak. He did not raise his head to see if it was his station. He saluted no one. Anyway, there was no one there but a muffled porter who silently waved a lantern over his head. As we moved off he was trudging in the middle of a road that glimmered with its own strange afterglow, passing between a row of pines whose sheltered sides were red and raw as with the cold. He was exactly like an old black mongrel loping home.

3

So I was left with the pool of water on the floor, dark under the carriage-light, and the snow crumbling into the corners of the windows outside, and beyond that only the light leaping and falling along the hedges. And in another two hours or so, when I got out, the carriage would be racing along, empty, through the night – three bits of separateness, the priest and the farmer and myself, flung off it like bits of the *disjecta membra* of the wheel of life.

For those two hours I tried to refute the talk of that priest, thinking that he had merely spoken out of the snowy landscape, which above all other conditions of nature is so powerful to make life seem lonely, and all work futile, and time itself a form of decay; or thinking that, had it been the green-dripping spring or the hot summer, we might all have shown different and more happy sides of our worlds; or thinking that the thin cheeks and the throbbing nerve of the man were nothing but the sign of twenty years of self-corrosion, and that even when he was a young man in his first parish, his heart must have been so bitter and vain that, like a leech, it began to destroy everything to preserve itself; or thinking that because of it he had joined us for a few moments until we seemed to crouch over a fire, and then deliberately scattered us and left us with his pox. But, though that might be all true, I could not deny to the wintry moment its own truth, and that under that white shroud, covering the whole of Ireland, life was lying broken and hardly breathing. His impress remained even when the train swished slowly into the city, where the arc-lamps sizzled in the snow, and the sounds were muffled, and through every street a sharp, pure wind blew down from the Wicklow hills. Once their distant convex gleamed, far away, beyond the vista of a street. There were few people abroad, and as they walked against the wind with huddled backs they, too, seemed to be shrouding something within them that slept, and barely palpitated, and was hurt by the cold. What image, I wondered, as I passed through them, could warm them as the Wicklow priest had warmed us for a few minutes in that carriage now chugging around the edge of the city to the sea? What image of life that would fire and fuse us all, what music bursting like the spring, what triumph, what engendering love, so that those breasting mountains that now looked cold should appear brilliant and gay, the white land that seemed to sleep should appear to smile, and these people who huddled over the embers of their lives should become like the peasants who held the hand of Faust with their singing one Easter morning? Perhaps it was foolish to wish for such an image – so magnificent that it would have the power of a resurrection call? Yet, there are times, as when we hear the percussion of some great music, or when we feel the shrivelling effect of the cold wind and snow, that leave us no other choice but to live splendidly, or gather up at least enough grace for a quick remove.

The train could be heard easily, in the rarefied air, chugging across the bridges that span the city, bearing with it an empty coach. In the morning, Ireland, under its snow, would be silent as a perpetual dawn.

The Old Master

I

When I was younger, and so, I suppose, in the nature of things, a little more cruel, I once tried to express John Aloysius Gonzaga O'Sullivan geometrically: a parabola of pomposity in a rectangle of gaslight. The quip pleased everybody who knew the reference – it was to his favourite stand, under the portico of the court-house, his huge bulk wedged into the very tall and slender doorway.

I said '*gaslight*' because John Aloysius rarely came to work before the afternoon when they lit the gas in the dim entrance-hall, and its greenish, wateryish light began to hiss high up in the dome. There he would stand, ten times in the afternoon, smoking, or watching the traffic, or gossiping with some idling clerk. He had a sinecure in the fusty-musty little law-library, a room no bigger than a box. He used to say, in his facetious way, that he left it often because he exhausted the air every half-hour.

As the Assizes came to us only four times each year, and the library was rarely used between the sessions, he was not hard worked. He was always at liberty to practise at the Bar, but he never did – he was a bachelor without attachments and he had a small private income.

The last time he took up his stand in the doorway was the Tuesday of the week the Russian Ballet came to town. That day he became a next-to-permanent feature of the portico. He wanted to talk to everybody about it, until we were sick of the sight of him.

Higgins the door-keeper got the brunt of it; he also got a relay of John A.'s best Egyptian cigarettes. Peter Cooney, Secretary of the Poor Law Guardians, got the remnants – invited specially to drink coffee with John Aloysius in the library, and look, for the thousandth time, at his naughty prints of Ingres' *La Source* (the naked girl with the pitcher), or Fragonard's *The Swing* (the shepherdess-lady being swung much too high above the gentlemen in silk knee-breeches and ribboned shirt). They were good listeners, the one because he had nothing else to do, the other because he liked the coffee – it was good coffee, ground in a special little French hand-mill, and flavoured with a fine liqueur brandy – and because, too, he loved the romantic flavour of the tiny library with its books stacked to the ceiling, and he really admired John Aloysius, and thought him a most cultivated man, and a most refined man – even if he did tell smutty stories and had a bad name with the women.

To Higgins the door-keeper, John Aloysius would say – with the cigarette poised before his mouth, and the fat, little finger cocked in the air – 'Higgins, I am outshone. Up to last night, Higgins, I was the sole particle of colour in this diminutive jakes of a town. I alone brought colour and culture into this kraal that goes by the name of Cork. But I am honourably outshone. Russia has eclipsed me.'

That was his regular way of talk. And if nobody took it seriously, nobody took it comically, either. For he always talked with a slightly cynical air, an ambiguous kind of self-mockery, and he never smiled. God alone knows if ever he said to himself, in the silence of the night, 'John Aloysius Gonzaga O'Sullivan, you're a sham!' Such men have no life but their own drama, and if you had dared say that to him he would probably have replied: 'Is it not as good a life as another?'

'Look at this court-house, Higgins!' John Aloysius would go on. 'Look at it! I have seen the Lord Chief Justice enter this building between files of cuirassiers with shining breast-plates, uplifted sabres, snowy plumes. A vision of scarlet and ermine, Higgins. But that was in the good old days, before these yahoos from the heath, these bog-trotters of Gaelic Leaguers, these bag-men, these Attacotti, these tin-pot patriots with the smell of dung on their boots, set the grass growing on the streets. But now, Higgins, what do we see? We see Justice arrive in a bowler hat and flannel-bags. My God, Higgins! It's a symbol. And I am left! I am left! I am left, Higgins, like an old master, lying forgotten in a deserted mansion.'

'Aye, aye, sir!' Higgins would respond, like the old navy-man he was.

And John Aloysius would pat his third and hairless chin, and tip his deep-bayed collar, with the tips of his pink fingers, and, in disgust at the changed world, fling his cigarette on the mossy steps of the court-house, lingering for a second to watch some ragged-pants pick it up – his jewel flung in largess. Then he would stalk away, his great torso swaying like a young elephant from side to side, and he would bid Peter Cooney come to the library, and lolling in his arm-chair, take up the tale again.

'Cooney, that fellow Higgins is a boor, a gun-room lout, a deck-swabber. Why must John Aloysius Gonzaga O'Sullivan associate with such offal? Can you tell me that, Cooney? You at least, however ignorant, have been to the ballet once – you have made your obeisance to that loveliness of which these, and these' (indicating the naughty prints, at which Cooney would be trying hard to look objectively), 'are but the whispering echoes. Think of it, Cooney! Russia is at our doors – the greatest civilization in the world, crushed under the elephant feet of these yahoos of Bolsheviks, these hairy moujiks from Siberia, these Circassian Huns who never knew what beauty was – that Russia is come to our city. And what happens, Cooney? Pwah! The swine do not even smell the pearls. Last night – a first night – the theatre – you saw it yourself – was *empty*!'

'O, bejaney, John A.,' Peter would mumble, ' 'tis a bloody shame.'

'My dear boy, we are ashamed before the civilized world. How can I lift my head again in London? Or in Paris? The name of this city will stink in the nostrils of every artist in Europe. Saint Petersburg comes to Cork – for so, in my dreams, I sometimes call that lovely city, and think to see again her lovely streets. . . . And Cork ignores her. The Nevsky Prospect, Cooney; the sleighs on the Voznesensky; the Gorokhovaya Ulitsa, lit from end to end by the rising sun! (It runs due south-east, Cooney.) The Neva frozen and glittering! All that! And Cork ignores it!'

(That was typical John Aloysius – he devoured travel-books to the point of believing himself that he had travelled the world.)

'Cooney! Will you tell me why do I live here? Why does John Aloysius Gonzaga O'Sullivan live in a sewer? You say nothing? I know why. You are saying to yourself – "But what an error!" you are saying. "Surely," you are saying, "the sewers of Paris, as compared with this chamber-pot of a town, are as a translucent Pierian spring?" And you are quite right. My boy, you show great intelligence.'

And so, having smoked Peter, and eased his own heart, off with him again to Higgins, and back again to his office, as restless as a hen with an egg, all that Tuesday afternoon, waiting until he should be seated again in the stalls, in his starched shirt and his tails – the only man, he was certain, who would dress for the event.

He knew he would be rubbing his paunch around and around, in an ecstasy, watching the limbs twine and untwine, the waves of *Les Sylphides* advance and retire, the heads nod, the knees rise, the arms upflinging. . . . In his library he blew little secret kisses at his vision. As he dressed he promised himself, 'fore God, that he would go around after the show to the stage-door and congratulate them in person. He might even take one of the ladies to supper. . . . He trembled at the thought. . . . And he knew that he was the only man left in all Ireland with a sense of beauty . . . the old master deserted in the abandoned house.

What a phrase! 'The old master on the walls – silent and dignified – while the bailiffs below-stairs drank their gin. . . .' As he walked to the theatre he polished the phrase, and he swayed on his hips like a young elephant.

2

Nobody knows if he said all that, but we can well infer it from what happened. For at the door of the theatre John Aloysius got a shock. He heard his name pronounced in full at his elbow – 'John Aloysius Gonzaga O'Sullivan,' spoken in a cold, malicious voice. Turning, he saw two men looking at him, one with a scornful frown, the other sheepishly. The frowner held a note-book in his hand and he was writing down the name. The other, of all people, was his satellite, Peter Cooney.

'What may this be?' stormed John Aloysius.

Cooney blushed and fidgeted, but the other spoke up.

'We're taking down the name of every man who enters the theatre tonight.'

He was a fine, healthy young man, with red, high cheek-bones, blue eyes, a soft mouth. John Aloysius recognized him; he was a doctor named Quill.

'And for what purpose, in the name of heaven?' asked John A., with a sick feeling beginning to crawl around his stomach.

'We think it's an indecent performance,' said Quill.

John Aloysius looked where he pointed and saw a little procession of young men marching around the square; among them were, also, some young women and boys. One man carried a placard which said:

> MEN OF SAINT MARK
>
> *We have Them Marked!*
>
> DOWN WITH IMMORAL PLAYS!

He thought quickly of his job. It was a nice job. But it had to be renewed by the County Council every year, and that was sometimes a delicate business.

'Dear me,' he said, and for Cooney's benefit he tried to say it as facetiously as possible. 'And is it as bad as all that? Have you, I mean to say, have you seen the performance?'

'I wouldn't be seen supporting it,' said Quill.

Cooney was restive. He drew John A. aside.

'To tell you the gospel truth, John A.' he said, wrinkling up his nose apologetically, 'Doctor Quill can say anything he likes, but it's the way I *couldn't* be seen supporting it. I'm in this all on account of Canon Paul. As you know, what he says goes. But take my advice now, John A., and let it alone. 'Twill be better for you.'

'And do you mean to stand there,' stormed John Aloysius, 'and admit to me that you are such a craven wretch . . .'

'None of that,' threatened Quill, turning on them like a flash. 'Mr Cooney has made up his own mind and you can make up yours, too, and as a matter of fact, I'm sure Mr Cooney doesn't really approve of this performance at all.'

It was on the tip of John A.'s tongue to abuse them both. As he caught the flaring lights of the foyer, the gold paint, the smell of the theatre's musk, like burned toast, he wanted to ask them if they realized that all the loveliness of Russia was behind those doors, to talk of the Gorokhovaya Ulitsa lit from end to end by the rising sun. He even thought of arguing that the ballet is, by nature, anti-Communistic. Rage swelled his neck. He thought of ten bad words to call Cooney – a moujik, a pimp, a blister, a PILE. . . .

'I see,' he said. 'Dear me. I must think it over.'

As he walked away from the door he heard the wretched Cooney say, 'Cross out that name. Mr O'Sullivan is with us.'

He felt he would choke, or cry. He went around the corner, and to a small newsboy who tried to sell him a paper he said all the ten bad words in a rush. Then he bethought himself and walked quickly to the stage-door, casting many glances behind him as he entered. He presented his card and a florin to the door-keeper, and was finally shown into the dressing-room of the dancer who did the part of the Rose in *Le Spectre de la Rose*. The room was full of excited men and women, all talking in loud voices at the same time.

'I have come, sir,' said John Aloysius to the dancer, 'to congratulate you, and to protest on behalf of my city against these disgraceful scenes outside. I do not wish you, sir, to form the idea that this city is an ignorant city, or a boorish city. It is a most cultivated centre of the arts. It always was. I am but one of thousands who feel that your ballet is a glorious thing, and if I may say so, an uplifting thing.'

The dancer was a small, lithe Lithuanian named Rachmanoff. He was no Nijinsky. Where Nijinsky would have hurled himself through the window, ten feet through the air, on to a mattress held by four scene-shifters, poor Rachmanoff jumped like any man. He was thirty-eight – near the end of his race as a dancer, and he was touring the small cities of the world, trying to lay up a little store of money against the time when he would dance no more. Eagerly he interpreted to the others, as they crowded around them to know what it all meant. John Aloysius saw the glowing lips, and coloured cheeks of the girls, their bare arms, their white backs, and smelled the scent of the powder. He felt the air in the musty dressing-room grow quick, as when lightning is about to explode the sky.

'It means so much to us,' pleaded Rachmanoff. 'It will ruin us. Last week in Sheffield we did not do well. And *Cardiff* – you remember *Cardiff?*' He turned to them all, and they all groaned the word '*Cardiff!*' 'Who are these young men?' implored Rachmanoff.

'They are young fools,' said John Aloysius. 'In fact, they are mere scum! In fact, they are the lowest of the low! As a matter of fact, they're really . . . what you might call, revolutionaries, That's what they are!'

'Not Communists?' begged Rachmanoff.

'Worse than Communists! Perhaps you might call them Fascists. Or Nationalists. It's very complicated.'

'What can you do for us?' pleaded the little dancer, and the girls put their white arms around John A.'s shoulders and peered at him beseechingly, as if he were their saviour.

'Pay no heed to them,' said John Aloysius, feeling the scent fume through his brain. 'I am a lawyer. There are ways and means. To-morrow night, I, John O'Sullivan, guarantee it, they will be swept off the streets. I can only apologize for them, now. As an old master, as one of the very few old masters, left on the walls of modern times, from the great eras, my friends, as you are of those great eras, I speak, so to speak, and I apologize for them. They will be swept from the streets like the dust before the wind.'

Then, hearing the singing of hymns outside the windows, and fearing the young men might come in and find him, he dragged himself away, followed by their beseeching eyes, their pleading smiles, their looks of fear and doubt. His heart was thumping as he left them. But he felt justified. He had given these yahoos their answer. The old master, so to speak, had leaned down from the walls, reproved their ignorance....

3

So thinking he found himself at the front of the theatre again. The procession had swollen to twice its size. Crowds of people were watching it circle round and round. Seeing them all, John Aloysius felt his resolution ebbing away. Suddenly he heard his name spoken again; this time it was Canon Paul, a lean, hollow-browed man with spectacles. With distaste John Aloysius noticed that the glass of the spectacles was dusted with little grains, and browned in the crevices of the frame.

'Mr O'Sullivan,' said the canon, 'Doctor Quill has told me how you refused to support this wretched business when you heard of our protest. That's the spirit. I'm so glad you are with us. Only three men have gone into the theatre – and, believe me, Mr O'Sullivan, we'll teach them a lesson.'

'Why,' muttered John Aloysius, 'I mean to say, it's . . . I was thinking . . . after all, it's all right for . . . adults, don't you think, Canon?'

'Ah, but it's the bad example, Mr O'Sullivan. That's what counts. The young people must be given good example.'

'Quite so,' said John Aloysius.

'And now, Mr O'Sullivan, we're going to start. We'll march through the city. Come with me.'

Gently but firmly he took John Aloysius by the arm, saying something about the value of educated men, and about ending this sort of thing, and before he could get out of it John Aloysius found himself beside Cooney in the procession with a hymn-book in his hand.

'Now, men!' shouted the canon.

At once John A. imagined himself standing out and denouncing them all. What a great story it would be! And while he thought of it the procession shuffled off and he had to march with it. He saw the crowds fall in behind, marshalled by stewards. They were singing. Cooney was bawling in his ear like a trumpeter. In his white paunch, he himself was the most conspicuous of them all, he was so big and fat, and his tall hat stuck up in the air.

The canon fell in by his side and smilingly urged him to sing. Then as the procession circled around towards the drawn doors of the theatre he saw the dancers clustered inside, overcoats over their shoulders, peering out, and they were gesticulating madly and pointing direct at him. He tried to hunch down his shoulders, and bend his knees. He took off his hat. But that looked as if he were trying to put more gusto into his singing, so he put it on again.

'Sing up, Mr O'Sullivan,' urged the canon, singing away himself right into his ear (as Cooney did on the other side), and banging his breviary to mark the time. Viciously John Aloysius sang.

'*Hark,*' he piped.

'Out with it,' from the canon.

'Hark, hear the sound
Those blessed strains are telling . . .'

'Fine,' said the canon. 'Louder!'

'Of that new life,' sang John Aloysius,
'When sin shall be no more. . . .'

They debouched out of the square into the principal street. Crowds gathered on the kerbs. Old shawled women bobbed to the canon, and said what a grand man he had with him.

'Somebody is waving to you,' cried the canon.

It was Higgins the door-keeper, waving cheerfully from the kerb. John Aloysius looked sideways out of his pince-nez and bawled away at the hymn, pretending not to see him at all. Presently the canon said:

'We're going to hold a protest meeting in the Grand Parade. You'll say a few words, of course?'

John Aloysius groaned. Sweat clamped his dress-shirt to his back. He felt he was going to assassinate the canon, pull out his lean neck the way you pull the neck of a hen. He saw, down a side-street, a little green, iron building. Pointing shyly to it, he excused himself to the canon, dived from the ranks, and with his tails in the air, raced down the street and took refuge inside the privy.

As he turned into it he saw Cooney racing after him.

'You vomit!' cried John Aloysius, mopping his brow inside the building.

'The canon wants you to speak!' protested Cooney.

'I have a colic,' said John Aloysius. 'A bad colic. I get them often,' and he began to unfasten his vest. 'Go away, you scoundrel, you . . .'

'But the canon!' cried Cooney.

'I'll follow after you,' said John Aloysius. 'Go now, please go. It's so embarrassing. I'll join you in five minutes. I swear it!'

Unwillingly Cooney went. There was an old man there, too. He had a belt across his knees. John Aloysius peered out.

'Wha's all the singin' about?' grunted the old man.

'Some damn yahoos!' said John Aloysius. 'Clod-hoppers! Protesting about something or other! Saying something is immoral.'

The old man grunted. John Aloysius decided it would be safer to join him. They were now sitting side by side.

'All nonsense, of course,' said John Aloysius. 'As one of the old world – an old master – left by the tide – as you might say. . . .' He peered out carefully and saw the procession pass the end of the street. 'They know nothing. The beauty of the world. The grace of the human body. All lost on them.'

The old man grunted. John Aloysius looked at him in disgust. He lit an Egyptian cigarette and thought of the white arms of the dancers.

'The rhythm of the human form,' he murmured. 'Lost to them. Its life. Its colour. Know nothing. Never will.'

The sun streamed down diagonally into them. It was September and it had the softness of spring in it. Far away they heard the singing, the clear voices of boys and young women rising through the air, and they were – though John Aloysius hardly thought so – also springlike and clear, sweet as a shower through sunlight.

'The Gorokhovaya Ulitsa,' murmured John Aloysius.

The voices sang:

> 'Though our hearts be wrapt in sorrow
> From the hope of dawn we borrow,
> Promise of a glad to-morrow,
>   All through the night.'

John Aloysius was left alone. The sun faded, but he was afraid to stir. He heard the sound of cheering. He formed the phrases he would use tomorrow to denounce Cooney. 'A man of no courage. I, at least, made my protest. Spoke my mind. To the dancers. Defended beauty.' It grew darker, and the soft voices rose again in another hymn. He stole away, wandering down devious side-streets, polishing his invective, swaying as he went.

In the end he never said a word to Peter Cooney. He got his death of cold out of it, and within two weeks pneumonia had him whipped. But the strange thing is that, somehow or other . . . John Aloysius had a good time . . . amused everyone . . . enjoyed life . . . but nobody ever thought of him as anything but a free, public show while he was alive, and we only began to think of him as a human being when he was gone.

Sinners

The canon, barely glancing at his two waiting penitents, entered the confessional. From inside he looked wearily across at the rows of penitents on each side of Father Deeley's box, all still as statues where they sat against the wall, or leaned forward to let the light of the single electric bulb, high up in the windy roof, fall on their prayer-books. Deeley would give each about ten minutes, and that meant he would not absolve the last until near midnight. 'More trouble with the sacristan,' sighed the canon, and closed the curtains and lifted his hand towards the slide of the grille.

He paused. To banish a sudden restiveness he said a prayer. He often said that prayer – an Aspiration against Anger. He had remembered that on the other side of the grille was a little serving-girl he had sent out of the box last Saturday night because she had been five years away from confession and did not seem to be a bit sorry for it. He lifted his hand, but paused again. To add to his difficulty – for it was no help to know what, under the *sigillum*, he must pretend not to know – he had just been told in the sacristy by her employer that a pair of her best boots was missing. Why on earth, he sighed, did people reveal such things to him? Did he *want* to know the sins of his penitents? Was the confession being made to him, or to God? Was it . . . He lowered his hand, ashamed of his irritation, and repeated the prayer. Then he drew the slide, cupped his ear in his palm to listen, and saw her hands clasping and unclasping as if her courage was a little bird between her palms trying to escape.

'My poor child,' he said, ever so gently, dutifully pretending to know nothing about her, 'tell me how long it is since your last confession.'

'It's a long time, father,' she whispered.

'How long?' To encourage her he added, 'Over a year?'

'Yes, father.'

'How much? Tell me, poor child, tell me. Two years?'

'More, father.'

'Three years?'

'More, father.'

'Well, well, you must tell me, you know.'

In spite of himself his voice was a little pettish. The title 'father' instead of 'canon' was annoying him, too. She noted the change of voice, for she said, hurriedly:

' 'Tis that, father.'

' 'Tis what?' asked the canon a shade too loudly.

'Over three years, father,' she prevaricated.

He wondered if he could dare let the prevarication go; but his conscience would not let him.

'My dear child, how much over three years is it?'

' 'Tis, 'tis, father, 'tis . . .'

The canon forestalled the lie.

'My dear child, how much over three years is it? Is it four years? And would you mind calling me *canon*?'

The breathing came faster.

' 'Tis, father. I mean, 'tis more, *canon*, father.'

'Well, how much? I can't make your confession for you, you know.'

' 'Tis a bit more, father.'

'Two months,' lied the maid, and her hands made a flutter of whiteness in the dark.

The canon almost wished he could break the seal of the confessional and reveal to her that he knew exactly who she was, and how long she had been away; all he dared say was:

'I suspect you're telling me a lie.'

'Oh, God, father, it's gospel truth.'

'But,' the canon tapped the cushion, 'there's no use in telling me if it's not the truth. For God's sake, my poor child,' he controlled himself, 'maybe it's five years?'

' 'Tis five years,' admitted the maid in so low a voice that he barely heard it.

He sighed with satisfaction. He straightened his hair on his forehead. Then he leaned nearer to hear her sins, nearer and nearer until his ear was pressed against the lattice.

'Now,' he warned, 'that is a long time, my child. But, thank God, you have come back at last. You must try hard to remember all – all – your sins. Let me help you. My poor little child! Take the first commandment.'

But when he heard the shudder of her breath he knew he had made a bad mistake; she would be seeing a long list of broken commandments before her and she would slur over many of her sins in order to shorten the ordeal.

'I mean to say,' went on the canon, annoyed with his own stupidity, 'that is one way of doing it. Do you wish to make your confession that way?'

'Yes, father.'

'Very well.'

'The first commandment . . .' She stopped in confusion and he realized that she did not even know what the commandment was.

'Did you ever miss Mass on Sundays?' he helped her out, although his knees were beginning to dance with impatience.

'Oh, never, never in my whole life.'

'Good. Did you ever swear? Take the Lord's name in vain?'

'Tututut!' said the girl in horror at the very idea.

'Did you ever disobey your parents, cause them pain in any way, give back-answers?'

'I have no parents, father. Mrs Higg – my mistress got me from the Orphanage.'

'Ah! Well . . . er . . . Lies? Anger? Have you told lies, or given way to anger?'

'Wisha, I suppose I did, father. I suppose I told a little lie now and again.'

'How often in those five years? On an average? I mean, is it a weakness you have? A habit?'

'God help us, father, I don't tell many. I only tell 'em when I do be afraid.'

'Well, we will say you told lies occasionally. Now the sixth commandment. Have you ever sinned in thought, word, or deed against Holy Purity? The opposite sex, for example. Have you ever misbehaved in any way with men?'

'Oh!' gasped the maid, and her voice thickened.

'Stealing?' prompted the canon, and he waited for her to say that she had stolen Mrs Higgins's boots.

'I never in my life, father, stole as much as the head off a pin.

Except when I was small I once stole an apple in the nuns' orchard. And then they caught me and gave me a flaking. And they took the last bite out of my mouth.'

'You never stole articles of dress?' threatened the canon, and he suddenly realized that there were only three very unlikely commandments left. 'Clothes? Hats? Gloves? Shoes?'

'Never, father.'

There was a long pause.

'Boots?' he whispered.

Suddenly the girl was sobbing violently.

'Father,' she wept, 'Mrs Higgins is telling you lies about me. I hate that wan. I . . . I . . . I hate her. I do. She's always prying and poking and prodding at me. She took me from the nuns five years ago and she never gave me a minute's rest. She calls me low names. She tells me I can't be good or wholesome to come out of an Orphanage. She is picking at me from dawn to dusk. She's an old bitch . . .'

'My child! My child!'

'I did take the boots. I took them. But I didn't steal them. Sure I haven't a boot on my foot and she has lashings and leavings of 'em. I was going to put them back.'

'My child, to take them is the same as to steal them.'

'What does she want them for? But she's that mean. Her own daughter ran away from her two years ago and married an Englishman who's half a Freemason. The poor girl told me with her own mouth, only last week, how she's half-starved by that husband of hers and they have no money to have a family. But do you think her mother would give her a penny?'

The girl sobbed on. The canon groaned and drew himself up to ease his chest. He could hear the wind whistling up in the roof and he could see the long queue on each side of Father Deeley's box, all still as statues in the dusk of the aisle. Seeing them he groaned again as much as to say, 'What's the use? They all deceive themselves. They all think everyone is sinful but themselves only. Or if they say they are sinners, and feel it – it only lasts while they are in the church. Then they go out and are filled with envy and pride and they have no charity.' He leaned back.

'My child, my child, my child! For five years you have stayed away from God. If you had died you would have died with that mortal sin on your soul and gone to hell for all eternity. It's the law of the Church, and the law of God, that you *must*, you *must* go to confession at least once a year. Why did you stay away? Look at the way your mind is deformed so that you can't even recognize a sin when you commit it. Is there some sin you haven't told me that you were ashamed to tell?'

'No, father.'

'Didn't your good mistress send you to confession at least every month during those five years?'

'She sent me every week. But it was always of a Saturday night. And one Saturday night I didn't go because I wanted to buy a blouse before the shops shut. Then it was six months before I knew it and I was afraid to go. And, anyway, sure what had I to tell?'

The canon waved his hands weakly and with great sarcasm he said:

'Did you *never* commit a sin?'

'I suppose I told a lie, father. And there was the apple in the nuns' orchard.'

Furiously the priest turned to her, determined to wring the truth from her. In her compartment he heard Lady Nolan-White, his second penitent, coughing impatiently.

'My dear child, you simply must have committed sins during those five years. Be honest with yourself. Come now! Look! Take the most common sin of all. Have you, ever, had what we, vulgarly, call a . . . er . . . call a boy?'

'I had – once – father.'

'Well, now!' He rubbed his forehead like a man in a great heat and he strained towards her as if he were struggling with her demon. 'You were, what do we say . . . er . . . walking out with him?'

'Yes,' panted the girl. 'In the back-lane.'

'Well, what shall we say? Did, what do you say, did, er, did any intimacy take place with him?'

'I don't know, father.'

'You know what it is to be immodest, don't you?' cried the canon.

Her breath was panting in and out. She said nothing. She stared at him.

'My poor, poor child, you seem to have small experience of the world. But we must get at the truth. Did he – did you – did either of you ever go beyond the bounds of propriety?'

'I dunno, father.'

Loudly the canon expelled his breath. He was becoming exhausted, but he would not give in. He rubbed his hair all the wrong way, which gave him a wild look. He took off his pince-nez and wiped them.

'You understand plain English, don't you? Now, tell me, tell Almighty God the truth of the thing. Did you ever allow him to take liberties with you?'

'Yes, father. I mean no, father. We were in the lane. No, father. We didn't do nothing. Nothing much, I mean.'

'Five years,' moaned the canon, and he hammered his thigh with his fist. 'And nothing to tell. What kind of Christians . . .' He determined to make one last effort – just one more effort. 'Did he ever touch your body?' he asked bluntly.

'No, father. Well, I mean – no, father.'

Seeing that she was beginning to whimper again he threw up his hands.

'All right, child,' he said gently. 'Say your Act of Contrition and I'll give you Absolution.'

'Father,' she whispered, her eyes black through the grille, 'I was in bed with him once.'

The canon looked at her. She drew back. He leaned away and looked from a distance at the criss-crossed face behind the grille. Then he began to smile, slowly expanding his mouth into a wide beam of relief.

'My child,' he whispered, 'did anyone ever tell you that you were a little deficient in the head? I mean, you weren't very smart at school, were you?'

'I was always at the top of the school, father. Mother Mary Gonzaga wanted to make a teacher of me.'

'And,' growled the canon, now utterly exasperated, and dancing his knees up and down on the balls of his feet like a man in the agony of toothache, 'do you kneel there and tell me that you think it no sin to go to bed with a man? Who,' he added, casually, 'isn't your husband?'

'I meant no harm, father,' she palpitated, 'and it's not what is in your mind at all, for we didn't do nothing, and if it wasn't for the thunder and lightning that terrified me, I wouldn't do it at all. Mrs Higgins was down in Crosshaven with Mrs Kinwall, that's her daughter, and I was all alone in the house, and I was afraid of the dark and the thunder, so Mickey said he'd stay with me, so he stayed, and then it was late and I was 'fraid to be by myself in the bed, so he said, "I'll mind you," so I said, "All right, Mikey, but none of that," and he said, "All right, Madgie, none of that," and there wasn't any of that, father.'

She stared at the canon, who was blowing and puffing and shaking his head as if the whole world were suddenly gone mad.

'It was no harm, father,' she wailed, seeing he did not believe her.

'Once?' asked the canon shortly. 'You did this once?'

'Yes, father.'

'Are you sorry for it?' he demanded briefly.

'If it was a sin. Was it, father?'

'It was,' he roared. 'People can't be allowed to do this kind of thing. It was a serious occasion of sin. Anything might have happened. Are you sorry?' – and he wondered if he should throw her out of the box again.

'I'm sorry, father.'

'Tell me a sin of your past life.'

'The apple in the orchard, father.'

'Say an Act of Contrition.'

She ran through it swiftly, staring at him all the while. There were beads of perspiration on her upper lip.

'Say three Rosarys for your penance.'

He shot the slide to and sank back, worn out. From force of habit he drew the opposite slide and at once he got the sweet scent of jasmine, but when Lady Nolan-White was in the middle of her *Confiteor* he waved his two hands madly in the air and said, hastily:

'Excuse me, one moment . . . I can't . . . It's all absurd . . . It's impossible . . .'

And he drew the slide on her astonished, beautiful, rouged face. He put on his biretta, low down on his nose, and stalked out into the aisle. He parted the curtains on Lady Nolan-White and said:

'It's quite impossible . . . You don't understand it . . . Good night!'

He stalked up the dim aisle, and when he met two urchins gossiping in a corner he banged their little skulls together, and at once he became disgusted with himself to see them cowering from him in fright. He passed on, his hand under the tail of his surplice, dancing it up and down. When he saw two old women by the great Calvary, rubbing spittle into the Magdalen's foot and then rubbing spittle to their eyes or throat, he groaned out, 'Oh, dear, oh dear,' and strode on towards Father Deeley's box. There he counted heads – fourteen penitents on one side and twelve on the other, looked at his gold watch and saw it was a quarter-past eight.

He strode back to the centre compartment and flung aside the curtains. Out of the dimness the warm, cherubic face of the young curate looked at him – a pink Italian saint. Slowly the glow of spiritual elevation died from his face as the canon's insistent whisper hissed down at him:

'Father Deeley, it won't do. I assure you it's absolutely impossible. Half-past eight and twenty-six people yet to hear confession. They're just deceiving you. They want to gabble. I am an old man and I understand them. Think of the sacristan. Electric light, too! And gas going until midnight. The organization of the Church . . .'

And so on. All the time he kept stretching and relaxing the mechanical bow of his genteel smile, and he spoke in the most polite voice. But Deeley's face grew troubled, and pained, and seeing it the canon groaned inwardly. He remembered a curate he had once who played the organ every day for hours on end, until the parishioners complained that they couldn't pray with the noise he made; the canon recalled how he had gone up into the loft to ask him to stop, and the curate had lifted to him a face like an angel, and how within one half-minute it had became the face of a cruel, bitter old man.

'All right, Father Deeley,' he said hastily, forestalling protests. 'You are young. I know. Still, you are young . . .'

'I am not young,' hissed Deeley furiously. 'I know my duty. It's a matter of conscience. I can sit in the dark if you are so mean that you . . .'

'All right, all right, all right,' waved the canon, smiling furiously. 'We are all old nowadays. Experience counts for nothing . . .'

'Canon,' said Deeley, intensely, putting his two fists on his chest, 'when I was in the seminary, I used to say to myself, "Deeley," I used to say, "when you are a priest . . ." '

'Oh,' begged the canon, cracking his face in a smile, 'don't, I beg you, please don't tell me your life-story!'

Whereupon he whirled away, his head in the air, switching on and off the electric light of his smile to penitents he did not know and had never seen in his life before. He found himself before the high altar. He saw the sacristan standing on a step-ladder before it arranging the flowers for the morning, and he thought it would be well to apologize to him for Deeley's late hours. But the sacristan kept turning a vase round and round and round, and at last he realized that the little man was cross with him already, was deliberately delaying up there, and would not come down until he was gone.

Sighing he went away, and after writing some letters he realized that his stomach had ceased to belong to him and would be out on its own devices until morning, like a hound that escapes from its kennel. Wearily he took his hat and cane and decided to take a long walk to calm his nerves.

It was tender night of floating moonlight, cosily damp, and it soothed him to look down on the city and see the roofs as white as if there was frost on them. More calm, he returned home. The river was like milk. The streets were asleep. He hummed quietly to himself and felt at peace with all men. The clocks of the city chimed at one another in a good-humoured mood, slow and with silvery, singing echoes. Then he heard a woman's voice talking from the high window of a cement-faced house, and he saw that it was Mrs Higgins's house. She was in a white nightdress.

'That's a fine story!' she cried down to the pavement. 'Ha! A cockalorum of a story! Wait until I see the canon. At confession, indeed! Wait until I see the nuns! Oh, you jade! You unfortunate, poor sinner!'

He saw the little girlish figure cowering down in the doorway.

'Mrs Higgins,' she wailed, 'it's gospel truth. The canon threw me out again. I told him all sorts of lies. I had to go to Father Deeley. He kept me half an hour. Oh, Mrs Higgins,' wailed the child. 'It's gospel truth.'

'Aha!' prated the nightdress. 'But you're a nice thing. Wait until I tell . . .'

The canon felt the hound of his stomach jump from the kennel again. His entrails came bodily up to his neck. He marched by, blowing and puffing.

'Oh, my God!' he whined. 'Have pity on me. Oh, my God! Have pity on me!'

He turned towards the dark presbytery deep among the darkest lanes.

Admiring the Scenery

From between the little wayside platforms the railway shot two shining arrows off into the vast bogland where they vanished over a rise that might have been imperceptible without them. It was just before sunset in early spring, a soft evening of evaporating moisture and tentative bird-song; for the birds seemed to be practising rather than singing, twirling and stopping, and twirling and stopping, and when the bold thrush rolled out a whirl of sound he might have been mocking all the other eager, stupid little fellows like the bullfinch or the tits who had not yet learned their songs.

The three men, leaning on the wooden railing along the platform, looked at the blush of the sun on the last drifted snow of the mountains, and though every rail was cut into an A shape on top, uncomfortable for arm or elbow, they found it restful to lean and look over the bog, speaking hardly at all. They had been walking all day and now were dog-tired. They were waiting for the last train to take them into the country town where they all three taught in the Diocesan College.

The priest stood in the middle, a young man, too fat for his years, with drooping lids, puffed lips, and a red face as if he suffered from blood pressure. The same features on another man might have suggested a sensual nature, but there was in his heavily-lidded eyes a look that was sometimes whimsical and sometimes sad, and that look, with the gentle turn to his mouth when he smiled, gave him the appearance of a man who had gone through many struggles and finally solved his problems in a spirit of good-humoured regret. So, now, as he pulled at his pipe and looked down into a cold bog-stream that flowed beneath them, his chin and his piggy jowls rested on his Roman collar, expanded around his little mouth as if he might at any moment break into a little, silent chuckle. Only, you might have felt, those tired eyes would not even then have changed: they would have mocked his own smile.

On his left, carrying the haversack, was a small dark man, with a slim small body and a button of a head and clipped dark moustaches. The main thing about him was that he did break occasionally into sudden talk, and when he did he banged the hard railings repeatedly or lifted his two fists in the air and slapped his forehead. He did all these things, suddenly, when he cried out:

'Why on earth is this ten-thousand times accursed station three miles from the village? What's it here for at all? My God, what a country! What – is – it – for?'

'To take us home,' said the third man, and the priest's belly shook a little, too tired to expel laughter.

There was nothing remarkable about this third man except that he had handlebar moustaches and a long black coat and a black hat that came down low on his forehead and shaded his melancholy face; when he spoke, however, his face was gentle as the fluting of a dove. There was nothing resigned about him; his oblong face was blackberry-coloured where he shaved and delicate as a woman's where he did not. His eyes were lined with a myriad of fine wrinkles. They were cranky, tormented eyes, and his mouth was thin and cold and hard.

'I know,' cried the small man. 'It's some bloody Czar that did it. Some fool of an Under-Secretary long ago or some ass of a flaming Lord-Lieutenant who took a ruler and drew a line across Ireland and said, "That shall be the route of the new railway!" God, what a flaming country!'

'I wonder,' said the sad man, Hanafan, in his slow voice, 'do the common people ever admire scenery?'

'Now that's very interesting, Hanafan,' cried the small man across the priest's chest. 'That's a most extraordinary thing. I often thought of that. Isn't that a coincidence.'

'Well,' said the sad Hanafan, blushing modestly, 'it's a common enough idea, you know.'

'Of course they do,' said the deep basso of the priest.

'But do they, do they, do they?' shouted the little man, hammering the railing.

The priest nodded, never taking his eyes from the stream or his pipe from his little mouth.

'How do you know?' demanded the small man, leaping backward

and whirling his head left, right, and up in the air, as if the answer were a bird.

'Why wouldn't they?' grunted the priest.

'I know what you mean,' interrupted the small man, and he wagged his finger into the priest's face. 'I know. I met men like that. Our gardener at home, for example. I'd say to him – he was an awful old drunkard – he'd be lying of a hot summer's afternoon under an apple-tree – a lazy old ruffian, "Grand day, Murphy," I'd say. "Oh, a grand day, God bless it," he'd say, "and isn't it good to be alive?" But that's not admiring the scenery,' went on the small man. 'It's not being *conscious* of it. It isn't, if you understand me, projecting the idea of the beauty of the scene, the idea, into one's own consciousness. Is it, now, Hanafan? And that's what you mean by admiring the scenery.'

'Well,' said Hanafan, and his words were like prize pigeons that he released one by one from his hands, 'I don't know. I'm not sure I mean that.'

'Then what the hell *do* you mean?'

'If a man said to me,' went on Hanafan, in his downy voice, ' "I do be sometimes sitting here, Mr Hanafan, enjoying the cool of the evening," I'd say that that man was enjoying the scenery even though he might not know he was doing so at all.'

The priest nodded. The small man looked contemptuously at Hanafan who now began to quote from Gray's 'Elegy' in his round, womanly voice, all the time looking sadly at the warmth of the sun fading from the distant grains of snow, and the mountains becoming black and cold:

> 'The lowing herd winds slowly o'er the lea. . . .'

'I know, I know,' interrupted the other, but Hanafan went on quietly:

> 'The ploughman homeward plods his weary way;
> And leaves the world to darkness, and to me.'

'You see I feel,' he said, 'that the ploughman responded to the sense of the end of the day, and the way the fields were all gentle, and dark, and quiet. Just like that bog there . . . is . . . all . . .'

His voice died out.

'Ah, damn it,' said the small man in disgust, 'that has nothing to do with it.'

'It has, Mr Governey,' murmured the priest. 'In a sense it has.'

'Every man,' cried Hanafan, aroused with such vigour that the other two glanced at him, 'lives out his own imagination of himself. And every imagination must have a background. I'll tell you a queer thing. It's about the station-master in this station a few years ago.'

The priest nodded and chuckled aloud.

'He was nearly sixty-five,' said Hanafan, 'And he was married, and had a grown-up son in New York, and a daughter, a nun in South America.'

'I sent her there,' said the priest. 'A nice poor girl she was, God rest her.'

'Did she die?' asked Hanafan, and when the priest said, 'Yes,' he fell silent and forgot his story until the other teacher reminded him crossly.

'Yes,' said Hanafan. But, again, he stopped because the station porter came out with two oil lamps, one of which he put into the frame of the standard near them.

'It's a grand evening, father,' he said as he turned up the wick.

'Is she late again?' asked the priest, and the porter looked up the line at the signal, and said:

'Aye, she's a trifle behindhand, I'm thinking.'

He got down and drew a great silver watch from his corduroy vest and held it up to the setting sun, peering through the yellow celluloid guard.

'She's due, bedad. Ah, she'll be here in a quarter of an hour all right.'

The small man groaned and said, 'What a country!' The other two looked up at the lamp and then away, and Hanafan said:

'Isn't it dark!'

The porter had walked away.

'Well,' resumed Hanafan suddenly, 'this old station-master! His name was Boyhan. He thought he had a great voice for singing. He was stationed at N——' (he mentioned the town where they all lived and taught in the college), 'and he used to come and sing in the choir with us. That was before your time, Mr Governey. And he sang in the parish choir. And he'd have sung in the Protestant choir and the Wesleyan choir and the tin-hut choir if they let him. There was not a concert in N—— that he wasn't the head and tail of it, and he always sang twice and three times, and it was all they could do to keep him from giving encores all night long. For,' sighed the teacher, 'he had no sense and the people used to make a hare of him. He couldn't sing any more than I could. He had a small little voice, a small range too, but it had no strength or sweetness; there was no richness in it.'

The teacher said these words, *strength, sweetness, richness,* with a luscious curl of his thin lips around the fruit of sound. His eyes widened. Clearly he was seeing nothing but the old station-master. Earnestly he went on, a small glow on each cheek:

'That was all right until they shifted poor Boyhan to this God-forsaken place. And if N—— is a lonely hole, this is the back of beyond. At the same time they started the new Broadcasting Station in Dublin and Boyhan conceived a great ambition to sing there. He formed the idea that some day or other a passenger would be on his way to Dublin, or from Dublin, and he would hear him singing and say, "My Heavens, who is that with the grand voice?" And he would make inquiries – some director or Government official – and stop the train to seek out Boyhan and say to him, "What's the meaning of this neglect? Why haven't you been asked to sing over the Radio?" Then there would be paragraphs in the newspapers about Discovery of Great Irish Baritone, and Romance of a Chance-heard Voice, and so on.

'The result of this was that whenever a train rolled in, Boyhan used to come out of his office singing. He'd be singing little trills up and down the scale, or a bar of *The Moon hath raised her Lamp Above*. He was known to all the passengers and, sure, they used to be looking out for him. And there he would always be, rubbing his hands and pretending he was doing his *Dohsohmedoh*, just for delight and jollity.

'Well, one hard, moonlight night in December, I was here, like this, waiting for the last train back to N——. The snow was white on the hills. It was blazing. There wasn't a sound but the wind in the telegraph wires. The clouds were in flitters, in bits. I well remember it. A rich night. A deep, rich night, and no harm in the winds but they puffing and blowing.'

Again Hanafan's cold thin lips sucked the sound of those words, *rich, deep,* and his eyes dilated under his black hat with the image of his memory. His eyes were not cranky now, but soft and big.

'I was here with a – a – I was here with a – a friend.'

He stopped for a second. The small man's eyes pounced on him, observing at once his strange embarrassment. He glanced at the priest, but he had lowered his face and his mouth was clamped. In that hesitant second he saw at once a piece of Hanafan's secret life revealed, a memory of something known also to the priest; the thought of a dead friend – or perhaps a woman – something or somebody that made the memory of that night so precious to Hanafan that he could not speak of it openly.

'Was this long ago?' probed the small man inquisitively.

'We walked up and down,' said Hanafan, 'looking at the snow under the moon and the clouds tumbling. Then Boyhan came out and he took us across the line. He had a fire and we sat around it. The smell of the peat, thick and slab, was stuck into everything in the room.'

'Was it only two of you?' prodded the small man, eager to know if it was a woman.

'He showed us photographs of his daughter, the nun, and of his son, Timsy, with, as he said, a lawn-tennis in his hand. He had no wife. She was dead. And there he was living alone, in the station, three miles from the village and his only two children in the world away in exile. I quoted Sir Thomas Browne for him, the passage in *The Quincunx*. We all looked out the little window at the stars of the Plough. "Think!" said I, "*The quincunx of heaven runs low and 'tis time to close the five ports of knowledge. . . . The huntsmen are up in America and they are already past their first sleep in Persia. But who can be drowsy at that hour which freed us from everlasting sleep, or have slumbering thoughts at that time, when sleep itself must end. . . .*"

'Then, by way of no harm, he began to talk about music and singing and he gave us one song after another. He sang us, *Oft in the stilly night* – and, you know, he sang it well. He sang, *The Moon hath raised her Lamp Above*. I heard the signal bell ring as he was in the middle of it and far away the train began to purr. He was singing it so heartily we didn't like to interrupt him, and as the train became a roar across the bog and the lights went flashing across the window, he rose and went out to the platform. By Heavens, that man saw the trainload as a vast audience whirled before him. He stood out on the platform singing to them.

'We rushed for the bridge, we had no tickets, he gave us no tickets, and as I ran I shouted back at him, "Hold the train!" He paid no heed, and when we were up on the middle of the bridge he got to the grand burst, the last crescendo, of –

"I come! . . . My heart's delight"

and waved the train on. We were left looking at it vanishing up the line. I roared at him for a fool, and a vain fool, but he only bowed to us, and he bowed to the porter, and he bowed his way backward to the office like a Caruso. The train purred into the distance and there we two were with the wind in the wires and the white moon on mountains.

'I went back to abuse him – it was the last train – but he only looked at me like a child you'd strike and said he couldn't hold back a train for anyone. The porter paid no heed to us. He outed the lamps and locked the place up. We left the old fellow alone in the station. We had to walk home. It was a grand, bright night. A lovely, thick night. . . .'

Hanafan's voice broke. Just then a signal bell rang. It was dark over the bog where far away the train murmured and it could easily be heard because the birds had stopped singing. There was nothing but the deep scent of the night air, and below them in a marsh, still deep from the March rains, a prattling as of a thousand tiny frogs.

'This is a lonely place he lived in,' whispered Hanafan. 'A lonely life. No children. No wife.'

The priest rose up and knocked out the ashes of his pipe as the train roared nearer.

'Yes,' he agreed.

'But,' cried Governey, 'what has all that got to do with admiring the scenery?'

'He sang to the night,' cried Hanafan passionately. 'He sang to the whole night. The moon was up.'

His voice fell and they barely heard him over the rumbling train at the end of the platform.

'We saw the moon in the flags of the Liffey as we left the station. In the flags of the river, through the trees.'

'Still and all,' cried the small man, 'he didn't form any intellectual concept....'

The train drowned his voice and its lights flitted across their faces. When they climbed into a carriage the windows were speckled with rain and the three men inside, who leaned back to let them pass, had a cold, damp look. They had been talking when the train stopped, but when they saw the priest they fell silent; looked at him under their brows; and shyly tipped their hats.

'Raining up the line?' asked the priest in a friendly voice.

'Oh, pouring in Dublin, father,' said one of the three men – an elderly, soldierly-looking man, probably a warder in the jail at M——.

The three teachers fell silent, sensing that they had interrupted a conversation. Then they were rolling through the night, looking at the lights racing along the little hedges beside the line. Suddenly the rain that had hit Dublin half an hour before swept down on them across the mountains, slapping the windows like a bucket of water. It kept trickling and shining on the windows.

'He died there last year,' said Hanafan suddenly, looking at the trickle outside the pane.

'I once asked him,' the priest leaned forward to say to the small man, 'what his favourite song was. Do you know what he said? *Scenes that are brightest.*'

The priest leaned back and gave a merry little laugh.

'Still,' cried the small man, thumping his knee, 'I can't see what this has to do with the question we were discussing!'

The priest looked at him, and kept looking at him, as he swayed with the carriage, but he said nothing. Angrily the small man looked back, and then he looked angrily at Hanafan, whose eyes had become cranky and tormented once more. He began to wonder why Hanafan was always so sour, and why he remained on in N—— if he didn't like the place, and why he had never married. His eye lit up a bit at that and he determined to get it all out of the priest when they were next alone. He tapped Hanafan on the knee and he began to ask him some question, but when he saw that Hanafan's eyes were closed he leaned back again. The priest was still looking at him, so he nodded towards Hanafan and winked. The priest's lidded eyes were as immovable as an owl's.

As they rolled on through the bog the small man kept looking around him restlessly, and at last he shifted over to the three countrymen, determined to find out if the common people really do admire the scenery. He started a conversation about turf-cutting, but before he could lead up to the question the train halted at a small station and the strangers got out. Then the three friends were left alone in the cold, damp carriage, listening to the battering rain. Tired and sleepy, nobody noticed that, in his corner, Hanafan was weeping to himself, the drops creeping through his tightly closed eyes.

Egotists

The young sailor was making his way hiking from Galveston to 'Frisco, and the professor was motoring east, from 'Frisco, with his niece. They met at the little hamlet of Santa Rosa, in Texas, not far from the border of New Mexico.

The professor halted his car there, because although Santa Rosa is little more than a handful of shacks, and he would have to sleep in the wayside camp, there is nothing much better in the four hundred miles between Santa Fé and Fort Worth. The sailor halted there because he was tired. It was hot and sticky. The sky was bronze with clouds sparring slowly around one another, promising storm during the night. Besides, he was afraid of snakes, and he had passed three of them on the road earlier in the afternoon, and they, like the slugs at home in Ireland, were a sure sign of rain.

Down beyond the six wooden huts of the camp was a makeshift bathing-pool under a group of magnificent maple-trees, and there he heard a girl's voice shouting and laughing. It was an English voice. He went down in the dusky light and saw the girl splashing about in the muddy water, and, on the grass bank, a tall elderly man watching her. His face, beard and bald head made a perfect egg-shape. His mouth was so soft that when it was closed it did not look closed.

'Very stuffy tonight, sir,' said the sailor.

The professor looked with interest at the man who had called him 'sir,' and said:

'It is very warm.'

The sailor looked down at the girl, and in his loneliness her English voice began to dissolve his bowels.

'I'm thinking it will be a storm, sir,' he said.

'I guess it will,' agreed the professor, looking southward at the brazen sky. Just then the girl scrambled up the ladder and ran dripping across the livid grass towards the huts.

'The young lady is English?' said the sailor.

'My niece is English,' said the professor, 'but,' he added pleasantly, 'she's been all around the world. I should have thought she'd have lost some of her accent by now. Are you English?'

On the vast edge of the Texan plain, quivers of lightning waved their hands madly, to and fro, and the thunder-pig came grunting across the horizon. The flashes lit up the *mesa* and its flat top stood for a second black against the sky.

'Yes,' said the sailor, 'I've hiked up from Galveston, down on the Gulf. I landed there from Southampton.'

A drop or two began to fall, so the professor edged towards the huts, and the sailor with him.

'Galveston? Where are you aiming for?'

' 'Frisco. I have a brother there that I didn't see for twenty years. But I won't make it. I'm turning back from here. Ah, I was dumb. I didn't realize how big this country is. I must have done up to seven hundred miles. Two weeks' walking, and still in Texas!'

He looked back south over the plain where it rolled down behind a fence, farther than a man could run without resting – and yet, that was not more than a mile away.

'Ah!' he went on. 'This country is too big.'

'It's big,' said the man who owned the camp.

They saw him sitting inside the netting of his porch, smoking at his ease. He was a powerful blond, probably a Swede. He looked at them, stolid, expressionless. The sailor gave him a dollar. The professor took out his wallet.

'Are you a Texan?' asked the professor as the man began to write out a receipt for the sailor.

'No,' said the man, without looking up. 'Chicago. I was a postman there for twenty-five years.'

'Oh, my!' murmured the professor. In his gentle way he was interested, but, as his training had long since put him beyond surprise, he was only mildly curious. However, as he considered the matter, he nodded and said again, 'Oh, my!' (It was as if he had said, 'That is surprising,' and then said, 'That is an interesting fact,' the tone of voice for each 'Oh, my!' had been so entirely different.)

'But,' cried the sailor, 'Chicago is thousands of miles away. It's a big city. Full of streets and people and . . . streets, you know, and . . . people.'

The ex-postman handed him his chit and took the professor's two dollars.

'Yeah,' he said, with interest. 'I remember the streets.'

'Still!' protested the sailor. 'You must want to get back!' Then thinking of what twenty-five years meant, he said: 'Yes – I suppose it was a long time.'

It was raining now, and the rain, as always at night, seemed to be murmuring and muttering to itself as if a vast crowd had suddenly filled the world.

'Still!' protested the sailor again, and then he stopped, thinking that a postman's life was a dull one, or, perhaps, impressed by the complete certitude of the man. 'Well, I suppose so,' he said, and scratched his curly hair.

The English girl raced in, laughing at the rain. She was firm-jawed and fair-haired. Flinging back her damp hair she smiled at them all. She looked down at the camp proprietor and said to her uncle:

'What about supper, uncle?'

'Yes,' he agreed, dreamily. 'Do you know, Helen, that this man has been a postman in Chicago for twenty-five years and he's not a bit lonely here.'

'Really?' cried the girl. 'Aren't you a bit lonely after all the gaiety and the noise and the fun and the excitement?'

'Why should I?' asked the man, leaning back in his rocker and looking from one to the other of the three people standing before him.

'How long are you here?' she asked, her eyes bright and wide, her white teeth showing, her r's very faint, her question put with a typical English mixture of assurance, politeness, kindness, and insolence.

'Twelve years,' he said easily. 'How old are you and where do you come from?'

'Berkshire, in England. I'm twenty-five.'

'Is that a big town?'

'It's not a town. It's a county. I live in Abingdon.'

'Big place?'

'Not very big.'

'Well, would you like to spend the next twenty-five years of your life there, without moving out of it?'

'Perhaps not without moving out of it.'

'I said,' he insisted, 'without moving out of it. If you got the chance, at the end of twenty-five years, of changing to some little place like this – in England – wouldn't you take it?'

'I don't think so, at all,' she said with assurance. 'For one thing I should miss my relatives. Didn't you when you left Chicago?'

'Young woman,' he said, 'in twenty-five years' time you won't have any relatives.'

She was going to say something, but instead she gave a little scream as the porch was illuminated by the lightning. They all looked out in time to see the *mesa* rise up and out of the darkness, and at the same instant the rumble broke, swelled, cracked. Iron doors were opening and shutting inside the mountain.

'Besides, I have friends here,' said the postman.

The girl stared at him unbelievingly, thinking of the vast distance between her and the sea, of the dull, wide boiling stretches of Arizona, and how the road since they entered Texas had become more and more uninteresting. In the clammy heat she lifted her breasts to breathe.

Then, as if to show that he was indifferent to company, the Swede said, in the same stolid voice:

'There's a café down the village. You'll pass the padre's bungalow on the way, at the turn of the road. You ought to call on him. He'd love to see you. He's a funny little cuss.'

The professor thanked him and they went out. At the porch he invited the lone sailor-man to eat with them and the old man said, 'Sure, that's nice of you,' and they scrambled into the car. Over their cold tea, ham sandwiches, and apple-pie, the professor said:

'Do you know, Helen, this man is walking from Galveston to 'Frisco. He came from Southampton. He's English.'

'Really?' said the girl. 'How nice!'

'Well,' explained the young man, 'I'm not really English. I'm Irish. But here it doesn't mean anything to say you're Irish. So I say I'm English.'

'My goodness,' cried the girl, 'but I always heard the Irish ran America! Isn't that so, uncle?'

'East,' he agreed, 'it would mean something to be Irish. In Texas, not so much. Though there are many fine Irishmen here, too. The man who owns the hotel in Albuquerque is named Murphy. I guess that's Irish enough.' He smiled with his mouth that was not so much a mouth as a loose opening above his neat beard.

'Are you going back to Ireland?' asked the girl.

'I am, that,' said the sailor. 'And,' he said, 'I'm going there now. You see, I wanted to see my brother here – I haven't seen him for twelve years. Then, I had a kind of idea, too, that I wanted to see the Mississippi. That's why I took a boat bound for Galveston. I thought it would be near the Mississippi. Somebody said it was near New Orleans, but you can't get any idea how big this country is until you begin to feel it. So now, I'm turning back from here. And I won't see the Mississippi, and I won't see the brother. Of course, I can always say I saw Texas. But I never wanted to see Texas.'

'And are you walking back to Galveston?' she asked.

'I must get to the coast,' he explained. 'Galveston is the nearest port. Well, I have plenty of time. I'll make it in a month. This country is too damn big. I don't like it. I come from County Cork. I thought that was a big county, but look at this place. Of course, I can always say I saw Texas,' he repeated, 'but I didn't want to see Texas, I wanted to see the Mississippi. And my brother.'

'It is big,' agreed the professor.

'It *is* big,' agreed the sailor warmly. 'It's big, and there's nothing in it. There's the Mississippi, of course. But I won't see the Mississippi, now.'

He laughed and she laughed.

'Yes!' cried the sailor, drawing out the word in a warm tone of approval. 'I'm going *back*. If it takes me a year! It's all in a day's work. Only I'd have liked to see the Mississippi. You see, I have a ferry in Cork, and I take an interest in rivers.'

They finished their meal and looked out at the empty plain. It was dark night, now, and the whole place was saturated and the thunder grunted continually. Their foreheads were damp with sweat.

They went down to the padre's bungalow, then, as the camp-man had suggested. He was sitting in the dark with an old Mexican who left when they came in. He was a very small, fat, jolly little priest, very dirty, without a collar, and his shirt was brown with snuff. He looked as if he washed in oil and then rolled in dust. The room was incredibly untidy but comfortable. With his easy smile and his *pantoufled* air of complete indifference to such things as cleanliness, or order, the little man had clearly rooted himself in that place as a thistle might root itself in a ditch. He was entirely at his ease with his visitors. He greeted them as if he had known them all his life. While he lit a candle the girl asked him about Texas. As he talked of it, he laughed and sighed by turns.

'You understand,' he explained, 'I'm not a Texan. I am French. I can never go back to France, now, because I did not do my period of military training, and I did not go to the war. Even if I could, it is too far.' Then he laughed, almost with pleasure, 'I have plenty to do here. My parish is three hundred square miles. Every Sunday I say three masses in different churches. Some of my people I say mass for only once a month. Some, once in three months. I ride horseback. The roads,' he chuckled, 'aren't there at all.'

He sighed deeply then, and went on:

'I would like to be here fifty years ago. It is all too quiet now.'

'Aren't there snakes and things?' asked the girl.

'Yes, there are snakes.' The padre shook all over with delight. He flung his fat podge of a hand out to the *mesa*. 'Up there. Thousands of them. When I came home in the old days I always shook my rug before I went to bed. Then I looked under the bed. Once there was a snake coiled on the handle of the door. But there are not so many now.'

'What makes it, as you say, quiet?' asked the professor.

'I don't know,' sighed the little priest. 'No bad men nowadays. But in the good days there were many of them. In the time of Billy the Kid. He was a dreadful scoundrel,' he chuckled. 'Of course,' he added quickly, trying hard to be solemn, 'he was a ruffian. He did terrible things. His father was shot by a red-headed man, so he went about shooting every red-headed man he met. Once' – the fat hand waved to the south – 'in a saloon in Estacado, on the Llano, he met a red-headed man. When he came in, everyone got out of the way and the bartender moved the glasses. "You drink with me," said Billy. He was a boy about eighteen. "No," said the red-headed man, "I don't know you." "You drink with me," said Billy. To avoid trouble the red-headed man drinks. When his head is lifted to drink, Billy shoots him, right through the mouth. The glass stuck in the unfortunate man's palate.'

The priest smiled broadly. But then he grew sad to think those wild days were gone.

'What about Indians?' asked the girl.

'Yes,' agreed the padre, and his voice grew cold. 'I have one small *pueblo*. But they are just like children and I let them go their own ways. They have a *kiva*, for instance (you have seen the *kivas* in New Mexico?), and they have their little practices in the *kiva*. I don't know what they do. No one knows what they do. I don't mind,' he smiled benignly. 'They do all sorts of little things. They put food in the coffins when they bury their dead. They are good people. They give no trouble.'

It was clear that he had small interest in these poor, mild Indians.

'Are you a Catholic priest?' asked the sailor with sudden suspicion.

The priest laughed so long at that that they all smiled.

'What else do you think? he cried. 'And what are you? You are not an American?'

Again the sailor talked about his brother, and about the Mississippi, and Galveston, and how big the country was, and how he was turning back in the morning. He spoke sadly. All this talk about strange people and strange doings made him feel more lonely than ever and the night was oppressive and the darkness mysterious.

'An Irishman?' said the fat padre. 'It was an Irishman that shot Billy the Kid. He met him and he just shot him. A dreadful scoundrel!' he chuckled.

'My uncle,' explained the English girl, 'knows all about the other Indian people. We are both back from there. We came by San Francisco.'

The professor nodded.

'Yes,' he said in his mild voice that they could hardly hear. 'Naturally they are wiser and more cultivated than our Indians here – even in the days of Cortez.'

'Them bloody Red Injuns,' said the sailor crossly, 'are savages.

'No, no,' reproved the professor in a whisper. 'They had a very high level of civilization until we white men reduced them to savagery. The race that came from below the Gulf, wandering like that storm that is blowing now over Mexico . . .'

They all looked at the curtains blown in on the wind.

'They came up to the Great Lakes. They were, often, a noble people who believed in one God, the Father, and saw in all earthly things a manifestation of His goodness.'

The padre rose and put out the guttering candle.

'God's candles will do,' he smiled, but the room was more musty than ever, and all they could see was the little beard of the professor. The white fire kept fluttering far away. 'You have studied their religion?' asked the padre, wiping his hand on his tail, and the sweat from his forehead, and again wiping his tail.

'Yes,' said the professor. 'For many years. I was for five years in Benares and for five years in Allahabad. I wish I could live there always. Noble poetry . . . noble imagery . . . In Allahabad; where the Jumna and the Ganges join – the holiest spot in the world. You wished' – he turned to where the sailor sat, heavily and silently, in the dark – 'to see the Mississippi. Since I was a boy I wished to see the Ganges. I have gone back there again and again. But now I am old, and I do not think I shall go back again. I shall not see the great festival when the pilgrims gather from as far away as the Himalayas, into the streets of Allahabad. And in the sun, after weeks of fasting and praying, they go down to the sacred river, all white-robed, to bathe . . .'

His voice was a mere breathing and they could hear the tremble in it. They were silent. The rain was silent.

'Never mind,' comforted the little priest innocently, 'if men are good-living, I always say, it doesn't matter what they do.'

Below the maple-trees was a great noise of cicadas, rubbing their thighs in a perpetual whistling, and far away the whiplash of a whip-poor-will. The thunder-pig had gone grunting off to the west.

The girl touched her uncle's arm as if to waken him from a trance.

'We should go to the camp,' she said softly.

The padre did not rise; he just waved his hand to them like a Pope and began to take snuff.

'Back?' said the man from Chicago. 'Did you meet the padre?' The girl said 'Yes,' and he added: 'He's a funny little cuss, isn't he? But he's a grand fist at dominoes.'

The girl and her uncle were gazing at the wind in the maples.

After a while she found herself sitting on the steps of her hut, and when she looked down the line, there was the eye of the sailor's cigarette at his door, and she could hear the ex-postman rocking quietly on his porch. She sat there for a long time, occasionally lifting her whole chest to breathe more easily.

Then she got up and walked down to the young sailor's hut to ask him for a light, and she sat on the step below him and smoked. He smiled down at her and she smiled back. She made him talk about Ireland because she wanted to hear an even slightly familiar voice and speech, and she liked the rough gutturals and the way he said 'I ran' as if it was 'I wron,' and his 'sure' that was so buttery after her uncle's twangy 'sheure.' Actually what he said she hardly knew. She kept lifting her chest. Her throat was heavy and her inside moved. She rose and gave him her hand and said 'Good night.' She wanted him to put his arms around her and crush her. Then shrugging a little – as if at him, and herself – she walked back to her hut.

For a long while they all sat there in silence, three of them smoking, and the postman rocking patiently on his porch. When he stopped, there was nothing. Or nothing that human ears could hear.

Kitty the Wren

I

The first thing the French sailor noticed about Connemara was that it smelled like a hospital. That was the reek of the turf-smoke, strong as iodoform.

But other smells were mingled with that smell of the turf-smoke; and when he leaped ashore and put his hand on a sod from the stack on the pier – his fingers went into the sod and he dropped it as if it were dung – those other smells made him straighten his back as if he had been kicked. He sniffed them, the uncovered seaweed, the hot summery air from the mountain at evening, the hundred scents of the little meadows, limed by the sun. He put out his chest, shook his ear-rings until they danced. He took a deep breath. He felt suddenly that they had put a hole in his stomach. They made him want something. And what he wanted was a girl.

'Before I meet Kitty the Wren,' the sailor used to say on that afterwards, 'turf remind me of a hospital. After – a hospital remind me of turf.'

Down the pier he went, and along the boreen to the pub. Inside, there were four fishermen, but the French sailor, without hesitation, selected an old but powerfully built man who was leaning over the counter, talking to the girl of the house. He greeted the pair of them, noted with distaste that the girl had a chest as flat as the back of your hand, and stood the man a pint of porter.

'My name is Peter,' he said, grinning.

'It's a damn good name,' laughed the old man, showing his rotted teeth. 'For Peter means a rock.'

The sailor smacked his chest, threw his roundy hat into the air, and laughed so merrily that the old man took a great liking to him.

'And what is your name?' asked Peter.

'My name and surname is Jamesy McCann. But the people all

know me around these parts as Jamesy Dinny John. That,' he explained solemnly, 'is after my father, and my grandfather.'

'Aha! Jamesy Dénijon!' flattered the sailor. 'That is a magnificent name. Have a cigar!'

Then the old man and the girl began to probe the stranger, and he told them so many entertaining lies that by the time the girl had brought a third drink – all paid for by the sailor – the three of them had their arms around one another, enveloped in a fog of cigar-smoke, and the talk was where the sailor wanted it.

'Is she a good girl?' he asked Jamesy Dénijon, winking at the barmaid.

'Is it Mary Con Jo Dubh?' asked the old toper, with his lower lip out in a blister of mockery, his eyes almost lost up under his ancient hat. He leaned down over the sailor's singlet, with one eye cocked up at the girl, who listened in delight, and he said, 'Listen to me, young man. You're inquiring now about a heifer would nuzzle no kish of brogues. It isn't today nor yesterday that one's tail waggled under her mother's belly!'

And while she screamed with laughter, and hammered his old hat with a glass-cloth, he prodded his head upward in imitation of a sucking lamb. Nevertheless, when it was all over, and the old lad was still laughing and sucking his cigar, the sailor persisted.

'But are you a good girl?' he asked her.

'I'd be very bad, now, then' (she tossed her head and flicked his cheek lightly with the cloth), 'if I'm not half as good as whoever you left behind where you last drew anchor.'

He could not catch that, so he tried to chuck her under the chin, and as she stalked away haughtily he cried out after her:

'And, my little one, if you are so good as all that, then I waste the beginning of a good night with you!'

That sealed the friendship between himself and Jamesy, who roared fit to burst, and slapped the counter, and took another pint.

'Jamesy,' sighed the sailor, coming to the point, 'when a man is on the sea he has no wife.'

'The divil a wife, by Jawsus!' croaked Jamesy at the top of his palate, 'but you're betther off not to be breaking your melt keeping time with them.'

'Jamesy,' coaxed the sailor, after as much polite laughter as he could manage for a joke of which he understood not a word, 'I have a feeling' – putting his lean hand on his stomach – 'that I want my arms to be around a girl.'

'A bad disorder,' commiserated Jamesy, 'but,' looking forward to a grand night of porter, 'we have the right way here to drown it.'

'Jamesy,' appealed the sailor, in exasperation, putting his two hands on his stomach, 'I am certain that many a time you have squeezed a girl under a bush.'

'The divils of hell hoist ye,' roared Jamesy in a rage that eddied at once into high good-humour. 'But maybe I did. I wouldn't say I didn't. I'd say again' it for no man. But, Pether, my lad, my son, my poor boy! There's no Kitty the Wrens in this part of the world.'

The sailor cocked his ear.

'Kitty the Wren? That is a nice girl? Where is she? Why is that her name? Tell me, quickly.'

'Aye!' nodded Jamesy wisely. 'You could hould her in your fist, she's that small. But,' daintily holding the cigar, whose end was by now a bog, horizontally under the sailor's eyes, he began to recite,

' "On Saint Stephenses day
She was caught in the furze,
Although she be little,
Her family's great . . ."

That is, if all we hear is true!' With a mighty wink. 'And as tidy, and as nate as a bullfinch, so she is. And living all alone where you wouldn't hear a sound but the stones falling on the mountain.'

'Jamesy,' whispered the sailor, 'where does she live?'

'Away behind Croghan.' Jamesy nodded his hat across the estuary that was already dark as a field. 'Twelve miles away. Behind in the hills.'

It took a great deal of whispering before the sailor found out all he wished to know. When he left the pub he left Jamesy staring down into his glass, whose froth and lees might have been an image of his youth – so deeply did the old man sigh as he stared into them.

2

The French sailor had a bicycle – he had borrowed it from one Jamesy Dinny John in Croghanbeag – and for two hours now he had been cycling over the mountain road. At first he sang. But as the glen grew dark, and the clouds gleaned the light of day, he grew silent. All he could hear was a sheep far up the valley. Still he went on, bumping and swaying. He crossed a railway, so covered with weeds and rust that it looked as if it had not been used for fifty years, and entered another valley. There he got tired of being bumped and walked for miles. Still the last cabin seemed hours ago, and still no sign of the grey rock by the mountain lake, that, so Jamesy said, was 'as near the house as if it fell out of the window.' Instead, he saw nothing around him, or before him, but grey rocks, and grey grass, and bog-pools the colour of porter. He rode on again, trying to avoid the slabs of outcrop, until the light grew so dim that he kept jagging into them. All he could see was black Croghan to his left. All he could hear was a lake clapping the stones, muttering to its froth.

There he met her, driving two spancelled goats whose beards almost touched the ground, and whose hair hung down like sails. He fell off his bicycle, flung it heartily into the ditch, cried out a *Hello!* and tried to see her face.

She was a slight creature, with handsome dark eyes – the only noticeable thing in her face – about forty, very shy but friendly. Her yellow hair thrust out about her in a bush. She walked with a slouch that reminded him of a little dinghy plunging in a fluking sea. He was greatly attracted by that gait of hers, and in anticipation of the fun before him he forgot the glen, the night, the distance from his ship.

'Kitty?' he said.

'Good night, sir,' she said, and she seemed to blush.

'I came to see you,' he smiled.

'To see me, sir? And what is your name, if you please?'

'My name is Peter. Your name is Kitty? I bring you a little present.'

He drew a parcel from his hip-pocket and held it out. She looked at it and at him. She hesitated, with many glancings all over him. At last she said: 'What is the message?'

'It is Jamesy Dénijon. He say to me – "Kitty is a nice girl. If you are lonely, talk to Kitty." '

Even in the dark her face went sullen, as if a cloud had slipped over a moon. Her head drooped away. Suddenly she cried out to the goats and slouched away after them.

'Kitty!' cried the French sailor, hastening after her. 'I am a poor sailor. I am a long time on the ocean. I have traversed the whole mountain, all the long way, to see you!'

She had seemed to him to be childish, undeveloped, in spite of her years, immature; he had thoughts she would be easy game because of that sluttish gait of hers. Quickly, now, he felt the fo'c'sle stove might be all he would have in the heel of the night. She paused on one leg.

'They're making a hare of you in Croghanbeag,' she muttered. 'So go back with yourself. The night is falling.'

A wind came rushing across the lake, bringing a mist out of the dark against his face. He saw her move away. In his mind's eye he saw rain over the mountains, and Jamesy Dénijon laughing loud at him.... He threw out his hands before her.

'Twelve miles! You say "Go back." I come over the hills and the valleys. All on an accursed road. On an accursed bicycle. Blessed Virgin! I cannot do it. I am tired out. Oh, my little one, please, I beg you, let me rest a while.'

She looked at him, weakening.

'Let me sit by your fire for a while,' he begged. 'For a little time. All I ask is to rest and talk with you for a little time.' He smiled his best smile, and finished – 'Then I go.'

'All right,' she yielded. 'But then,' she warned sternly, raising one finger, 'you take your road on yourself, sure and certain.'

'Of course!' he assured her. 'What else?'

3

They were sitting by the fire, each holding a cup of goat's milk. She had no tea, she said with a blush. She sat with her knees spread like a man, and held her cup like a man in her fist, and she leaned her elbow on her knee like a man. She pleased him just because she was so like a man, though afterwards he thought she did everything like that merely because her brothers and her father did it in that way.

He coaxed her, casting his line gently lest he should as much as ruffle the quiet moment.

'I'm sure you're never lonely here,' he said.

'Why do you say that?'

'I'm sure you're never lonely. You must have lots of fine lads calling in to give you the time of day.'

She sipped her milk and looked at the glowing turf.

'And living all alone,' he said, drawing out the words seductively.

'Tell me,' she said, 'what things do they be saying about me in Croghanbeag?'

'They say,' the sailor leaned eagerly towards her, 'that you are a fine girl, a lovely girl, warm as a thrush, and that you live alone. That is all. And it is all true.'

'Aren't they the bitter people in Croghanbeag!' she mused. 'And it isn't all true, nor half of it.' Her mournful glance held him. 'I don't live alone.'

He looked over his shoulder to where the firelight edged a few bits of delph on some kind of shapeless dresser. His straw-rope chair creaked as if the angry hand rattling the door from across the lake had shaken the whole cabin. The wind died down.

'But what matter?' she sighed.

In the silence there came from the room, beyond the darkness, a little wail. Hugging her elbow to support her cup-hand she was looking at the stranger with curiosity, forgetting her shyness. She was examining with her eyes his curious dress – the blouse, the round cap, the blue trousers, the canvas shoes.

'That's my brother,' she said. 'He does be here always. He goes out when the wind changes. Then I stay awake the whole night although I go to bed.'

'Where does he go to?' whispered the sailor.

'He goes down to the school. It do be shut, of course; but he has a wish to be there. I always find him there, in the morning, sitting by the wall.'

'Is he . . . is he not well?' whispered the sailor.

'God help us, he's not himself these ten years.' Suddenly she leaned forward to his blouse and began to finger it with pleasure. 'That's a queer yoke of a jacket you have. Where did you get it?'

He wanted to go away. He spoke shortly, not caring if she understood. 'Marseilles.'

'I'd like a blouse of that stuff. Why do you wear them things? – pointing to his ear-rings. 'Show me.'

He took one off and put it in her palm. She turned it over and over, and looking at it forgot him. As she did so, he looked into the heel of the kitchen. She laughed, and it frightened him. She was wagging her head to feel the ear-ring against her cheek.

'Give me the other,' she smiled.

She put that on, too, and because she had no mirror in the house he took out his little pocket-mirror and she looked at herself in it, and kept looking at it, and putting it down, and taking it up.

'You like pretty things?' he said. 'To wear in the village.'

'I never leave the glen.'

'You go to the village?'

'No.'

'But you go there sometimes?'

'No.'

'But for food – you must, sometimes.'

'The brother do go, when he's any way well. Sure, what would we want? There's always the goat's milk and the bit of flour. Times, there doesn't be any flour. But what matter? God is good.'

'Still,' insisted the sailor, 'sometimes you go?' And when she could no longer turn aside his whys and why-nots, she said she had no boots. The sailor's eye fell on a crucifix on the wall, and he said:

'You go to the Holy Mass?'

'I don't.' She hung her head over the mirror. 'And sure a person might as well be an animal if they don't go to Mass. But you're a Protestant, I suppose?'

'I am not. I am a Catholic.'

'You're a liar.'

'But I am a Catholic,' he protested, and, for the first time, saw something like fear creep into her eyes.

'But you couldn't be!' she cried.

'But I am,' he said.

'You came here,' she muttered, 'tonight, with bad things in your head.' He waved his hands at that.

'It's no harm,' he tried, with a last flicker of playfulness, 'to come to see a nice girl.'

As if it climbed up from the bottom of her mind the answer took a long time to come.

'It's no good thing people learn in foreign countries.' Again she delved and said, solemnly, 'It's a mortal sin.'

Thereupon she gave him back the mirror and the rings, one by one. To return the mirror to his pocket he had to take out a folded paper story-book he had been reading. She put out her hand for it.

'I do read too,' she said. 'But I have only one book.'

Leaning forward under the tarred, soot-caked log that was the chimney-tree, she drew, from a clevvy in the wall, a book with black shamrocks printed all over the green cover. It was a school-reader with her name inside, in childish handwriting.

> Kitty Canavan,
> Carrigadoura National School,
> Lochawnaphooka,
> Connemara.

'I read that often to myself.' She took the book from him and turning the pages began to chant in a high monotone, with rests after each group of words, just as if she were reciting it in the classroom. ' "The rhineoycayros – is a wild bashte – he would ate – a human being – he is the largest – and the strongest – of all the bashtes – that inhabit the earth." '

'If I ever come back to Ireland, Kitty,' murmured the French sailor, 'I will bring you books to read.'

'Oh, God, do!' she cried. 'Books with pictures.'

'Yes,' promised the sailor, wishing he had all the books in the world to give her at that moment.

'I forgot,' he said, then, bringing out again the little parcel she had refused earlier, 'It is for you.'

She unfolded the paper. It was a pair of slippers, so soft as to be quite useless to her – living as she did. They had furry edges and a design on the instep. Her face grew transparent with delight as she held them in her hands.

'Try them on,' whispered the sailor.

Biting her lip as if she was afraid to speak, she put her foot into the slipper. She arched her foot, and moved it this way and that, and admired it, so utterly a child, that the French sailor leaped up, dug his two fists into his hair, then shook them up to the roof, and sitting down, groaned into his palms.

'Kitty,' he cried, taking her knee, 'I come tomorrow, and I bring you shoes. I bring you clothes. That is Saturday. I bring you all the bloody shoes in Croghanbeag. Then, on Sunday, you go to Mass! It is settled? Yes, it is settled!'

And, after a little while of arguing, it was settled. He said good-bye, kissed her hand and ran out of the door. As he ran, the wail from the room came to him, the wail as of a sick man, and the wind sighed a little when he opened the door, as if it had intended to roar but remained to watch. Indeed, when he had closed the door and was becoming accustomed to the dark, the mountain seemed to be leaning forward over him, and the white mouth of the lake whispering up to him from the shore.

He opened the door again to give her the mirror. She was standing with her dress over her bare knees, gazing at the slippers on her feet. She laughed out.

'I'm looking at them.'

He gave her the mirror, and looked at her and looked at her, and even then he wondered could he coax her, but he knew that all he wanted, now, was to kiss her and hear her laugh. He banged the door and raced down the boreen, where he groped for his bicycle, and rode the twenty miles back to his ship, torn by emotions as dark and twisting as the wind.

It was the first dawn before the bog-myrtle gave way to the old stink of the sea. The clouds were blue-black over the hills.

4

In the afternoon of the Saturday he went to the pub; but as soon as he mentioned the name of Kitty Canavan the barmaid's lanky face grew as cold as the rain spattering the windows.

'Who was blathering to you about Kitty the Wren?' she asked sharply.

'It was Jamesy Dénijon. But I think he told me a lot of lies.'

' 'Twouldn't be much harder for him than to tell the truth.'

'Where does this girl live?' he asked.

'Away back in the hills.'

'With her father and mother?'

'Her father is dead. He wasn't right when he died.'

'Does she never come to the village now?'

'I never saw her. Is there anything you want?' She let her eyes rove over the shelves.

From her he went down to the shop, where he bought three red handkerchiefs that he didn't want. There, beginning to learn the ways of the country, he tacked against the wind towards his question. Yet, even at that, the man's face grew into a knot when her name was spoken.

'Aye!' he said, as if he grudged having to admit that she as much as existed. 'There is such a family.'

'Are they well off?' asked the sailor.

'They were one time,' admitted the man, and stopped dead.

Then, as if in a sudden gush of confidence, he leaned forward with a great show of secrecy.

'There was a class of a dispute about land. And then . . .'

He touched his forehead, and winked, and said no more.

'But this girl? Is she not . . . what do they say here?' – and the sailor fluttered his fingers towards his forehead.

The man beckoned and whispered around the corner of the sailor's ear.

'She's sound enough in the head. But she got into trouble, thereabout ten years ago. There was a child. One of the lads from around this place it was, as a matter of fact. He ran to America. 'Twas then her father, poor man, went wild. He drank himself into a fury and he was missing for three days. They found the body, God help him, in a bog-hole. Ah,' cried the man, reverting to his work at the counter, 'not a nice business at all, no, not nice at all, at all. Women like that,' he muttered, 'should be hunted out of the country.'

A dark wind from Kitty's night-valley might have crept over the sailor, he shivered so violently. He saw he would get no more from this man, so he left him in search of Jamesy Dénijon. But when the old toper saw him he turned away up the road, was lost behind a thorn hedge, and the sailor never saw him thereafter. From that the sailor went, idly, towards the little whitewashed chapel on the hill, and sat there smoking under the lee of the wall, looking out moodily. The hairy clouds brushed the sea with rain until it seemed covered with dust. He cursed aloud.

There the old priest came on him, and they talked for a while, and the old man was so kind and genial that the sailor burst out with:

'Father, do you know a girl called Kitty Canavan?'

The sailor thought he would say, 'Yes, what about her?' Instead the priest stroked his nose with his finger and thumb, and said, slowly:

'Tell me. What do you know about Kitty Canavan?'

The sailor talked so fast that the old priest lifted a fin of a hand.

'One moment. What I want to know is, did you ever meet Kitty Canavan?'

'Yes, I did,' said the sailor. 'I went out to her last night.'

'Why?' asked the priest, and the look that came whenever her name was mentioned darkened his face.

'Because,' cried the sailor with bravado, 'I wanted a woman. But I got nothing for my journey except a sore behind. She said it was a mortal sin.'

The old priest grunted between derision and satisfaction, and looked long at the sailor.

'Tell me, young man,' he said, 'how long is your boat going to be in Croghanbeag?'

'Until the high tide tomorrow morning.'

'And tell me this. What do you propose to do with yourself tonight?'

'I had thought that I would take her a pair of shoes so that she could come to Holy Mass. But – '

'Yes?'

'I think I will get drunk instead.'

There was a long pause.

'I see. Tell me, my child. How drunk do you get when you get drunk?'

The sailor flew into a rage and waved his fist under the priest's nose.

'I get so drunk that I cannot stand,' he shouted. 'I become a dead pig.'

'I see.' Then, patting the young man's shoulder, the priest said, 'You could do worse.'

'But,' shouted the sailor, as the old man began to move away, 'what about Kitty the Wren?'

Half turning, the old priest took the sailor by the arm. He spoke so gently and earnestly that the sailor was impressed.

'Are you a Catholic, my child?'

The sailor shrugged his shoulders and said, 'Yes.'

'Have you talked at all to the people hereabouts – I mean talked about this girl?'

The sailor shrugged again, eloquently.

'My child, I am her priest. Regularly, once a year, I visit this girl. I go to her for my dues – I don't want them – they are a shilling or at most two – but I take them from her. I go every May Day, and she is expecting me, and she is fasting, and I hear her confession, and I give her Holy Communion. I cannot tell you what she confesses to me, but, young man, if you had as little to confess as Kitty the Wren it would be well for you. Yet never once have I asked that girl to come here to Mass, and never once has she asked me about it. The poor girl will never enter this village again.' The old priest looked at the mottled stones of the graveyard as he added: 'And 'tis better that way.'

'She told me,' grumbled the sailor, 'that there is nothing on earth she would like better than to come to Mass.'

'No doubt,' sighed the old priest, as he looked away over the sea. 'But it's the least part of her punishment. Leave her, my child,' he patted, 'to her solitude. It's a lonely glen, but it can be lovely. God, my child, deals with His little creatures in His own way – a more kindly way than our way. Take her from where she is, and . . .'

His eyes roved to the handful of houses that made up Croghanbeag. Then they grew bright and a wickedly merry glint appeared in them.

'My child, if you get tired of Flaherty's liquor, come up to me. We'll make a night of it.'

Tottering, he went away, while the sailor leaned over the stone wall and waited until the mist that was making Croghan invisible damped him. Then he cursed, dreadfully, Jamesy, and the priest, and the barmaid, and Connemara, and he tried to understand why the priest should be so lenient with him and so stern with Kitty, and he ended by cursing the whole of Ireland, lock, stock and barrel, and he went down to the pub, where he drank himself into the darkness of the night – the worst bout of drinking ever seen in Croghanbeag; so that, afterwards, they would say of a man 'he was as drunk as the French sailor.'

He woke when the people were crowding down the hill from Mass on Sunday morning, their faces shining and their clothes as black as the gale that was howling up from the north. The tide was soon at the full. A rain-squall, in the afternoon, veered the wind to the west, and they sailed on it. He sat at the tiller until the sunset was holding up its five fingers to the clouds, and then he went below.

When he looked out again they were veering towards land, but he could see nothing, for dusk, but the water clapping against the prow and a few faint pricks of light along the coast. They came nearer and nearer until they could smell the peat-smoke, and they finally moored in a little harbour that might have been a smaller Croghanbeag. After the supper the sailor sat before the stove crumbling a lump of turf between his hands. The captain joked him, but his replies were growled.

'*Tu vas t'amuser ce soir? Une bonne petite femme?*'

'*Ca n'existe pas dans ce pays.*'

'*Tiens, tiens. Tu le crois?*'

The sailor tore the turf to pieces, and said:

'*Non. 'Ny a pas des filles en Irelande. Mais les hommes. . . . Ce sont des crevasses, des moules, des . . .*'

' '*Ta gueule!*' roared the captain at the filthy words.

With any angry look he beckoned the third man of the crew. They went ashore and left him by the stove, still grinding the little bit of turf into tiny fragments. When they came back, he was lying asleep in his bunk, his face as gentle, his lips as soft as a child's.

My Son Austin

I suppose very few people here now remember poor Father Tom Owens. He left the priesthood in or around 1921, when the Troubles in Ireland were at their height. He told the Bishop he was suffering from nerves and must go away for a rest, and the Bishop, like a decent old skin, gave him twenty quid and told him to go off to London for a month. The truth of the matter was that Father Tom's mother died just about that time. Right enough, he suffered from nerves too, though not so much on account of the shootings and the ambushes and the rest of it as because, simply, he had known for years that he was a square peg in a round hole. He told me himself when I met him in London that his mother had made him become a priest; so that, when she died, he felt it was now or never. He said goodbye to the Bishop – he did not tell His Lordship what he was going to do – and he set out for London, intending never to return. He had about six months of freedom, and then, one morning, he was found dead in bed from heart disease.

All that is another story – the devices he employed to get a lounge-suit; the fibs he told his tailor; how he never did destroy his black trousseau; the time it took him to knot his tie every morning; the way he worried about his investments; above all, the extraordinary ideas he had about women – terrified out of his wits of them. I mention him only because it was from him, and in London, that I gathered the truth about Dinny Fagan and his son Austin.

I had called one morning on Father Tom . . . I must mention that I never could get used to calling him plain Tom. I had known him as Father Tom ever since I was a child, when I used to imitate his earnest, lugubrious, up-and-down way of saying the prayers, running clean up the scale until he spoke with the intake of his breath, and then down the scale again to take in more breath at the very bottom. It had a great effect of piety and impressed every parish he went to.

C.S.S.O.—H

I had called on Father Tom, then, in his flat on Primrose Hill one morning in June, just as the postman on his second rounds left the house. He greeted me, finished reading the letter, stuck it into his pocket, filled me out two jorums of Irish, and at once began to fiddle nervously with his glass. It was about eleven o'clock in the morning, and the wireless was braying out its music from some wretched cinema organ in Shepherd's Bush. Down the hill a delivery van was jolting quietly from door to door, and the clank of milk-bottles told us that the dairyman was still on his rounds: from time to time we heard his cuckoo cry of Mi-ULK . . . Mi-ULK. Whenever the cinema organ paused, the hum of London rose from the distance like a dust.

'You mentioned ould Dinny Fagan the other night,' said Father Tom suddenly.

'That's right. You said you didn't know much about him.'

'A priest,' said Tom – *Father* Tom (I can't help it!) – 'knows everything. And he knows nothing. I have a letter in my pocket, now, that refers to him. You know,' he went on, nervously, 'I was never quite easy in my conscience about that family. I know I did my best for them. But . . .'

While he shook his head and looked out at the sun on the limes I saw old Dinny Fagan. He was just another like Crainquebille, in that lovely story of Anatole France, only, being Irish and Catholic and reared in Kerry in the Black Forties, he was ten times more stupid, and gentle, and shy. When I knew him he was already old, barely able to run his rounds for a city butcher. Under each arm he would have a lump of meat wrapped up in newspaper (which he would sometimes pause to read, lifting the leg of mutton close to his nose). I used to see him, too, every Monday night toddling down the nave at the Holy Family Confraternity, his phiz screwed into a rictus from peering, his face as scrubbed as a butcher's block on a Saturday night, and his fingers trying to unfold his red ribbon and leaden medal from the bit of brown paper in which he kept it clean from week to week. It was, I used to think, the widest, brightest, cleanest ribbon in the church. Sometimes Father Tom, who conducted the Confraternity in his easy, lazy way (reading us, maybe, a bit of Dickens instead of a sermon, and keeping us together more by the way he roared out the hymns and banged his breviary on the pulpit cushion, than by good advice), would stop the old man in his toddling haste and in his hearty way greet him loudly as the oldest member of the Confraternity. But Dinny would look up at him, in fright, and go red, and hurry on, as if he were afraid even of his priest.

'You remember,' Father Tom interrupted me suddenly, 'how he used to come to the Holy Family Confraternity? Well, now, there's a case in point. Would you believe it, I used to hate to see him there? I knew, too well, the kind of family life he had in Harper's Lane. Eight of them living in two rooms – Dinny and his son Austin, and his son Bill, and his daughter-in-law, Bill's wife, and their four children. What with Bill drinking, and the wife drinking, and the pair of them nagging at him, and even beating him, it's no exaggeration to say that the old chap lived the life of the damned in that house from the time his own wife died. And – Godfathers! – the dirt of the place. . . . The only years of peace he had were the last few years of his life, when his son Austin took him away from it all over to the North side of the city. Did you ever talk to Dinny?'

I nodded, and said, 'A few times.'

'Then you know all about him. Because, apart from that home of his, which he was always – poor fellow – trying to keep secret, there was little enough to know. I used to often stop him in the street for a chat, and I'd mention the weather, or politics, or something that happened in Dublin or London, a murder or a procession or something big like the coronation. And he'd know about them, all right, too . . . he'd know they happened, anyway. But he'd mention every single thing, Dublin or Timbuctoo, king or criminal, in exactly the same tone of voice. I don't really believe that he was quite convinced that they existed. You know the feeling you get when you read about witchcraft in the Balkans? That, I imagine, is the way Dinny felt about everything outside his native Cork.

'But . . . if you mentioned his son Austin! The eyes would stop peering, and the voice was as soft as a hand laid on the head. He'd say "My son Austin" the way a man would mention his birthplace. You'd have to listen, then, to all the books on history that Austin had at home in the lane, the maps of old Cork that had been copied from books in the Free Library, the plaster model of the old city, painted "*by hand*," the modellings of flowers and designs, and all the rest of it – for Austin, you know, was a very fine modeller. Dinny would tell you things that never appeared in any books; and never would – some of them; and always it was "So my son Austin tells me," until you could never be sure whether what you heard came from the mind of the son or the mind of the father.

'He'd say, shifting the leg of mutton (God forgive me, I often thought of the dinners we delayed with our old gossiping):

' "Did you ever know, father, that this street, here, Paul Street, has a river flowing underneath it? D'chever know that before? It was a quay, long ago, d'chesee? Ships from all parts of the world used to come up to it. Oh, it was the most famous river in history. And, since by, look!"

'He'd shift the lump of meat to the other arm, then, and begin to list on his fingers.

' "Look, father. Look at all the tradesmen that are in it! There's a cork-maker. There's a frame-maker. There's a boot-maker. A basket-weaver. A tinsmith. A statue-maker, a cabinet-maker, and a wood-carver! And around the corner, there's a farrier . . . and a man makin' vinegar. And," suddenly remembering in huge delight, "bejimininy, there's ould Carey the cooper!"

'And mind you, those tradesmen were there, just as he said, and I had never noticed them for all my years in the parish. Another time he stopped me, and he said without preamble –

' "Father, do you know who was a great man? Aristotle."

' "He was, indeed, Dinny," says I.

' "Do you know who was another great man, father? Plato."

' "So he was, Dinny."

' "Ah, a great man," sighed Dinny. "And my son Austin tells me he's up in the Cork Madhouse, now."

'Another time:

' "Father, I suppose you do be reading a lot at night? I wonder now, could you tell me where I'd get a good lamp cheap. That son of mine is a terror for the books."

'I knew,' added Father Tom, here, 'what books Austin was reading. A priest, as I say, knows everything. Lessing's *Laocoön*, Renan's *Life of Jesus*, the atheistical one. Books from the Rationalist Press, Bob Ingersoll, and such-like.

' "He's a terror for the books," says Dinny, "and the poor boy do be complaining how he can't come out to the Confraternity with me on account of all the study he wants to do. For my son Austin isn't going to be a common plasterer all his life, father."

'And then,' sighed Father Tom, again nervously turning his glass round and round, 'the last touch to the story – the old chap would appear about twice a year with his face all cut and his eye a deep purple. Always he made up some lie about it (and I suppose he'd confess the lie after to me in confession) concealing that foul home-life, the termagant daughter-in-law, the boozing eldest son – concealing what we all knew. Ah, dear! Ah, dear!' said Father Tom. 'And worse later on, when he got too old for the butcher and he was bringing no money at all into the house. Yes,' he sighed, 'yes . . .'

I could see that, to him, that old man babbling out his innocent lies was not merely the contents of one life, but the contents of all human life – a tiny purse of it, with all the coins there, well rubbed, much treasured. And I knew that even if I rebelled for Father Tom, supposed this old babbler a youth, a courtship, a love-making, something more than he seemed ever to have had, it wouldn't make a scrap of difference; because I never could have supposed the old man enough ambition to make either youth, or courtship, an act of his own will, something grabbed by him from life to add to – *to what?*

'Well,' I said, 'that's one subject, anyway, that you seem to know everything about.'

Again he let the sun on the limes outside mesmerize him, staring at them with those fine, sad eyes of his that, once upon a time, made him such a popular priest with the women and children.

'Yes!' he said. 'But take that son Austin! There was a fellow no one ever fathomed! I always said Dinny was a saint. I say, now – though you might think it a strange thing to say – that Austin Fagan was a bit of a saint, too, in his own queer way.'

The mild eyes grew very troubled as he said this, and he had the bothered air of a man who, in acknowledging that there are more worlds than one, acknowledges also that he can never decide which one of them he will choose for himself. Suddenly his eyes cleared as he went on, smiling:

'One good thing that young man did, anyway, for which I'll always be thankful to him – he married Lily Long. In fact, the night we heard it, there were five of us in the presbytery, and we opened a bottle of sherry and the five of us drank his health. For Miss Long, not to put a tooth in it, was the loose lady of the parish, and for years she had us crucified running after her. And we weren't the only ones who celebrated. The night he proposed to her in public – yes, in public! – became a legend in the lane, and I suppose it's still a stock story in the parish.

'I knew it was coming, because Dinny had me worried about it for weeks beforehand. When I'd see him coming along the street, at his snail-pace, and his face . . .'

Father Tom threw up his hand.

'I used to try my best to comfort him; and had he only foreseen it, it was the best thing ever happened to him; but they had the life pestered out of him down in Kelleher's pub. They'd say . . . A priest knows everything,' winked Father Tom. 'They'd say, "Well, Dinny, that's a fine hoult of a daughter-in-law you're going to have, aw?" Or, "Have she him hooked yet, Dinny-boy; have she him clammed?" '

(Tom was excellent at the sing-song, slender, Cork accent, and he trolled it with delight. He must have been a grand priest for the lanes.)

'Or they'd say: "Have she him out tonight, Dinny-boy? A good night for the larks in the fields, aw, Dinny?" And poor Dinny, what between not knowing the half of what they were hinting, and not daring to ask, and not knowing where to turn for comfort, and being afraid to go home to the other termagant, would come wandering round to me, his heart as heavy as lead. So he was, one evening, when the three met in the lane. It was a grand summer's evening and I was stuck inside on duty listening to the kids howling around the streets . . .'

The eyes were lost, once more. In their pupils, Cork . . . the slender finger of Shandon, plumb against the clouds, rising across the river, exactly in the centre of the canyon lane . . . Dusty streets . . . The old crones and the young girls sitting in their doorways on each side of the passage-way; the girls with their flaxen hair caught into a wave at the nook of the neck by their shawls . . .

'The old man saw the two of them coming along the lane, arm-in-arm. And he began to cry.

' "What's wrong with you, now, da?" says Austin.

'The old man said nothing, only looking down at the ground.

' "Is there somebody tormenting you?" asks the son.

'Still, Dinny couldn't get a word out of himself.

' "Speak up, da!" says Austin.

('My spies told it well,' said Father Tom. ' "At that moment, father dear, didn't Shandon strike the hour and the dead-bell in the chapel begin to toll?")

' "Austin," says Dinny at last. "Who's the girl?"

' "Is it Lily?" says Austin. He was a queer, mocking, cheek-sucking kind of fellow. "Lily is my girl," says he. "She's going to marry me. Aren't you, Lily?"

(' "Father dear, it was the queerest proposal you ever heard. And, father dear, sure if we all begin to laugh, who'd blame us?")

' "Ooh, Austin!" says Dinny. "Not marry!"

' "Come on up home, da," orders the young fellow, at that, "and we'll talk it over."

(' "And when we made for to follow them, father dear, what does he do but turn on us with a look that'd skin you, and says he, as if he was God Almighty – This is our affair, says he, and we intend, says he, to discuss it in private.")

'You know,' chuckled Father Tom, now thoroughly enjoying the story, 'it was like a scene in the French Revolution. There was I, up in the presbytery, and the gossips running in with despatches every five minutes. "Oh, fader, dere'll be holy war in deh lane tonight." And, "Fader, Bill Fagan and deh wife is paralatic." And then, "Fader, he's clammed, he's done, she have him, fader, there's not a winda in the lane but have three heads in it. Fader, fader, poor Dinny is out of his mind – dey're inside in deh house this last two hours and dere's ructions going on with Bill and the missus."

'It was four o'clock in the morning before I was finally called out. There was Dinny, stretched out inside in the house, and he was, indeed, *paralatic*. Everyone was gone home, by then, except Austin and his future wife – a shy, soft, foolish sort of a girl. I gathered that not only was Dinny persuaded into agreeing to the marriage – and agreeing was a good word with a fellow like Austin Fagan who'd have had his will of Satan – but *delighted* with it! For Austin had money saved, and was going to start as a builder himself, and he was willing to take his father with him to a new house. At that point his brother and sister-in-law had raised the ructions; the Guards had been called in; they all, apparently, went down to Kelleher's until Kelleher threw them out at closing-time, and then they took a half-tierce into a stable, and made a night of it.

'What between the excitement and the drinking it was all too much for Dinny, and I was very much afraid it might well be his last night on earth.

'It was the most extraordinary scene I ever saw. There in that room, while I anointed him. The dawn all blue and white, and the blessed candles were lighting, and the girl stood like a beautiful madonna looking out the dirty window at the sky. Austin sat in a corner, reading a book, and by the way he glared at the page, and his two cheeks meeting inside his mouth, I could see he wasn't reading a word of it. I spoke in a whisper, when I spoke at all, for the rest of the Fagans were snoring next door and there wasn't a cackle in the lane. When I went away it was about five in the morning, and there wasn't a window lit but theirs.

'A month later Austin married the girl, and there was very nearly a scandal about that too, because the fellow actually wanted to marry her in a Registry Office . . .'

Father Tom was so cross at the bare memory of it that I had to smile. He saw me and grew red. He waved his hands. I stopped him by patting his knee and saying:

'I'm only teasing you. Go on.'

'You can see, of course,' he expostulated, 'what a scandal it would be for these poor people. In the end I married them myself, and when they were in the sacristy signing the book, Austin says, very sarcastically, "Well, I suppose you expect the usual twenty pounds for this?" "I want nothing whatever," said I, "only to see the pair of you happy. But I think you should pay ten shillings, anyway, to the parish." He looked at me very hard – and he gave me three quid. It was the decent streak in him breaking out in spite of himself. He took his father with him, then, up to the North side of the city, and the old man was in the seventh heaven.

'They had a nice little house, with a yard where Austin put his building materials. Lily turned out quite well – at first, at any rate, when I visited them – and there was Dinny, inside in the spotless little kitchen, sitting beside the fire, gazing into the bars, one palm on his knee rubbing it round and round, and the old cat, inside the fender, washing its puss. One little thing only troubled him. He was too far from the centre parish ever to come to the Confraternity. And also he used to sometimes miss the little things that had meant much to him in the lane – a hole-in-the-wall where he bought his baccy and had a little chat, or the fishermen tarring their nets who'd give him the time of day, and so on and so forth.

'But he wouldn't go back! Many times the other son and his wife invited him – for they felt the disgrace of his being away from them, and once he actually did go there for a week; he left it after two nights, old and infirm as he was, with the drum of his ear broken. After that, so I was told later, he would wake the house, crying out like a little pup, thinking he was shouting: "Don't hit me! Don't hit me!" Austin would have to come in to him and shake him out of the nightmare and he would sink back then breathing relief.

'The years went by. Two, three, four . . . I forgot all about them, and then, suddenly, a message came to me from one of the priests on the North side to come up and do something with the Fagan household, for the sake of the children and the sake of the parish. I went up, and I called into the house on my way, and though there wasn't any great difference there – except that now there were four children, and it's not so easy to keep a house tidy with four small things crawling around it – I very quickly sensed that there was something wrong.

'There was Dinny, sitting by the fire, the hand rubbing the knee as always, but though I could see he was dying to say something to me he never let out a word. I talked, then, to the wife, and at once she began to defend herself . . . It is hard to blame girls of that type. She was a warm-blooded piece, and she liked her bit of gaiety, and on the other side her only anchor was the Church and the priest – and Austin, he derided the Church. Then, too, the building was not going too well. Austin considered himself too good for it, and if a city contractor asked him to come down and do a bit of modelling for him, an acanthus leaf or a trellis of vine-shoots for some wine-merchant's shop, he would drop whatever bit of plastering he had on hand and race away at once. The result is that here and there all over Cork you can still see examples of his work on other men's houses, and not a building, not even a slum cottage, built by himself. As for the children, he simply said two of them weren't his, and he paid no attention to them, and he was never at home any night before twelve or one o'clock. He used to go to the School of Art every night to draw from the model. Nobody there, except one other student, seemed to know him well. That other student was a clever young draughtsman with a queer, twitching, sensitive face.

I remember he had a magnificent profile. They called him The Knight of the Rueful Countenance. Those two used to go home together, and at the bridge they would halt, wet or fine, and stand for hours plastered into the parapet. Once, coming back from a sick-call at two o'clock on a February morning, I passed over the bridge, and there were the two of them, hunched against the wind and rain, talking, their fists in one another's faces. I asked The Knight, after, what on earth the dispute was about.

' "Ha!" he laughed, and he smote his forehead, and his face twitched all over, "the old dispute. Adams or Franchini. We were studying the Georgian stucco-work in the big houses of Cork and Dublin, and it was the 1740's against the 1790's all over again. Fagan is very good on Adams, and his own designs and his own modelling are topping – first-class. It's a crime to have that man plastering houses. But, in Cork, well . . . You know Cork . . ." And The Knight twitched his face and shrugged his shoulders and ate his moustache and then, in sorrow for Fagan, he made a terrible face and nearly tore his ear and walked away, tails flying, hands flung up into the air.'

Father Tom's sorrow expressed itself in a three-step descent of the scale.

'Yes,' he sighed, and he turned off the music. 'Yes,' and the faint clacking of a lawn-mower. 'Yes,' and we heard a fly on the pane. 'And I should have helped Austin. But . . . ah, well . . . I didn't. The thing went its way and 'twas on a Christmas Eve it finished. I went up there, in response to another appeal of the canon's – a hard, frosty morning it was, with the holly piled along the kerb for sale. I came to the old wooden gate just as Shandon blared out the nine o'clock – the old blistered, grey gate, with the half-circle on it – *Austin Fagan,* and the line underneath – *Builder and Contractor.* There was a little crowd of people at the gate watching the milkman hammering at it with his measure.

' "What's wrong here?" said I, and the milkman told me he could get no answer, and some of the neighbours began to tell me how the dog had been wailing all night long, and the hens cackling since dawn.

' "Father," says one old woman – and she whispered it – "I think we'd better burst in that gate, I don't like the look of things at all."

'I borrowed a step-ladder and the milkman climbed in and unbarred the gate. In we went, about ten of us, up the cinder-path; and when we came to the house the blinds were down. We went around the back, and there was the old dog in his kennel, growling at us, and in the hen-run the fowl lined up clucking for food.

' "Father," says the milkman, "look at this."

'I looked in the window and there was Dinny, in the kitchen, sitting by the cold range, his hand motionless on his knee and a suitcase on the floor by his side. Leaning against the case was a little plaster cast of Shandon tower. When we got in, there wasn't a soul in the house, nor a stick of furniture but the chair he was sitting on.'

Father Tom was a man who suffered from blood pressure, and his face was normally like a ripe strawberry. Now he was dirty and grey. I filled him a glass and he took it, shaking.

'But where were they gone to?'

'Somewhere in America. The day before, a van had gone in and come out. That was, no doubt, the furniture. All they left Dinny to take back to the home in the lane was the suitcase – it had a few books of Austin's in it – and the little plaster model. He had taken them. And when they were gone he packed his few little traps, and took the model of Shandon in memory of the great cleverness of his son. Then he sat down for a last warm by the old fire.'

'And went back,' I said, 'to live in the lane . . .'

Father Tom looked at me out of his big, soft dog's eye: a beaten dog. He said:

'The fire was gone cold . . . I buried him on Boxing Day. The only mourner. It was a damn windy day.'

'I know the Cork wind.'

' 'Tis cold.'

'Up from the harbour.'

A Born Genius

I

Prout Lane (better known as Little Hell) was wrapped in a softly-waving veil of mist and Pat Lenihan, leaning against his doorpost, was staring into it; even as earlier in the afternoon when he had been caught by old Phillips, at the office-window of the vinegar factory, staring down into the darkening marshes.

'Lenihan,' he had raged, 'if I came into this office twenty times a day I'd find you eating your pen with your gob to that window. What the blazes do you be looking at, anyway?'

And shoving up his glasses, he had peered out at the brown evening fog rising through the pollarded willows, mingling as it rose with the barely descending rain. Then he had looked back at Lenihan, and as if slightly in doubt of his clerk's sanity, he had left the room with a low, minatory 'Get on with it.'

Lenihan smiled to himself as he recalled the question. What had he been looking at, indeed, but at his boat – when it would be finished – chugging out between the forts at the harbour mouth, cutting through the waves and the mists over the open sea.

He was clerk to the old vinegar factory – an easy, even a pleasant job. There was not a great deal of work to be done; the factory was on the outskirts of the city, one might almost say in the country, and Phillips, the manager and owner, was easy to get on with. Besides, Lenihan knew he was not a very satisfactory clerk and not every employer would have put up with him. That afternoon incident at the window was typical. There were other times when Phillips had been known to roar up from the yard to the office-window:

'Lenihan, will you stop that blasted singing?'

And the sweet, tenor voice, that like a thrush in full music had been trilling up and down the scales with swollen throat for the last half-hour, would fall silent in the middle of a run. Then old Phillips would sniff through his great red beak of a nose and with a sigh the workmen would take up their shovels or their hods again, and up in his office Lenihan would raise his shoulders as if to bear a sudden weight before he returned with a sigh to his ledgers.

Even the workmen knew he was not a satisfactory clerk. When they came to the office-window on Saturday for the week's pay they might find him sweating with excitement and nervousness over a pile of notes and silver, counting the amounts over and over again, forgetting to which envelope each little pile belonged, making wrong calculations, and finally getting so utterly confused that the men themselves would have to come to his aid before he got it all correct.

In return he occasionally sang for them. If he passed by as they lay resting after the midday meal they would grasp his hands and sleeves and legs and beseech him for a song. They did not care what song he sang – anything so long as they heard him. Not that he always agreed: he would explain that a singer must be very careful of his voice, *so* careful. If he did sing, he would draw himself up, take the key from a tuning-fork, puff out his voice in a little cough, face the marsh, the sluggish stream and the leaning poplars, as if they were an audience, and with as much care as if he were in the greatest theatre in the world, sing for the four or five old workers lying about him, all stained white with magnesia. He would give them *Flow on thou Silent River*, or *The Gypsy's Warning*, which is, he explained, really a song for a contralto, or their favourite, the tenor's part from *The Moon hath raised her Lamp Above* out of Benedict's *Lily of Killarney*. Gently he would sing:

> 'Do not trust him, gentle maiden,
> Gentle maiden, trust him not . . .'

while the men swung their heads in time and winked at one another in delight and admiration.

> 'Over in the green grave yonder,
> Lies the gypsy's only child . . .
> Soon she perished, now she's sleeping,
> In that cold and silent grave. . . .'

When he finished he would go away at once with a little bow and a military salute, blushing faintly if he overheard their praise as he went.

'Ah! God!' one would say. 'He have a massive voice.'

'A marvel!' they would reply in unison.

'But, of course,' the first would lean forward to whisper confidentially, 'he's a born genius!'

Only Flyer, his brother, would lean back very stiffly, silent as a waxwork image. Presently, he knew, they would turn to him for the latest news of Pat's doings, and then he would tell them – what matter if they had heard it all fifty times before. Meanwhile he sat silent, his two hands holding his paunch, his two swivel eyes gazing sadly into one another.

'Well, Flyer!' they ask at last. 'What is he up to now?'

Before he began Flyer would shake his head mightily by way of emphasis, as if he were trying to shake his eyes straight or fix his head down properly into his shoulders.

'Pat,' he whispers very solemnly and oracularly, 'is a marvel!' Then with a sudden roar he leans forward to them – 'He's after painting two swans,' he bellows dramatically, 'on deh kitchen windas. Wan is facing wan way and d'oder is facing d'oder way. And I swear to God,' Flyer continues with the gestures of an orator speaking to thousands, 'I swear to God dis day' – here he looks both ways to the sky – 'ye'd tink dey'd fly away while ye'd be looking at 'em. And what's more, he's after making a sunny-house outside o' deh winda, and he have geraniums, and lilies, and posies, and nasturtiums and I dunno what else put growin' dere. So dat so help me God dis day' – again Flyer implores the sky – 'you'd tink deh swans was floatin' in a garden! And deh garden was floating in through deh winda! And dere was no winda! But you all flowers' – here he swims through the air with his outflung hands – 'and all swans and all garden ...'

He never finished his account of anything, his head taken by a kind of gigantic Vitus's dance and his eyes starting from his head. He was subnormal, the factory liar. Pat scarcely ever spoke to him, he was ashamed of him.

The men firmly believed Flyer's tales; wasn't there, at the back of the drying-shed where the white chunks of magnesia were stacked on shelves to cake, and had been, for years now, the monument he carved for his sister's grave? It was a huge block of grey vermicular stone which the rains of winter had begun to peel and crumble as if it were plaster. For almost a year he had toiled at it, day and night, in every spare moment, lying on his stomach on the cold stone, kneeling beside it in the clay, getting into all sorts of postures as he hacked away. For that year he never went to a concert or exercised his voice. He worked so hard that old Phillips, seeing him tapping away at the stone during the spare moments of the lunch-hour, used to sniff and say, 'If you worked as hard as that for me, Lenihan, by George, you'd nearly be worth your hire!'

But when it was all ready except the inscription he had spoiled it. He went at his sister's name in a fury of impatience to be finished, working into the night by candlelight, with the bull-frogs croaking below him in the moon-blanched marsh. Then he stared in horror at the result: all the S's and N's were upside down – it read like Russian script. A month later he began at the name again, carving out a horizontal piece to obliterate what he had done. This time, he got all the S's and N's right, but by some accursed fate he forgot everything else, and the name now read,

SUSANNANAN LENINAN.

He never completed his task and the monument now lay – as he said bitterly, like a huge letter-box to Heaven for *Susannanan Leninan* – covered with a sack, forgotten, unfinished behind the drying-sheds. And now, wasn't he making a motor-boat!

*

The veils of mist continued to float in from the sea, as solid as a fog. With a sigh he closed the door and returned to the fire. Summer was ending. He took up a piece of wood-carving that he had begun last winter and with a small gouge he scraped at the vein in a leaf. He had the house to himself – Flyer was boozing in the pub at the end of the lane and his mother was gone to the chapel to her Confraternity. He laid the piece of wood aside and lit a cigarette and hummed a bar or two from a song – Schubert's Serenade. Then he turned to his baby grand piano, and when he had searched for and found the key and shook out the music, he dusted the worn keys with his silk handkerchief.

2

Directly opposite the narrow mouth of Little Hell, or so it appears to the eye, are the slopes of Montenotte – tonight no more than a crowd of winking lights hanging, like the stars, but in a lower darkness. From where she had stepped on a mound of ruins somewhere behind Prout Lane, Mrs John Delaney looked across at those hundred faint lights of which at least a couple might be the windows of her home and the lamps at her lodge-gates. She could even distinguish the lay of her own road where the lamps curved in a steady series. Far down to the right, too, she could see through the mists another faint line of lights where the river swung out to meet the harbour, and she halted for an extra second to stare into the impenetrable darkness beyond all, from where the wind blew chill about her legs and blew the mist into her eyes and penetrated her furs. It would be hard for her to say which view of the harbour was more familiar to her – from this side of the city, a narrow ribbon of river threading between factory chimneys and the roofs of houses; from her garden, there across the valley, widening and narrowing to river-lochs, the great country-houses scattered deep in trees into which she could almost fling a pebble. For it was not really so long ago since, from a lane-way door not a mile from this lane, she had stood as a young girl looking at this self-same night-view, taking a breath of air after hours of practice at the piano, and at the Jewel Song from *Faust*, and *Absent*, and *Flow on thou Silent River*, and *The Gypsy's Warning*, and all the rest of them, to be allowed to sing one of which was her reward for an hour Oh'ing and Ah'ing at the scales. Leaning against a crumbling wall she hummed to herself:

> 'Do not trust him, gentle maiden,
> Gentle maiden, trust him not . . .
> Soon she perished – '

She pulled herself up suddenly – at this rate she would not get her calls finished by midnight. She saw a solitary lamp ahead of her at the end of a passage and made for it: perhaps Ninety-Two B was at that end of the lane, and for the sixth time she smacked her lips in annoyance at not having had the sense to ask for precise directions, or, at least, to bring some kind of torch.

And yet they were always telling her at the Society that she was their best woman for dispensing charity. Occasionally she wondered why. There were occasions on which she forgot she had been a lane-child herself, or tried to persuade herself that the Society and the lane-people did not know that it was her voice, and the help of the nuns in her school, that had lifted her out of the rut, that it was her voice alone that had opened the way for her into amateur theatricals where she met her husband. It was her one vanity, her one hopeless self-deception. For even if they had not remembered her, the lanes would have seen the mark of their kind in her deep chest, and her strong arms, and her frosty complexion, and her hard lips – her only inheritance from her mother, a woman who had carried a basket of fish on her back around Cork, day after day, for thirty years. That was the real reason why the Society always sent her to the worst lanes; they knew well that the lane-people knew, and would not try to impose on her with a sorrowful tale and a whining voice; that the only weapon left to the poor people was flattery, and that would not succeed with such as her. It was because of that lane-cunning, as strong in her as in them, that she would not knock now at a door to ask the way. It was old wisdom to her – 'What they didn't know didn't trouble them.'

But when she reached the lamp and its light fell on the number to her left, she knew she was utterly lost in this forest of slummery. She was about to walk back the way she had come when suddenly from behind the lighted cabin-window by her shoulder a piano flung out in great strong drops of sound the prelude to an old familiar arrangement of Schubert's Serenade and immediately a fine tenor voice opened the duet, though where the contralto or baritone should reply there was silence except for the gently throbbing beat of the accompaniment. Her heart beat faster than the time of the music as in one of these half-silences she knocked at that door. The music halted and the door opened. Because the light was strong behind him she could not see Lenihan's face.

'Can you tell me,' she said, 'where I can find number Ninety-Two B?'

At the first word she recognized the voice.

'Yes, of course. But I'm afraid you won't find it yourself. Wait one minute,' he said, diving back into the kitchen, 'and I'll get my hat and show you.'

She lowered her head to step down into the earthen-floored cabin. She saw the baby grand, almost as long as the whole room; it was grey with a layer of dust and coal-ash. A smoke-darkened plaster-cast of an angel hung over the wide, low grate. Pieces of wood shaped like monstrous bones leaned in a corner – the ribs of his boat. When he turned she gave him one quick look, and he, caught by the full shock of surprise, cried out:

'Trixie Flynn!'

'Pat Lenihan!' she reproached. 'Why did you never come to see me and welcome me home?'

Her voice was deep, rich, pouting.

'I couldn't, Trixie. I couldn't somehow. What brings you here at this hour of the night?'

'The Saint Vincent de Pauls sent me. Mrs Cahill in Ninety-Two B is sick.'

She had recovered completely from her surprise and she arranged her hair as she looked at him from under her eyebrows.

'Sit down!' he said.

His voice was shaking and he shut the door and leaned against it.

'The old favourite,' she said, looking at the score on the piano.

'I haven't sung for nearly a year and a half,' he said.

'Why?'

'I'm making a boat,' he murmured, almost as if he were a child caught wrong-doing.

'A boat!'

She was shocked.

'Pat Lenihan! A boat! And you with your voice!'

'Ah!' he cried miserably. 'It's all very well for you, Trixie. You caught the tide. You've been to Paris and Milan. I read about your concert last March, below in the Opera House.'

She grimaced with lips and eyebrows and shrugged her shoulders in disdain.

'*Un rien*. A bagatelle.'

'And you got married, too,' he whispered.

'Aha!' she trilled. 'I often thought we'd get together, Pat. But, *chi lo sa?*'

His lips twitched and his eyes strayed to a photograph on the piano. She went over to it, and he followed. There she, as a buxom Marguerite, knelt and looked up at Lenihan in the tights and doublet of Faust.

'And you've been singing in Manchester and Liverpool,' he said, looking at her as she looked at the photograph.

'It's my wonderful year,' she laughed. 'Back from Milan! Married! Several recitals! But' – she pouted again in a deep, said voice – 'you never came to see *ta petite* Marguerite!'

'See what?' asked Lenihan.

'Me!' she pouted, swaying before him.

'Oh! You don't want me now,' cried Lenihan.

He slammed down the lid of the piano. The wires vibrated.

'I'll never sing another song!' he declared.

She was about to argue with him, but he interrupted her savagely.

'What's the use?' he cried. 'Who hears me? And if they did, what difference would it make? Who could tell in this hole of a city whether I was good or bad? I suppose if the truth were known I wouldn't be taken in the chorus of a travelling Moody-Manners.'

'I heard you outside the window,' she said. 'You were in good voice.'

'I'm not. I couldn't be. I haven't practised for eighteen months. It's all a lot of damned tomfoolery. Look at all the hours I've wasted – the nights. And what good did it do me? I know I have a voice. But it isn't a great voice. I never even got as much as a penny out of it. Not that I want it. Of course the Opera House is a bagatelle to you, as you call it. What are we here but a lot of country boys playing at amateur operatics?'

'Why don't you sing in a choir, Pat?' she asked. 'You'd make some money that way.'

'A choir!'

His voice was like the sour beer that stank in the vinegar factory.

'And what would I sing in a choir?'

Through his nose he began to intone horribly:

'Tantum ergo
Sacramentum

Novo cedat
  Ritui . . .'

'Stop, Pat!'

They were silent for a minute or two.

'I want to sing my old part in that serenade, Pat,' she said gently.

'No.'

'Please, Pat!'

'No! No! No!'

She went to the piano and, leaving a wave of scent in the air as she swished by him, began to turn the music with the ample gestures of a *prima donna*. As she sat, and with her white fingers plucked out the modulated sounds, the music seemed to mingle sweetly with the scent. She saw, looking over her shoulder at him, that he was wavering.

'Have you never been to any of my concerts, Pat?'

He shook his head. She flung out a few notes like a blackbird full of pride in its song.

'Come on, Pat!' She smiled at him again.

He flung his mood aside and stood by her, his hands clasped tremblingly across his chest, his eyes lost in the dark corner of the room. They began:

'Leise flehen meine Lieder
  Durch die Nacht zu dir,
In die stillen Hain hernieder,
  Liebchen komm zu mir' . . .

Her rich, finely trained voice poured into the room and out of it through the lanes. Responding to it his body swayed to and fro as he drew up from his chest the most powerful volume of song he could command. Once where she had a bar or two to sing alone he glanced down at her. Her great bosom, too, rose to the notes, and it was white and suède-smooth in the lamplight. Looking at her, he almost missed a note. He sang with an almost uncontrolled passion the remainder of the song.

When it was finished he fell into a chair by the piano and covered his eyes with his hands.

'My God!' he said. 'What a voice! What a marvellous voice!'

He thought he caught the vibration of triumph and pity in her throat as she said:

'Pat! You really have a very nice voice.'

Outside the window, in spite of the rain, they suddenly heard a chattering group of men, women, and children, trying to peep through the window-slits and the key-hole. He was glad of the interruption and, jerking his head, he led her to the back-door and across the yard to another lane.

'Come and see me, Pat!' she said. He did not reply. From time to time she said, 'Isn't it wet?' Or, 'Mind this hole!' But still he did not reply. At the door of Ninety-Two B, she said again:

'Won't you come to see me? Ah! *S'il vous plaît? Mon cher* Pat? *Mon petit Pat?*'

'Yes, yes, yes,' he said shortly. 'I'll come. Maybe. Good night, Trixie.'

'Au revoir, *mon petit* Pat.'

The light of the cabin windows fell on him at intervals, as he went. Then the mist and the dark covered him from her sight.

3

To her surprise, when she heard from him, three months later just before the Christmas holidays, he was in New York. It was a picture postcard of the New York Philharmonic Orchestra with his address and two sentences:

> *Having a grand time. Richard Trübner has taken me in hand and has great hopes of me. Pat.*

With the cunning of the born guttersnipe she went at once to Little Hell on two or three entirely superfluous calls and at each house she said when leaving – 'I hear you've lost Mr Lenihan from the lane.'

Before she left the slum she had heard more about him than he would ever have written to her in a hundred letters, and as she was driven back to Montenotte she smiled to think how neatly everything she had heard fitted in with all her previous knowledge of Pat Lenihan – his silence about himself, his poverty, the strain of bitterness and irreligion in him. He had never told her, for example, that he lived in Prout Lane or that he had for years supported his mother and sister. And she recalled, suddenly, how when five years before they were meeting frequently for some amateur operetta he had told her of the monument he was going to carve for his sister's grave. She had said, probing inquisitively:

'And you'll put your father's name on it, too, of course?'

'No! I will not,' he had snapped back, and, flushing, walked away.

Well! Here was the secret out at last.

'Ah, sure, Mrs Delaney,' they had said to her in Prout Lane. 'That boy could do any mortal thing he liked. D'ye see his house? 'Twould take the sight of your eyes, Mrs Delaney. It's massive. Oh, sure, his father will make a Cruso out of him. The two of ye will charm Cork.'

She had to halt their flattery several times. She wanted to hear about Pat Lenihan.

'His father? 'Nt ye know? Fifteen years ago – No! I'm tellin' a lie – twelve years ago his fader ran away from his mother to America. He left her with five children, the blackguard. Three of 'em died since. Susie was the last to go. An' all this time the father is sending for the boy. His mother says, an' Flyer says – but you wouldn't mind Flyer – his mother says the father is rotten with money. But the blackguard never sent a penny since the day he left. Oh, Pat's future is cut out for him. Sure he's a genius. He'd charm the married women. And' – with a burst of hypocritical and delighted laughter – 'sure you'd charm the married men, Mrs Delaney!'

She envied him. She was to have her first child in the spring and her singing days, she felt, were nearly done. For all her promise of triumphant nights and audiences applauding in the gloom across the footlights, she was falling into the routine of a little tawdry provincial city. From this on the most she could hope for would be an occasional recital in Cork, with more frequent gratis appearances at charity concerts to help her husband to get contracts for churches or convent buildings or for hospitals or schools managed by religious. She did not reply to the postcard.

4

New York was wine to Pat Lenihan, and because it was under snow the silence of it filled into his heart. All he could hear above the perpetual whistling of the chains on the automobiles, and the muffled honk of their horns, was the long sad squawk of a train-siren cleaving the frozen air, and the low tolling of a bell where an engine drew its load through Manhattan, somewhere to the north. The air was cold, exhilarating and pure. A few last gentle flakes were added to those clotting the trees in the Park, and the low sun, a burning moon, blazed on every twig. The tall, tapering buildings, dim and pale, glittered with their own thousand lights as they rose through the sky.

He was driving in a taxi, back from his singing-lesson, to his room in a little down-town Theological Seminary on Ninth Avenue and Twenty-First Street. He had laughed to think what they would say in Cork if they heard he was living in such a place. But two weeks after his arrival in New York his father had got him a letter to the Dean, and because it was cheaper and less frigid than a hotel he had stayed there ever since. Not that he saw his father; the introduction was sent to him, and though that was nearly four months ago he was about to meet his father tonight for the first time.

Ever since the tender disappeared into the early-morning mist at Queenstown four months or so ago, leaving him on the liner, he had been filled by that miracle of elation that comes only once in life to every man, that fills him when chance at last opens for him some long-desired road. He had never in all his life been so excited as when he stepped off the boat and looked expectantly around the wharf; for half his dreams had been of the day when his father would return with him, successful and wealthy, to live, reconciled to his mother, in Ireland. But he saw nobody and nobody came to meet him. He was planning to go to his father's business address, the only one he knew, when at the customs desk they handed him a letter in which his father explained that he had been called away suddenly to Cleveland on business and they would see one another in a few weeks' time.

'There is, to be sure,' his father wrote, 'a good deal of money in singing and my Pat must have the best teachers money can buy. Meanwhile you must have a good time.'

The letter mentioned several theatres; one called *Earl Carroll's Vanities* was a 'real bully show.' Lenihan smiled at the Americanese, and because he could not meet his father, went that evening to see something that his father had liked. He came out, unhappy and troubled, his eyes and mind soiled by gaudy images of red and purple curtains and sham marble pillars and naked women. Had he not come by chance on a symphony concert and snatched an hour filled with the thunder and whisper of a Beethoven concerto (it was *The Emperor*) he would have had nothing but an unpleasant memory for his first night in New York, a memory that might have shattered his miracle for ever.

After that he lived his own life and the miraculous elation of hope blossomed once more. After another three weeks his father wrote again. He was now in Chicago and in a few weeks they would meet. Meanwhile Pat must begin to study; 'for my Pat must make a name for himself and I'll help my boy to it while I have a dollar left.' Things went on like that for another three months, some of the letters containing large cheques, and still Lenihan had not met his father. By now, too, his mother was writing long letters from Cork, charging him in an agony of fear with hiding something from her, and Lenihan spent a good part of his leisure time writing long letters to both of them. But his master was by now much more hopeful, and even enthusiastic, and Lenihan could already see, a year away, perhaps, the night of his début – the little concert-hall, for it would be a very modest beginning, the accompanist looking to him for the signal, the scattered audience of connoisseurs and critics, and then the notices the following morning in the Press giving him the taste of fame or failure.

It was characteristic of his elation that he found even Ninth Avenue beautiful. And yet, at any rate around Twenty-First Street, it is merely a dirty, paper-strewn cobbled street, darkened and made raucous by an overhead railway. There is the usual Greek fruit-store, the usual wide-windowed restaurant and lunch-counter, white-tiled like a public lavatory at home in Ireland, and with such names as *Charlie's Lunch* or *The Coffee Pot*; an old-clothes shop, a cheap Sicilian haberdasher strayed up from MacDougall Street; there was a *Palmist and Phrenologist*, with big-breasted Polish gypsies always offering themselves in the doorway. The tram-cars raced along the avenue under the thunder of the overhead railway. Only when the snow covers the dirt and the smells and dulls the noise is the place really tolerable. Yet, to Lenihan, it had the charm of a foreign city, the one place that remained indelible in all its details on his memory when he returned to Ireland, that filthy avenue banked in snow, made doubly white by the black girders of the overhead; and side by side for all its length all those vital struggling immigrant homes. That long noisy street remained with him as a poignantly lovely memory, a thing more vital and brutal than he could ever explain.

And it was all the more poignant and bitter when he discovered that for all the four months he was in New York his father had watched him coming out of the archway of the Seminary in the morning and going in, often very late at night, getting no more in return for his patient vigil than the briefest glance at his son's face raised questioningly to the sky, or, after dark, the outline of his son's back under the lamplight.

In the hall, now, by the telephone booth he stood waiting, and though it was twelve years since they had met, and the old man had grown scant-haired and yellow-skinned and hard-mouthed, they recognized each other at once. But they could say nothing but, 'How are you, my son?' and, 'How are you, father?' – looking shyly at each other, smiling and saying nothing, because they had nothing in common they dared talk about.

'Let's go and have a cup of cawfee,' said the father at last, and he took his son by the arm and led him across to the white counter of *Charlie's Lunch*.

In the bright light of the restaurant Lenihan noticed that his father's hands were trembling, and that they were rough with work, and that his suit was odorous of the steam-press.

'You've come from Detroit, father?'

'What?' said the father, taken by surprise.

'You wrote me from Detroit last time, father,' said Lenihan.

'Yeah!'

As the white-hatted curate brought them the coffee the father spoke about Detroit to his son, inventing the names of the streets and the squares and the parks.

' 'Nt you like New Yawrk?' he asked then, and in spite of the succession of nasals his intonation was pure Cork.

'I do, indeed,' said Lenihan. 'It's marvellous!'

The old man began at once in a very fast voice to make his confession to his son, but he went round and round it and he could not approach the actual point. He talked instead in a confused way about America and its customs, about democracy and the liberties of America, about freedom of thought and tolerance and cosmo-politanism, and though Lenihan tried very hard to follow him he could not, and finally he gave it up and, barely listening, merely said, 'Yes,' or 'No,' or 'Indeed?' or 'Do you say so?' He was trying to think how he could get to the point of suggesting to his father that he ought to return to his home and wife in Cork. Suddenly he observed how excited and nervous the old man was, and how his eyes were shifting here and there as his talk grew slower and more deliberate. He felt his father was coming to the point, and he waited for his opportunity, almost trembling himself with hope and expectation.

'Of course,' his father was saying, 'you are a young maan still, Pat. A very young maan. And in Ireland a maan has little chance of meeting with experience. But you are a clever young maan and I hope you have understanding.'

'I hope so, sir,' said Lenihan.

The old man looked at him from eye to eye, and said solemnly and deliberately:

'A maan's married life is sacred to him.'

'Father!' said Lenihan, grasping his father's hand. How rough it was and how it shook as he held it!

'Yes, Pat?'

'Father, come home to my mother.'

With a shock he realized that he had often and often said those words before to his father when he used to meet him as a child, wandering drunk in the streets. His father looked at him. There was silence for a moment and then an overhead train thundered by.

'Pat!' said his father.

'Yes.'

'Pat, I want you to stay here.'

'But you can go home without me,' he was beginning to argue when the old man interrupted him.

'Pat, boy, I'll make a success of you. I'm very fond of you, and I always was. Aren't you my first son, and why shouldn't I? I have a father's love for you, Pat. My boy! I've done a lot of rotten things, Pat, but you don't hold them against me? You wouldn't hold things out against your old dad?'

A group of men came in and sat at the counter near them.

'Come upstairs, Pat,' said the father, taking his hand.

'Upstairs?' said Lenihan.

'Yes,' said the father, leading him through the shop. 'I know the man here,' he explained.

He was like a hare doubling before the dog. He lied at every hand's turn. Upstairs in the room over the shop the first thing Lenihan saw was a panorama of Queenstown and in surprise he turned to his father.

'Yes, Pat?' faltered the old man.

'Queenstown!' said Lenihan in delight.

'Aye,' smiled his father, still unable to confess.

'How did it get here?'

'Yes, Pat.'

And he laughed with foolish delight, in spite of his nervousness, because at last someone else besides himself was enjoying the old familiar scene.

'Look at the old Deepwater Quay!' said Lenihan. 'And look at Spike! and Haulbowline! Isn't it grand!'

Then he stopped, his eyes wandering to the fireplace over which hung an Irish flag, the old green with the yellow harp, and crossing it an Italian flag, the quartered shield in the white centre. Beneath it on the mantelpiece was a photograph. He went towards it. It was himself and Trixie Flynn as Faust and Marguerite. When he wheeled on his father the old man was looking up at him like a dog about to be kicked or a schoolboy waiting for punishment. But before the confession could come the door was flung open and in raced two lovely little black-haired boys, and after them strode a dark-eyed, big-chested Italian woman.

'Whoo! Pop!' cried the children, leaping up joyously at old Lenihan. 'We been shoppin'!'

And they began to show him their New Year toys until, seeing the stranger, they fell suddenly quiet.

'Anita!' said old Lenihan. 'This is Pat.'

It was plain that he had told her at least some of the truth – how much Lenihan never knew; probably that he was a widower and this was his son. Afterwards it tore Lenihan's heart to think the old man had not been able to keep it secret that he had a son whom he loved. Now, however, as the woman looked at him, searching his face for the face of his mother, Lenihan began to think of Prout Lane, wrapped in its veils of mist, and of his mother, hurrying to the chapel to her Confraternity at night, and he let his eyes fall, and taking his hat he went slowly out of the room. His father raced down the stairs to stop him, persuading and entreating him, step by step, as he insisted on descending to the street.

That night when he had at last got rid of his father Lenihan packed his bag and took the Shore Line midnight to Boston, his taxi racing with whistling chains through the snow-covered avenues, past the great flood-lit towers of the city's buildings, closed for the night, past the theatres he had begun to know so well, dark now and silent, and empty, the shops at rest, the side-walks deserted, into the great station where the foyer was full of light and life, and the waiting line of Pullmans beyond stood silent and dark, ready for its journey, under the sad whistle of the siren and the low tolling of its bell.

He stayed in Boston for the better part of a year, abandoning all his ambitions and hopes. There was no looking out of the office window here, no singing at the lunch-hour for the workmen, no intervals in which he might at his ease exercise his voice. Having saved his fare, and a little more, he returned to Ireland for Christmas.

Not until he was seated in the train from Queenstown to Cork did it occur to him that in those four months in New York his father must have spent on him the best part of his life's savings, that his father was a poor man – that his father probably was truly fond of him. A light snow, rare event in Southern Ireland, was blowing past the carriage windows, and in it he saw Ninth Avenue and the black girders of the overhead and, for the first time, his father's face at the window of *Charlie's Lunch* peering out anxiously to see him leave the Seminary in the morning, peering out at night in the hope of seeing him return, and doing that day after day, week after week, afraid to meet his son, and yet aching to talk with him and maybe persuade him to stay with him for the rest of his life. The old fellow, thought Lenihan, must have gone to a great deal of trouble and humiliation persuading the Dean to allow me to stay at the Seminary; and then he thought of all the devices, all the lies, all the subterfuges his father had employed, and all to no greater result than five minutes' painful argument as they stepped down the stairs of the restaurant-cum-haberdasher's shop in Ninth Avenue; and, afterwards, still more painful because bitter and insulting, the pleading and the quarrelling in the little room of the Theological Seminary over the way. Through the whirling snowflakes, curling about the bare beech-boughs, and melting on the dark drooping laurels and the tattered hedges, he saw only, and now with a sudden but tardy pity, that his father's sin had borne bitter fruit.

The train rolled into the city, over the red bridge into the railway station, and as he stepped from it and saw his mother coming forward in search of him through the crowd, full of joy at the thought that she was about to see her son again – the sorrow of her husband's early desertion long since forgotten – Lenihan realized that he was divided in pity between these two, and that, for being divided, he could never as long as he lived be at ease again with either.

In the old covered car, as they drove into the city, and up the hills again to Prout Lane, Lenihan told his mother the truth about her husband. But when she began to weep for herself and curse her husband with sudden blasphemy, Lenihan found that he had no longer any hate or resentment left in him. After that, when the news spread through the lane, he refused to talk of it with anybody, and if they insisted on upbraiding his father he would merely say 'I pity him sometimes.'

5

All that day a stream of lane-people kept trickling in to welcome the genius home. They had expected a night of jollification, but they were just as pleased with the drama of the weeping mother, Flyer drunken and fractious on the porter intended for the feast, and Pat sitting glum and silent by the fire. His piano he had sold before he went to America, never thinking to need it again; his window-flowers were withered stumps; the fire had taken his wood-carvings one by one, as well as the unfinished portions of his boat that used to lean in the corners of the kitchen.

'Didn't I have a clean kitchen for you, Pat?' his mother wailed. 'And what news you brought me! Look at that lovely red marbled wallpaper we got for you, fourpence a dozen, and Flyer to put it up for you with his own two hands. Oh! What a home-coming!' she wailed at each new comforting gossip, until at last he drove out of the house and down to the river's edge to look at the skeleton of his boat, and to look, in the dusk, at the marshes of the vinegar factory. Then the only shelter from the night and his loneliness was the dark lights of Montenotte and Trixie Flynn.

It was no pleasure to him to visit her. Earlier in the afternoon he had observed from an old poster that they were now calling her 'Madame Flynn-Delaney, Cork's Own Nightingale,' and as he read it he had groaned aloud, like a man in pain. This rat-eaten place still had, he thought bitterly, as he walked through its tawdry front streets whose finery was only the thickness of a brick, and into its warehouse back streets that looked as if they had been rusting and crumbling for centuries, all the mannerisms and unconscious humour ascribed to it by the sniggering Levers and Prouts and Thackerays of a hundred years ago. With a kind of sour joy he began to roam about the city, trying to keep from visiting Montenotte – O romantic mount of Night! – associating his own misery with the shades of the Spensers and the Warbecks and the Walters – for he refused to ally even his thoughts with the people themselves – the Dukes and Earls and Lords-Lieutenant and Secretaries whose petty glories were the only ones the place had ever seen. Everywhere he went he sought with deliberate malice for the signs of decayed grandeur – streets of Georgian houses full of cheap shops, a puny bridge called after Wellington, a wide street dubbed a Square and given to Nelson, a horse-trough presented to a Berwick, a wretched slum street to the whole House of Hanover, and every sooty, mud-deep quay partitioned off here to a Grenville, or a Wandesford, or a Camden, or a Lancaster, a George, a Charlotte, an Albert. Every exiled down-at-heel sighing for St James's and Pall Mall, with their flea-bitten servants and tarnished finery, had been offered the immortality of their names on the walls of a jakes in this city of exile. But all the time, as if in spite of himself, he approached nearer and nearer to Montenotte. The bored souls of provincial towns are all like that – feeding on one another without pleasure like leeches.

He had been afraid that she would ask him too many questions about his father and his own plans. She seemed far more interested in showing him her baby and in telling him about the contract for the new cathedral that all the architects in Cork were trying to wheedle out of the Bishop. Then her husband came in for dinner and with him her sister-in-law and her brother, and they prevailed on Lenihan to stay. It was a good dinner but noisy with cross-talk, and

Delaney bored them with talk about the cathedral – the people who were manoeuvring for the contract, distant relations of the Bishop that were being approached by this person and that, the best sites for the cathedral, the soil, the stone, the style, explaining the advantages of Romanesque with his knife and his napkin and a loaf of bread, deriding Pugin because he had filled Ireland with plaster Gothic.

'My God! I'd rather concrete,' he would declare. 'Though concrete wasn't as popular once as it is now. That's what your Americans' – to Lenihan – 'did for us. I remember a competition twelve years ago and I was the first student to suggest a concrete church. "How in the name of God," said the adjudicator – it was Sir Edward Lutyens – "how in the name of almighty God," says he, "could that roof stand?" "Oh, it's concrete, Sir Edward," says I. "Indeed," says Sir Edward, "an' I suppose the spire is made of cast-iron?" But, you know,' Delaney went on in spite of the laughter, 'you could have a concrete roof in a Romanesque church. And it wouldn't be a smaller church. You'd make in the height what you'd lose in the width; you could have galleries . . .'

And so on and on Lenihan kept thinking, 'I'm back; back in garrulous, windbag Cork.' And his mind filled with images of New York and Boston and he ceased to hear Delaney's talk except as the babble of a stream.

After dinner, whisky and port and coffee were handed around and there was much sniggering in a corner over a *risqué* French pictorial. But Lenihan put such a good face on things that he managed to lift out of his mood into a good humour, and while the rain blown up from the harbour lashed the streaming panes and the fire crackled with drops falling in the chimney he and Trixie sang a comical duet from the *Yeomen of the Guard* while Delaney pranced around the room holding his glass to the ceiling, coming in on the refrain very flat and out of tune. Then he went off to drive his guests home and Lenihan and Trixie were left alone, boasting by the fire in a darkened room, of the great singers they had heard, she of Melba, and Patti, and Tonnalerre, and Clara Butt, he of Kennerley Rumford and Caruso and his master Trübner. She began to complain sadly of her life in Cork and he said he could well believe her.

'I have my child, of course,' she said, 'and I'd die for her. I'd lay down the last drop of my blood for that child,' she declared with flashing eyes, and her bosom panted and her voice rose.

The wine was going to both their heads, and Lenihan found himself telling her that her sentiments did her great honour. But then, there was her husband, she said, and her voice fell. There was John gone off to the club now and he wouldn't be back until morning; and she allowed Lenihan to kiss her on the hand. He felt he had never liked her so much as tonight, and as she leaned forward and encouraged him to speak he told her readily all about his father. As he left they halted in the door to hum a bar from the Serenade, and he kissed her hand in goodbye.

Then, as he tramped in a midnight downpour back up to the little sleeping cabins of Prout Lane he felt that he had no right to betray the old man's shame, and late as it was he wrote and posted a letter to his Trixie warning that she had his confidence and imploring her to tell nobody what she had heard. She wrote a long and warm letter in reply saying that she was honoured by his confidence and would respect it. She wrote:

> 'Don't I understand, Pat, only too well that such things are best kept quiet in a town like this. There are always people trying to dig out your past in Cork. As for your father, have nothing to do with the old devil. You never know what he'd try to make out of this. Leave him severely alone, neither writing to him nor communicating with him in any way . . .'

Again Lenihan saw his father peering out of *Charlie's Lunch* for that morning and evening glimpse of himself leaving the Seminary, and thinking of it he decided he would never again visit this coarse woman, wandering instead at night, in and out of the back streets, searching always for old names and old memories, sometimes for snatches of accidental beauty where the shadows of a lamp in an archway made a design of glooms, or lights that were more like shadows, or where an empty blank gable-end towered dark over a lane, or a whitewashed cottage shone like snow under its purple roof. What was he, after all, but another like those Sydneys and Coburgs and Adelaides and the rest of them, whoever they were, another exile tortured by empty days and the companionless nights?

In the end he went back to her. After all, they were the only two people in Cork who really knew what singing meant. And when he did go, late one evening, she was so childishly glad to see him, and so unhappy about her husband, that he felt he had been harsh and unkind and readily agreed to sing with her at a forthcoming concert. But it happened that just that night a priest called to bless the house. ('Father Shanahan,' she whispered to Lenihan as he came in, 'the Bishop's secretary;' and, as he went upstairs to pray over the house, 'God forgive me I have my house blessed by half the priests in Cork.) He was a pale-haired saturnine man, with a voice as high-pitched as a girl's, and his eyes were soft with innocence or humility, and immediately he entered the room Trixie began to be charming to him and flirt with him in a loud voice and with much winking. His answers, however, were so awkward that to Lenihan Trixie's talk seemed improper and gross. He pretended to be playing with the baby, leaning over the pram and glaring down at it as if he were about to choke it. Presently he found himself being intrigued into giving a half-promise to sing the *Adeste* with Trixie at the parish choir next Sunday, though it enraged him to see his half-promise passed on at once as if it were a personal gift of Trixie's to the parish. But she was so charming about it that the little priest grew more and more awkward and finally took his leave, and Lenihan, who had disliked priests at all times, preferred to go with him. Yet the following night he was back at her house again. Again she was delighted to see him. After that he took to visiting her regularly. There was no other house open to him.

6

In April he was taken back in the vinegar factory, and little by little the marshes under the office window began to sprout in green patches, and at the lunch-hour he could walk abroad in the fields more and more often under dry skies and broken clouds and work longer and longer in the evenings at his boat. He began to feel less resentful of Cork. The loveliness of the country encroaching on and compensating for the empty town, the promise of long Sundays in summer among the inlets within and without the harbour, where the bright green hills dipped down to the blue sea, and the white line of waves seemed never to move – all this weaned him gradually back to his old self, and the memory of the heavy winter passed from him.

He was in that happy mood one Sunday as he went to sing at a charity matinée with Trixie. She was waiting for him in the corridor and at once she called him aside to her dressing-room. In the artificial light her hair shone – so much bronze wire piled on her head – and her rich bosom displayed generously in her low-cut evening-gown of pink and silver looked as if a touch would reveal that it had a nap on it like a peach or snow-white suède. He took her by her bare, braceleted arm.

'Is it the contract?' he asked eagerly.

'No.'

She was awkward. He felt there was something wrong.

'Pat! They are beginning to talk about us. You mustn't come so often.'

The music of the orchestra rolled up to them as the stage-door was opened and shut.

'Who is talking about us?' he asked, flushing with shame.

'Well! Father Shanahan is dropping hints.'

'Oh!'

'My husband says it's unwise.'

'It's the contract you're thinking of, Trixie.'

'I'm not, Pat. But you know Cork?'

With a sudden impulse of defiance of the mean, tattling city he put his arms around her and kissed her, and she did not resist him, returning his kiss even more warmly than he gave it. It seemed natural to her to kiss him, to hold him in her great maternal arms. A knock on the door called them to their duet and they went down the corridor to the stage whispering to each other to be calm, to be calm. But as on that first night when she came to his house in Prout Lane, they sang the duet in a rivalry of almost wild passion, accelerating the tempo of the melancholy serenade until the accompanist found himself never nearer than a quarter of a bar behind. The audience sensed their emotion in Lenihan's flushed cheeks and in the woman by her high-flung chin and flashing eyes, and sharing in that emotion, several seconds before the song ended, they sent their clamorous, thundering applause up from the gloom beyond the bright encircling footlights. In the wings, Delaney, trembling for his contract, waited for his wife: he implored her to be careful – the Bishop was in the house and Shanahan was somewhere on the stage. But beyond the billowing curtain the applause rose and fell in wave on wave until they came forward to sing again, choosing with an almost incredible lack of discretion the love-duet from *The Lily of Killarney*. By the prompter's box Father Shanahan looked on with tightened lips and disapproving eyes as Lenihan rose breathlessly to:

> 'I come, I come, my heart's delight!
> My heart's delight!
> My heart's delight ...'

sung so feelingly that when it was over and he reached the side of the stage he collapsed in a chair. They brought him a glass of water, and as he sipped it mechanically he saw Delaney come in from the auditorium, in a fury, and lead his wife to her room, and little Father Shanahan looking at them with a cold look in his innocent eyes.

After that painful scene he dared not visit her again, and indeed she wrote to warn him not to come to her. Fortunately it was summer and he could now work for long hours in the evenings at his boat. As he saw it, as it were, come to life under his hands he became as happy as a woman with child. July came and the trestles under his boat were deep in buttercups, and as he worked the salmon leaped up the falls, splashing, bow-bent silver. During those days he seemed to be tireless, and when the darkness drove him home to his cabin-kitchen he worked late into the night making cabinets to exchange with a local firm of furnishers for the timber and the brass and iron and glass fittings he needed. It was August and a woodbine trailed its tendrils from the hedges over the flank of his boat. As with his sister's tombstone he worked in a fever of impatience to be finished. It was so hot that he had to put a tarpaulin over the keel and it burned his hand to lean on it. September came and under his boat the yellow musk, and the wild-arum in its tight wrapping. October followed and the denuded trees showed the red berry of the dog-rose, burning like the holly-berry on its branch. It seemed as if he would not have his boat launched that autumn, but before the month died he had painted the name on her prow – *The Trickster*;

and dared write to Delaney asking if he and his wife would come to launch his boat.

That Sunday, after singing in the choir, she came, and the boat was lowered down the slip and it breasted the water and floated there in broken ripples of colour. Lenihan rushed forward to thank her, but her husband was impatient to be gone and she would not delay.

All he could say was:

'Thanks. Is he still angry?'

'Yes. He says you lost him that contract.'

'Didn't you get it after all?' he cried.

'No,' she said. 'We heard last night that Cassidy got it.'

But Delaney sounded his horn impatiently and she turned to go.

For a week Lenihan was delighted with his boat. He almost slept in it. He visited it before his work every morning. He raced down at the lunch-hour to see and fondle it. Then the engineers from whom he had ordered the engine told him it would never be of any use to him. He argued with them for hours, but they only shrugged their shoulders at him. The timbers were too far apart and flimsy to bed the engine on them; the stern-post would not bear piercing for the propeller-shaft; the sheer of the quarter made it impossible to lead the shaft through at the proper angle.

As in the case of his sister's tombstone he never went near it again. It lay moored under the alders until marauding boys knocked a hole in it, and sinking half-way in the shallow mud, it grew slimy and green and hulk-like. You can see it there today – for it has outlived poor Lenihan – but only if you peer closely enough into the fibrous shadows of the bank, where it is almost indistinguishable from the air-searching roots of the trees.

The evening Lenihan discovered that it would never take him out to the misty sea, never nuzzle the swaying flowers that glisten in the carmined inlets of the harbour, it was grey with the first cold rains of November. He stood by his door in Prout Lane, biting his nails, and staring across the dark valley of the Lee at the hanging lights of Montenotte, while the slowly waving mist veiled the moon – a warm haze floated up from the sea, persistent as a fog. Winter had begun again, and again the boredom of the empty days and nights. He could hear the people talking beyond the dividing wall. His mother was gone to the chapel to her Confraternity. Flyer was boozing in the pub at the end of the lane.

Searching for the key of his piano – a second-hand, cheap affair – he wiped the dust from the yellow keys and sat to play the Schubert Serenade. As the worn keys plucked out the drops of sound his voice rose gently to the words. Suddenly he stopped and listened. He rushed to the door and flung it wide. He saw the mist curling about the gas-lamp overhead and the lighted cabin-windows as they vanished down the winding lane. Slowly he closed the door and returned to his song. The voices in the next house had fallen silent: his fingers drew the notes in slow procession.

'Lass auch dir die Brust bewegen,
  Liebchen höre mich,
Bebend harr' ich dir entgegen,
  Komm, beglücke mich . . .'

He could not finish. Was that a tapping at the door?

Sullivan's Trousers

I

When I first came to know poor Roger Sullivan he had the reputation and the face of a jolly man. He travelled for cured pigs' heads and he had a face like a pig's head, only his face was red, and a pig's face, when cured, is pale, and nothing would cure Sullivan's face but a régime that he could not have borne: he loved his drop.

It is the misfortune of fat people, with red faces, and a quick tongue, that nobody takes them seriously. But during the troubled times in Ireland it was a useful misfortune to Roger. Nobody on earth could have suspected that men 'on the run' used Roger's house even in the toughest times; that he had secreted guns for them, carried messages for them, collected money for them, guarded, at one time, under the floor of his bedroom, as much as ten thousand pounds in gold coins.

But time came when it was a misfortune to be a traveller for pigs' heads. There was only one thing worse than pigs' heads that he could have peddled, and that was English boots, clothes, furniture or anything else forbidden entry into the country. It meant that he saw revolutionary politics in terms of hard-cash. And this, in a country which was gone mad on them, was aggravating to himself, and more aggravating to the patriots he tried to persuade to his point of view.

'But,' Roger would argue, 'the trade of the country-shops is being ruined. There's no credit. There's no buying....'

'Credit,' they would reply, 'is a fetish. People will buy what they need. They can do without what they don't buy.'

'But there's no money in circulation,' Roger would cry.

'Money,' they would say, 'is a fetish. Values are correcting themselves at last.'

'But I can't get my debts in,' Roger would shout. 'I can't pay my own creditors.'

'Debts,' they would point out, 'are a fetish. You cannot collect your debts. Well, what of it? This man, from whom you cannot collect your debts, cannot collect his debts from some other man who cannot collect his debts from another man who cannot collect HIS debts from you. You see, it all adjusts itself quite easily in time. Let us all wipe out our debts and begin again on a cash basis. Nobody will really suffer.'

At that stage – and such arguments were as common as sunrise – Sullivan would become sarcastic and the bitter side of him come out.

'I see,' he would say. 'Well, *you* will begin, no doubt. You are owed a month's wages by your employer. If we decide to consider all debts wiped out, will you forgo the wages of that month?'

Blandly they would agree.

'Why not? My grocer will also agree to forgive my debts. It could easily be done.'

'And then you will not allow your employers to go into debt with you again? Eh? And if a trader orders a hundred pigs' heads from me he will pay cash? Eh? And if a miller orders four hundred tons of wheat from the Argentine, will you tell me when will he pay, and where will he pay, and at what rate will he pay? Eh?'

'My dear chap,' they would smile, 'we shan't import any wheat. And as to the price of it – the Government will control all that. I don't think,' they might add gently, 'that you have quite thought it out.'

'And what about the stuff you export?' Roger would say between cold terror that the world was going mad and rage that was threatening to drive himself mad.

'Pooh! We shan't have any exports. We shall be absolutely self-contained.'

'I see,' Roger would whisper. 'And by that time I suppose we'll all be drinking spring-water for tea, and reading the newspapers of twenty years back for news. Yes. Perhaps I haven't thought it all out. It will be a very interesting country. Very. Hahahahahaha!'

And off he would go in a perfect whirl of laughter that was so acid and so rancid and so scornful that they would turn red with irritation and declare the fellow was a danger to the State and should (like all debts) be 'wiped out'.

2

Finally, after twenty years of selling pigs' heads, Roger found he could sell no more. Why that was so nobody could tell. There were no more Danish pigs or Russian pigs or Chinese pigs, and the price of bacon went up, and yet the farmers couldn't sell their pigs and began to eat them. Everybody said that was sensible except Roger. However, he gave up selling pigs to the towns and began to sell seeds to the farmers, and for a while that worked just as well. But then the farmers stopped buying seeds, also. They were now so poor that they garnered their own seeds. And everybody pointed out how sensible that was, too.

'Imagine the folly of the old system,' they said. 'A farmer goes into the town to buy what's growing on his own land! Towns are clearly a fetish. The land is the only reality.'

'It may be,' Roger would cry. 'But where am I? I'll tell you where I am. I'm up the bloody spout.'

And he would think of his wife and child at home living on what their relations could give them and go mad with rage. He came to cursing the Government and the shopkeepers joined him in his cursing and enjoyed themselves immensely. But it meant that Roger would find himself outside their doors just as poor as when he went in.

He now looked what he was becoming, a dangerous man. He would start an argument in the best possible humour, trying to get to the bottom of the new economics – for he was a serious man, and he had a real interest in his country – and he would end by tearing open his coat and crying:

'Me shirt is made in Ireland. Me vest is made in Ireland. The hair on me chest is like catgut from Irish whisky. Me very skin is made out of Irish food. But do ye know what it is? I'm turning to hate the bloody country and all in it. As for this so-and-so Government, and its so-and-so president, and its so-and-so ministry, well, be heavens, my, you, oh!, then, I, ah! . . . Oh!' he would groan, 'if Roger Sullivan was only God Almighty for five minutes!'

And then – after one of his worst quarrels . . .

3

I remember the quarrel well – on the journey to Limerick. I got in at the Junction and the carriage was already steaming with argument. Every place was full and they all with faces as long as a wet week. It was a dismal journey and a dismal day and a dismal argument. Roger was in one corner and he was talking to a black-faced man diagonally across from him – old Phil McCarthy, who travelled for Irish beer.

'Dev's New Economic Policy,' says the black-faced commercial – in the most melancholy voice imaginable, 'is a Christian policy.'

'Primitive Christian,' snaps Roger. 'The sort they had in the Libyan desert.'

'And what's wrong with the Libyan desert?' challenged the melancholy man, almost with fire. 'I suppose a man could be happy in the Libyan desert too?'

'You'd be happy there, I suppose,' said Roger to McCarthy, 'selling your Irish beer? Bloody stuff that'd take the paint off a door. But would I be happy there trying to sell me canary-seed?'

'Ah, no!' said the melancholy man with the suavity of one of the saved. 'Under Dev's policy you wouldn't be selling canary-seed. After all, canaries are a fetish. For instance, now, during the War I had a cousin in Liverpool who had three parrots. And for patriotic reasons do you know what she did with them?'

What Roger said she did with them is not printable.

'She did not,' said the melancholy McCarthy. 'She killed them and ate them. And they were dear to her. And in that way she was able to save quite a few shillings on seed every year. Now, why haven't we that spirit? Our forefathers,' he wagged his lean finger solemnly, 'were happy, and they had no canaries. They had no parrots. They lived simply and they were happy.'

'Happy-me-arm,' roars Roger. 'Living on rotten potatoes in 'forty-seven?'

'That,' said the sad man with a mild reproof of his finger, 'was due to English policy. We exported our corn while we were starving. But under Dev's New Economic Policy we'd export nothing.'

With fury and contempt Roger jumped up and down on his seat.

'In the first place,' he cried, 'if we export nothing we can import nothing. We can have no machinery. In the second place, if we begin to manufacture machinery the price of every machine-made product would go up like a rocket. In the third place we couldn't manufacture machinery. In the fourth place we'd be living in a state of barbarism. We'd have no motor-cars, no motor-buses, no lorries, no trains, no aeroplanes, no big guns, no fountain-pens, no watches, no safety-pins, no nothing. Isn't that right?' he implored the whole carriage-load of commercials.

All those who were travelling for safety-pins or watches or the like hummed a cautious agreement.

'What need have we,' asked the beer-man pityingly, 'for these things? Our forefathers had no buses, and they were happy. If I were the President I'd pass a law forbidding the use of all motor-vehicles. Why can't we use horses? Look at the help that would immediately give to the horse-breeding industry. Take yourself, for example. You'd be far better off riding a horse than travelling in this stuffy train. And what do we want with safety-pins? Our forefathers had no safety-pins, and oh!' he groaned with his eyes to heaven and in a rising wail, 'they were good and they were happy . . .'

'You can't get on without watches!' shouted Roger in despair.

'Our forefathers,' said the commercial traveller.

'Your forefathers-me-arm!' howled Roger.

'I remember,' said the beer-man . . .

'Ah, yes, and I remember,' said Roger. . . .

'I remember,' said McCarthy, unperturbed, 'my own poor mother to say, I think it's dinner-time, children, because the sun is on the dresser. And she was a good and holy woman who . . .'

'Begobs,' gritted Roger, 'then it's kind son for her. What we'll be saying now is the sun is on the dresser, children, but there's nothing on the table. Oh, yes! Oh, yes! I know the sort of Ireland ye want. We'll all be going around living in beehive huts and wearing kilts and having our newspapers like the Book of Kells on goatskin. Yah! Do you know what I'd do with that sort of country? I'd run out of it to the Isle of Man.'

'I am informed,' said McCarthy with a joyous misery, 'that last summer twelve people committed suicide in the Isle of Man. You see – they're not happy. They don't lead the simple life. They live like pagans and they die like pagans.'

The whole carriage murmured approval at that and looked sadly at Roger as at a pagan already doomed to die.

'Pagans my so-and-so!' said Roger, and he went out to the corridor lest he should say worse, while they all looked pityingly after him.

'That man,' said the beer-traveller, 'is a danger to the country.'

'As a matter of fact,' whispered McCarthy to the carriage, 'I heard the man is being watched by the police, and not for that.'

'As a matter of fact,' said a traveller for school requirements, 'he's in the pay of the British.'

'As a matter of fact,' said the jeweller confidentially – but he said nothing else, only tapped his head.

Three days after he did go mad. We were travelling back from Limerick for the weekend on the morning train, and when the train halted at Mallow who should we see on the platform but Roger, and he dressed in kilts, with a feather out of his bonnet and a big card in his hand – BUY ONLY IRISH GOODS. We hailed him and he got in.

'I was down in Tralee,' he began. 'It's a noble town, but decadent. Oh, quite decadent. The heart of Ireland gone rotten. I thought I'd hear nothing but Irish spoken. Not at all. Anglicized. I ran out of the place in disgust. I went to Dingle. The most westerly town in Europe. Was that Irish? Did they talk Irish? Not a bit of it. Most disheartening. I ran out of that. I went on out to Dunquin. It was a dark night and the breakers were roaring under Slea Head. And the lights of Blasket against the black Atlantic. There I was at home. The O'Suileabháin blood in me boiled with delight. Do ye know what I did? I walked down to the rocks and I took off every stitch I had. I thrun my duds into the sea. They were made in Ireland, but the cut was the cut of Cromwell. Naked I ran to the priest's house and naked I knelt to him and naked made him rechristen me in the tongue of my forefathers. He rose me up and he said – "Ruadhri O'Suileabháin, put on your pants." "Never," says I. "Well," says he, "you'll catch yer death of cold." "Nothing but kilts will I wear from this day on," says I, "if I was to die for it ten times over." '

Well, apparently they searched Dunquin high and low with Roger sitting in his pelt by the fire and the housekeeper peeping through the keyhole, and by the grace of God there was a boy there was a piper in Killarney once and for the sake of decency they gave Roger the suit. He tore the buttons off one by one. 'Our forefathers,' Roger cried, 'had no buttons and neither will I.' He showed them then how to use pieces of twigs for clasps and with that he was prickly with twigs all over him.

'And are you still in seeds?' they asked him in the carriage.

He produced a clay pipe made in Tralee, and filled it with tobacco grown in Millstreet, and lit it with a flint and steel he got in an old curiosity shop in Killarney.

'All commerce,' he explained patiently, 'is a fetish. Our forefathers didn't have commercial travellers and they were happy. There is no record of Irish coinage before Elizabeth. It will all adjust itself according to the natural life. This is my last journey in a train,' he apologized, 'and I wouldn't be taking it only I'm in a hurry to bring my wife and child to Sceilg.'

'The Sceilg,' cried McCarthy the beer-man. 'Is it the Sceilg Rock?'

'It is,' said Roger. 'I'm gathering a community of Irishmen who'll be prepared to live the life our forefathers lived. Away with all forms of paganism. Away with trousers. Back to the desert!'

In no time there were all sorts of accounts of Roger's community in every paper in the British Isles, for, naturally, it was better than either a murder or a monster. But of course his wife wouldn't go with him and she had him pestered with priests and policemen trying to persuade him to come home and have sense. However, so far he was breaking no law, and though the Government didn't like it at all because it was bringing their Economic Policy into disrepute, they saw no way to interfere. Then, unfortunately, Roger began to reeve. He and the other lunatics began to go out at night and drive the cattle from the mainland farms down into the sea. That was the end of him. He was arrested and they gave him six months' hard in Mountjoy. After his release he became a familiar figure around Dublin, with his bonnet and his kilts and he living down in the Iveagh House with what pennies people put into his hand for the love of God. And then . . .

4

I remember well the day we heard it. We were travelling up to a Congress of the Commercial Travellers' Benefit Society when McCarthy bought an *Evening Herald* at Ballybrophy and the next thing he was crying out that Poor Roger – as everyone called him now – was dead.

'Is it Roger Sullivan who used to sell pigs' heads?' says we.

'Oh, it is, indeed, the poor lad,' says McCarthy in his miserable voice. 'And he died nobly, too, in the end of all. It appears there was an ambush down in Ballymuggena – a foul attack on the President's car. There by Cooney's pub (sure ye all know it). "And the deceased," he read out, "rushing forward recklessly with outspread hands, faced the attackers. The firing, however, did not cease until the car had passed. The man was then picked up dead. On inquiring at the police-barrack our correspondent was told the matter was well in hand." '

'But is the President safe?' says everybody in one breath; for everybody loved the President.

'Quite safe, thank God.'

'Well, well,' they sighed. 'So there was good stuff in Poor Roger all through.'

'And to think,' says a traveller for ready-mades, 'that it was only under a year ago since we were arguing with him that day on the Limerick train about the New Economic Policy. He was an upright fighter whatever he believed. I had to admire the poor fellow that day the way he stood up for his point against us all.'

' "Imports," says he' – put in the traveller for jewellery, ' "must pay for exports." We can't progress without machinery. I felt the truth of it at the time. But I said nothing.'

'I think,' said the traveller for school requirements, 'that we have a lot to answer for. It was you, now, for example,' he challenged McCarthy, 'that put it into his head to go back to the ways of our forefathers. And have you gone back to the ways of your forefathers yourself? I think he was at his best when he stood for the development of a modern Ireland.'

'Ah, no,' said McCarthy, 'he was at his peak when he put on the kilts at Dunquin. I say here and now, without fear of contradiction, that when Roger Sullivan took off his trousers the course of Irish civilization was changed. It was an historic date. And an historic spot. He was a pioneer.'

'Yes!' protested the jeweller (who was beginning to find it hard to sell even Ingersoll alarm-clocks). 'But why the hell don't you take off your trousers?'

'In time,' defended McCarthy, flushing. 'All in good time. Bit by bit is the keynote of progress. We can agree to differ on his merits. But we can all agree to commemorate him and I propose we do something about it here and now. I am going to move a motion at the Congress that we institute a collection at once to erect a monument on the Rocks of Dunquin showing Roger Sullivan taking off his trousers and casting them into the sea, under it to be written:

HIBERNIA JUGUM ANGLICUM DEPONET.'

'Never,' said the jeweller hotly. 'I'll oppose it. The man's trousers are a symbol. He was right about exports. I believe when he threw his trousers into the sea he was symbolizing the folly of Ireland in abandoning its export trade.'

'Let's have the monument, anyway,' said McCarthy. 'Every comer can interpret it as he wishes.'

'Agreed,' said the jeweller. 'It's a long time, anyway, since anyone had a statue in Ireland.'

Well, the thing was proposed and it was passed, and more than passed, for nothing would do McCarthy but to march four-deep to College Green and have a public demonstration in memory of Roger. At first they did not approve of this. But when McCarthy put in the bit about 'four-deep' he swept the crowd with him. For there isn't an Irishman living who would not march from here to Hong Kong if only he is allowed to do it in military formation.

Of the meeting little is remembered now but its queer ending. McCarthy was in grand oratorical form, and at the critical moment he had just come to the question of the monument.

'And there, a cháirde, near where Grattan points to the future,' he was saying, 'and in the presence of the figures of Goldsmith and Tom Moore, we propose to raise a mighty monolith, to commemorate eternally the moment in which Roger Sullivan on the peak point of the peninsula of Dingle, in the name of Ireland and the future, took down his trousers. Though it's a deed, mind you, I wouldn't, and few of us would, be prepared to do here in College Green. He is to be commemorated not merely for his courage but for his honesty, because he expressed his opinion without rancour or rant – (hear, hear) – because he was a man of independent judgment – (hear, hear) – and because in agreeing to commemorate a man who differed from many of us we erect a monument for ever, also, to the spirit of Irish tolerance. (Cheers.)'

And then McCarthy stopped dead. For there through the excited and cheering crowd he saw coming towards him the furious face of the Man that Died. About his head a neat bandage, and over it a bowler hat, and, worst of all, he was wearing his trousers!

'Ye bloody set of yahoos,' yelled Roger. 'I'll have ye up for libel.'

'What's wrong?' cried the crowd. 'Who's this man? What's this about?'

'It's Roger Sullivan,' shouted McCarthy. 'He's safe. He's with us again. Three cheers for the saviour of his country!'

And the crowd cheered like mad, and McCarthy threw his arms around Roger, and dragged him up on the wagonette, though all he wanted to do, really, was to hide the fact that Roger was wearing trousers like everybody else.

'A speech, a speech, a speech!' howled the mob. 'Tell us about the ambush.'

'Ye Hottentots of Hell!' screamed Roger, and he beside himself with rage. 'There was no ambush. I'll have ye all in jail for this.'

'But you saved the President,' cried McCarthy, and he trying to drape his overcoat around Roger's waist, for he knew that if the crowd saw the trousers the whole lot of them would be killed dead.

'There was no President,' screamed Roger. 'We were just having cockshots at a porter-bottle on the ditch with an airgun. And as for saving the President, do ye think that I'd lift one solitary finger to save a scoundrel that's ruining the country? Do ye know that for wan six months I didn't sell a single package of canary-seed? And for the six months before that I only sold two and a half pigs' heads.'

Then he turned in a fury to McCarthy, who was behind him all this time trying to take down his trousers, unknown to him.

'That policy,' howled Roger to the crowd (and it was clear that whether with the wound, or with all his previous sufferings, he was back to sanity once more), 'that policy is the policy of retrogression. It is a return to barbarism.'

By this time McCarthy had all the buttons open and he was now down on his knees and he pulling like blazes at the legs of Sullivan's pants.

'No, no,' he cried, poking out his head between Roger's legs.

'If you don't balance your exports and imports,' howled Roger –

too excited to take notice – 'you are heading for economic ruin.'

'No, no!' cried McCarthy, who had by now got Sullivan's pants down to his ankles.

'Stop, stop,' cried the crowd. 'This is all wrong. That's not Roger Sullivan. Where's his kilts? His bonnet and feather?'

'Wages,' shouted Roger, hammering the side of the wagonette, 'will fall and prices will rise.'

'Traitor,' shouted the crowd. 'Pull him down. Tear him. That's not Sullivan. That man is a fraud. He's an impostor.'

'He's no impostor,' poked McCarthy, giving Roger a sudden heave, and whipping the trousers off him he waved them in the air.

'Sullivan's trousers!' he cried triumphantly. 'Sullivan's trousers!'

Whereupon the crowd, carried completely away, cheered fit to split the sky. But, unfortunately, at this point some apple-women near the wagonette caught sight of Roger and they screamed out murder when they saw he had no trousers on. And when Roger began again at exports and imports everything went to pieces. The crowd rushed the wagonette. McCarthy shouted to Roger to run. And Roger ran. He broke through the people and bebbled down a side street and off down through the slums near Trinity College, with his shirt-tails flying and the slum-women after him, their hair waving like mænads, the men hurling paving-stones after him, the children screaming with delight at the man's white legs twinkling in the sun, and down from the windows of the brothels the pious prostitutes flung flower-pots at the man without any pants.

A Meeting

Many towns in Ireland, after fifty or sixty years of prosperity, suddenly begin to decay; and 'decay' is the word for it, because they become not so much old as, in literal truth, decayed. Houses fall idle. Then they fall down. The street becomes gapped like an old man's mouth.

Burnt Hall is like that. From being a mere coach-stop on the road to Limerick it suddenly became quite a large town after the Crimea when the English cavalry began to train there. Now, the English cavalry is gone. The barrack (Crimean tent-canvas become stone) is crumbling to pieces. Facing this metamorphosed canvas is a broken line of shops – the sutlers' booths – staring emptily at the mirror of their own future.

I walked down this melancholy street one afternoon this summer. The river was as calm as a dream; it slept among the pebbles of the shore. Fishing was out of the question, so I decided to go for a walk on the bogs, where I heard the hum of a hay machine. Outside one shop (one of the few with any real purpose now) were the usual bundles of hayforks and rakes and spade-handles, tied in lots, all sunburnt. My mind was so idle as I smelled the dinner-bones burning in the cabins, and looked at the loungers extended on the grass under the barrack-wall, that I struck against these farming implements. At the clatter every door became a cuckoo-clock. A man strolled out of the mossy gateway of the barracks and looked at me with suspicion. The loungers actually turned their heads and peeped under their caps that had been shading their faces from the sun. Then I saw a woman staring at me, and I realized that, after twelve years, I was re-meeting Sally Dunn.

When I first knew Sally she was up to her eyes in the Revolution. If there was a dangerous despatch, or a bomb or two, or a gun to be carried through the British patrols, she was the safest girl in Limerick for the job. If there was an important mission to Paris or

America, she was certain to be chosen – the tomboy, the dare-devil, the travelled woman, and the best story-teller I ever met. We used to look up to her, then, as a woman of the world – she was about thirty, older than most of us – so that we always fell silent when she began.

I shall always associate her with her marvellous yarn about her school-days in Paris when, at the age of eighteen, she lost her companions in some big hotel. She took the wrong stairs and found herself suddenly in what must have been a basement *brasserie*, surrounded by red-coated cavalrymen. Her hands would flag as she talked:

'I was flattened, I needn't tell you. Imagine! Only eighteen! I had long golden hair . . .'

'You still have,' somebody would admire.

'Oh, but then it was yards and yards! Down to my knees, girl! They gathered about me. Big men with black moustaches and clanking sabres. They made a circle around me, and they drew their swords and they held them in the air. One of them wound my golden hair around my throat. Then they caught hands, and danced around me. I was limp. Limp!'

Or her story about the Persian princess, told with the most casual reference to Wagons-Lit, the Interlaken and Kandersteg, F. D. trains, the Engadine Express, and 'I said to the gendarme at the frontier' – or, 'Then, at Linz, her maid came in with the coffee' – ending with:

' "*Gar nichts,*" said I, and "*Gar nichts,*" said she. So he went through our things. And the two of us trying to keep looking out the window! He found nothing and he went away and we nearly lost the connection trying to pack at the last moment and dodge out. "Well, anyway," says I to her, "if it hadn't been for your damned old diamonds in the wash basin I could have washed myself." And says she, "If it hadn't been for your stupid papers down my knickers I could have dressed myself." "Pooh to you," says I. "Pooh to you, whatever it is," says she, and I never saw her after. Of course, I don't believe she was a princess at all. And anyway, I'm *sure* she was up to something underhand.'

Even now, as we strolled along the street of Burnt Hall, she talked and talked, and she said she would love to walk with me over the bogs. But first we went to her home; she had married into the little town – her husband was a dentist – and she had three children. It was only when we sat in the front parlour of her little villa (originally built by some English colonel) that I began to feel a lack in her talk. She would drop a subject almost as quickly as she took it up, and race off on a bit of domestic gossip. There were embarrassing pauses.

Once, she went out of the room to appease a crying child, and as I looked about me I felt the same lack. Only on the little book-shelf did I find any memories of the old days – pamphlets from Russia, poems by this rebel leader who was shot in action, and that one who died on a hunger-strike – and even they were down on the lowest shelf behind the armchair. When she ran in to say she was ready she caught me fiddling with them, and she just laughed and lifted her eyes comically to the ceiling, and shook her head a little as if to say . . . I did not know what. I promised myself to find out while we walked in the fields.

The bog was dry as dust and in the heat it trembled like a mirage. For miles and miles it stretched across Ireland, dark purple with heather, and bright with furze. Only a few tattered poplars broke the horizon. There was one little hill – the cone of Cobdur, lonely as a stranded bottle on a beach. The only sign of life was the occasional plume of smoke from a turf-cutter's fire. It was all as quiet as the waters of the shallows back in the village, asleep among the stones. But although it was lovely, not merely old but immemorable, not merely unchanged but unchangeable, it began to weigh heavily on me; and to that feeling, partly of the day, partly of doubt about my friend, was added a sense of other hidden lives when I saw the bog-cabins with the dark water lapping to their doors, just like arks, all sinking back into the mould. We saw a woman inside one door, her eyes as dark as bog-pools, and as patient and as still.

Not, again, that Sally was not full of talk – except for those sudden pauses – and delighted to have somebody to fill with old tales; and I made her tell me again the yarn of the Persian princess, and I tried to rouse her with talk of current politics.

'Aha,' she cried, 'we're still good at heart!'

But then she asked me some question or other that showed me that he had not read a paper for days. She was passionate and angry, too, about the village life, saying that it would drive a saint to sin; but she did not play golf ('an English game'), or play cards ('the women are as silly as geese'); or even go to the annual Point-to-Point that everybody associates with Burnt Hall.

Repeatedly I drew her back and back to the old rebelly days and nights. Once or twice she told a grand story – like that one about the morning she woke up to see a man on the platform at Munich being greeted by an absolutely infuriated woman; simply because on his fur collar was *her* Spanish comb. It had got stuck there when she slept with her head on his shoulder during the journey.

'And you know, I said to myself, I must not lean over that way if I begin to fall asleep. I simply mustn't. And all the time that I was nodding I was keeping myself from that lovely fur collar! But wasn't he a dear to have let me sleep there all the time? For of course he had a private sleeping-compartment of his own – only – The dear! he wouldn't disturb me.'

'How do you know he had?' I asked, sceptically.

'Good Heavens, didn't I tell you who he was? It was only a year after I found it out. I saw his photograph in the papers.'

'Who *was* he, Sally?'

'My child, it was Basil Zaharoff!'

I always did enjoy that story; although the first time she told it to me the man was Fritz Kreisler.

Once or twice, too, she took out her old battle-weapons and, as it were, spat on them saying:

'We're having an auction on Monday at Lady Banks's place in Mount Prospect. That's one of the last of the old gang to leave the country. Thank God for that, anyway.'

'Sally, girl,' I protested, 'don't say you're gone Bolshie?'

There was a pause. She turned and waved her hands wildly, and let them fall.

'I don't know. We are going to have a factory now in the disused barracks. The slum-people have taken over all the living-quarters. And they're turning it into another slum. I don't know. Honest to God, I don't know! I wonder ought we have factories spreading like that all over Ireland? We might end with cities like Manchester or Glasgow? And look at all these vulgar people making money out of it all. It's hard to tell . . . You know, it's . . .' – another pause.

So we talked for an hour, sitting low under one of the high causeway roads, chewing dry rush-stalks. Somehow it was she who seemed to do most of the listening, until I felt like a person giving a transfusion of blood. She was draining me. Life – these few hours of it, anyway – was become like music in the distance, as quiet as the bees wandering near us into the thistle-flowers and the furze. As we walked back our talk was like the dusty smell of the boreens – a musk – hardly a scent, something so faint and slight that it really hardly touched the senses. It was just pleasant, companionable talk – getting its meaning from old memories – nothing more. We might otherwise be strangers.

Then she was suddenly imploring me to meet her again, some day, in Limerick, when we must talk and talk.

'Oh!' she cried. 'We'll talk like the old days. There's so much I want to talk about I can't remember it now. We'll talk until the cows come home! And then talk again until the cocks begin to crow! Won't we?'

'We will!' I laughed. 'Of course we will!'

I knew that if I had met her six or seven years before I could have said:

'Sally, are you really happy here?'

And she would have said:

'Jesus, I'm fed to the bloody eye-teeth with this bloody hole and all in it!'

As we walked to the station a faint, sweet, evening wind came down over Ireland. When I had waved goodbye and was looking back through the window there was already, behind her, a light or two in the little country town, and the bog into which it all sank behind the train was already whispering and dim.

We never met again. I doubt if either of us wanted it or expected it. You cannot have your memories and eat them.

Discord

At the square and low-pitched window of the priest's room high under the eaves and overlooking the city, the two lovers – they had been married only yesterday and were in Dublin for the honeymoon – clutched the window-frame level with their chins and saw the field of roofs. The moving panorama of the sky had blown with it all but the final dusk of smoke. Down in the street a tin-can rolled on the flags with a bright clanking. Behind them Father Peter, his black arm pointing between their heads, led their eyes over the aerial plain.

'That's Saint Michan's with the spire. There's the Protestant Saint Michan's with the square tower.'

Always awkward with the newly-wedded, he had led them straight to the window immediately they entered his room. He now said Pro*test*ant for a joke, hiding his own shyness.

'That?'

To a query of the girl's.

'The Dominican Church. But there now is a very interesting old place, Saint Mary's Abbey. Its real name is Saint Mary's Ostmanby – the East Men, do you see, the Danes. It was a Benedictine church to begin and then the Cistercians took it over. It's all the old Dublin as you know, there in front of us across the river.'

'Girt around by prayer,' said the young man, whose eye picked out the spires and towers all around the horizon.

'And girt around by pubs,' said Father Peter cynically. 'It's wonderful there at night, though, with all the lights. It's like Paris from Montmartre. Those old roofs of that slum-house there between us and the river . . .'

One could have spat down across the narrow street at the humped and twisted dents and downs of the roof-top.

'. . . they're ugly enough with their lumps of plaster between the slates, but you have no idea how lovely they are if there's a fall of snow. Oh, it's very lovely. Last winter there was a heavy fall and those little crevices of roofs were . . . Ah!'

They could almost see the whirling gentle fall darkening over Dublin as they heard him gurgle behind them with delight. He was forgetting his shyness. Through the windows of the slum-house they could see three floors and on each floor iron bed-legs. Seeing the poor drabness of it Angela turned away.

'Well, well,' teased the girl as she looked over the cosy room with its big mannish furniture and its low roof, 'who wouldn't be a priest?'

They sat down in the deep armchairs, their minds brought back by her to the present.

'This is the best of it ye're seeing now,' laughed Peter. 'Not that I have such a bad time, mind you.'

'Are you kept very busy, father?' she asked kindly.

'No,' he said, a bit doubtfully; and then, more positively, 'No!' He poked the fire, and leaned back in the capacious settee, and supported his paunch, for it was a cold autumn and he liked his comfort. He lit a cigar and gave them cigarettes, to celebrate the occasion as he said. 'I have two Confraternities, the women's every Monday night, and then the first Sunday of each month I have the Bona Mors. That,' he explained, 'is for the old people. For a happy death. It's mainly the old weak people who come to that, as you might understand.'

The young lovers nodded as if they did understand.

'Then we have a week on and a week off on duty, sick-calls and the like. We share that between us. Day and night. I'm unlucky at that. I seem to get more sick-calls than any other priest.'

'That's because you're so popular, father,' laughed the girl.

'Faith, 'tis not. 'Tis just the way things come. I have one old lad there now in Watling Street and he gets uræmic fits. Even if he had me in twice that day and it was three in the morning he'd have me in again.'

'And you have to go?' asked the youth.

'Oh,' said the priest solemnly, 'you couldn't refuse.'

'Some of them are divils,' commiserated the youth.

'Aha,' teased his girl, 'wait till you're on your bed of death and you'll be howling for a priest like the worst of them.'

'Bedad,' laughed Father Peter, 'a uræmic fit is a pretty bad thing.'

'I suppose,' she said, 'you'd wish sometimes for a little parish down the country?'

'I do,' he agreed eagerly. 'I do. It's good here. And I meet all sorts of people. And it's interesting work. But – ah, you know . . .'

'Still,' said Frank with equal eagerness, 'I envy you. You meet people, you're in contact with life. There's that fear always over me – being isolated – getting away from life – getting wrapped into myself. Everyone living in the country has that feeling sometimes. It's a bit terrifying.'

His eyes wandered to the sea of roofs. His girl looked at him, as if surprised by some cavern in him that she had not seen before and must, maybe, yet explore. She did not guess that in his mind that image of a vast Dublin, growing and decaying, was still dilating like a smoke in wind.

'There's that indeed,' said the priest. 'You must keep on meeting people. But, then, you know, too, here it's always a certain kind of people. Sad stories. Rotten stories. Down-and-out stories. Always the same. Drunks, paupers, prostitutes – ach!'

'You have a lot of books?' said the girl, again drawing their minds back with hers.

'I'm bankrupt from them. But they're a great refuge for me. As you see, I have no room for any more.'

He rolled out of his settee and picked out a volume.

'This *Life of Mangan* reminds me. This room is full of associations. Mangan wrote most of his poetry here: he and Davis and the rest of the writers of *The Nation* used to come here and talk and argue into the dawn. John Mitchel was in this room. That was when the famous Father Meehan – C. P., you remember – lived here. He kept open house for the lot of them. It was called The Attics. They had Attic Nights!'

'Is that a fact?' cried the youth. 'James Clarence Mangan in this room?'

He rose and walked about it excitedly. It would have been just the same then – the low ceiling, the windows crushed under it, the green baize door, the cosy fire, the books from floor to roof, and all that poor, decayed city full of life and fashion and movement and colour. His mind flooded with vague associations of eighteenth- and nineteenth-century Dublin.

'Surely Wolfe Tone was born somewhere hereabouts?' he pointed.

'And Lord Edward Fitzgerald, where did he live?'

His hands seemed to grope with his memory.

'Why, man,' cried Father Peter, 'Thomas Street is just behind us. Emmet had his depot for making bombs a stone's-throw away. They hanged him in the street – you can see Saint Catherine's spire just over the spot from my bedroom window. The street between us and the Castle is Lord Edward Street.'

'Mangan!' said the young man, and he recited, moodily but finely, while his wife looked at him, troubled, and at the priest almost with distrust:

> 'I saw her once, one little while, and then no more:
> 'Twas paradise on earth awhile, and then no more.
> Ah, what avails my vigil pale, my magic lore?
> She shone before mine eyes awhile and then no more.
> The shallop of my peace is wrecked on Beauty's shore.
> Near Hope's fair isle it rode awhile, and then no more . . .'

'He was a fine poet,' said Father Peter, and then, thinking this too melancholy for honeymoon days, he said, 'They had one great night here, I believe, when they had an argument on Shakespeare. Davis was reciting Antony's speech to the mob, "Lend me your ears . . ." "What nonsense," cries Mangan. "That's a misreading. He said, 'Lend me your cars.' Sure, they were going to a funeral." '

They laughed lightly at that, but the fume of memory was still in the young man's brain.

> 'I saw her once, one little while, and then no more;
> The earth was Peri-land awhile, and then no more.
> Oh, might I see but once again as once before,
> Through chance or wile, that shape awhile, and then no more!
> Death soon would heal my griefs! This heart now sad and sore
> Would beat anew a little while, and then no more...'

'Aye,' said Father Peter, 'and the O'Hussey's *Ode to the Maguire* is magnificent.'

> 'An awful, a tremendous night is this meseems,
> The floodgates of the rivers of heaven, I think, have been burst
> wide...'

The girl had fallen silent. The priest noticed it.

'Come and see the chapel,' he said. 'Or the crypt.'

'What's there to be seen?' asked the girl distrustfully.

'Why,' cried the priest, 'it's most historic. There's maybe a hundred people buried there. Great huge vaults there like wine-cellars. Do you know who's buried there? Leonard MacNally.'

MacNally the spy. The scrubby lawyer who was the friend of the Earl of Clare, the traitor who used to eat his nails and was so dirty the bar-mess would not admit him. The friend of Tone. The friend of Emmet. He had defended him and betrayed him. Not until he was dead did the people discover it. The priest laughed.

'Yes, he's down there. And his coffin falling to pieces. Every time I go down I give it another kick. When he was being brought there I believe the poor of the city crowded the vaults to be sure he wasn't laid near or nigh to one of their own. Come on and let's have a look at the church.'

After descending the long dark stairs and entering the chapel by a side-door they were surprised to find the high altar so marble-white and glittering. As they looked reverently at it a young man with his hands joined and his eyes cast down approached the priest. The lovers moved away, but they heard the man's request; his wife was outside and she wanted her baby to be baptized. Father Peter gruffly told him the name of the priest on duty. In one place an old woman was muttering prayers under her shawl. An old man told his beads under the light of the candles by the Virgin's altar. They were all poor and ragged. Suddenly they saw a wild-bearded, hollow-faced man standing away back in the nave, praying devoutly. His beard was soft but tangled; his hair was to his shoulders; he held his two arms aloft as he prayed; his eyes shone. Curiously they watched him, a little frightened.

'Who is he?' asked the girl of the priest.

'He's daft,' whispered the priest. 'An ex-soldier. He sometimes preaches to the empty church. Come this way.'

'He'd terrify me,' said the girl.

Peter laughed again as he led them down another flight of stairs through an old trap-door.

'You'd go off your nut here if you took too much notice of things. Wait till I light this candle.'

Down they went and the air was close and it was pitch-dark beyond the candle gleam. In that little light they saw the vaults open right and left of the great supporting arches. She took her man's hand as the shapes of the coffins emerged out of the dark. A hanging bit of rusted wire caught in her hair and she gave a little scream.

'That's a bit of wire,' said the priest cheerfully.

Two eyes of light from the street-level stared at them.

'Do you see those holes?' he said, and they were all stooping. 'The cats come in there from the street.'

Before them the wall under the high altar was pierced by two tiny arches. Behind was a tiny enclosure in which they barely fitted. 'Here we are.' He held the candle sideways to show the lettering on a coffin-plate. With his spittle he tried to rub the name clear.

'*Philip Betagh*,' he read out. 'That was the first man to be buried here. He was a hedge-schoolmaster who brought the property and set up a school here. This (he was speaking like a guide), I forgot to say, is the site of the old Smock Alley Theatre where Peg Woffington used to foot it one time. Betagh bought the site and afterwards the church was built on it. The land belongs to the Protestants, so we still pay them a hundred and sixty pounds a year for ground rent. Think of it – nearly two hundred thousand pounds they have from us by now. Isn't it a shame!'

They felt hot and clammy. The candle smelt of its own grease. They clambered out of the place, and he showed them another and another coffin.

'I smell putrefaction,' said Frank.

The priest showed them a pile of tiny coffins.

'There's something the Gas people never put in their front window. An explosion that wiped out a whole slum tenement.'

The girl clung, horrified, to her lover. She thought of the young wife whose baby had to be baptized, as she looked at the tiny little boxes, now falling apart and immovable.

'Oh!' she cried. 'Come out, come out.'

'I want to see MacNally,' said Frank obstinately.

'There you are.'

It lay all alone in a great vault. It was unusually large because of the lead casing. The wood was a fine red dust. A finger on it left a hole. To show them that it was of lead the priest kicked it, and for bravado the young man kicked it,

'Come, come,' said the girl. 'I'm baking.'

They went back as they had come. The wild eyes of the mad soldier had not deflected from the high altar. The youth who had intercepted them still stood by the side-door, his fingers peaked, his eyes downcast.

'Why didn't you come at the right time?' said the priest to him as he passed out to the windy, sunny September air: outside the young girl waited with her baby in an old battered pram.

The priest spoke to her more gently. 'You should have come at twelve o'clock,' he said.

'We were late, father,' said the girl humbly. 'I was workin'.'

They re-entered the presbytery and Father Peter challenged them to race him up the stairs. He took it three steps at a time. He left them in the room while he went for his hat and overcoat. He was going to take them out for a 'bit of fun to celebrate.'

They did not speak while he was away. She sat looking into the fire and he stood by the window, looking over the city. A light or two had begun to twinkle. The roofs were melting into one another. Somehow since they had met the priest several years had been added to both of them. They had come upon one of those moments of life when, like the winter butterflies in the high corners, they felt the hurt of cold. Breezily the priest returned, coated, buttoned, slapping his hands.

'Well, now, boys and girls, we'll see what Dublin has to offer in the way of life.'

Meekly and slowly they followed him and on the stairs they groped for one another's fingers, and when they met they held and clutched. Outside the dusk was fallen and the night air was blue and the water of the river held an autumn mist.

While they were with him they tried hard to be gay, and they delayed him when he wanted to go, and Frank even made him promise to meet them in the morning; but, once he was gone, they hurried to their hotel along the quays, faster and faster, their hands clasped like children lost in a wood. Not until they were quite alone, and he had drawn down the window-blinds, and closed the windows, shutting out the faint cry of a barking dog, did they begin to laugh; and they laughed and laughed over Peter, with his penny candle, until they had him turned into a fat Punch like the Devil in the play.

Then he closed the old-fashioned plush curtains so as to shut out the last glow from the arc-lamp. They lay beside one another in the dark. Their passion was wild in its unrestraint.

In the morning the river glittered in the sun, and she made him bring Peter to the Zoo. There she was so gay and comical with the animals that they were delighted by her innocence, and Peter, leaving them at the gate of the Park, took Frank by the arm and said, 'A grand girl, Frankie, boy!' However, nobody but she saw the joke, and even she, in her wisdom, as women do with their wisdom, never thought about it when she recalled it, as she never forgot it when it had long passed out of her silly little head.

The Confessional

In the wide nave the wintry evening light was faint as gloom and in the shadows of the aisle it was like early night. There was no sound in the chapel but the wind blowing up from the river-valley, or an occasional tiny noise when a brass socket creaked under the great heat of a dying flame. To the three small boys crouched together in a bench in the farther aisle, holding each other's hands, listening timidly to the crying wind, staring wide-eyed at the candles, it seemed odd that in such a storm the bright flames never moved.

Suddenly the eldest of the three, a red-headed little ruffian, whispered loudly; but the other two, staring at the distant face of the statue, silenced him with a great hiss like a breaking wave. In another moment the lad in the centre, crouching down in fear and gripping the hand on each side of him, whispered so quietly that they barely heard: 'She's moving.'

For a second or two they did not even breathe. Then all three expelled a deep sigh of disappointment.

It was Monday afternoon, and every Monday as they had each heard tell over and over again in their homes, Father Hanafin spoke with the Blessed Virgin in the grotto. Some said she came late at night; some said in the early morning before the chapel was opened; some said it was at the time when the sun goes down, but until now nobody had dared to watch. To be sure Father Hanafin was not in the chapel now, but for all that the three little spies had come filled with high hope. The eldest spoke their bitter disappointment aloud.

'It's all my eye,' he said angrily. The other two felt that what he said was true, but they pretended to be deeply shocked.

'That's an awful thing you said, Foxer,' whispered the boy in the middle.

'Go away, you, Philpot!' said Foxer.

'God! I think it's a cause for confession, Foxer!' whispered Philpot again.

'It's a mortal sin, Foxer!' said the third, leaning over to say it.

'Don't try to cod me, Cooney, or I'd bust yer jaw!' cried Foxer angrily.

Philpot hushed them sternly and swiftly, but the spell was broken. They all leaned back in the bench.

Beside them was Father Hanafin's confession-box, its worn purple curtain partly drawn back, his worn purple stole hanging on a crook on the wall inside, and as Foxer gazed into the box with curiosity the Adversary tempted him in his heart.

'Come on, Cooney!' he invited at last, 'come on, and I'll hear yer confession.'

'Gor! Come on,' said Cooney, rising.

'That's a sin,' said Philpot, though secretly eager to sit in the priest's chair.

'You're an awful ould Aunt Mary!' jeered Foxer, whereupon all Philpot's scruples vanished and the three scrambled for the conressor's seat. But Foxer was there before either of them, and at once he swished the curtains together as he had seen Father Hanafin do, and put the long stole about his neck. It was so nice in there in the dark that he forgot his two penitents waiting beyond the closed grilles on either side, and he was putting imaginary snuff into his nostrils and flicking imaginary specks of snuff from his chest when Cooney's angry face appeared between the curtains.

'Are you going to hear me confession, Foxer, or are yeh not?' he cried in a rage, eager for his turn to be priest.

'Go back, my child,' said Foxer crossly, and he swished the curtains together again. Then, as if in spite, he leaned over to the opposite grille and slowly and solemnly he drew the slide and peered into the frightened eyes of Philpot.

'Tell me how long since your last confession, my child,' he said gravely.

'Twenty years,' whispered Philpot in awe.

'What have you done since then?' intoned Foxer sadly.

'I stole sweets, father. And I forgot my prayers. And I cursed, father.'

'You cursed!' thundered Foxer. 'What curse did you say?'

'I said that our master was an ould sod, father,' murmured Philpot timidly.

'So he is, my child. Is there anything else?'

'No, father.'

'For your penance say two hundred and forty-nine rosaries, and four hundred and seventy Our Fathers, and three hundred and thirty-two Hail Marys. And now be a good obedient boy. And pray for me, won't you? Gawd bless you, my child.'

And with that Foxer drew the slide slowly before the small astonished face.

As he turned to the other side his hand fell on a little box – it was Father Hanafin's consolation during the long hours spent in that stuffy confessional listening to the sins and sorrows of his parishioners. Foxer's awkward fingers lifted the cover and the sweet scent rose powerfully through the darkness as he coaxed the loose snuff down from the cover. Then drawing the slide on Cooney, he gravely inhaled a pinch and leaned his ear to the cool iron of the grille.

Outside a footstep sounded on the marble floor, and peering out Foxer saw the priest walk slowly up the farther aisle, turn and walk slowly down again, his breviary held high to the slanting radiance of the Virgin's altar.

'It's Father Hanafin,' whispered Foxer to Cooney; and to Philpot – 'Keep quiet or we're all ruined.'

Up and down the solemn footsteps went, and high above their heads in the windows of the clerestory and along the lath and plaster of the roof the wind moaned and fingered the loose slates, and now and again they heard the priest murmur aloud the deep, open vowels of his prayer, Gaudiamus Domine, or Domine, Domine meo, in a long breathing sigh.

'He's talking to the Virgin,' breathed Cooney to Foxer.

'He's talking to the Virgin,' breathed Foxer in turn to Philpot.

'Amen,' sighed the priest, and went on his knees before the candles that shone steadily and were reflected brilliantly in the burnished brass.

The three spies had begun to peep from their hiding-place when the snuff fell on Foxer's lap and the grains began to titillate his nose. In agony he held his mouth for a full minute and then burst into a furious sneeze. In astonishment the priest gazed about him and once again Foxer held his breath and once again he sneezed. At the third sneeze the priest gazed straight at the box.

'Come out!' he said in a loud voice. 'Come out of that box!'

And as the three guilty forms crept from the three portals he commanded again, 'Come here!'

Awkwardly they stumbled forward through the seats, trying to hide behind one another, pushing and upbraiding one another until they stood before him.

'What were you doing in there?' he asked Foxer.

'I was hearing their confession, father,' trembled Foxer, and half raised his arm as if to ward off a blow.

For a moment the priest glared at him and then he asked, 'And what penance did you give?'

'I – I gave three hundred and thirty Hail Marys, father, and I think it was four hundred Our Fathers, father, and two hundred and forty-nine rosaries, father.'

'Well!' pronounced the priest in a solemn voice, 'go home and let each one of ye say that penance three times over before nine o'clock tomorrow morning.'

Stumbling over one another's heels the three crept down the dark aisle and crushed out through the green baize door and into the falling night that was torn by the storm. The street-lamps were lit and under one of these they halted and looked at each other, angry and crestfallen.

'Nine hundred and ninety Hail Marys!' wailed Philpot, and Cooney squared up to Foxer with clenched fists.

'Yerrah!' said Foxer. 'It's all a cod!'

And he raced suddenly away to his supper, followed by the shouts and feet of the other two.

Mother Matilda's Book

I

In their starched and pointed coifs, beak-like, their winged blue sleeves, their skirts pouched about them like balloons, the sisters of Saint John of the Cross look for all the world like geese. As they talk their cowls slew about in the air. They move as if on castors.

But, in her hey-day, Mother Matilda simply was a goose. She was shapeless as a ball of fur; she clucked and stuttered – her teeth never fitted her – and as the smiling novices hopped about her, she was for ever waving her hands up and down in the air as if she were winging water through the air from the tips of her little fat hands. And as in her youth she had been a goose, in her years she was a wretched little gosling. Her clothes hung from her, she had developed a dropped eyelid, her cowl fell over her blind eye; her voice was a pip-cough. When she slept in the sun, with her breath coming in gusts through her mouth, her face red with sun and sleep, her bibulous coif, and her teeth sinking slowly down to her lower lip, she was a picture nobody in the convent, least of all the novices over whom she once held power, cared to look at. She was become one of those pensioners of religion that you find in every convent, and whose doings are a constant worry to their House. She was come to that stage when the new Reverend Mother – the third since her day – began to conspire with the sisters against her; as she had in her time conspired against the pensioners above in the graveyard.

Daily they gossiped about her, looking over their shoulders lest she should come on them unawares; they said, nodding many times over it, that she was a dear old soul, everyone in the convent knew that. But after all (we get old, and she can't help it, poor dear), this latest habit of losing her teeth was too much. Why, you might walk on them! And Sister Eunice said that if she straightened Mother Matilda's coif once a day, she straightened it twenty times. And

Sister Agnes whispered behind their backs that it was a pity she dropped tea on her gimp. And Sister Ignatius thrust in her red, country face with the two buck-teeth, and cried that yesterday as she was walking by the oratory with Father Kennedy they almost fell over her legs, where she had them stretched out right in front of her like a man, and she sitting on the grass-bank snoring like a trooper. They all laughed at that, but Mother John sighed impatiently and hushed them away to their tasks. They were no help to her.

Then as she stood in the green distempered hall and looked up at the portrait of their foundress, her eye fell on the list of Mothers of this House framed beneath it. There was Matilda's name and two other names after it, and then, last of all, her own name, Mother John O'Connell. Poor old Matilda had inscribed that list herself, in a firm uncial hand with grotesque Celtic capitals – she had been drawing mistress in her day; and as the name *Mother John O'Connell* showed – clear and soft and flowing – inscribed only a few months ago, she had not yet lost her skill. Mother John noted all that; but she noted, too, with a little start of fright, the date beside the first name of all. In five years' time that house of the North Abbey would be seventy-five years in existence. At once she turned and went smiling in search of Matilda.

She found her telling her beads in a shady corner, sheltering from the summer sun and wind. She straightened her coif and, holding her hand, led the talk to the history of the Order. From their nook the city roofs fell into the valley, hung there in a swaying hammock of smoke. From the near backyards, with the shirts and shifts drying in the wind, and the cries of the lane children and the mothers calling them at the tops of their voices, that aerial plain narrowed out and up to the farthest smoke-rim beyond. There they could barely see another piece of churchyard calm, the second house of Saint John of the Cross – the South Abbey.

'Do you realize, mother,' said Mother John, 'that in five years' time it will be the Jubilee of this House?'

'I do,' said Mother Matilda.

'We must begin to prepare for it,' said Mother John.

At the word 'we' Matilda looked up with a faint hope; then she said humbly:

'Indeed, you must, mother.'

Quickly John began to talk about their foundress, the wealthy and charitable spinster Georgina Tinsely, whose people had made their money out of sweet Kerry butter and lived, through the last century, in the North Abbey. That was her portrait in the hall, a sharp, long-jawed face, shadowed by its frilled coif. Mother John began to complain that in spite of the interdictions of generations of Reverend Mothers, the frame beneath was worn shapeless by 'the lanes' about.

'Year after year,' she wailed, 'they rub their dirty fingers on the wood. I even saw a woman scraping off a piece of gilt the other day and blessing herself with it. As if it were Holy Water or a bit of the True Cross!'

'Ah, wisha, sure,' soothed Matilda, 'it's no wonder. She did great work for them.'

'They don't do it in the South Abbey,' said John, looking across at it.

'She didn't live in the South Abbey,' said Matilda.

'She founded it,' said John.

'Well, in a way she did,' said Matilda, 'but it was her sister gave her wealth to it.'

Gabbling away, while John listened cutely, she began to trace the spread of the Order all over Ireland, recalling how a third house had been founded by a convert, how a parish priest in Kinsale had asked for a fourth, because he wanted free schools for the soldiers' children, how a bishop gave land for a fifth near Cashel, and how the Order had prayed night and day when a lawsuit was being fought to get money for a sixth.

'I often heard Mother Mary, God rest her,' said Matilda, 'tell about the Novenas they said that time. If we lost that case we'd be beggared for the next fifty years, aye, and longer!'

John looked at her – she was a bright old woman, yet, she thought. Yes, she could do it all right. And if she didn't, what harm was done.

'Mother Matilda,' she ordered, and she straightened the dropped coif once more, 'you shall write the history of the North Abbey and the Order. The book will be like the Book of Kells. It must be ready for the Jubilee, and every house in the country will see it and pride in it.'

She rose and looked down smilingly at the old pensioner. Matilda, like an old cat rejoicing in a sudden wave of sunshine, had stuck out her tongue between her teeth and was gazing over the city and the hills beyond. She clapped her little hands and waved the tiny sausages of fingers up and down in the air. Then her hands fell and she sighed.

'I'll begin it, mother. But I'll never live to see the Jubilee, mind you.'

'You'll live to see the Centenary,' laughed Mother John, as she raced away, delighted with her plan.

2

For the first couple of years Matilda did quite well at the History. She got a huge vellum book, bound in tooled leather, a book so huge and heavy that she always had a novice beside her to lift and move it. (This was part of Mother John's cunning – it gave her an excellent excuse for putting a warder over the old nun.) With the most perdurable inks, of scarlet and violet and gallblack, with Chinese white and tiny drops of gold, Matilda framed each small block of handwriting. She would spend a month tracing out the convolutions of the patterns in which she bedded her capitals, peering at them for hours through a magnifying-glass held out by the trembling hand of the novice. She copied these designs from Irish manuscripts of the tenth and eleventh centuries, the great period of manuscript illumination, and she expended so much patience in making her plant-like animals brilliant and glittering, after their long voyage through their own deformities, that by the time she had spent three years on the book and covered twenty years of history, there was not a convent of the Order that had not borrowed the unfinished manuscript, to show it to their sisters and patrons. Nobody cared now if she snored over her work, or if her coif fell on her neck, or if she mislaid her teeth. For she did all these things in the privacy of her cell, and if she escaped to do them elsewhere they could chide the novice to their hearts' content.

Alas! she then grew ill and her eyes began to fail her, and she grew weary of her work. She had copied all the more interesting pieces of illumination and she grew perverse and headstrong and began to invent designs for herself. But they were always the same kind of thing – vines twined about a trellis with bunches of purple grapes and great vine-leaves wandering into the body of the text. A little later on she ceased to make capitals, and her round uncial declined into a ragged minuscule, from that into an angular running hand, and lastly into a childish typescript of her own. Because she was too lazy to rule her page it sloped out of the horizontal. There were several errors in spelling and the leaves were often smudged.

It grew so bad that by the time Mother Philomena succeeded Mother John the book could no longer be sent out of the North Abbey. They tried to suggest to her that she was tired and should allow somebody else to finish the book, for by now it had become, in their minds, a prized possession of the House. They would cluster over her as she worked, sighing at one another behind her back, while the novice stared at them all with a stony face, or looked at the old nun as one might look at a strange animal. Or they would hint that she needed more light; or one of them would lend her a ruler that was 'nicer than her own'; or the more daring ones brought new pieces of illuminated work that they 'thought she might like to get ideas from.' She would just raise her fat face with the greying moustaches and smile her thanks and go on ruining the book.

With the approach of the Jubilee the last step was reached. She hurried and scurried over the page like a rabbit, scarcely seeing what she wrote. Her vines became leafless; their staffs sagged; the grape-bunches were either pills or big as onions. She did not even notice if her sleeve suddenly swept a whole page into a mist. But that was not the worst of it. She talked of nothing but the Jubilee day. Clacking her teeth like an enraged monkey, she would peer up suddenly at the novice through the thick lenses of her spectacles and cry:

'I think we ought to exhibit it in the chapel!'

Then she would turn the half-filled page, with a stuttering, tremulous:

'Where did I leave off? What last? What last?'

Or she would jump up and, wrapping her glasses in her sleeve, hobble off to search out the new Reverend Mother – Philomena.

'The hall, mother,' she would grin. 'That's the best place. I just thought of it. In the hall! Can I show it in the hall?'

Whereupon Philomena, who was a shrewish city woman with a cocked nose and a lisp, would see His Lordship stooping in amazement over the childish efforts of the old nun, or the visiting Mothers smiling sweetly at her and telling her what a great work the mother-house had done for the Order, and how well they could understand now why the book was kept from them during the last three years.

'No, dear,' snapped Philomena – red to the summit of her nose – 'it is a very bad place. Do straighten your cowl, mother dear. What? In the hall? In everybody's way! Sister Agnes!' (she calls out to a nun flitting by). 'You know, dear, you have no right to be . . .'

So she leaves the old pensioner drooping like a broken plant, and that afternoon three separate sisters come privately to her to tell her that 'poor Mother Matilda is weeping all alone in the oratory and will not leave it for anybody.'

'Why,' she implores Mother John (already sinking to the stage of pensioner herself), 'why did you ever suggest to that poor soul to write a history of the Order?'

'Oh!' cries John. 'How can you be so hard on the old dear? Why, the whole convent knows she is a born saint. Please, mother, let me tell her you will exhibit the book somewhere.'

'Tell her anything you like,' cried Philomena. 'This Jubilee will be the death of me.'

And before she could retract her promise, off goes John to fetch the scribe, and off goes Philomena to conspire against the pair of them. From her office-window she could see them, a few minutes later, coming hand-in-hand down the rosary, Matilda shining like a moon, as she unwrapped her glasses to add a few more smudges and a few more monstrous grapes to her manuscript.

3

It was the Reverend Mother, as usual, who settled the problem. She took Matilda aside and told her she had made special arrangements for the book. They would have a lectern sent up from the North Cathedral. They would drape it in purple velvet. She could have candles about it and flowers. They would give her the best room in the school, where everybody could see it in comfort.

The result was that the novice watched in terror while Matilda madly filled page after page, composing now as she went, making the most loving personal remarks about everybody in the convent, down to the new washer-woman, whose steam was even then rising from the basement.

'A most praiseworthy and Christian woman,' read the novice

over her shoulder. 'She is married, we are informed on the best authority, to the most disgraceful . . .'

'Disgraceful?' popped Matilda back at the novice, while her hand made impatient circles over the page. 'What else is he?'

'Mother, I don't know him!' wailed the novice.

'Oh! What else? What else? Disgraceful? What else could he be?' Her hand raced on.

'. . . and disreputable drunkard of a man. She has ten children, she tells us, all by different husbands. But the hand of God has watched over her and lighted her a way out of the . . .

'The what?' she cries. 'The what?'

'I don't know, mother?'

'What do you get lit out of? What? What?'

'. . . pit!' writes the hand.

'Pit of what?' she cries again. 'Of what?'

'. . . iniquity,' writes the hand, while the novice groans and tells her beads.

They finished the book so late on the eve of the Jubilee day that Matilda was too exhausted to question if anybody would ever come to the Geography Room to see her masterpiece. It was three storeys up, and all that evening they tramped up and down stairs, carrying flowers and candles, and bickering with other nuns who wanted the same flowers and candles for something else.

They barely had the room and the book prepared as the first guests arrived the following morning. The lawns were green after a providential night of showers and a morning of burning sun. The Chinese lanterns barely swayed on their strings and the tablecloths barely flapped a lazy wing under the jellies and the wines and the teacups and the cones of sweetcake. The gentle wind had cleared the city roofs of smoke and the clouds were building castles in the air. The two nuns, the old nun and the young novice, remained for hours watching the greens grow black with priests as if a flock of crows had alighted there and were pecking on the lawn. They all had shiny tall-hats; a neat circle of white cuff on every wrist; here and there a warm ribbon of scarlet marked out a canon or a dean.

Then His Lordship came with Mother Philomena on his right and her second-in-charge on his left, and the Mistress of Novices accompanied his secretary behind. As he passed through the crowd of clergy and lay people, he was like some giant walking through a field of rushes; at every step they sank before him on a half-knee. Then he went indoors and the two nuns fluttered about their book and lit the candles and tipped the flowers.

But he did not come to their room – and no priest came to their room, and through the livelong day nobody came. Until, several hours after lunch, Mother John managed to round up two giggling schoolgirls who looked and blushed at one another, and were heard giggling louder than ever as soon as they got outside the door. John had tried hard (so she whispered to the novice), but Philomena had her cohorts so well deployed that it was impossible to get anybody even as far as the door of the school.

4

Then, from their window-perch, the novice suddenly saw a friend of still earlier novitiate days entering with the Reverend Mother of the Kilcrea House. After being cooped up in that room all day, far from the fun and excitement below, her flesh weakened and she ran to seek her. ('Just for one minute, mother dear, you won't go away, will you, his lordship might come?') It was ten minutes, however, before she did find her, and then, hand-in-hand, the two young nuns went wandering under the lilacs by the gardener's shed, pressing one another's fingers under cover of their long sleeves, and smiling foolishly, as if they were both a little tipsy, and sometimes pausing to kiss when they recalled some particularly happy morning in Kilcrea. They were so full of joy that they lost all sense of time.

Left to herself, Matilda blew out the candles and wandered down, painfully, step by step, to the main parlour, and from that to the guests' parlour, and so from room to room. One or two nuns, sitting there with friends, smiled at her coldly and she retired at once. Then she heard voices in the Common Room, and peeping in, she saw that it was filled with priests, standing or sitting about comfortably, sipping tea or wine or smoking cigarettes. There were two or three nuns there, but though they stared at her, she did not retire. With a little croak of joy she had spied old Father Mulligan in a far corner, a parish priest she had known years ago, and she was beckoning to him and making noises like a bird to attract his attention.

At last somebody pointed her out to him and with delight he came forward and drew her in. He was a hearty, rude-faced man who had been given a small parish twenty years before in a village by the sea and he had never left it. Whiskers stood out of his ears and a kind of invading wilderness of white hair was stopped on each cheek by the razor. He was the only priest there smoking a pipe. He bowed over her and flattered her, and they talked for a while over everybody they knew – though it was one long litany of God-rest-them! – until his curate came by and he was led forward to meet the old nun.

'The oldest sister in the House,' boomed Father Mulligan.

'Interesting!' murmured the curate humbly. 'It should be commemorated. The doyen of the House.'

The next thing Matilda knew was a sudden fall in the clamour of talk about her and they were all listening to old Father Mulligan calling on them to drink 'in wine, whisky, or good strong tay' the health of the doyen of the North Abbey.

'And she's still at work, I may say. She had completed the History of the Order of Saint John of the Cross.'

'History?' one or two murmured with interest.

'Illuminated like the Book of Kells,' palpitated Matilda. 'It's on exhibition in the Geography Room and I wish you'd all come and see it.'

'Let's all go and see it,' said Father Mulligan, while the three nuns looked at one another in horror.

'This way,' piped Matilda, turning round and round like a peg-top, unable, in her excitement, to find the door.

But then she clapped her hands to her mouth and stared around at them in fright.

'What's wrong, mother?' asked the curate in his miserable, whining, too-humble voice.

'My teeth,' wailed Matilda. 'I've lost my teeth. I think I had them in my hand when I came into the Common Room.'

'Let's find them,' cried a merry little man with a bush of curly hair.

He had drunk just a shade too much Beaune in the wine-tent.

'A search! A search!' he cried.

Whereupon they all began to wave their hands in the air and lift cushions and flower-pots, and stooping, they raised their behinds before armchairs and peeped under settees, and they opened cupboards that they should not have opened, while the three nuns fled for Philomena and her cohorts, and above all for the wretched novice who had allowed Matilda to escape.

'Lost! A row of delf!' cried curly-mop.

'Aurora's pearls,' said the classical scholar.

'Upper and lower?' teased Father Mulligan, while Matilda in a corner searched herself all over.

The fun and scurry was at its height when His Lordship entered, ushered in by Philomena's second-in-charge.

'Oh, my!' he said in his gentle country brogue that broke every word into an iambic sigh. 'O-oh! m-my!'

'It's Mother Matilda,' explained Father Mulligan's curate in a sad voice, dropping his cigarette behind him where a friend deftly crushed it under his toe. 'She has mislaid her denture,' he went on, and he said it like a naughty schoolboy, looking up at the bishop under his fair eyebrows.

'Oh, my!' groaned his lordship sympathetically.

'And who,' he croaked in his graveyard voice, that with time had become gentle and slow, because nobody had ever dared to interrupt him, 'who may Mother Matilda be?'

'She is Father Mulligan's friend,' said the curate wickedly, as if he were saying, 'It's poor old Mulligan at it again, milord.'

But Father Mulligan did not mind. He led her forward.

'The oldest sister of the Order,' he said. 'The doyen of the abbey.'

Matilda dropped on her two knees and kissed the extended ruby, once, twice, three times.

'Once for a man,' murmured the curate under his breath, 'twice for a woman, three times for a fool.'

'Well, well!' smiled his lordship, and the first 'well' was up in a tree, and the second 'well' was as deep as a well. 'Well, well!'

'Give me your blessing, your lordship,' pleaded Matilda.

His hand wavered it over her crooked coif. The priests gathered near, away from the wine-glasses, and watched with interest.

'I hope, my child,' smiled the bishop, 'that you will have many more long and happy years.'

The face of Philomena appeared in the door, behind it a bunch of dismayed faces peeping over her shoulder.

'Dear Mother Matilda,' greeted Philomena, coming forward. 'I hear Sister Kieran left you. It was naughty of her.'

She smiled at the bishop and led Kieran forward.

'Sister Kieran wants to show you a pigeon's egg,' she went on to Matilda.

The round face of the little novice was pale as a mushroom.

'A lovely little pigeon's blue and white spotted egg,' she babbled, 'such a lovely little egg, come and see it.'

Matilda looked blankly at her.

'Go,' croaked his lordship, and he smilingly patted Matilda's arm, 'go and see the pigeon's EGG!'

'It's green with blue spots on it,' said the novice eagerly. 'It's marvellous! It's lovely!'

She led her charge out and away down the corridor. She almost dragged her in her haste.

'But my teeth,' wailed Matilda, stumbling after her. 'And the book.'

'In the Geography Room,' said Kieran. 'You left them there, maybe.'

'And the book?' wailed Matilda. 'They are coming to see the book.'

'You left that in the Geography Room, too. We must light the candles. Hurry. Hurry.'

Matilda was panting before she reached the room. While Kieran lit the candles she drew her breath at the window. From there she saw the bishop go out into the garden and then down the alley to the main gate. The priests, like cockchafers, flowed in his wake. Matilda said nothing, but her coif slewed after them as they passed out of sight.

The rumble of the evening of the city came to her, and near at hand a mother calling loudly to her child. A gentle mist was beginning to fall and Matilda lost herself in gazing out through that shimmer of haze. The novice was looking at the flame of a candle, and her eyes were soft and her mouth trembling. She snivelled.

'He's a lovely priest,' said Matilda suddenly. 'And he gave me his blessing. But,' she gulped, 'he never saw the book.'

Suddenly she noticed the tears in the novice's eyes.

'Never mind, dear. We'll show the book another day,' encouraged the old nun.

'It isn't that,' wept the novice, who was thinking of her little friend in Kilcrea. 'But Sister Mary Michael is – is – is as thin as a latch.'

And she wept openly at the thought that her friend might die.

For a moment Matilda tried to understand, but then she began to pick at her back tooth and look over the misted roof and her eyes, once more enlarged with her own little grief, went grey with the light of the falling rain.

'Ja-a-a-anie!' screamed the mother below in the lane. 'Come ho-o-a-ame! I'll give you lamb-and-sally when I ca-a-a-atch yeh! Ja-a-a-anie!'

Faintly in the distance a child's voice replied. Then they heard, far away, the rumble of the town. One by one the novice extinguished the candles and led the old nun down to the babble of the refectory for her supper. As she had not found her teeth, however, she could eat nothing, so she spent the whole hour listening vacantly to everyone talking of the excitement of the day.

There's a Birdie in the Cage

I

While the case was being tried at the court-house, Lolly Black thought it would be a good time to see Pomfret's house. Her father would be at the court; the town would be at the court; poor old Mrs Pom would be at the court. So with her Phil she went there.

Immediately they got inside the house they realized it was too big for them. It rose like a Norman castle from the garden, a square of red brick like one of the grain elevators down in the harbour, or the queer concrete thing at the chemical works, all red from iron ore. It was lavish in its waste of space – wide passages, many cupboards, two dozen or more rooms. They could never hope either to furnish it or make it look cosy. What Pomfret wanted it all for they could not guess.

'Well,' said Lolly, 'it's easy to see what ruined this fellow.'

Their feet resounded across the bare corridor.

'Look,' she said.

It was a small, square room on the second landing. It was papered in deep blue, walls and ceiling, with golden stars stuck all over the paper, and in between them some silver butterflies. The glass in the arched window was a livid yellow and red. The floor had been painted black at some time; the mark of a square of linoleum or carpet was in the centre of the floor. Candle-grease spotted the floor in one corner.

'Was he a Freemason?' he asked.

'Was he a Catholic?' she whispered. 'It looks like an oratory.'

'*Was* he? Why *was*?'

'Well, is he?'

'They both are. Or rather, she is – or was – I don't know . . .'

They laughed. In a big room facing the sea they came on a mantel-piece laden with books. They fingered one or two. Byron's works.

A cream-covered notebook like a bank pass-book. It had to do with the distillery.

'No wonder he messed your father's affairs,' said Phil. 'Look at the scrap of a book. Poor devil – he let it all go to blazes at the end. Didn't even clear out of the house properly.'

He was pointing to the back of the door where trousers hung on a peg. A little wind from the sea made it wave feebly as if in a Pomfretian protest.

He lifted the window and they sat on the sill and looked out where the two brigs in the little harbour swayed and a cart rolled over the hump-backed bridge. In a backyard a cock crowed. A beech shed two leaves.

'Was it drink?' asked Phil.

He came from the city and he knew little about the town or its people.

'He drank,' said Lolly. 'But she drank like a blooming fish. But it wasn't that, I think. Just expensive living.'

'In Barronloe! But what is there to spend money on, here?'

'This house, parties, an expensive car, and two pianos, and holidays abroad: cruises, tours, expensive education for the daughters, clothes. The town says he gave a party last summer down there in the garden. At supper one of the fireworks went down instead of up – they were probably tipsy – and burnt a hole in the tablecloth: it had to be sent away to Brussels to be mended and cost twenty pounds to repair.'

He thought he caught a note of envy in her voice.

'He enjoyed himself?' he tested.

'Chinese lanterns in the apple-trees,' she went on, 'and he had three kind-of-tramp musicians in the summer-house, playing the melodeon and the concertina. The town was up till all hours, watching the fireworks, and listening. They talked of it for weeks. I heard the parish priest hinted at them in a sermon. Helen and myself were walking the Harbour Road that evening and we saw a good deal of their goings-on.'

He knew what 'walking the Harbour Road' meant. Every time he came to Barronloe and found the sisters out he was told he would be sure to meet them 'walking the Harbour Road.'

'How much did he get from your father per annum?' he wanted to ask. Instead he said:

'Had his wife money?'

'Ph!'

'Had he private means?'

'I knew his father when I was a child. He was a cobbler.'

'Isn't that amazing?'

'He speculated. On grain. With father's money. That will all be coming out by now in the court. He left pappy with fifteen thousand tons of maize, with the market falling. Too clever!'

'Where did he get the high notions?'

'I say it is from her. She was really a nobody. She can be very grand, but sometimes a terrific cockney accent jumps out. I believe it is true she used to dance. He said she was famous at one time, and that her name was Violet von Evremont. But I never met anybody who heard of her. Helena says her name was Lizzy Boggs. If she ever danced, it was a long time ago.'

'What a wicked little puss we are!' he teased.

'She made an awful show of herself on the beach at that party, I'm certain. She's forty-five if she's a day, and fourteen stone, and they say she was half-undressed, doing Greek dances.'

'Did you like her?'

She looked at him.

'What does Helena see in her?' he asked.

'Helena is soft.'

They closed the window and went down into the garden. It was gone wild already. Pomfret had been arrested in April, and everything collapsed at once. One good wet spring had turned the place into a jungle, docks three feet high, giant nettles, bishopsweed in the beds, speedwell, dandelions seeding on the wind. Apples lay rotting on the paths. Here and there they shone white in the high grass. Lolly Black could not stop talking of Mrs Pomfret.

'Really, she's an awful heap, and the town is well rid of her. He isn't a bad fellow. He keeps himself well. I have often seen him with a different suit every day. And he told me he ordered his shirts direct from London. (He has good taste and good manners.) But she *was* a heap. The first time we called on her she was all right. But the next time Helena and I dropped in unexpectedly. We were sick of the Harbour Road. She was all frowsy, with a dirty old dressing-gown on her, smoking cigarettes and drinking whisky. That at twelve o'clock in the day. She began to tell us – phew! the smell of the whisky – all about Buenos Aires, and how you pay five shillings for a bottle of Bass there. "And you must 'ave it, dearie. You come out from a hard night with the ballet and you're just simply dying for it. Of course, we didn't always have to *buy* it, dearie!" '

'Ho-ho!' whistled Phil.

'You may well ho-ho. It angered me to hear her talk that way, especially to Helena. "Hellow, Helen, dearie. Aren't you looking clean and fresh! That dress shows off your figure, Helen. You know, Helen, you have a lovely figure." And Helen would blush, and try to look at some picture or other. "What are you staring at, Helen? How warm you look. Let me hold your hand. Oh, that? That's *The Tweed*. A clipper that licked the steamer from Hong Kong to Singapore by a day and a half. That other one was decorated by the Viceroy of Madras from this-or-the-other. You know, Helen, I can't keep my eyes off you. You have a lovely body, darling. Let me look at you . . ." Ach! Then the way she'd pull her dressing-gown tight around her and shiver. And lean on the mantel, looking you up and down with heavy lids, talking of marriage and men, and the way life goes slipping away from you, and the loneliness of Barronloe, and what a lovely body Helen had if she only knew it, and she blowing smoke through her nose at every sigh.'

'Forty-five? Fifty? Fifty-five?'

'At least. She married twice, you know. Her first husband was a planter in Sumatra. That house' – they both looked up at its bald red back – 'was full of things from the Indies. Lumps of teak and ivory. The shipyards of Johore, dearie. Heads of wild beasts. The Burmese jungles, dearie. All mixed up with spears and skin shields and pictures and bottles of sacred water. Straight from Lourdes, dearie. That day she offered us whisky before she thought of herself, and then tea. Then she ended up by producing an enormous box of chocolates. The outside smelt of eau-de-Cologne. She pulled it out of a drawer in her bedroom. It was awful. Please don't ask me to *remember* it. The chocolates cost at least a pound. Have 'em, dearie. I don't eat 'em. A boy-friend gave 'em to me. She said he was a silly ass. I couldn't touch them. Straight from her bedroom, dearie. But Helen didn't mind. She said I was a silly ass.

'The barracks in the town knew her like a bad penny. The jarveys were always driving officers to the house. And the extraordinary thing is that Pomfret never seems to have known about her goings-on. He was too often away.'

'Shall I be too often away?'

She slapped his hand playfully.

'Our gardener, who knows everything about everybody, told pappy, when he had Pomfret arrested for embezzlement, that the clerks in the distillery always knew they could be late if they saw light in Pomfret's windows after twelve. That meant *he* was out of town. And he told me that: "Yerrah, sure, miss, the poachers on the river used her house for a lighthouse!" He said, too, that the priests were always taking maids away from the house.'

'It sounds a nasty kind of house to me,' said Phil. 'Where did Pomfret meet this woman? He's a town boy, isn't he?'

'Yes. He met her here. One summer when she came on holidays with her first husband. He had some job connected with oil. He was a Major Gilfillan. They took the house for two months for their children. Pomfret was only a clerk with us, then. The first time anyone ever heard of her was one pouring wet night – she must have taken the house for August and September – when the Rowleys, they're the only neighbours we speak to, heard a most frightful row coming up from the beach. Then they heard a window being smashed and Violet von Evremont, or Mrs Gilfillan, or Mrs Pomfret, or Lizzy Boggs or whatever the creature's name is, screaming out at the top of her voice that her husband was killing her. The next thing there was her ladyship, breasting in the door with the two older children, Bel and Pickaninny, by the hands. She sobbed out that Gilfillan had stabbed her with his sword and that nothing but her corset saved her. And the maid running off with Donna in a blanket to the police barrack. We didn't hear about this until long after, for it was hushed up, or, I needn't tell you, we shouldn't have called on her. I think it was very wrong of the Rowleys. But once she told Helen that *she* had first stabbed *him* with the carving-knife, in the hand! And one of her maids that came to us told me it all began when the dog ate her false fringe and she beat the dog. I think the truth of the matter is that she was drinking his brandy. Though the gardener says it was the way he found her with an officer in the house. One doesn't know what to believe. That was when Pomfret met her. He used to play cards there. I suppose he had nowhere better to go – it's a small town. Then when the Major died suddenly he met her again and married her. That was twelve years ago. They had two children. That's five altogether. But now she does nothing but mope and drink, and race off to Dublin. She just let herself go to pieces. Honestly, she lives half her life in a pig-sty. And, of course – officers always. Helena and I, when we go for a walk down the Harbour Road, see her hanging out of the window, smoking and mooning, her hair done up beautifully, rouged, and all the rest of it. But we always said she was probably in rags from the neck down.'

'She probably hadn't enough to occupy her time,' suggested Phil, who was tired of the subject. 'We must give you enough to keep you busy.'

Lolly looked at him and then began to blush slowly, deeply, and not knowing where to look, until suddenly understanding her blush he caught her to himself and kissed her hair and brow. With soft, dreamy, sensuous eyes she looked over the sparkling sea, all her little pert and youthful hardness dissolving in her love.

2

Her hands and her hair lit by the sun through the slats of the venetian blind, Helen strummed with too much *rallentando* and too much *molle* and *piano*, at her favourite largo from her favourite Beethoven – the *Concerto in C Minor* – a thing more soft and more tender than air or dew, humming where the flute and the bassoon should moan out the *andante*. But then, instead of going on to the *rondo*, she lifted her hands from the keys as a mother might lift her hands from a cradle. She looked at the dust-motes in the barred sun.

'It's too sweet,' wept Mrs Pomfret from the sofa. 'Thank you, darling.'

Helen rose, on her mouth a twisted smile. She clicked the blinds level so that the sun poured in, and she could see the heat-haze on the ocean, and far away through it as through milky water the clouds falling like rose-petals in late autumn. A cart lumped over the bridge. On the hillock, in the chapel grounds, to her left, the chapel-woman was tolling a dead bell.

Behind her Mrs Pomfret blessed herself hastily, and when Helen turned suddenly and saw her, she explained:

'The Angelus is such a lovely thought. It always reminds me of Fra Angelica. Like the Rosary. The hours I've spent with thee, dear heart.'

Helen twisted her fingers passionately.

'It comforts me in my misfortune, Helen. I didn't know the hardness of human beings. You know I always thought you Irish were so kind and soft. But it isn't so! I dropped into the bank just now to cash a cheque I got from a good friend. You don't know, Helen, what it is to be looked at the way they looked at me, and at that cheque, and the questions and the delay. I had to sell our Bechstein this morning for ten pounds, Helen, to pay a lawyer for my husband. Think of it! My Bechstein in Murphy's front parlour. You know what that skinny daughter of his will do with it. She'll play 'ymns on it. And put a red antimacassar on it, and the family photographs. Anytime . . . Oh, well! It does rile me! And I sold my last bit of jewellery to Cooney for another ten. My engagement ring that Jim bought in London for fifty guineas. And if I didn't sell 'em Jim wouldn't have any counsel at all to open 'is bleedin' mouth for 'im.'

'I'm sorry, Violet.'

'It's nice to hear you call me Violet,' groaned Mrs Pomfret.

'I wish I could lend you some money,' sighed Helen.

'That's good of you, dearie; but we owe nearly five hundred in town.'

At that Helen, in spite of herself, gave a little gasp of annoyance and disapproval, and at that sign from so young and ignorant a critic Mrs Pomfret's dams began to crack.

'Oh, I know it ain't nice. But everybody does it. It isn't that that worries me. I don't mind for my own sake. I've been through it before. I don't give a damn even for Jim's sake. He'll come through it in his good time. It's the kiddies. Mary and Patrick are just ready to get something out of their schooling now. And Donna, in the middle of her course at the university. But wot can I do? Where can I take 'em? I can go and live with my sister in Blackpool. But you cawn't fit children reared in an Irish village, I might say, into an English town.'

She banged her fist into the sofa and let herself go utterly.

'Oh, Christ, wot a fool that man was! Wot a bloody fool I was to marry 'im. Oh, don't look at me like that, dearie. I know I didn't ort to use bad language opposite you. You're so good. But it's the bad stuff comin' out. I don't care. I don't care. I must 'ave a good cry. And damn, damn, damn, damn, damn! So there! Think of me what you like.'

And the big, fat, powdered and painted wreck of a danseuse broke into a storm of tears. Suddenly she stopped and dried them.

'Here I am, after all my years, and I haven't as much sense as one of the chorus in her first pantomime. Here I am. And wot brought me 'ere? I ask you. I *awsk* you! Even if I was back in Sumatra with my old man I'd be better off – and I know it's hell, the sweating heat, the stink, the water that's always hot and tasting of iron. Though you should 'ave seen me, Helen. I was slim. You 'ad to be slim in them places. The heat made you slim. I'll tell the world. All in white. Pure w'ite. He called me 'is lily. Ha, don't make me larf. And look at me now; yes, do look at me. I see you looking at me, and I know what you're thinkin'; you're thinkin' I'm a fat, coarse lump of a woman, with false hair and sweaty armpits, and a complexion at two-and-six a jar. And you're right. It is right. It is so. But time was when the Johnnies in the stalls threw golden sovereigns at my feet. You should have seen me do the can-can. I could kick me legs as high as that bloody chandelier, I could. Swish, frouf, kick, boys, kick! And the Johnnies in Rio shouting at me to kick it higher. I'll say I kicked. I did it though I bust me braces! Last year I tried to do it on the beach, for our tin wedding. I know I made a fool of myself. I didn't need Jim to tell me that. I saw them smirking at one another while I did it. And yet I just couldn't stop. And why couldn't I stop? I couldn't stop because I thought I was back in Java, doing it for my old man for our tin wedding on the beach, and the niggers beating with their feet and clapping hands like a lot of bloody lunatics. Oh, Helen! The moon, and the water making a little – you know – hush – hush . . .'

And again the tears. With Helen staring at her, between shame, and horror, and pity.

'Come, now, Mrs Pomfret,' she stammered. 'It's all – I mean – Java is . . . Well, your husband is dead now . . .'

'Ho, indeed? Is he? I bet he ain't. Yes, yes, yes, yes! I know he's supposed to be. That's the yarn I spread about here. I suppose it's bigamy. But I don't care. What a show I'm after making of myself before you, girlie. But somehow – I don't know – I've always found you so – so innocent, Helen. Coo! The things I've done. What's the differ now? I came here to try and give you a bit of advice, and here I am splitting on myself, and you'll hate me all your life. Well, I deserve it.'

'But why . . .'

'Oh, I was down and out – that's why. I had three kids on my hands. My old man left them to me, and he left me, that's all. Then Jim Pomfret came along. And I say it's all his fault. He had no right to marry me. I didn't know wot kind of life was before me, with him. He ought to have known. It's all right for him. He had his business at your daddy's place. He had his friends at the club. But wot about me? I used to sit up in the window of our bedroom, day after day after day after day and look out. And wot would I see? I tell you. I see an empty ocean. Or I see a little ship come now and again with pyrites for the chemical factory. Ships from Rio Tinto. And I've been in Rio Tinto. And when I'd look at them through the bloody rain I'd see Rio Tinto. Or else wot would I see? The harbour lighthouse in the fog of the water. That's all. That's my life for ten years. Do you know wot I've done? I've done the Stations of the Cross. I used to look up at the Virgin's face and say – yes, I'm a mother of sorrows, too. I've looked up at the face of Father McCarthy giving sermons to the Women's Confraternity – me in the Confraternity! Think of it! – Shades of Rio! – and I'd say to myself, "Gawd bless you, father, you're a bleedin' innocent," I'd say, "and if that's sin then I'm a bleedin' saint." '

And she tried to calm herself, but her hair was crooked and her hat was crooked, and her eyes were gone red and her lips wet.

'Oh, well. Never mind. I shouldn't talk like this to you, Helen. You're such a kid.' There was a pause. 'Helen, you ought to get married. It's so easy for you. You've got such a lovely figure, and with your hair. All men are alike when it comes to that! You could get any man you liked – if you – you know – don't be so shy. That's what I came to say. And I say it 'cos I like you. You've never turned your back on me. Of course,' she said bitterly, 'you might if you'd known.'

Helen said in a low voice:

'I did know.'

The woman peered at her.

'Wot did you know?'

'I knew everything. Bel told me.'

'Wot's everything?' cried Mrs Pomfret in terror. 'Whatche mean? About my husband?'

'Yes.'

Mrs Pomfret rose in a fury.

'Bel didn't tell you. Bel's my son. Bel didn't know. What you bloody well mean? Come off it. He didn't know. I tell you he didn't know! How could he know? Bel's my son – my son, my son!'

The girl grew pale.

'I shouldn't – I shouldn't . . .'

The big woman stood over her. Her fist was clenched.

'What did Bel tell you?'

But she, too, was going pale, and there was fright and shame in her eyes.

'Bel knew. I knew about the house. I mean. Bel knew. That's why he left.'

The woman looked at her, peering furiously, searching her young face.

'I don't believe Bel knew. You're telling me a lie, Helen.'

'I am not telling you a lie,' said Helen angrily. 'I beg your pardon, Mrs Pomfret; but I am not telling you a lie.'

Pomfret collapsed.

'Don't be angry, dearie,' she wheedled. 'But Bel didn't really tell you, did he? I mean, you picked it up from him. Guessed like. Isn't that all?'

Helen shook her head. The older woman sank into a chair.

'So you *were* great with him? I was right about that anyway. You're all together. You're all one. You're all just the same! The only person in the whole damn' town to stick by me was that little rat of a Shinnick woman. A rat of a woman. The cook's wife in the asylum!'

Again she collapsed.

'Oh, I wish I 'adn't come to say goodbye to you. But I'm not sure, mind you. No, I don't care what you say; I don't believe it. I don't believe Bel knows. It's all lies. All lies. I'll tell you why Bel went away. I sent him away. Now!'

The girl looked at her, doubtfully.

'Yes, I did. I'll tell you the way of it. If you get my meaning. Just about the time the trouble came with the distillery, Bel told Jim right off the bloody reel that he wanted to marry you. That he was in love with you. You're . . .'

'Yes?'

'Well . . .'

'I know what you were going to say.'

'I wasn't going to say it.'

'What?'

'Oh, don't be an idiot, girl. He said he was going to ask you some day to marry him. His father – I mean – well – if you must know it – told Bel to remember you are a Protestant. I don't mind so much really about religion myself. I have my own way of getting on. I don't always hold with the Church . . .'

Helen was looking at her wildly. The old woman went on hurriedly with her lies.

'Anyway, his father and I and he had a hell of a row. Jim was on bail at this time, remember. I said: "Send the boy away for a year or two and then see if he still wants the girl." It so happened I had an offer of a job from a friend in Sumatra for any young lad that wanted a start in life. And I put it up to Bel.'

'I see,' said Helen in a dull voice.

'I pity the boy. It's no place for a white man. Bad enough for a white woman. Out at dawn to get something done before the heat of the day.'

She shook her head at the thought of it.

'No wonder I'm what I am. Only time I ever slept in that place was between noon and half-past four in the afternoon. And sweat? Only for the nights I couldn't have stuck it. I tell you, we made them hum!'

Helen turned on the piano-stool and sank her head in her hands. The keys jangled under elbows, horribly.

'I'm getting batty,' said Pomfret. 'I wanted to tell you about Bel.'

'I don't want to hear about Bel.' Helen whirled proudly. 'I'm not interested.'

Pomfret leaned over her and took her chin in her palm and looked at her face as at a mirror.

'Helen! Are you still in love with him?'

One second's hesitation would have meant yes. Helen hesitated far longer. Pomfret dropped her hand.

'I'm sorry, Helen. It's all Jim's doing. Though it's not that either. You're . . .'

'You said it before,' wailed Helen.

'What?'

'You said I'm too old for him.'

'Well, it is the truth. There – you have it at last.'

Helen shook her large and lovely head, knowing that she would never know the truth from this woman.

'You were always telling me I should get married!' she cried. 'Why did he go?'

'Yes, but . . .'

'Yes, but not to Bel. Is that it?'

'Well . . .'

The old woman was silent. The girl had hit on the only piece of truth left in that heavy carcass. The woman was proud of it, and she was ashamed of it. But because it was a piece of truth she decided to surrender on good terms.

'He's my only boy, Helen, dearie. If you married him he'd be sure to find out everything. You see – your daddy knows all about me.'

Revelation broke on the girl. It was her father who had sent Bel away. She tried hard to hold her pride, but her pride broke her. Pomfret bent over the child and kissed her quivering neck.

'Darling!' she said, 'I came to give you advice and I've made a mess of it. Everything comes out in the wash. Your daddy sent him away.'

Then she stole from the room. In the hall she pulled herself together and walked like a lady down the Main Street of Barronloe, thanking her stars that she had not, at least, confessed that she had sold the girl for twenty-five pounds and the education of her own daughter.

3

Through the slats Helen looked across the bay, where the sun was pouring shadows into the little valley of the distant river. The cottages on the far shore were like mushrooms. There, only last April in the late afternoon of a day so soft that between the tides the surface of the mud cracked in the sudden heat, she and Bel had gone exploring the first open tributary of the Barron Beag. They had sighed with pleasure to see the cool breeze come crawling over the water and race suddenly down their spines. As they passed under the cold slimy bridge, the waters rushed at them around the quoins.

'Floods after the rains,' grunted Bel.

On either side the woods swept down to the edge of the gravel. Far ahead the smoke of a village clung to the pine-tops. It had been hard pulling against the current, so that they were glad to moor by the steps at the back of a pub and drink lemonade that Bel brought out in two enormous glasses. It was a picture she would never forget – the boy standing there, balancing the glasses, in a doorway set in a pink, sunlit wall. For, as she had looked up at him over the necks of the hens pecking corn on the landing-stage, she had realized, with a flooding of sudden excitement in her throat, how young and manly he was, with his fair glib of hair falling into his eyes, his soiled shirt climbing out of his baggy trousers, and in his ways plain almost to rudeness. He did not take the slightest notice of her as he handed her the glass and with a grin slugged down his own, spitting afterwards with gusto at the clucking hens.

Leaving the boat there they had walked through the village and sat on a tree-trunk outside a sweet-shop and sucked bull's-eyes. Bel fired pebbles at the sweet-shop hens until the shop woman strode out to them and called them 'little Proteshtant shnots' and other rougher names that made them fly, red with laughter, back to their boat.

'Though why,' chuckled Bel, 'I should look like a Protestant!'

'Do I?' she had challenged.

'You have their cold look about you,' he taunted.

Then they had pulled slowly into the stream, smooth and colourless in the after-glow. They were stopped by the weirs of an abandoned mill, where the tide, dim with corn-dust, curled as slowly as the hands of a clock.

Far away across the distant lock they heard the clanking of the last train out of Barronloe, and coming on the clear air from the hills above the rattle of a cart.

'Nice place,' commented Bel, where he lay chewing sweets on his back in the prow.

' 'M,' said Helen, and she remembered how she had tried to write her name in the dust of the water.

'Must have a picnic here,' he nad suggested then. 'Will you come?'

'I'd love to.'

She bent lower over the water, afraid she had said it too eagerly.

'Are you cold?' he asked. 'You have a thin dress on. You look like a lump of ice to me.'

'Lump?' she bandied. 'Thank you.'

He laughed and scratched his stomach and giggled again over the joke.

'Pole us home,' he suggested.

She stood and poled them around easily, and they began to float back through the grassbanks to the village.

'You're not really a lump,' he said critically.

She blushed, remembering how often Mrs Pomfret had said the same thing, though more nicely. She tossed her head.

'Getting dark,' she said.

The Harbour Road would be deserted, the lovers gathering under the trees. Bel was now poling beside her. It would be lovely on the estuary as they rowed back. Suddenly he saw the reflected lights of the village were dulled by a mudbank.

'Cripes!' he said. 'The tide is falling.'

Down they floated lower and lower between mudbanks, where tributaries now opened right and left, wide almost as the main stream. When he stood on a thwart to see ahead a star twinkled in a ring of mud.

'Safer to let me pole,' he advised, and as he stepped back the boat rocked under his feet.

'Shall I try to steer?'

'No, no, it can't be done.'

It was quite dusk now. The stars were coming out. The pinewoods might have housed wolves, so black they were. They ran aground.

'Blast!' she heard him curse under his breath.

He stood up and heaved the nose free. The stern ran aground now. The stars shuddered in the water.

'Can't see much!' he muttered.

His voice sounded hollow and distant, and when he paused to wipe the sweat from his brow she heard only the mud whispering in its ooze. He pushed off and for the last time she stuck.

'Bel! Swing her stern into that side-stream.'

'What good is that?' he snapped.

'We can sail out again,' she mocked, as shy people always mock.

He shoved her about and her stern fouled again. He sat down, and in despair flung his oar into the boat.

'We're done,' he said. 'We can't get off until the tide rises. I am a fool. That wasn't the floodwater pulling against us at the bridge. It was the falling tide.'

'We can't stay here all night,' she said firmly.

He was drying his face with his handkerchief.

'There's nothing for it but to get into the water. It's deep enough at the prow. But it's damnably cold. Just turn around, Helen, I'm going to undress.'

A few moments later she heard the splash of his body descending into the water, and the blubbering sound he made with his mouth at the cold. She saw his ten fingers clutching the side of the boat and his naked shoulders heaving against it.

'No good,' he shouted at last. 'I'm coming in. Turn away.'

She felt him clambering in and the smack of his wet feet on the thwart and his teeth chattering. She turned her head slowly – against her will – to look. She saw him forked against the stars, the water glistening on his thighs, one arm whirling to bring back the blood. Her cheeks burned, but she continued to look.

'All right, I'm dressed,' he said at last.

Almost in a whisper, she asked:

'When does the tide rise?'

'About dawn I should say.'

He took out a diary and lit several matches to see. They sizzled when they fell.

'Four twenty-two,' he said. 'Can you swim?'

'No. Why?'

'Ach!' He snapped. 'What does it matter if you can't? We might try to swim ashore up a side-stream. Wade, rather. Nice sight we'd be then, though, and a mile to the village after.'

He seemed to be turning over all possible plans in his mind.

'It's no good. Have a bull's-eye.'

'No, thanks!'

He crunched.

'Sorry, Helen!' he mumbled at last.

'It's all right. Father will be worried to death.'

They sat silent for about half an hour. Then her teeth began to dance.

'Take my coat,' he commanded, peeling it off.

'No.'

He thrust it at her. She flung it back.

'No!'

They sat silent for another spell, and he guessed she was holding her jaws tightly because when she took a breath her teeth chattered again. He went forward to where she sat and put his arm on her shoulder.

'Helen, you'll get your death of cold.'

He took off his coat and put it about them both and sat near her. She was too miserable to remove his arms. Across the far mouth of the valley a faint moonlight came from behind the clouds. About half an hour more and he suggested they must lie on the floorboards, and began to bale. She said she would not, but when he was beside her again an owl screamed suddenly in the woods, and she shivered violently in his arms. He became serious then and made her lie down. She said he must share the coat, so they lay side by side. She thought of the Harbour Road again, and the lovers clinging together under the trees. ('Helen, dearie, you have a lovely body.') When she felt his arms pressing her more closely she did not resist, nor when she felt his mouth pressing on her hair and forehead. They lay like that all night, and from time to time his hand strayed gently over her. That was when he told her all he knew of his mother's life.

When she awoke they were in the middle of the loch, the sky clouded over, the estuary filled as with milk, and the houses on the far shore watching her. The mist clung low on the shore.

As she was ill for three weeks after that she did not know that he had gone until she received his letter from Cairo. That lovely May night she went down the road to the strand, slipping on the stones and the slime, out to the very point and the first ripple. A yawl was entering the harbour, its boom creaking, a light from its hold cast upward on the brown sail. There, with a dead dog to her left and a stranded basket to her right, she looked where the tide held the winking town of Barronloe on a plate, and again and again she returned to that letter and its opening words – 'Darlingest Helen.' Of course she would wait for him. Sumatra? She would go to Siberia with him. He was the first person she had loved. She felt he would be the only one she would ever love. She spent all the following day writing a reply, but to that she received only a long letter telling about life in Sumatra, the loneliness of plantation life there, and he wondered many times if she would ever be able to exist there. That was the only letter she received from him since he landed. As she watched another sunset filling the valley across the bay with its shadows, she knew she would not hear from him again.

*

Her father came in. With a start she turned from the window.

'That's over!' he said.

'Did – what . . .?' (She had lost all sense of time and place.)

'Three years he got. I'm glad it's finished.'

'Oh!'

He sank into the sofa and wiped his cheek wearily with his palm.

'Play me something, Helen.'

For a minute she sat without playing. He thought she was deciding what to play. She was thinking, really, if she ought to speak to him about Bel. Then she remembered that Bel had not written for four months.

She began again at that pathetic largo, music that is like the sound of human tears. She played it gently and slowly, but with more understanding than she had ever played it in her life before. When she had finished, she went to the window and sat there for so long a time without stirring that she did not notice her father go. Quite clearly, and with absolute honesty and accuracy, she saw her life stretched out before her; and she faced it with courage, for there were many dreams that allured her by the way, and many hopeless possibilities that delayed her. If she had not known Mrs Pomfret – if she had met Bel far sooner – if Mrs Pomfret were a good woman, that above all – if her father had not found out about Mrs Pomfret – she even thought wildly of going off to Sumatra, and thereby came to the end of her vain turning and twisting. It wasn't that she didn't even know where his place was, thousands and thousands of miles away, lost even on the largest map. It was just that he was gone.

He was gone. And she was here, and would be here always. He was free – yet. But she was caught as, sooner or later, all human beings are caught in that coil of things from which there is no escape.

Now and again she saw the dumb gulls fly inland over the house, and in the harbour the fog breathing on the full water. High over the tide the clouds, warmed by the sunset, were bursting like roses, and as she, a statue by the window, looked at them over the ocean, she saw, without moving either eye or head, the antique lamplighter on the road beneath confess the autumn evening.

*

The door opened gently and the maid appeared.

'Tea is ready, miss. Your father is waiting.'

The statue scarcely nodded. Then, dissolving into a woman, it went downstairs to tea. Lolly and her young man were there. Her father sat quickly to table. She could see that they were all irritable for being kept waiting.

'You know I like you to pour,' chided her father.

Absently she poured. As she sipped, she saw the moisture on the window-panes.

Teresa

I

On the platform at Dieppe, at a corner so near the sea and the boat as to be part of the quay, there stood a small nun, flanked by three shapeless bags of that old-fashioned kind known as portmanteaux. Lovely as a black wallflower, large-eyed by nature, her eyes were now enormous: for she was looking across the quays with delight at the sun-blazing confections of houses on the other side. Now and again an old nun came hobbling up to her from the busier end of the platform, muttering something that drew a shadow across the lovely face, and then hobbling away again, head down, to this official and that official, wavering around like a top as each one hurriedly threw a few words at her and rushed past. At last the old nun came back to the novice, with her two hands out in appeal. The novice, followed by the old nun, at once walked straight down to the first official she saw and said in clear English:

'Where is the train for Rouen?'

The official glanced at her, then smiled, then bowed, and said politely, indeed with deference:

'There it is, mademoiselle,' and pointed to it.

'Mais non, non,' babbled the old nun. 'Pas aller à Rouen! Aller à Leesoo!'

'That's all right, Sister Patrick,' said the other. 'We change at Rouen.' And taking charge of the situation, she led the still-protesting nun up to the waiting train, put in the bags, helped – almost pushed – the old woman before her, and settled herself for the journey. The old woman clambered out again, red with fluster. Once more she ambushed official after official, all of whom said a word so like 'Wrong' that she insisted on hauling out her companion.

'Listen, Sister Patrick,' begged the novice, with saintly patience. 'I know the route backwards. It's Dieppe, Rouen, Elbeuf St Aubin, Serquigny, and then Lisieux. This is the train.'

The guard confirmed this, as far as concerned Rouen, and they clambered in at the last moment; but the old woman was still saying that they would never get to 'Leesoo', that they would find themselves landed in Paris in the middle of the night, that she had told Mother Mary Mell not to send her, that thirty-one years is too long out of a country for anyone to remember the language, and so on and so on, while the younger nun gazed wide-eyed out of the window at the passing fields.

'Our pilgrimage has begun,' she said in a dreamy voice, almost to herself.

'And what's going to be the end of it at this rate?' snapped the old woman. But then she gave a frightened look at the little face before her. The big eyes had lowered. A tremble was flitting across the red lips. The old woman immediately calmed down, laid a rough hand on the novice's knee, and said, gently, 'Sure, don't mind me, Sister Teresa. I'm all of a flusther. We're on the road now. Just as you say. When we get to Leesoo, 'twill be all right, a gilly. Saint Teresa will look after you and . . . Look't, I have no sense. We should be eating our lunch.'

'I'd love a cup of tea!' said the girl. 'I have a raging headache.'

'Tut tut,' clucked the old woman, and then she grabbed the girl's flank. 'Are ye wearing your double petticoat, Sister Teresa?'

'Yes, Sister,' said Teresa, with a blush and a warning look into the corner of the carriage, where an old Frenchman was devouring a roll and slugging red wine.

'Have ye the red-flannel drawers on ye?' demanded the old nun.

'Yes, Sister. Sssh!'

'There's nothing like red flannel next the skin,' said the nun, fiddling with the lunch-parcel. ' 'Tis a touch of cold you've got.'

' 'Twas the heat down under that deck,' said Teresa, and big floods of water entered her eyes. Her chaperone did not notice. 'I never saw Dieppe from the sea,' she whimpered. 'And Mother Mary Mell says that it's lovely from the sea.'

'Will ye have egg and cress, or tomato?' asked the old woman, too intent on her own appetite to take notice of anything else. 'We earned it,' she laughed, with a happy look about her and a countrywoman's smile and nod to the old Clemenceau in the corner. He just dug a chunk of his roll off with his penknife, wiped the back of his hand right and left across his moustaches, and with an idle glance at her, opened both mouth and eyes simultaneously to devour the chunk.

The nuns began to nibble their food. Two hens could not have pecked more nimbly or neatly. Their travelling-companion finished his lunch almost before they had well begun. He carefully stowed away his bottle, produced a long cheroot, and began to fill the carriage with smoke. Then, to the dismay of the novice, he leaned across and closed the window tightly. By the time she had finished eating, she had already begun to lean her aching head on her palm. In minute imitation of the Frenchman, the old woman rubbed her moustaches and her beard clean of crubs, leaned back, closed her eyes, began to eat chocolates and to breathe through her nose. She woke with a start to hear Teresa say to the Frenchman:

'C'est assez chaud, monsieur. Veuillex bien ouvrir la fenêtre.'

The old tiger-face glared, growled, tapped his chest fiercely, poured out a flood of uncompromising French, and leaned back. His sideward glare thereafter was like a cat ready to pounce.

'What's that?' asked the old nun apprehensively.

'My head,' groaned Teresa.

'Offer it up, girl,' advised the old woman. 'Offer it up to Saint Teresa for the success of your intention.'

'I've offered it up on the boat the whole way over,' retorted the novice.

' 'Tis a cross,' said the old woman easily. ' 'Tis put on you by Saint Teresa to try you. Suffer it for her sake.'

The girl looked at her coldly. Then she observed that they had a second travelling-companion. He was a cavalry officer, who, with more consideration than their 'Clemenceau', was walking up and down in the corridor to smoke his pipe. Each time he passed the door he glanced up at his luggage on the rack. She raised her eyes appealingly the next time he passed. He paused, glanced at her, was about to pass on, paused again to look. A tiny gesture of her hand, a widening of her eyes held him. He came in, sat down, looked around him, and stared at her.

'Monsieur,' she begged. 'J'ai mal à la tête. La fenêtre. Est ce que nous pouvons l'ouvrir?'

'With pleasure,' he said, in English, stalked over to it and slapped it down.

A raucous argument started up at once between the officer and his fellow-countryman. Sister Patrick sat up, glared at her charge, and drew herself in from the combatants. The argument ended with the abrupt flight of the old man, cursing as he went, a laugh from the officer, and a frightened smile from the novice, accompanied by a glance at her chaperone, who, in the greatest suspicion of the officer, had lowered her head to look crookedly at him, like a duck, out under her coif. He was stroking his little line of moustache and smiling at Teresa. When Patrick slewed full around to survey her charge, Teresa had cast her eyes down demurely on her clasped hands.

Presently the officer got up, and went out to smoke another pipe. Every time he passed, he bowed in to the two nuns. Teresa never looked higher than his knees. When he had passed for about the sixth time, Patrick said:

'Sister, do you realize that officer is bowing to us every two minutes?'

'He is very kind,' said the little nun. 'Everybody is very kind,' she sighed, and began to pray on her beads.

But when he passed again, and bowed, the old nun said crossly:

'I believe you're looking at him, Sister Teresa!'

Teresa shook her head sadly and looked out of her big eyes at her chaperone.

'It is sad,' she said. 'He will be killed in the wars,' and her eyes swam with tears.

'And what's that to you?' whispered the old nun angrily.

'He reminds me of my brother, Jim, in the army,' said Teresa. 'He will be killed on the battlefield too. Oh, let us pray for the pair of them.'

The old nun could not refuse to do this, so they prayed together, and when the officer passed, and bowed, and smiled, the two nuns bowed and smiled back, and went on with their prayers for the repose of his soul when he would be killed in the wars. But he was useful at Rouen. He bought them two lovely cartons of café-au-lait, with buttered rolls, and showed them where the auto-rail would start. Then for the last time he bowed, and smiled, and went away, and they never saw him again.

2

It was the fading hour of day before their little auto-rail came and took the two travellers (and about eight others) trotting out of Rouen. A light haze of rain began to float down through the air. They passed a village deep in trees. There the first lights were beginning to contest the supremacy of the day. Soon the rain shone in rivulets on the lighted windows of the auto. The other travellers leaned closer together in a kind of animal companionship and chattered in loud voices, as if to keep the night at bay.

'I wonder,' murmured Teresa, 'what are they doing now back in Saint Anthony's?'

'Ah, yes!' sighed the old nun wearily. 'It makes England seem very far away to think of Saint Anthony's now.'

'And Dublin?' smiled the novice sadly.

'Ha!' said the old nun, with a yawn that dropped the subject into vacancy. Her youth and her friends were too remote for serious reflection.

'I know what my sisters are doing now in Dublin,' whispered Teresa. 'Having tea and making plans for the night.' And she looked out at the evening shower and the thickening night. 'I wish I never came,' she said suddenly. 'I feel terribly lonely.'

'Sssh! Tut tut!' chided the old nun; she had begun to eat more chocolates, and did not want to talk.

'It's all right for you,' complained the novice. 'You're going to meet your aunt. I'll know nobody in Lisieux. And if I find out there that I have no vocation, what'll I do?'

'Now, now, now,' grumbled the old woman, 'you know you'll get peace and calm in Leesoo. The saint will reveal your heart to you. You'll quieten down. You'll know that all these scruples of yours mean nothing at all. Sure, we all had them!' In spite of herself she became impatient. Her soothing voice gradually took on an edge. 'And anyway, goodness knows, you were eager enough to come! And let me tell you it isn't every Reverend Mother would let you. And it's not a holiday you're on, Miss. It's thinking of the holy saint you should be, and not of gillygooseys in Dublin.'

The novice withdrew into herself. She was too tired to pray; from sheer repetition the words were becoming meaningless.

Presently the old nun said, as if she were thinking aloud:

'And even if I have an aunt . . . Ha! . . . I suppose she won't know me.'

She stopped again and folded her hands deep into her sleeves.

'Thirty-one years,' she mused to the window.

The auto-rail rattled along for several miles. Then, Patrick leaned over and said comfortably:

'A terror for the hot milk at night. She'd drink two pints of it. Sure, 'twas enough to kill a plough-horse.'

From that on she kept on letting occasional little gasps of laughter escape her. It was as if somebody tickled her every three minutes. Then, after a protracted giggle out of each side of her mouth, she went off into a beatific sleep and the broad smile never left her face until they stopped abruptly in Lisieux.

As they left the station and emerged on the great square, Teresa cried in delight:

'But it's really a big place!'

Through the rain the little town shone into the station like a prismatic waterfall. She saw a green neon light flitting through the wetness over the hotel door. She saw a vis-à-vis crawling shiningly across the Place, and it made the town seem both cosy and intimate, and at the same time enormous and important. But Patrick had flown into a hurry and scurry, fumbling with her umbrella, and clutching her bags, and gazing all around her in a new rush of timidity; the two, in this conflict of absorption, nearly lost one another in the crush. The novice said:

'Oh, Sister Patrick! Couldn't we have one cup of tea in a restaurant before we go to the Hostel?'

'Wha-a-t?' cried Patrick, hunching up her shoulders, and laying her hand on her guimp like a stage Frenchwoman. 'Mon Pethite, que dites vous? Du thé? Vous savez bien . . . Vous savez bien que nous . . . Il faut . . . Il faut . . .' She groaned furiously. 'I can't talk French. I told Mother Mary Mell . . . Are you talking about tea? Do you realize, Miss, that you're on a pilgrimage? Gosthering in the middle of the street! Hurry! Hurry!'

They did hurry, under their black umbrellas, like two ants with top-heavy loads. Suddenly Teresa stopped and sneezed resolutely; once . . . twice . . . four times. Patrick towered over her. She started to gibber at her like a baboon.

'You're after getting a cold on me! That's yourself, and your window, and your fine officer!' Teresa sneezed a fifth time. 'Are you sure,' demanded Patrick, 'that you have the double petticoat?'

The novice's big eyes were directed miserably into a confectioner's window. It was bright with the brightest cakes.

'Dear Sister Patrick!' she wheedled. 'Don't you think we could have one small, tiny little cup of tea?'

The nun opened her mouth to say 'No,' looked at the window, looked at Teresa, and after a struggle said:

'Well! Since you have a cold coming on you, I'll let you have just one hot cup of coffee. Just one, mind you!'

It was warm in the café. Patrick had an éclair. Over their heads a radio kept weaving waltzes that made the novice sway gently on her chair. Patrick had two éclairs. The novice made her coffee last as long as possible. Patrick had a third éclair. Then, in spite of a fleck of cream on her jaw, Patrick's face was unusually forbidding as she looked up and said:

'Well, Miss, I hope you're feeling better now?'

'Thank you very much, Sister,' said Teresa, and rose with an air of firm resignation. 'We must go to the Hostel.'

A bell rang eight o'clock as they emerged. They wasted ten minutes searching for the Hostel, a bald faced house rising plumb from the pavement. Its brass tipped, reed-woven half-screens were damply inhospitable. Its closed door and iron grille were shining with the rain. The lay-sister who drew the slide of the grille spoke in unintelligible, provincial French, of which they understood only one word, 'Impossible!'

'Quoi?' squawked Patrick, clawing the grille, as the slide shot to in her face. 'What did that wan say?'

The bell jangled down the hall again. This time the lay-sister was even more emphatic, and therefore even less intelligible, and she became still less intelligible as Patrick hung to the grille and blustered in Franco-English. Teresa firmly pushed her aside, with a calm sanity:

'Vous ne comprenez pas. Tout est bien arrangé. Notre mère a écrit une lettre à votre mère. . . .'

The lay-sister interrupted. She said, 'Trop tard.' She said, 'Huit heures.' She said these words several times. She closed the grille with the slowness of a curiosity that commented on the folly of the two foolish virgins who had come too late. Teresa turned to Patrick, and burst into peals of laughter at the look of horror on her face.

'We're too late!' she cried, joyously. 'Now we must go to a hotel!'

Patrick rent her.

'You and your tea! You did it deliberately! Wait until we get back to Mother Mary Mell! I'll tell her you're not fit to be a nun! You're a little flitthermouse! You're a gillygoosey! What a pilgrim we have in you! There's your answer for you! You're not fit to be a nun! You're a slip! You're a miss! What're we going to do? What'll my aunt say to me? What'll Mother Mary Mell say to me? What's going to happen to us?'

Teresa began to cry. Patrick at once hushed her tirade, unfurled her umbrella (it was as big as a bookmaker's), dragged up two of the bags and set off, in a mouth-buttoned fury, to find a hotel. The rain was now a downpour. Their bags weighted them down. She halted. She gave the girl a look that was worse than a blow, shoved her into a doorway, and said, 'Don't stir from there till I came back.' She left the bags in her care, and butted out into the rain.

Men kept approaching the door, and seeing the nun, they would stop dead, and push away. At first this merely frightened her for she did not realize her predicament: but suddenly a cistern flushed noisily behind her and she recognized that she was standing in the doorway of a *cabinet*. Clutching her bags, she fled down the street, down a side street, another side street, and halted panting under a café awning.

The old proprietor came out and looked at her, cocked his head to one side, bowed, considered her, smiled, said that it was a bad night, and wiped his indifference on to the tabletop. Then he gazed around him, looked at her again, shrugged, and went indoors. More men passed her, on their way in or out, always pausing, after the first glance, to smile and bow. Twice she got up to fly, wondered whether Patrick would ever find her, sat again on the damp iron chair. A drunken old man with a beard finally put her to flight by taking off his hat, leaning on the tabletop, and starting a flowery speech. She ran into a gendarme who was accompanying Sister Patrick down the street. Patrick threw her two hands up to the sky preparatory to a tornado of abuse. She was soaked; her guimp was a rag; her coif hung around her face like lace. Before she could speak, Teresa hurled herself on the old woman's breast and sobbed out all her awful adventures, so that the gendarme and the nun calmed her with difficulty. They took her bag, then, and led her, whimpering, to the little pension-pub that Patrick had chosen for their night's lodging. There Patrick put her into bed, in a cosy little room all to herself, with red stuff curtains and a dusty-looking carpet – it was nearly threadbare – and with her own two hands Patrick lit a fire, brought an omelette, rolls, and coffee, and tucked her in for the night; and all the time Patrick kept begging her pardon for that outburst at the hostel. What with the comfort, the kindness, and the vestigial excitement, the little novice was melted to tears of happiness.

'Our pilgrimage is beginning,' she whispered happily to Patrick. 'Isn't it, dear Sister Patrick?'

' 'Twill begin in the morning,' temporized Patrick. 'And then the saint will smoothen everything out.'

Right cheek touched right cheek, and left cheek touched left cheek, in the way of all nuns kissing. Old fingers laid out her glossy black hair on the pillow. The light went out. A rough palm smoothed her forehead. The door clicked. The flames flickered on the ceiling.

In Kent, at Saint Anthony's, the only sound around the convent at night had been the crackle of twigs in the damp wood, the hoo-hoo of an owl. Here she heard footsteps in the street below, an occasional motor-car swishing over the cobbles, the soft, whispering downfall of April rain. Looking up at the wavering ceiling, she attended to those sounds, whose tumult, and whose unfamiliarity, and whose suggestiveness made England and her convent, Dublin and her home, utterly remote – less part of another country than part of another life. More than anything else they said, 'The pilgrimage has begun!' They said, 'O dear Saint Thérèse, I will leave all things in thy hands.' They said, 'O most omnipotent God, I yield all the world to Thee.'

'I want to be a saint!' she cried out, and beat the coverlet with her palm. And at that fell asleep, curled up in bed as softly as a cat.

3

Only the hens were awake as they walked to first Mass at Saint Pierre. The sun was glittering in the water between the cobblestones. Teresa felt that she alone possessed the town. She felt that all things converged on the forthcoming visit to the shrine. Even the warm prophecy of the steam rising from the streets and the cloudless whiteness of the sky seemed not something general to everybody in the world, but particular to her life alone. She whispered to Patrick, 'Thérèse is calling! I hear her!' Patrick nodded, too excited to speak.

After breakfast they began the ritual of Lisieux. Les Buisonnets, the Martin home (Saint Thérèse Martin), was exactly as they had foreseen it, just like all the photos and descriptions in biographies of the saint. They saw the 'trim lawn in front of the house', and 'the useful kitchen-garden at the back'. From the attic windows there was the expected 'distant view over the plain'. Teresa said to Patrick, with a sign of happiness:

'It was all made for her. If I had lived here, I, too, would have been a saint!'

Patrick nodded in agreement with the general proposition. For the novice to say that she could have been a saint was merely a way of saying that God had chosen one and could easily have chosen another.

' 'Tis Heaven!' she murmured, and clasped Teresa's hand.

It was the same in the sacristy of the Carmelite convent, where the saint's hair lies strewn under glass in its reliquary, and the walls are covered by mementoes of those who have paid honour to her memory – decorations, orders, swords, letters from all over the world. Here, where Patrick became almost incoherent at the prospect of meeting her aunt, thirty-one years after, now a Reverend Mother in the Carmelites, Teresa filled with sadness.

'The folly of the world!' she murmured, sighing again and again. 'They honour her now. They did not know the sorrow of her heart while she was alive.'

The two touched cheek to cheek again.

A Carmelite lay-sister next led them to the grave of the saint. From that they would go on to the convent proper to meet Patrick's aunt. They began to palpitate in mutual sympathy. The grave calmed them by its simplicity.

When they rose, the aunt stood beside them. Patrick toddled to her with cries of joy. The aged woman, her head a mere skull, her hands bony and ridged, gave no sign of recognition other than to say, 'God bless you, my child.' Old Patrick drew back like a frightened child. Timidly she introduced the novice. She explained falteringly why they had come.

'She's not sure if she wants to be a nun, Mother.'

The Carmelite looked at the novice. She, too, at once drew back. But the Carmelite smiled to hear the English name, Teresa, and took her hand gently and led her (Patrick following) across the garden to the convent ante-room. On the way she talked of simple things like the budding shrubs and the blessing of the rain. They sat in the ante-room and the Carmelite rang a bell.

They talked of the price of vegetables, until a faint passage of light in one wall drew their eyes to the grille – the last portal of the inner Carmelite hermitage. Behind the grille was a gauze, and presently Teresa's eyes made out, behind the gauze, a still face from which the gauze had eroded all recognizable character. All she could see was the vaguest outline of a countenance. As if she realized in that second how the discipline of the Order must have likewise eroded from the little girl of Les Buissonets all human emotion, and in a flash of understanding knew what sacrifice really means, she flung herself at the Carmelite's knees and cried out hysterically:

'Ma mère! I have no vocation!'

Patrick intervened hurriedly:

'Pay no heed to her. She's upset and sick in herself. The child doesn't know what she wants.'

The aged Carmelite waved her aside and lifted the novice to her feet. Looking into her face with a clear eye, she said, after a frightening silence:

'Could you be a Carmelite?'

'No!' panted the novice, and she drew back, as if she were at that moment about to be imprisoned behind the grille.

'If you cannot be a Carmelite, my child, you can be nothing.'

'She'd be happy enough,' intervened Patrick comfortably, 'in an easier Order.'

'She will be happy – we will all be happy – only in Heaven,' said the Carmelite coldly. 'Could you not even try to be a Carmelite?' asked the aged woman.

'No!' begged the novice. 'I couldn't do it!'

'Why not?'

'To be always shut in?' trembled the girl.

'It is an enclosed Order,' agreed the Superioress calmly.

'I couldn't stand it!'

'How do you know?' catechized the Superioress.

For answer the girl burst into such a sobbing wail that Patrick drew her to her broad bosom and turned on her aunt.

'Ye have no heart!' she upbraided. 'Badgering the poor child! 'Tisn't that we expected from you! Don't heed her,' she comforted Teresa. 'My poor little girsha! Don't mind her. Sure we can't all be saints. You'll do your best. You can't do more.'

'But,' sobbed Teresa, 'I want to be a saint. 'Tis to . . . to . . . to be a saint I joined the nuns.' Her voice came out through her nose, miserably. 'If I can't be a saint, I don't *want* to be a nun!'

The old woman comforted her, and finally restored her to a whimpering silence. Looking up, they saw they were alone. The grille was closed. The veil was hidden. The Superioress had gone.

The two pilgrims went back to their pension. That afternoon, without discussion, they went on to Saint Malo. There the novice was expected to find bodily rest, as at Lisieux she had been expected to find calm of soul.

4

Saint Malo faces across a wide estuary the modern watering-place of Dinard. At night they saw the lights in the hotels, and cafés, and more coloured lights beaded all around the roof of the casino; and sometimes they heard music across the still surface of water. Steamers from Southampton and the Channel Islands floated in the bay at anchor. Patrick was charmed with her room in the convent where they stayed. It looked directly across at Dinard. She wrote to Mother Mary Mell that she had a 'grand-stand', and that she was thinking of going across in a row-boat some night to gamble in the Casino and make the fortune of the Order. Becoming serious in a postscript, she said that Teresa had not yet made up her mind, but that she was 'behaving with the most edifying devotion'.

Not only did the novice attend every service in the convent, but she had become pious beyond description, daily spending long hours alone in adoration in the chapel. But when Patrick noticed that she left her lunch untouched on her table on the third day of her arrival, and went up to the novice's cell to ask if this were wise, she made a frightening discovery. She found that the mattress and bedclothes had been rolled up and put away under the bed, and all the girl's flannel underclothing was hanging in her cupboard. At once she went down to the chapel, and hissed at the solitary worshipper to come out, beckoning madly with her bony finger.

'Sister Teresa,' she said severely, 'you are refusing your food. Is there any reason for this?'

The novice hung her head and said nothing.

'Answer me, Sister.'

Still the novice kept her eyes on the parquet.

'I command you, Sister, to answer me.'

'There is no reason,' whispered the novice.

'Then eat up your food in future,' ordered the nun. 'Do you want to make a skeleton out of yourself?' And she added more easily, 'Don't you know right well I'm supposed to bring you home as plump as a duck?'

The novice raised two large, sad eyes.

'Sister Patrick,' she begged, 'I will obey if you command me. But I want to do penance for my sins, and for the sins of the world. I feel I have received a higher command.'

'What higher command?' blustered the old woman, taken aback. 'What on earth are you talking about, Sister?'

Teresa sighed.

'The sins of the world are all about us,' she smiled sadly. 'I see them every night from my window, across the water, in the dens and gambling-houses. All lit up like the fires of Hell to lure poor souls astray. I dreamed the first night I came here that the Devil lives over there. I saw his red eyes in the air. I saw that this convent was put here specially to atone for the wickedness that surrounds it.'

'Holy Mother!' cried the nun. 'What are you talking about, girl? Sister Teresa, let me tell you that if you ate a proper supper . . . And by the same token, Miss, no wonder you have dreams if you sleep on the laths of the bed. Do you,' she threatened, 'sleep on the laths of the bed?'

The novice once more hung her head, and once more she had to be bullied into replying.

'I do, Sister,' she confessed unhappily.

'Well, then, let there be an end of it! What right have you to be going on with these andrewmartins off of your own bat? You know right well you must ask permission of your superior before you do the like. And that reminds me,' she cried, grabbing the girl's flank, and then standing back from her in horror, with her gummy mouth open. 'You haven't a stitch on you! Go upstairs at once, miss, and dress yourself properly. I'll be after you in two minutes. I'm worn out and tormented with your vagaries! Ten times I told Mother Mary Mell . . .'

She pointed upstairs – a figure of Justice.

The novice went, tearful, head-hanging. In two minutes the old nun followed. She opened the door of the cell. The girl lay on the ground, her arms stretched out like a crucifix, her dilated eyes fixed as on a vision over her head. The old nun entered the room, closed the door, and thundered:

'Get up out o' that!'

The novice did not move.

'Miss!' said the old woman, pale as a sheet, 'how dare you disobey me!'

The novice trembled as if a wind had ruffled her spirit. With her heart battering inside in her, Patrick walked over and looked down. The big brown eyes, so strikingly dark in that pale pink-and-white face, stared up past her. Patrick looked up at the electric light bulb. She looked all about her. The thick-moted afternoon sun slanted in across the bed. A hissing suspiration below the window was followed by the little groan of the gravel dragging back under the wave. Then she saw a slimy brown insect, with wavering head, creep to the white ear of the novice, and she screamed:

'An earwig! Climbing into your ear!'

Teresa sat up as if she was stung. The fright passed. The two looked at each other with hate in their eyes. At the door, Patrick said:

'I'll wait in the garden.'

In complete silence they walked four miles that afternoon. They did the same the following morning. That was their last full day. On the final afternoon Patrick spoke:

'We will be in Saint Anthony's tomorrow night. Do you know, yet, my dear, if you have a vocation?'

'I have decided to join the Carmelites,' said the novice.

They halted. They looked across the sea-wall into the blue of Dinard. A few lights were already springing up over there – the first dots in the long, golden necklet that already they had come to know so well. A lone seagull squawked over the glassy water. The sunset behind the blue pinnacles of the resort was russet.

'And what's wrong with our own Order, Sister dear?' asked Patrick of the vacancy before her.

'I feel, dear Sister Patrick,' judged the novice, staring ahead of her, 'that it is too worldly.'

'How is it too worldly?' asked Patrick in a whisper.

'Well, dear Sister Patrick,' pronounced the novice, 'I see, for example, that you all eat too much.'

The little wavelets fell almost inaudibly, drunken with the fullness of the tide, exhausted and soothed by their own completion.

'I shall tell Mother Mary Mell that you think so,' whispered the old nun.

'There is no need, dear Sister. It will be my duty to tell her myself. I will pray for you all when I am in the Carmelites. I love you all. You are all kind and generous. But, dear Sister, I feel that very few nuns really have the right vocation to be nuns.' Patrick closed her eyes tightly. The novice continued: 'I will surrender myself to the divine Love. The death I desire is the death of Love. The death of the Cross.'

They heard only the baby tongues of the waves. The evening star blazed in the russet sky. The old nun saw it, and she said, in part a statement, in part a prayer, in part a retort:

'Sweet Star of the Sea!'

Teresa raised her dark eyes to the star and she intoned in her girlish voice the poem of Saint Thérèse:

> 'Come, Mother, once again,
> Who camest first to chide.
> Come once again, but then
> To smile – at eventide.'

The old nun fiddled with her beads. She drew long breaths through her nose. She tried several times to speak. She gestured that they must go back. They turned and walked slowly back to the convent, side by side; the old nun as restless as if she were in bodily agony, the novice as sedate and calm as a statue. After a while Patrick fumbled in her pocket, and found a chocolate, and popped it into her mouth. Then she stopped chewing, and threw an eye at her companion. At the look of intense sorrow in the face beside her, she hunched up her shoulders and as silently as she could, she gulped the fragments whole.

On the journey homeward they did not speak one word to each other: all the way to Rouen in the trotting auto-rail; in the clanking train to Dieppe; on the boat; in the English train. In silence they arrived at Saint Anthony's, among the dank beechwoods, now softly dripping, in time to hear the first hoo-hoo of the owl, and to troop in with the rest of the community for evening chapel. Mother Mary Mell barely had time to ask the old nun how she had enjoyed her holiday – that first holiday in thirty-one years. Patrick's eyes fluttered. She recalled the lights of Dinard.

'It was lovely, Mother!'

Mary Mell caught the flicker of hesitation. Just as they crossed the tessellated threshold of the chapel, she whispered quickly, 'And Teresa?'

Patrick who had been waiting for that question ever since the final afternoon in Saint Malo, and yet had no answer ready, took refuge behind the chapel's interdiction of silence. She smiled reassuringly, nodded, smiled, nodded again, and then, very solemn and pious, she walked in with her head down. She said her prayers badly. She slept hardly at all that night. She heard every crackling branch and fluttering night-bird. For what, in the name of the Most High, was she to say to Mary Mell? And what was she to say to the community in the morning? As she tossed and tumbled, she thought of Teresa sleeping peacefully in her cell, and the old woman burst into tears of rage.

In the morning there was no Teresa. She had left the convent, through a ground-floor window, before anybody was awake, and gone on the milk-train to London. She had walked across the city at that hour when the sun emphasizes the position of the East End, and the sleepers in the parks that she traversed are unwrapping their newspaper-blankets. A sister-in-law coming out to collect the morning milk found a nun sitting on the doorstep. She had breakfast, in a tennis-frock, along with the family.

She saw the convent only once again – about two years later when she brought her husband to see it. As they got out of the train she looked up into the familiar beeches at the steam of the engine caught in the branches, and she remembered how every train used to make the woods seem infinitely lonely and the convent darker and more melancholy, because that white steam suggested people travelling, and the luxury of the world she had renounced. Her George, who was a Protestant, and who was much excited by this expedition, nodded solemnly, and began to get an uncomfortable feeling that he was married to a nun. They were entertained politely. Old Sister Patrick did not appear. As they left, the starting train again sent its gushes of steam into the branches, and now those branches again seemed to Teresa to clutch not only at the white smoke but at her own heart. She felt that the woods enclosed a refuge from the world of which she had, irrevocably, become a part. As she snuggled down into her fur collar she gazed out of her big eyes at her husband, and said, with a shake of her little head:

'Ah, George! George! You will never know what I gave up to marry you!'

He smiled adoringly at her as, in obedience to a gesture, he leaned over to put a cigarette between her rouged lips.

'My precious Teresa,' he murmured softly, and patted her knee.

She shook her head at him again, with a pitying smile.

'Has it upset you, my sweet?' he asked dismally.

Saying never a word, she kept gazing at him fixedly, as if he were a stranger. He huffed, and hawed, and hedged himself behind his newspaper, looking as despondent as he considered proper. For as he explained to his colleagues in the morning, his wife was 'a very spiritual woman' and on occasions like this she always made him feel that he had the soul of a hog.

The Man Who Invented Sin

In our youth when we used to pour into the mountains to learn Irish, places that were lonely and silent for the rest of the year became full of gaiety during the summer months. Every day there were picnics and expeditions; every night there were dances, moonlight boating parties, sing-songs in the cottages. The village street became a crowded promenade; its windows never went black before one in the morning; the pub was never empty. Where once you could have been utterly alone half a mile off the road, in the bog or up the mountain, you could not now be sure of privacy anywhere. If you went up the mountain to bathe naked in some tiny loch you might suddenly see a file of young students like Alpineers coming laughing down on you over the next scarp; you might turn the corner of a lonely mountain-pass courting your girl and burst upon a bevy of nuns sedately singing choruses among the rocks – for every kind of teacher, laymen and women, nuns, priests and monks were encouraged in those years to come out into the hills.

How we all got accommodation I do not know. The priests took lodgings in the villages. The monks and nuns purchased derelict houses which had been abandoned by the landlords after the Revolution. The people gave up their best rooms to the rest of us, turned lofts into dormitories, one or two even set up second-hand bell tents. One July, so stifling was the house where I stayed – six at least to every room – that I used to take a rug every night and climb into the high hay in the barn; and there were always four or five like me who preferred to be bitten by the ticks and wakened early by the birds and the mountain air than to be half-suffocated in feather-beds under the baking slates. By the end of the month, however, I got so tired of digging the little crab-like ticks from under my skin that I moved two miles out the road to a place called Ryder's, a small house on the lower lake, which usually took nobody at all. Indeed, only by great cajoling did I persuade Mrs Ryder to take me in. My only fear, then, was that I might be lonely. But before she knew what had happened Mrs Ryder had not merely one lodger but five, for with the beginning of August the monks' hostel overflowed, and the nuns' hostel overflowed, and she had to take in two of the monks and two of the nuns.

There was nothing remarkable about my fellow-students, except, perhaps, that little Sister Magdalen was so dainty and gay and spirited that it seemed a shame to lock her away from the world in a convent. Sister Crysostom was tall, delicate, with big hands and a blotchy skin, and she walked with her toes turned in. She was a bit of a Miss Prim, and I think she had been chosen as companion for Sister Magdalen because she was so prim. Brother Virgilius was a countryman with a powerful frame and a powerful voice, round red cheeks, and no nerves, and why he had chosen to be a monk was hard to understand. It seemed to me that he would have made a better farmer than a teacher. However, I found that he was a fine hurler and I am sure the boys loved him for his natural ways. Brother Majellan was very different, a gentle, apple-cheeked man with big glasses, a complexion like a girl, teeth as white as a hound's, and soft, beaming eyes. He was an intelligent, sensitive man. I took to him immediately.

At first we saw very little of one another. They had their principal meal at their own hostels, were studying most of the day, and the only time we all met was in the evenings, when we sat in the little garden and passed discreet remarks across the path about politics or the weather; or, if there was rain, we would meet in the drawing-room where there was a turf fire, and talk of the day's lessons. They kept convent hours, were off to their rooms by nine at the latest, and long before I rose were gone down to the village to morning Mass. That year, however, the weather broke suddenly in the middle of August so that we found ourselves in the drawing-room almost every evening, over our notebooks and dictionaries and grammars. We had, by then, become like travellers on a long railway-journey who have broken the silence and are beginning to chat companionably. We might still sit silent for, say, a quarter of an hour, but then somebody would say something and we would all get going. One night for instance, Majellan lifted his eager, earnest, doggy eyes, and said:

'Sister Magdalen, how do you pronounce the word which I call *cearrbhach?*'

'Oh, Brother Majellan,' she laughed, shocked at herself, entertained by her own folly, 'I am afraid I do not even know what the word means!'

Virgilius clapped his two big countryman's paws together and roared out laughing.

'Sister Magdalen, I'm surprised at you! I'm surprised at you! Not know the word *cearrbhach*? It means a card-player or a gambler.'

'And is that what it means? *Cearrbhach*.' And she pronounced the guttural word as daintily as if it rhymed with *peruke*.

She was a city-girl and had never before heard Irish spoken by anybody but city-people.

'No! You're not saying it right at all. You're too ladylike about it. Say it the way the people say it. *This* way.'

'I see.' And again the dainty pronunciation like *peruke*. 'Like that?'

'Listen, Sister. I'll show you the way to talk Irish. If you'll pardon the expression, make a great big shpit inside in your mouth and gurgle it. Like this. Carrrwoochhhk.'

Crysostom immediately protested.

'Please, Brother Virgilius! If we cannot speak our own language like ladies let us not speak it at all.'

'But,' from Majellan, 'that really is the way the people speak. It is a guttural language. Like German.'

'Not Bavarian German. It is true that the Prussians . . .'

And off they went into a heated argument – the sort of argument we were always having in those days, about whether Ireland must always be a peasant country, and what other countries had achieved, and Virgilius, who hated arguments, blew out his lips and looked gloomily at his two big feet stretched out before him, and Majellan and Magdalen got so excited that Crysostom had to stop it with her usual: 'Sister, I really think it is our hour to retire.'

One day at the College, as we called the sunbaked tin building where we studied from ten to one, we were asked to write an essay on a proverb to which the nearest Saxon equivalent is 'The Child is Father to the Man'. I remember, that evening, how the mists lifted from the hills, and the sun began to raise gentle wisps of steam from the rocks, and the trout were leaping from a lake as blue as the patches of sky between the dissolving clouds. We spread newspapers on the two damp garden seats, and as we discussed the proper Irish terms to be used, the four of them began, without noticing it, to speak of their own childhood; where they had been born, where they went to school, and so on. Sister Magdalen sucked the end of her silver pencil and said:

'I know the Gaelic for "I was born", that is *Do rugadh mé*. And the place – Templemore. Of course, that is *An Teampall Môr*. The Great Temple. Or the big church. Though the Lord knows there's no big temple in Templemore.' She sighed. Then she cocked her head suddenly. 'I suppose you were never in Templemore, Brother Majellan? But, sure, why would you! It's an out-of-the-way little place.'

Crysostom tapped my fingers irritably with her pencil. I was idly pulling a fuchsia flower to pieces:

'How would you say that, Sister?'

'Which? What? What was it you said, Sister Crysostom?'

' "It's an out-of-the-way little place." You see I want to say that, too. I was born in a small little place like Templemore.'

'Where was that?' asked Virgilius idly. He had been staring solemnly at the fuchsia that I threw into his lap.

'Kilfinnane,' said Crysostom, 'in County Limerick.'

At once Virgilius whirled and slapped her thigh.

'Yerrah, Crysostom, do you mean to tell me that you come from Kilfinnane!'

'Brother!' And she held his arm excitedly. 'Do you know Kilfinnane?'

'Do I know my own father? Wasn't I born just below in Kilmallock? Oh, wisha, then, 'tis many the fine Sunday I took the old bicycle out to Kilfinnane hunting hares behind the rath. If you come from Kilfinnane you must surely know the rath?'

'The rath is on our land!'

'Ah, no?' – in a huge childish delight.

'Often and often I stood on the rath and looked down at the smoke of the train coming into Kilmallock – in and out of the woods – the little white smoke. And I could watch it again for another half an hour after it left Kilmallock, puffing away down towards Cork.'

'I well believe you! It's a wonderful view. They say you can see six counties?'

'For a whole hour,' she remembered. 'The little white smoke. I used to wonder who might be in it, and would I ever travel away in it myself.'

'Didn't I go every night to meet it at the station and gather the Dublin papers, for my uncle kept a paper shop in the Main Street? The Cork train we called it. Majellan, you're a Corkman, aren't you?'

Majellan was not listening to us. He was gazing across the darkening lake whose headlands were faint as smoke.

'My father,' said Sister Magdalen thoughtfully, 'was a doctor. I know how to say that, too. My mother died when I was fourteen . . . I was a lone child . . . My father married a second time.'

Majellan kept staring over the lake. She said something about a notebook and flitted indoors. I got tired of listening to Virgilius and Crysostom and got up to go to the dance. It was only then I noticed that Majellan and Magdalen were in the hall. She was dabbing her eyes with his big red handkerchief.

When I came back from the dance the half moon had vaporized the moist land with a melancholy, filmy light. The house was black and silent.

I think it was Virgilius who first began to play pitch-and-toss along the garden path, and it was that evening that Magdalen called Majellan 'Jelly'. I came on them laughing over the game, which Brother Virgilius was trying to teach to the other three. Brother Majellan was, by then, calling Sister Magdalen 'Maggie', Crysostom naturally became 'Chrissy', and Virgilius, of course, joined Jelly as 'Jilly'. How they laughed over that! I crowned the night for them by taking them up to the drawing-room piano and teaching them all a song with a chorus:

'Bab Eró 'gus O mo mhíle grá.'

And Chrissy so surprised us by the strength and sweetness of her voice that at the end Virgilius clapped his hands and shouted, 'I wouldn't doubt you, Chrissy. I knew you had it in you,' and made her sing the song again alone. As she sang we heard a clear echo: it was a boating party out on the lake. They took up the chorus and gave it back to her until they faded around a headland still singing.

'But you know,' gurgled Magdalen, 'I really don't know what it all means. Can you translate it for me, Jelly?'

'No trouble at all,' said Majellan. 'It is a young fellow singing a song to his lady and this is what he says.'

As he translated he gradually blushed redder and redder, and Virgilius winked at the big, rolling eyes of Magdalen, and her rounded little mouth, just ready to burst into laughter. When Majellan stuck his head right out through the window to look at the lake Magdalen burst. Crysostom said: 'I really think, Sister, it is our hour to retire.'

'Jelly,' said Virgilius, when they were gone, 'you big gom! You have as much sense as a child of two.'

When monks and nuns quarrel, I found, they seem to be astonished and shocked rather than angry: like children who have bumped against a door or a calf who has tried his first nettle. Grown men would have ended it with a curse or a clout. I escaped down to the kitchen to practise my Irish on Mrs Ryder. She was baking a cake, and humming '*Bab Eró* . . .' Her cousin, who was the clerk in the Post Office, was sitting on the settle. She asked me which had the lovely voice. Mrs Ryder said her house was blessed.

'The creatures! Isn't it grand to hear them enjoying themselves? Four saints I have in the house.'

'Only four?' I protested.

'What time did *you* come in last night?' she asked, and the conversation became exuberantly coarse.

The next evening too, was exquisitely silent. The tiny trout-splashes could be heard clearly, and the cattle lying on the dry strand across the water chewing the cud. We were all upstairs, I playing the piano, Virgilius seated in the open window singing and beating time with a silver tankard that young Ryder won in a tug-of-war, Jelly and Maggie trying to waltz, and when Crissy was not laughing at poor Jelly's efforts to learn the steps she, too, was singing, at *Bab Eró*, like a blackbird. The music must have carried a long way over the water.

The door was slashed open with a bang that made the piano hum, and there was our local curate's black barrel of a body blocking the opening: for though he was not more than twenty-five – I believe it was his first parish – he was very fat. He was also pompous and cocksure. In the College we called him Lispeen, which is the Irish for a frog. For that second it was as if a camera-reel stopped dead – the tankard held in the air, the two dancers like a waxworks, and Crissy with her mouth open.

'Glory be to God,' he moaned. 'So I have been informed correctly.'

(It was only after that I thought of the postmistress on the settle the night before; you might as well talk to a microphone as to a postmistress.) 'To think that this kind of thing has been going on under my nose for weeks.' He let his voice fall solemnly, even secretively. 'Unknown to anybody!' He roared then: 'To think I cannot go for a summer walk to read my office without hearing this kind of caterwauling!' His voice fell again. 'If Martin Luther could only see this! What's your name?' he stabbed at Crissy. She had turned as pale as her coif.

'Sissster Cryssossostom, father.'

'And your name, Sister?'

'My name is Sister Mary Magdalen,' said Maggie, very dignified and entirely self-possessed, and looking very angry.

'Well-named,' he growled. I saw Jelly grow red with fury. 'Go to your rooms, please. I'll talk to these gentlemen.' With a scornful emphasis on the last word.

They fluttered out obediently, Magdalen with her head in the air, Crysostom with terror in her eyes. Majellan turned on him. I held his arm. He was only a monk, and no match for a curate in his own parish.

'You had no right, father, to talk to the sisters like that.'

The curate swelled.

'Are you daring to answer me back, young man?'

Majellan's voice shook but he held his ground.

'We are doing no harm.'

Even Virgilius spoke up, though more respectfully – he knew the power before him.

'Sure we were only having a bit of sing-song, father?'

The curate gasped, melodramatically – I swear he had taken a prize for elocution at his seminary – then dropped into a wonderful tone of sarcasm.

'Only having a bit of a sing-song? *Only* having a bit of a sing-song? Well, well!' He put his stick behind him like a shooting-stick and teetered back and fro on it. He was very sure of himself. 'Perhaps, gentlemen, we think that we are back in the days of the Reformation?' Then he did his roar again. 'Singing? Dancing? Drinking?' He whirled his stick and cracked the tankard.

Virgilius stared into the tankard, and sighed: 'Shweepstake Tickets.'

That sent the blood to Lispeen's forehead.

'I'll talk to you young bucks in the morning when I've had a word with your Superior. Good evening to you.'

The door slammed. We heard him go downstairs. His voice boomed in the kitchen at the Ryders. Then we saw his shadow passing across the paling sheen of the lake.

'The bosthoon,' hissed Majellan.

'Jelly,' moaned Virgilius, who had seized the situation at once, 'we're for the long drop!'

With that we stole down the corridor and tapped at the sisters' doors and conferred in a huddle, and Virgilius and Crysostom blamed Majellan for speaking back but Magdalen said, 'You were quite right, Brother. He is no gentleman.' But Crysostom kept pulling her fingers and looking at each of us in turn. She knew, too, how all this would appear back in the city where the Bishop and their Superiors would say, 'What is this! Nuns and monks living in the same house? Dancing together? Singing choruses? Playing pitch-and-toss out in the garden? And what's all this about *a tankard*?'

Magdalen said next morning that she heard Crysostom crying late into the night.

Actually nothing at all happened. Old Ryder and the Parish Priest between them must have put a stop to the curate's gallop. After all curates come and curates go but parish priests, like the brook, go on for ever. But the story spread, and the students gathered round the four to comfort and encourage them, and of evenings people started to walk out to Ryder's and, in spite of Sister Crysostom's warnings and tremors, we began to have regular concerts in the garden. The four even began to go out on surreptitious boating-parties, and the bed-at-nine rule gradually became bed-at-ten, and even bed-at-eleven, until they were soon having as happy a time as anybody. Or should have, if their consciences were at ease. But were they? For, looking back at it now, I think I understand what had occurred. The Serpent had come into the garden with the most wily of temptations. He had said, 'How dare you eat this apple?' And straightaway they began to eat it. They swallowed the last morsel of their apple the night before they were due to return to the city, perhaps for a lifetime, among the smelly slums about their schools.

We were moody that evening in the garden.

'I suppose this will be the last time we'll see the moon on the lake,' said Sister Magdalen.

But the moon would not be up until after eleven, and a fairy-wind in the reeds, ruffling the stars in the water into a fuzz, meant that even then there might be a clouded night.

'Our bus goes at seven,' said Sister Crysostom. 'When does yours go, Brother Virgilius?'

By anticipation they were already becoming formal with one another.

'Half-past seven,' Brother Virgilius.

'Who'll walk as far as the lake?' suggested Brother Majellan.

They went down the white road. Autumn was coming already. A white mist hung low over the river. The lake was dim as a ghost. They stood at the edge of it and looked at the low hills beyond.

'Sure, we can be looking forward to next year,' said Brother Virgilius cheerfully.

'If there are any summer courses next year,' murmured Sister Magdalen.

The soft sound of oars was heard and a boat appeared out on the water. The people in it were singing quietly; a last boating-party. It was one of those big, barge-like boats built for excursion parties, and there must have been twenty people in it, crushed shoulder to shoulder. Majellan hailed them and they approached and when they invited the four out for a row even Crissy hardly demurred. The presence of the two monks and the two nuns seemed to cheer them up, for as they rowed away towards the narrows, making for the upper lake, the songs became louder and more merry. The lights of the village overflowed into the lake. Promenaders there heard them and sang back. Doubtless the curate heard them, too, and thanked God they would all be gone in the morning.

Time ceases to exist on a lake: every fisherman knows that. Somebody said that the moon would be up at eleven and would light them home. Crissy whispered to Maggie that that would be very late, and what would happen if some message came from the Hostel? But Maggie hushed her passionately, and Virgilius cried, 'Let the last night be the longest.'

It was much later than eleven before they got through the narrows – the old barge stuck there as it always did. Then the grey mountain slowly swelled up like a ghost against the spreading moon, and the whole land became black and white. On the bright side of the land the white cottages shone under their tarry roofs, and on the dark hills their scattered yellow lights invited us home. It became cold on the water. Rowing back against the current was a slow business. Heavy drops of phosphorescence fell from the blades. Presently a voice said, 'It is near twelve, lads, put your backs into it.' Now they were not singing at all; nor did they sing again until they saw the remaining village lights – only one or two left now. And they did not sing Irish songs, which are nearly all melancholy, but old music-hall songs like *Daisy, Daisy*, and *The Girls you Can't Forget*, and *I'm One of the Knuts of Barcelona*. The barge was not much more than twelve feet from the shore when they saw, clear in the moon-light, the black figure standing on the causeway. Majellan yelled, 'Backwater!' The barge slewed around.

'I suppose, my dear ladies and gentlemen, that it does not matter to you that you are keeping the whole village awake?'

Nobody replied. The rowers set off for the opposite shore. The two brothers turned up their coat collars to hide their Roman collars. The two nuns hid their guimps and coifs with borrowed coats. Every-body was feeling cross and tired. As they neared the far shore the same black figure awaited them. He had raced round by the bridge, and gone leaping over heather and bog-pool.

'You won't land here tonight until I have the name of every person on that boat!'

The midnight mountains cried back, 'On – that – boat.'

The boat pushed off again and in mid-lake they held a conference: for even lay-teachers do not like falling out with a priest. And the four religious? There was only one thing to do. It was easy to dis-guise Majellan and Virgilius: caps for black hats, and the Roman collars ripped off. The nuns had to remove guimps, and cowls, put on kerchiefs and pin up their skirts. Then the boat again rowed to the landing-place, the men crushed around the priest arguing loudly, and the rest ran. In five minutes he was alone on the causeway. At his feet he saw a white object on the stones: a nun's starched guimp. As he looked at it he trembled like a dog.

He was no longer alone by the moon-flooded lake. He was roaring in the pulpit, holding up the guimp: he was in the Bishop's Palace quietly unfolding a pale linen object out of brown paper: he was in the Parish Priest's sitting-room and the white thing lay between them on the table: he was knocking at Ryder's door – yes, even if it was nearly one o'clock in the morning. He might have done all these things if, when he got back to his cottage, there was not a sick-call before him, and he had to get out his car and drive at once three and a half miles into the heart of the hills. Half an hour later he was tearing back. He had been hoaxed. The window of his cottage was open. The guimp was gone. It was the one good deed I did for my four friends.

I was awakened by the supernaturally bright light: it was not the sunrise: it was the sinking moon. My watch showed me that it was barely turned five o'clock. Dew and mist were all around the silent house: the lake was frosty; the sky pallid. The trees were weighted with sleep. Only the ceaseless mountain-stream and the deceived birds made a sweet noise. Below in the garden, by the wooden gate, stood Majellan and Magdalen, talking...

I never saw Magdalen again; I never saw Virgilius again; I never saw Crysostom again.

That was nineteen hundred and twenty, and not for twenty-three years did I meet Majellan. He was, of course, still a monk, and will always be: he was greying, and a little stooped, and much thinner. His eager, doggy eyes lit up for me: until I began to joke about those days, and then the light faded. I asked him about the others, and he told me that Virgilius was now a Principal somewhere. He had not heard of the two nuns since that night on the lake.

'Ah!' I sighed. 'Great days! But nobody wants to learn the language now. The mountains are empty.'

'Yes. The mountains are empty.'

'What a shame!'

'Mind you,' he said, after a moment, 'I'm not sure that I altogether approve of young people going out to these places. I hope I'm not being puritanical or anything like that, but . . . well, you know the sort of thing that goes on there.'

I was so shocked that I could not reply for a moment.

'But, surely, it's all very harmless?'

He shook his head seriously.

'Maybe. You *never* know.'

I said something idle. Then I asked him did he go out there at all nowadays.

'That was our last year.'

'I hope it wasn't any trouble with your superiors?' I asked anxiously.

'Oh, nothing like that. No. It was just . . .' He looked away. Then he said over his shoulder, 'I didn't much want to, really.' Then he looked at me, and in a little gush of confidence he said, 'You mightn't understand it, now! But it's not good to take people out of their rut. I didn't enjoy that summer.'

I said I understand that. After a few more words, we parted. He smiled, said he was delighted to see I was looking so well, and went off, stooping his way back to his monastery in the slum.

By coincidence, two hours later, I found myself side by side with Lispeen, looking into a bookshop window. He was scarcely changed, except for a faint brush of grey at each ear; he wore a tall silk hat and carried a silver-headed umbrella. When I spoke to him and he turned, the sunset struck his rosy face and lit the sides of his hat so that they glowed and shone. With difficulty I brought his mind back to those years, but when I did he greeted me as heartily as if I was his best friend, and laughed so merrily at the memory of those old days that I almost expected him to clap me on the back.

'Of course, you know,' he confided, with wide eyes, 'they were only children. Such innocents!' He laughed at the thought of the innocents. 'Of course, I *had* to frighten them!' And he laughed again, and then threw up his head and said heigh-ho in a big sigh. Then he shook my hand, and beamed at me, told me I was looking grand, and went his cheerful way. He bowed benevolently to every respectful salute along the glowing street, and when he did his elongated shadow waved behind him like a tail.

Unholy Living and Half Dying

Jacky Cardew is one of those club bachelors who are so well-groomed, well-preserved, pomaded, medicated, and self-cosseted that they seem ageless – the sort of fixture about whom his pals will say when he comes unstuck around the age of eighty, 'Well, well! Didn't poor old Jacky Cardew go off *very* fast in the end?'

For thirty years or so he has lived in what are called Private Hotels; last winter he said to his friends, 'These bloody kips are neither private nor hotels, I'm going to take a flat.' What he got in the end was the sort of makeshift thing that goes by the name of a flat in Irish cities – two rooms (that is, one room cut in two), with the W.C. on the ground floor and the bathroom on the top floor; and in the bathroom an unpleasant, greasy-looking gas-stove such as Prince Albert might have unveiled at the Great Crystal Palace Exhibition of 1851.

But Jacky was delighted. At least he now had privacy. Nobody lived in the house but himself and his own landlady, for a tinsmith had the ground floor (rather noisy and smelling of solder), there were solicitors' offices on the second floor, the old lady lived under the slates, above Jacky's flat, and he hardly ever saw her except when he paid his rent.

About two o'clock one bad February morning just as Jacky and a few friends were settling down for the fourth time to their last game of solo they gradually became aware that a dog was beating his tail on the floor above. There was no other sound then – for a while – but the flick of the cards and the rain spitting on the window and the slight exclamations of the players. Then they heard the rapping again.

'Better go easy, boys,' somebody said, playing a card, 'we're keeping the old lady upstairs awake.'

They played on intently. Again they heard the rapping, this time insistent and loud. Jacky glanced around at the lifted eyebrows, at his wrist-watch, at the dying fire, at the drops sparkling on the pane in the arclight of the Square below, and went out with the sort of frown he would have turned on a junior in the bank who had not been soapy enough. Striking matches he climbed the stairs. The nail-heads shone. Hearing him stumble and curse she called his name, and he made his way towards the voice, stooping under the great rafters of the attics, elbowing aside the damp washing that she had hung there to dry, feeling the cold within a few inches of his poll. He found her room, a bare attic. He was affronted by its poverty, its cold stuffiness, its sloping attic-window that wept in ripples with the lights of the city.

In the matchlight he saw her pale eyes staring up at him in terror from the pillow; he saw her hollowed cheeks; the white beard on her chin; her two pigtails tied with bits of red wool. The match burned his fingers. Through the dark he heard her whisper:

'Mr Cardew, I'm dying.'

He was so frightened that he immediately lit another match. He was even more frightened by what she replied when he asked her if he could call in one of her friends:

'God help us,' she panted. 'Friends how are ye? I haven't a friend to wet me lips. Not a friend. In the world.'

He raced down the stairs. One of his pals was a doctor; he went up and examined her, soothed her, came down, said there was nothing much wrong with her except old age and perhaps a touch of indigestion, and ordered two aspirins and a hot-water bottle on her stomach. They made her comfortable for the night and the party went home, heads down to the rain, shouting commiserations all round.

Jacky came back to his dishevelled room and sat by the cold fireplace. He heard every quarter-hour strike from the City Hall, sometimes bold and clear, sometimes faint and sad, according to the mood of the wintry wind. He suddenly remembered that his own mother had gone on a night like this. He wondered who would attend to the old woman if she died, and for the first time he took notice of the family photographs hung around the walls, mainly young men and women and vacant-looking babies with their mouths open. There was a big black enlargement of a man with a grey moustache and a bald head. He reminded him of old Cassidy, his last Manager, who now dined regularly every Tuesday of the year with another retired banker called Enright. As Jacky poked the dead cinders it came to him that Cassidy probably had no other friend in the world, and, begod, anyway, once you turn fifty what is it but a gallop down the bloody straight?

At half-past three he went up to have another look at her. She was asleep, breathing heavily. He tried to feel her pulse but could not remember what a normal beat is and felt hers was as low as a hearse. He returned to his cold room. The rain still spat. The Square outside shone. He felt a dull pain in his groin and wondered, could it be appendicitis? He thought that he should have called in the priest to her and he counted the years since he last went to Confession. At half-past four he had another look at her and found her breathing easily and decided she was all right. As he pulled up his pyjamas he gave his paunch a dirty look.

He was awakened at his usual hour by the old lady herself, bringing him his usual hot cup of tea and buttered toast. She had a prayer-book under one arm and was dressed for the street.

'Good Heavens,' he gulped, 'I thought you were . . .'

Her tall lean body swayed over like a reed with the gusts of laughter.

'Mr Cardew, 'tis well known you can't kill a bad thing. My little hot seat in Purgatory isn't ready for me yet. Ah, I knew I'd pay for that load of bacon and cabbage I ate yesterday.' An inelegant gesture from her stomach to her throat made him hastily lay down the buttered toast. 'I was all swelled up with it the day long.'

Jacky dressed, blaspheming. On his way out he decided to have a serious word with the woman. She had returned from chapel and was sitting in her kitchen sucking up a big basin of soup.

'Look here, Mrs Canty,' he said severely, 'is it an actual fact that you have no friends whatsoever?'

'I have plenty friends, Mr Cardew,' she smiled happily. 'The best friends any woman ever had.' She laid her bony hands on a pile of prayer-books – there must have been about twelve of them, a pile a foot high, all in shiny black cloth coverings. 'Haven't I the souls suffering in Purgatory? I have Saint Anthony.' Her glance directed his to a big brown-and-cream statue on the dresser. 'And haven't I the Sacred Heart?' He eyed the red-and-gold statue over the sink with the withered palms of last Easter crossed before it. 'Look at the Little Flower smiling at me. And what about Saint Joseph and Saint Monica?'

Jacky's head was going around like a weather-cock.

'And amn't I only after coming in from praying to the Left Shoulder? Friends, Mr Cardew?'

She smiled pityingly at him. He strode out, to prevent himself from saying, 'Then why the hell didn't you call on them last night instead of rapping me up to you?' Instead he took it out of his secretary at the bank.

'Pure damn superstition, that's what I call it. Craw-thumpin' by day and bellyachin' by night. The usual Irish miserere. All based on fear of hellfire and damnation. It would turn anybody into an atheist!'

The girl talked up to him; they almost quarrelled; she told him he should be ashamed of himself; she even told him his 'day would come'; she drove him beside himself by telling him she 'would pray for him'. At lunch he got into a violent argument about religion during which he kept on using the word, 'Benighted! Benighted!' He was still at it that night in the club, but he had to go easy there as most of the members were Knights of Columbanus and business is business. He took the middle line of:

'Mind you, I have a great regard for what I call *real* religion. And, mind you, I'm no saint. I'm honest about that. Though I suppose I'm no worse than the general run, and maybe a bit better if the truth were told. And I'll say this for it, religion is a great consolation for old age. But if religion doesn't go with *character* – character first and before all – then it crumbles away into formalism and superstition!'

They all considered it safe to agree with that. He surveyed his cards contentedly.

'I think it's your lead, Maguire.'

He found himself strolling homewards with Maguire: a gentle night after all the rain, and a delicate spring touch in the air.

'We won't know where we are now,' said Maguire, 'until Easter is on us.' And he gave an uncomfortable little laugh.

'What's the joke?'

'Wisha, I was just thinking there tonight when you were gassing about religion that . . . begod, do you know, 'tis a year since I was at confession. With Easter coming on now I suppose we'll have to get the ould skillet cleaned again. Easter Duty, you know. Where do you go? I always pop up to Rathfarnham to the S.J.'s. Men of the world. Nobody like 'em.'

'I usually go there, too,' lied Jacky. 'You can talk to those fellows.'

And he began to wonder, would he or would he not make a dash for it this year?

On the Thursday of Holy Week, just after midnight, Jacky and the boys were in the middle of a hot game of nap when a faint knocking percolated through the ceiling.

'No bloody fear,' he grunted. 'Once bitten twice shy. More cod-acting.'

They gathered up their hands and began to play. Through the slap of the cards the rapping came again, this time more faintly.

'That one now,' said Jacky. 'You play, Jim. That one . . . God, have you nothing but the Ace? That one is a typical example of the modern Irish crawthumper. Behind all this piety, believe you me . . . Who said I reneged? What are you talking about, didn't I put the seven on Redmond's deuce? Behind all this so-called piety there's nothing but a child's fear of the dark.'

Maguire laughed at him.

'Now, Jacky, there's no earthly use your beefing about religion. The stamp of the Church is on you. 'Tis on all of us. 'Tis on you since the day you were born and sooner or later they'll get you and you may as well give in and be done with it. Mark my words, I'll live to see the day you'll have holy pictures all around your bloody bedroom! The stamp is on you! The stamp is on you.'

Jacky flared. Here was a fellow who barely confessed once a year and he was talking as if he were a blooming saint.

'Stop wagging your finger at me, please. And, anyway, with all your guff, when were you at confession last, I'd like to know?'

Maguire laughed smugly.

'I don't in the least mind telling you. I was there three days ago. A grand old priest.' He clicked his fingers and looked around him at the group. 'He let me off like that. I think if I'd told him I'd committed murder all he'd say would be, "Any other little thing troubling you, my child?" '

They laughed approvingly.

'Ah, there's nothing like an S.J.,' Maguire went on. 'Listen, did ye ever hear the one about the fellow that went to confession the time of the Troubles here and said, "Father, I shot a Black and Tan." Do you know what the priest said? "My child," says he, "you may omit your venial sins." Honest to God, I believe 'tis a fact.'

They all laughed again although they had heard the yarn many times before: it is the sort of story every hardy sinner likes to hear. Through their laughter the knocking came again.

'I'm afraid, Jacky,' said another of them, a commercial named Sullivan, 'you'll have to have a look at the ould geezer.'

With a curse Jacky flung down his cards. He climbed to the attic. He struck a match and gave one look at her and at once he knew that she was bad. Her forehead was beaded. Her chest rose and fell rapidly.

'Mr Cardew. I'm finished. Get me the priest. For God's sake.'

'Certainly. Certainly. Right away. And I'll get the doctor.'

He belted down the stairs and burst in on them.

'God, lads, 'tis no joke this time. She's for it. I can tell it. I can see it. Maguire, run out for the priest like a good man. Sullivan, there's a telephone down by the kiosk, call the doctor, get Cantillon, Hanley, Casey, any of 'em. Hurry, hurry!'

He brought her up a stiff whisky but she was too weak to sip it. When the priest came, a young man with the sad eyes and bent head of a Saint Francis, the gamblers huddled outside under the rafters, looking through the skylight at the wide Easter moon. They were all middle-aged men, younger than Jacky, but replicas in every other way.

'Oh,' whispered Maguire. ' 'Tis true. Just as the old priest told me. Like a thief in the night. We never know the day or the hour.'

' 'Twas a terrible winter,' whispered Sullivan. 'I never saw so many people popping off. I see where old Sir John Philpott went off yesterday.'

'Ah, God, no?' begged Jacky, shocked at the news. 'You don't mean Philpott of Potter and Philpotts? I was talking to him in the club only three days ago.' (He said it as if he were affronted at Sir John's giving him no previous warning of the event.) 'But he was a comparatively young man! Was he sixty-two itself?'

'Heart,' whispered Wilson. 'He went off very fast in the end.'

'Here today,' sighed Maguire. 'Gone tomorrow.'

'The best way to go,' murmured Sullivan. 'No trouble to anybody.'

'That is,' whispered Maguire, 'provided our ticket's been punched for – ' And he pointed respectfully upwards. 'I heard a preacher say one time that he knew a man who came into his confession-box after being twenty years away. He said he had just lifted his finger and said the *Absolvo te*' – here Maguire lifted his two first fingers – 'when the man dropped dead at his feet in the box! There was a close shave for you!'

Jacky moved uneasily; he knew the story was just a preacher's yarn, but he had not the spirit to say it.

'The best death of all,' murmured Sullivan, 'is the soldier's. I believe, just before a battle, a priest can give a whole regiment a General Absolution, and if a man is killed he goes straight up to heaven. That's what makes Irishmen such good soldiers. Straight up to heaven!'

'Grand in attack,' said Jacky judiciously, 'not so good in defence.'

'And that's why!' said Sullivan. 'And, what's more, I wouldn't be surprised if that isn't why the English are better on the defensive than in the charge. Sure any man would fight like a divil if he knew what was coming after? Death has no terrors for a man in a situation like that.'

They fell silent. A cloudlet crossed the moon. Then all their faces were illumined again. The city's roofs shone. The priest's voice murmured softly.

'He's taking a long time,' said Jacky. 'And it isn't,' he whispered, trying to make a little joke, 'as if she had so much to tell. *She's* all right anyway.'

'And,' said Maguire piously, 'on Good Friday. A lovely death!'

'So it is,' said Wilson. 'Good Friday!'

They all sighed deeply. The priest came out, stooping under the beams, removing his stole and kissing it. Maguire asked him, 'Will she last, father?' The priest sighed, 'A saint, a saint,' as if he were sighing for all the sinners of the world. Jacky showed him out, and as he walked away the doctor came down. Jacky shut him into his car and shoved in his head anxiously.

'Is she bad, doctor?'

'Anno Domini. We can't live for ever. The works give out – just like an old motor-car. All we can do at that age is wait for the call,' and he beckoned with one finger. Jacky drew back hastily. The headlamps whirled and the car purred away across the empty Square as if its red tail-lights were running away with somebody.

Jacky was left alone in his room. He sank into an armchair by the open window. The spring night was gentle. The blood of life was pulsing through everything. Even the three old London planes in the middle of the Square had their little throb and the high Easter moon was delicately transparent as if with youth. He leaped up and began to circle the room. He had never seen anything so lovely, it seemed to him, as those little babies gazing at him out of their big eyes, with their soft little lips parted. He was looking again over the shining roofs and the blank chimney-pots, and as if a shutter flicked he felt for one moment the intense vacancy and loneliness of his life and saw it, as the years went by, becoming more lonely and more empty. And when he was gone, the moon out there, the old trees below, would still be there, still throbbing. A little wind scurried furtively in the dust of the Square. He looked at the decanter. Low tide. Like his own life. He'd be able to rest tomorrow anyway. He paused before the black enlargement. Good Friday morning. One more day to Easter. A veined, red face with a blue nose, thin ruffled hair, bags under the eyes was looking at him out of the mirror. He licked his lips and got a horrible taste in his mouth and felt an uneven thumping in his heart.

He sat down heavily by the open window, before the moon's indifferent beauty, and began to go back over the years. There were a couple of things it wasn't going to be too easy to . . .

'Not, mind you,' he assured the empty Square, with bravado, 'that I'm going to hand myself over to some bogtrot from the County Meath. Pick the right man and . . . "Well, Father," he rehearsed, flicking a grain of ash from his pants and pulling his ear, "I'm afraid, er, I've got more than a few little peccadilloes to tell you. We're only human, Father. Children of Adam, and all to that and so on." That was the ticket. Frank and open. Two men of the world. "Of course, there's been a spot of liquor, Father. And, er . . . Well, er . . . I mean, er . . ." ' Jacky coughed and ran his finger around inside his collar. This thing was going to take a bit of doing. He closed his eyes and began to think of all those nights that had seemed such grand nights – at the time.

When he opened his eyes again the sun was warm on his face, the Square was gay with sunlight, somebody was shaking his shoulder. It was his landlady smilingly handing him his tea and buttered toast.

'Well, Mr Cardew,' she cackled, 'since I didn't go last night I'll live to be a hundred!'

As Jacky looked blearily down at the three plane trees the misery of the night flooded on him. He gave her one maddened look, banged down the cup, and started up to tell her just what he thought of her. An unholy gripe pierced a red-hot needle through the small of his back.

'Oh, Mr Cardew, what on earth made you sit by the open window!'

But now the pain ran across the back of his neck, and with hand to his back and a hand to his neck all he could do was to crawl away moaning and cursing to his bed.

As he lay there through the holidays he found himself being petted and cosseted as he had never been in his life before. She rubbed his back and she rubbed his chest and she brought him hot punch and fed him with Easter delicacies until, gradually, if sourly, he decided that he would be a fool to change his landlady. At the same time, and especially on Easter Sunday morning as he lay with the sun slanting warmly across his chest, his hands behind his head, smoking his after-breakfast cigarette, his Sunday paper on his lap, listening to the silvery bells of all the churches of the city, he was aware of a certain slight feeling of discomfort – nothing much, just a coiled shadow at the back of his mind, the merest hint of apprehension. Cautiously he turned his stiff shoulders to look at the mantelpiece where she had placed a little spray of Palm in a glass vase, and beside it a little glass bowl of Holy Water. He grunted as he considered them. He'd get rid of those things all right when he got on his feet again! Just then he remembered Maguire, and all that about the stamp being on you. He smiled uncomfortably. Oh, well! He flicked his ash on the carpet. Some day, no doubt. Some day.

How lovely the sun was. It was nice to hear all the footsteps across the Square below, going to Mass. Their shadowy reflections passed softly on the ceiling, and the silvery bells went on calling everybody to be happy because Christ was risen.

He took up the paper and began to study Form.

The Silence of the Valley

Only in the one or two farmhouses about the lake, or in the fishing hotel at its edge – preoccupations of work and pleasure – does one ever forget the silence of the valley. Even in the winter, when the great cataracts slide down the mountain-face, the echoes of falling water are fitful: the winds fetch and carry them. In the summer a fisherman will hear the tinkle of the ghost of one of those falls only if he steals among the mirrored reeds under the pent of the cliffs, and withholds the plash of his oars. These tiny muted sounds will awe and delight him by the vacancy out of which they creep, intermittently.

One May evening a relaxed group of early visitors were helping themselves to drink in the hotel-bar, throwing the coins into a pint glass. There were five of them all looking out the door at the lake, the rhododendrons on the hermit's island, the mountain towering beyond it, and the wall of blue air above the mountain line. Behind the counter was an American soldier, blond, blankly handsome, his wide-vision glasses convexing the sky against his face. Leaning against the counter was a priest; jovial, fat, ruddy, his Roman-collar off and his trousers stuck into his socks – he had been up the mountain all day rough-shooting. Leaning against the pink-washed wall was a dark young man with pince-nez; he had the smouldering ill-disposed eyes of the incorrigible Celt – 'always eager to take offence' as the fourth of the party had privately cracked. She was a sturdy, red-mopped young woman in blue slacks now sitting on the counter drinking whisky. She sometimes seemed not at all beautiful, and sometimes her heavy features seemed to have a strong beauty of their own, for she was on a hair-trigger between a glowering Beethoven and The Laughing Cavalier. Sometimes her mouth was broody; suddenly it would expand into a half-batty gaiety. Her deep-set eyes ran from gloom to irony, to challenge, to wild humour. She had severe eyebrows that floated as gently as a veil in the wind. She was a Scot. The fifth of the group was a sack of a man, a big fat school-inspector, also with his collar off. He had cute ingratiating eyes. He leaned against the opposite pink-washed wall.

In the middle of the tiled floor was a very small man, a tramp with a fluent black beard, long black curls, a billycock hat, a mackintosh to his toes, and a gnarled stick with a hairy paw. The tramp (a whisper from the priest had informed them all that he had once been a waiter on the Holyhead–Euston Express) held a pint of porter in his free hand and was singing to them in a fine tenor voice a ballad called *Lonely I wandered from the Scenes of my Childhood.* They heard him in quizzical boredom. He had been singing ballads to them on and off for nearly two hours now.

Outside, the sun was seeping away behind the far end of the valley. From the bar they could see it touching the tips of the tallest rowans on the island. Across the lake the tip of a green cornfield on a hillock blazed and went out. Then vast beams, cutting through lesser defiles, flowed like a yellow searchlight for miles to the open land to the east, picking out great escarpments and odd projections of the mountains. The wavelets were by now blowing in sullenly on the shore, edging it with froth.

The tramp ended. They applauded perfunctorily. He knew they were sated and when the red-headed young woman cried, 'Tommy, give us *The Inchigeela Puck Goat,*' he demurred politely.

'I think, miss, ye have enough of me now, and sure I'm as dry as a lime-kiln.'

'More porter for the singer,' cried the priest with lazy authority, and the lieutenant willingly poured out another bottle of stout and rattled a coin into the pint-glass.

'I suppose,' asked the Celtic-looking young man, in a slightly critical voice, 'you have no songs in Irish?'

'Now,' soothed the school-inspector, 'haven't you the Irish the whole bloody year round? Leave us to take a holiday from it while we can.'

'I had been under the impression,' yielded the Celt, with a – for him – amicable smile, 'that we came out here to learn the language of our forefathers? Far be it from me to insist pedantically on the point.' And he smiled again like a stage curate.

'Tell me, brother,' asked the American, as he filled up the tramp's glass, 'do you remain on the road the whole year round?'

'Summer and winter, for fifteen years come next September, and no roof over my head but the field of stars. And would you believe it, sur, never wance did I get as much as a shiver of a cold in my head.'

'That is certainly a remarkable record.'

The proprietor of the hotel entered the bar from the kitchen behind it and planked a saucepan full of fowls' guts on the counter. He was accompanied by a small boy, long-lashed, almost pretty, obviously a city-child, who kept dodging excitedly about him.

'Have any of ye a match?' he asked. He was a powerful man, with the shoulders of a horse. He wore neither coat nor vest. His cap was on his poll. His face was round and weather-beaten as a mangold. He had a mouthful of false-teeth.

'What do you want a match for, Dinny?' asked the priest with a wink at the others.

The American produced a match. Dinny deftly pinched a fold of his trousers between the eye of his suspenders and inserted the match through the fold: there it effectively did the work of a button. The priest twisted him around familiarly. A nail had performed the same service behind. They all laughed, but Dinny was too preoccupied to heed.

'What's this mess for?' The American pointed to the stinking saucepan.

Dinny paid no attention. He stretched up over the top of the shelves and after much fumbling brought down a fishing-rod.

'Give it to me, Dinny, give it to me,' shouted the child.

Dinny ignored him also as he fiddled with the line. He glanced out the door, turned to the kitchen and roared:

'Kitty cows coming home tell Patsy James have ye the buckets scalded blosht it boys the day is gone.'

Or he said something like that, for he mouthed all his words in his gullet and his teeth clacked and he spoke too fast. They all turned back to watch the frieze of small black cows passing slowly before the scalloped water, the fawny froth, the wall of mountain.

'The cobbler won't lasht the night,' said Dinny, pulling with his teeth at the tangled pike-line. The priest whirled.

'Is he bad? Did you see him? Should I go down?'

'Still unconscious, Father. No use for you. Timeen was up. He was buying the drink.'

'Drink?' asked the Scots girl grinning hopefully.

'For the wake,' explained the Celt.

'Well, do you know what it is, by Harry?' cried the inspector earnestly to them all. 'He's making a great fight for it.'

'He may as well go now and be done with it,' said Dinny. 'Gimme the guts. We're fishing for eels.'

'Gimme the rod, Dinny, gimme the rod,' screamed the child and taking it he dashed off like a lancer, shouting with joy. Dinny lumbered after him with the saucepan.

'I reckon these people are pretty heartless?' suggested the soldier.

'We Irish,' explained the Celt, 'are indifferent to the affairs of the body. We are a spiritual people.'

'What enchanting nonsense,' laughed the young woman and threw back her whisky delightedly.

'It is none the less true,' reprimanded the Celt.

'You make me feel so old,' sighed the young woman, 'so old and so wise.'

'Are you a Catholic?' asked the Celt suspiciously.

'Yes, but what on earth has that to do with anything?'

'Well, I reckon I don't know much about the spirit, but you may be right about the body. Did you see those hens' guts?'

The priest intervened diplomatically.

'Did you ever see them fishing for eels? It's great fun. Come and watch them.'

All but the tramp walked idly to the edge of the lake. The waves were beating in among the stones, pushing a little wrack of straw and broken reeds before them. Dinny had stuck a long string of windpipe to the hook and the boy had slung it out about twelve feet from the shore. To lure the eels a few random bits of guts had been thrown into the brown shallows at their feet and there swayed like seaweed. The group peered. Nothing happened. Suddenly Dinny shouted as fast as a machine-gun's burst.

'Look at 'em look at 'em look at the divils blosht it look at 'em look at 'em.'

A string of intestines was streaking away out into the lake. Dark serpentine shapes whirled snakily in and out of the brown water. The eels had smelled the rank bait and were converging on it.

'By golly,' cried the American, 'they must smell that bait a mile away.'

The reel whirred, the line flew, the rod bent, they all began to shout, the child trembled with excitement.

'You have him pull him you divil,' roared Dinny and seized the rod and whirled a long white belly in over their dodging heads. The girl gave a cry of disgust as the five men leaped on the eel, now lashing in the dust, and hammered savagely at it with heels, stones, a stick, screaming, laughing, shoving. The eel seemed immortal. Though filthy and bleeding it squirmed galvanically. The child circled dancing around the struggling group, half-delighted, half-terrified.

'Well, Jo,' said the young woman as she looked disdainfully at the last wriggles of the corpse, 'it seems that boys will be boys. Dinny, do you really eat eels?'

'Christ gurl I wouldn't touch one of 'em for a hundred pounds.'

'Then why catch them?'

'For fun.'

Her face gathered, ceased to be The Laughing Cavalier and became Beethoven in Labour. She saw that the men had now become absorbed entirely in the sport. The American had thrown out the line again and they were all peering excitedly into the water. The sun left the last tips of the mountains. The lake grew sullen. Its waves still hissed. They did not weary of the game until eight eels lay writhing in the dust.

Just as they were becoming bored they observed a silent countryman at the edge of the ring looking down at the eels. The priest spoke to him saying, 'Well, Timeen, how is he?' He was a lithe, lean, hollow-cheeked young man with his cap pulled low over his eyes. He lifted his face and they saw that he was weeping.

'He's gone, Father,' he said in a low voice.

'The Lord have mercy on him,' said the priest and his own eyes filled and the others murmured the prayer after him. 'The poor old cobbler. I must go and see herself.'

He hastened away and presently, tidy and brushed and in his Roman collar, they saw him cycle down the road. The child called after him, 'Will you roast the eels for me tonight?' and over his shoulder the priest called, 'I will, Jo, after supper,' and disappeared wobblingly over the first hill.

'By Harry,' cried the inspector, 'there'll be a powerful gathering of the clans tonight.'

'How's that?' from the American.

'For the wake,' explained the Celt.

'I'd certainly like to see a wake.'

'You'll be very welcome, sur,' said Timeen.

'Did he go easy?' asked the inspector.

Dinny threw the guts into the lake and took Timeen by the arm.

'He went out like a candle,' said Timeen, and let Dinny lead him away gently to some private part of the house.

The group dissolved.

'I do wish,' said the American, 'they wouldn't throw guts into the lake. After all we swim in it.'

'It's very unsanitary all right,' the inspector agreed.

'What are we all,' said the Celt philosophically, 'but a perambulating parcel of guts.'

The girl sighed heavily and said, 'The lamp is lighting.'

In the hotel window the round globe of the lamp was like a full moon. A blue haze had gathered over everything. They strolled back to the bar for a last drink, the child staggering after them with the heavy saucepan of dead eels.

The cobbler's cottage was on the brow of a hill about a mile down the road. It was naked, slated, whitewashed, two-storeyed. It had a sunken haggard in front and a few fuchsias and hollies behind it, blown almost horizontally by the storms. On three sides lay an expanse of moor, now softened by the haze of evening. From his front door the dead cobbler used to look across this barren moor at the jagged mountain-range, but he could also see where the valley opened out and faded into the tentative and varying horizons of forty miles away.

When the priest entered the kitchen the wife was alone – the news had not yet travelled. She was a tiny, aged woman who looked as if her whole body from scalp to soles was wrinkled and yellow; her face, her bare arms, her bare chest were as golden as a dried apple; even her eyeballs seemed wrinkled. But her white hair flowed upward all about her like a Fury in magnificent wild snakes from under an old fisherman's tweed hat, and her mobile mouth and her loud – too loud – voice gave out a tremendous vitality. When she was a young girl she must have been as lively as a minnow in a mountain-stream. The priest had known her for most of his adult life as a woman whose ribald tongue had made the neighbours delight in her and fear her: he was stirred to tears to find her looking up at him now like a child who has been beaten. She was seated on the long settle underneath the red lamp before the picture of the Sacred Heart.

He sat beside her and took her hand.

'Can I go up and pray for him?'

'Katey Dan is readying him,' she whispered, and the priest became aware of footsteps moving in the room over their heads.

She lumbered up the ladder-like stairs to see if everything was ready. While he waited he looked at the cobbler's tools by the window – the last, and the worn hammer, and the old butter-box by the fire where the cobbler used to sit. Everything in the kitchen had the same worn look of time and use, and everything was dusted with the grey dust of turf – the kettle over the peat fire, the varied pot-hooks on the crane, the bright metal of the tongs, the dresser with its pieces of delph, a scalded churn-lid leaning in the window to dry. There was nothing there that was not necessary; unless, perhaps, the red lamp and the oleograph of the Sacred Heart, and even that had the stiff and frozen prescription of an ikon. The only unusual thing was two plates on the table under the window, one of snuff and one of shredded tobacco for the visitors who would soon be coming down from every corner of the glens. The only light in the cottage came from the turf-fire.

As he sat and looked at the blue smoke curling up against the brown soot of the chimney's maw he became aware, for the first time in his life, of the silence of this moor. He heard the hollow feet above the rafters. A cricket chirruped somewhere behind the fire. Always up to now he had thought of this cottage as a place full of the cobbler's satirical talk, his wife's echoes and contradictions. Somebody had once told the old man that he was not only the valley's storyteller but its 'gossip-columnist'; the old chap had cocked a suspicious eye, too vain to admit that he did not know the phrase, and skated off into one of his yarns about the days when he had cobbled for the Irish workers laying rails out of Glasgow along the Clyde. The priest smiled at the incident. Then he frowned as he looked at the fire, a quiet disintegration: a turf-fire never emits even the slightest whisper. He realized that this cottage would be completely silent from now on. Although it was May he had a sudden poignant sensation of autumn, why he could not tell.

The old woman called him up. After the dusk of the kitchen this upper room was brilliant. She had lighted five wax-candles about her husband's head. Snowy sheets made a canopy about his face. The neighbour-woman had just finished the last delicately fluted fold on the lacey counterpane that lay ridged over the stomach and toes. Silently the three knelt and prayed.

When they rose the old woman said, looking down at the calm countenance on the pillow:

'He's a fine corse and a heavy corse.'

'He was a great man. I loved him.'

'He had a fierce veneration for you, Father.'

They lumbered down the steep stairs. She was as quiet as if the business in hand was something that had happened outside the course of nature. She thanked God for the fine weather. She asked him were there many staying at the hotel. When he told her, she muttered, 'We must be satisfied,' as if she were talking about the hotel and not about her man. When two more neighbour-women came and stood looking at them from the doorway, he took leave of her saying that he would return later in the night.

The hollies at the door were rubbing squeakingly against each other. The moon was rising serenely over the Pass to the East. He felt the cold wind as he rode back to the lake.

They were at supper when he entered the hotel. He joined them about the round table in the bay window through which he could barely discern the stars above the mountains. The rest of the long room, beyond the globe of the lamp, was in shadow. He mentioned that he had seen the cobbler, that they must go down later to the wake, and then set about his food. He paid small heed to the conversation although he gathered that they were loud in discussion over the delay in serving supper.

'Just the same,' the American was saying, 'I cannot see why it would not be perfectly simple to hang up a card on the wall announcing meal-times. Breakfast, eight to ten. Luncheon, one to three. And so on. It's quite simple.'

'Just as they do,' suggested the young Scotswoman, 'in the Regent Palace Hotel?'

'Exactly,' he agreed, and then looked in puzzlement at her because she was giggling happily to herself.

'You must admit,' the inspector assured her, following his usual role of trying to agree with everybody, 'that they have a wonderful opportunity here if they only availed of it. Why don't they cater more for the wealthy clientèle? I mean, now, suppose they advertised Special Duck Dinners, think of the crowds that would come motoring out of Cork for them on summer afternoons. It's only about forty miles, a nice run.'

'Gee, how often have I driven forty miles and more for a barbecue supper down the coast? I can see those lobster suppers at Cohasset, now, two dollars fifty, and the rows and rows of automobiles lined outside on the concrete.'

'What does our Celt say to this perfectly hideous picture?' asked the redmop.

'I can see no objection – provided the language spoken is Gaelic.'

She broke into peals of laughter.

'We,' the Celt went on, dark with anger, 'envisage an Ireland both modern and progressive. Christianity,' he went on, proud both of the rightness and intellectual tolerance of his argument, 'is not opposed to modernity, or to comfort, or to culture. I should not mind,' his voice was savage, for she was chuckling like a zany, 'if seaplanes landed on that lake outside. Why should I? All this admiration for backwardness and inefficiency is merely so much romantic nonsense. Ireland has had enough of it.'

She groaned comically.

'Fascist type. Definitely schizoid. Slight sadistic tendency. Would probably be Socialist in Britain, if not – ' she wagged her flaming head warningly and made eyes of mock horror – 'dare I say it, C.P.?'

'You,' cried the Celt scornfully, 'merely like the primitive so long as it is not in your own country. Let's go to Nigeria and love the simple ways of the niggers. Let's holiday in Ireland among the beautiful peasants. Imperialist!'

'I beg your pardon,' she cried, quite offended. 'I am just as happy in the Shetlands or the Hebrides as I am here. Britain's pockets of primitiveness are her salvation. If she ever loses them she's doomed. I very much fear she's doomed already with all these moth-eaten church-wardens in Parliament trying to tidy us up!'

And she drew out her cigar-case and pulling her coffee towards her lit a long Panatella. As she puffed she was sullen and unbeautiful again as if his hate had quenched her loveliness as well as her humour.

'Well, now, now, after all,' soothed the inspector, 'it's all very well for you. Your country is a great country with all the most modern conveniences . . .'

'Heaven help it!'

'. . . whereas we have a long leeway to make up. Now, to take even a small thing. Those guts in the lake.'

'O God!' she groaned. 'What a fuss you make over one poor little chicken's guts! Damn it, it's all phosphates. The Chinese use human phosphates for manure.'

The priest shook in his fat with laughter – it was a joke exactly to his liking – but the other three took the discussion from her and she smoked in dudgeon until the priest too was pulling his pipe and telling her about the dead cobbler, and how every night in winter his cottage used to be full of men coming to hear his views on Hitler and Mussolini and the Prophecies of Saint Columcille which foretold that the last battle of the last world-war would be fought at Ballylickey Bridge. The others began to listen as he retold some of the cobbler's more earthy stories that were as innocent and sweaty as any Norse or Celtic yarn of the Golden Age: such as the dilemma of the sow eating the eel which slipped out of her as fast as it went into her until, at last, the sow shouted in a fury: 'I'll settle you, you slippery divil!' and at one and the same moment snapped up the eel and clapped her backside to the wall.

Laughing they rose and wandered, as usual, into the kitchen for the night. They expected to find it empty, thinking that everybody would be going down to the wakehouse; instead it was more crowded than ever, it had become a sort of clearing-house where the people called on their way to and from the cobbler's cottage, either too shy to go there directly or unwilling to go home after visiting their old friend.

The small boy was eagerly awaiting them with the saucepan of eels. The priest set to. He took off his clerical jacket and put on a green wind-jammer, whose brevity put an equator around his enormous paunch, so that when he stooped over the fire he looked like one of those global toys that one cannot knock over. When the resinous fir-stumps on the great flat hearth flamed up – the only light in the kitchen – he swelled up, shadows and all, like a necromancer. He put an eel down on the stone floor and with his penknife slit it to its tail and gutted it. The offal glistened oilily. While he was cutting the eel its tail had slowly wound about his wrist, and when he tied its nose to a pothook and dangled it over a leaning flame and its oil began to drip and sizzle in the blaze the eel again slowly curved as if in agony. The visitors amused themselves by making sarcastic comments on the priest as cook, but four countrymen who lined the settle in the darkness with their caps on and their hands in their pockets watched him, perfectly immobile, not speaking, apparently not interested.

'Aha, you divil, you,' taunted the priest, 'now will you squirm? If the cobbler's sow was here now she would make short work of you!'

That was the only time any of the countrymen spoke: from the darkness of a far corner an old man said:

'I wonder is the cobbler telling that story to Hitler now?'

'I sincerely hope,' said the Scots girl, 'that they're not in the same place.'

The old man said:

'God is good. I heard a priesht say wan time that even Judas might be saved.'

'Jo,' said the inspector, steering as usual into pleasant channels, 'do you think that eel is alive?'

The small boy was too absorbed to heed, lost in his own delight.

Now and again a handsome, dark serving-girl came to the fire to tend the pots or renew the sods, for meals were eaten in this house at all hours: she seemed fascinated by the eel and every time she came she made disgusted noises. The men loved these expressions of disgust and tried various ways to provoke more of them, offering her a bite or holding up the entangled saucepan to her nose. Once the American chased her laughingly with an eel in his fist and from the dark back-kitchen they could hear them scuffling playfully. By this time many more neighbours had come into the kitchen and into the bar and into the second back-kitchen, and two more serving-girls became busy as drinks and teas and dishes of ham passed to and fro, so that the shadows of the men about the fire, the scurrying girls, the wandering neighbours fluttered continually on the white walls and the babble of voices clucked through the house like ducks clacking at a nightpond.

Above this murmuring and clattering they heard the tramp singing in the bar a merry dancing tune, partly in Gaelic and partly in English:

So, little soldier of my heart
Will you marry, marry me now,
With a heigh and a ho
And a sound of drum now?

'So the little bastard does know Irish,' cried the Celt much affronted as the song broke into Gaelic:

A chailin óg mo chroidhe
Conus a phósfainn-se thú
Agus gan pioc de'n bhróg do chur orm . . .

'Perhaps he suits his language to his company?' the red-haired girl suggested.

I went to the cobbler
The besht in the town
For a fine pair of shoes
For my soldiereen brown,
So-o-o . . .
Little soldier of my heart,
Will you marry, marry me now . . .

The girl peered around the jamb of the door into the bar and then scurried back dismayed. The tramp had spotted her and at once came dancing fantastically into the kitchen on her heels. His long mackintosh tails leaped, and their shadows with them. His black beard flowed left and right as his head swayed to the tune and his black locks swung with it. His hands expressively flicked left and right as he capered about the girl. His billy-cock hat hopped.

But O girl of my heart
How could I marry you
And I without a shirt
Either white or blue?

'Would you ate an eel?' asked the green-jacketed porpoise by the fire holding up the shrivelled carcase to the dancer, who at once gaily doffed his hat (into which the priest dropped the eel) and went on his way back to the bar dancing and singing, followed in delight by the boy:

So chuadhas dti an tailliúr
The besht to be found
And I bought a silken shirt
For my saighdiúrin donn

'Come, lads,' cried the priest, suddenly serious, 'it's time for us to visit the poor cobbler.'

It was full moonlight. The lake crawled livingly under it. The mountains were like the mouth of hell. It seemed to the priest as if the dark would come down and claw at them. He said so to the Celt who had become wildly excited at the sight of the dark and the light and the creeping lake and strode down to the beach and threw up his arms crying,

'O Love! O Terror! O Death!' – and he broke into Balfe's song to the moon from *The Lily of Killarney*:

The Moon hath raised her lamp above.

'If you don't stop that emotional ass,' growled the girl as she wheeled out her bicycle, 'he'll start singing The Barcarolle,' and showed her own emotion by cycling madly away by herself.

'Grim! Grim!' said the American and the inspector agreed with, 'In the winter! Ah! In the winter!'

They were cycling now in single file switchbacking up and down over the little hills until the glow of the cobbler's window eyed them from the dark. Near the cottage dark shapes of men and boys huddled under the hedges and near the walls and as they alighted drew aside to let them pass, fingers to caps for the priest. The causeway to the kitchen door was crowded, unexpectedly noisy with talk, smelling of turf-smoke and pipe-smoke and bogwater and sweat and hens.

In her corner by the enormous peat-fire, the little old woman seemed almost to be holding pleasant court, her spirits roused by the friendliness and excitement of the crowds of neighbours.

The babble fell as the strangers entered. It rose again as they disappeared up the ladder-stairs to pay their respects to the cobbler. It sank again when they clambered down. Then gradually it rose and steadied as they settled into the company. They were handed whisky or stout or tea by Timeen, and the priest began to chat pleasantly and unconcernedly with the nearest men to him. To the three Irishmen all this was so familiar that they made no wonder of it, and they left the American and the girl to the cobbler's wife who at once talked to them about America and Scotland with such a fantastic mixture of ignorance and personal knowledge – gleaned from years upon years of visitors – that all their embarrassment vanished in their pleasure at her wise and foolish talk.

Only twice did her thoughts stray upstairs. A neighbour lifted a red coal in the tongs to kindle his pipe: she glanced sharply and drew a sharp breath.

'Light away, Dan Frank,' she encouraged then. 'Lasht week my ould divil used to be ever reddening his pipe, God rest him, although I used to be scolding him for burning his poor ould belly with all the shmoking.'

Once when the babble suddenly fell into a trough of silence they heard a dog across the moor baying at the moon. She said:

'Times now I do be thinking that with the cobbler gone from me I'll be afraid to be by meself in the house with all the idle shtallions going the road.'

It was her commonest word for men, shtalls or shtallions, and all the neighbours who heard her must have pictured a lone tramp or a tinker walking the mountain road, and she inside listening through the barred door to the passing feet.

Elsewise she talked of things like hens and of prices and several times seemed to forget the nature of the occasion entirely. Then, in her most ribald vein she became scabrous in her comments on her visitors, to the delight of everybody except the victims, who could only scuttle red-faced out the door without, in respect for her, as much as the satisfaction of a curse. It was after one of these sallies that the priest decided to close his visit with a laughing command to them all to kneel for the Rosary. With a lot of scuffling they huddled over chairs or sank on one knee, hiding their faces reverently in their caps.

Only the soldier did not join them. He went out and found more men, all along the causeway and under the hedges, kneeling likewise, so that the mumbling litany of prayer mingled with the tireless baying of the dog. All about them the encircling jags of mountains were bright and jet, brilliant craters, quarries of blackness, gleaming rocks, grey undergrowth.

The journey back was even more eerie than the journey out, the moon now behind them, their shadows before, and as they climbed the hills the mountains climbed before them as if to bar their way and when they rushed downward to the leaden bowl that was the lake, and into the closed gully of the coom, it was as if they were cycling not through space but through a maw of Time that would never move.

The kitchen was empty. The eels lay in the pot. Two old boots lay on their sides drying before the fading fire. The crickets whistled loudly in the crannies. They took their candles and went in their stockinged feet up the stairs to bed, whispering.

The morning was a blaze of heat. The island was a floating red flower. The rhododendrons around the edges of the island were replicated in the smooth lee-water which they barely touched. As the American, the girl, and the Celt set off for their pre-breakfast swim from the island they heard the sounds of spades striking against gravel. They saw the tall thin figure of an aged man, with grey side-chops, in a roundy black hat and a swallow-tailed coat, standing against the sky. He held a piece of twig in his hand like a water-diviner. He was measuring, taking bearings, solicitously encouraging the grave-diggers below him to be accurate in their lines. He greeted the strangers politely, but they could see that they were distracting him and that he was weighed down by the importance of his task.

'For do you see, gentlemen, the cobbler was most particular about where he would be buried. I had a long talk with him about it lasht week and the one thing he laid down was for him to be buried in the one line with all the Cronins from Baurlinn.'

'But,' demurred the American, 'would a foot or two make all that difference?'

'It is an old graveyard,' the old man admonished him solemnly, 'and there are many laid here before him, and there will be many another after him.'

They left him to his task. The water was icy and they could only bear to dive in and clamber out. To get warm again they had to race up and down the brief sward before they dressed, hooting with pleasure in the comfort of the sun, the blue sky, the smells of the island and the prospect of trout and bacon-and-eggs for breakfast. As they stepped back on the mainland they met a mountainy lad coming from the depths of the coom, carrying a weighted sack. His grey tweed trousers were as dark with wetness to his hips as if he had jumped into a boghole. He walked with them to the hotel and explained that he was wet from the dew on the mountain-heather and the young plantations. He had just crossed from the next valley, about two hours away. He halted and opened the mouth of the sack to show them, with a grin of satisfaction, the curved silver and blue of a salmon. He said he would be content to sell it to the hotel for five shillings and they agreed heartily with him when he said, 'Sure what is it only a night's sport and a walk over the mountains?' Over breakfast they upbraided one another for their lie-abed laziness on such a glorious day.

The day continued summer-hot burning itself away past high noon. The inspector got his car and drove away to visit some distant school. The American took his rod and rowed out of sight to the head of the lake. The girl walked away alone. The Celt went fishing from the far shore. The priest sat on the garden-seat before the hotel and read his Office and put a handkerchief over his head and dozed, and when the postman came took the morning paper from him. Once a farm-cart made a crockety-crock down the eastern road and he wondered if it was bringing the coffin. In the farmyard behind the hotel the milk-separator whirred. For most of the time everything was still – the sparkling lake, the idle shore, the tiny fields, the sleeping hermit's island, the towering mountains, the flawless sky. 'It is as still,' thought the priest, 'as the world before life began.' All the hours that the priest sat there, or walked slowly up and down reading his breviary, or opened a lazy eye under his handkerchief, he saw only one sign of life – a woman came on top of a hillock across the lake, looked about her for man or animal and went back to her chores.

Towards two o'clock the red-headed girl returned from her walk and sat near him. She was too tired or lazy to talk: but she did ask after a time:

'Do you think they really believe that the cobbler is talking to Hitler?'

'They know no more about Hitler than they do about Cromwell. But I'm sure they believe that the cobbler is having nice little chats with his old pals Jerry Coakley and Shamus Cronin – that's Dinny's father that he will be lying next to – up there in the graveyard – in a half an hour's time.'

She smiled happily.

'I wish I had their faith.'

'If you were born here you would.'

'I'd also have ten children,' she laughed. 'Will you join me in a drink?'

He could not because he must await the funeral and the local curate at the chapel on the island, and, rising, he went off there. She went alone into the bar and helped herself to a whisky, and leaned over the morning paper. She was joined presently by the Celt, radiant at having caught nothing. To pass the time she started a discussion about large families and the ethics of birth-control. He said that he believed that everybody 'practised it in secret', a remark which put her into such good humour that, in gratitude, she made him happy by assuring him that in ten years' time the birth-rate in England would be the lowest in the world and for the innocent joy he showed at this she glowed with so much good-feeling towards him that she told him also how hateful birth-control is to the poor in the East End of London.

'I always knew it,' he cried joyfully. 'Religion has nothing to do with these things. All that counts is the Natural Law. For, as I hope you do realize, there is a Law of Nature!'

And he filled out two more whiskies and settled down to the unburthening of his soul.

'You see, I'm not really an orthodox Catholic at all. To me Religion is valid only because and in so far as it is based on Nature. That is why Ireland has a great message for the world. Everywhere else but here civilization has taken the wrong turning. Here Nature still rules Man, and Man still obeys Nature. . . .'

'As in the East End?' she said.

He hurried on, frowning crossly.

'I worship these mountains and these lakes and these simple Gaelic people because they alone still possess . . .'

'But you were angry last night when I defended primitive life. You wanted sea-planes on the lake and tourists from Manchester in Austin Sevens parked in front of . . .'

'I have already explained to you,' he reproved her, 'that to be natural doesn't mean that we must be primitive! That's the romantic illusion. What I mean to say is – that is in very simple words of course . . .'

And his dark face buttoned up and he became ill-disposed again as he laboured to resolve his own contradictions.

She was about to fly from him when, through the wide-open door, she saw a dark group top the hillock to the east. As the sky stirred between their limbs she saw that they were a silhouette of six men lumbering under a coffin. Its brass plate caught the sun. They were followed by a darker huddle of women. After these came more men, and then a double file of horsemen descended out of the blue sky. On the hermit's island some watcher began to toll a bell.

'I'm going to the island,' she said. He followed her, nattering about Darwin and Lamarck.

The priest stood under the barrel-arch of the little Romanesque chapel, distent in his white surplice, impressive, a magician. The two went shyly among the trees and watched the procession dissolving by the lakeside. The priest went out to meet the local curate.

Presently the coffin lumbered forward towards the chapel on the six shoulders and was laid rockingly on four chairs. The crowd seeped in among the trees. The widow sat in the centre of the chapel steps, flanked on each side by three women. She was the only one who spoke and it was plain from the way her attendants covered their faces with their hands that she was being ribald about each new arrival; the men knew it too, for as each one came forward on the sward, to meet the judgment of her dancing, wicked eyes, he skipped hastily into the undergrowth, with a wink or a grin at his neighbours. There was now a prolonged delay. The men looked around at the weather, or across the lake at the crops. Some turned their heads where, far up the lake, the American in his boat was rhythmically casting his invisible line. Then the two priests returned and entered the chapel. Their voices mumbling the *De Profundis* was like the buzzing of bees. The men bowed their heads, as usual holding their caps before their faces. Silence fell again as the procession reformed.

In the graveyard the familiar voices of the men lowering the dead into the earth outraged the silence. Nobody else made a sound until the first shovel of earth struck the brass-plate on the lid and then the widow, defeated at last, cried out without restraint. As the earth began to fall more softly her wailing became more quiet. The last act of the burial was when the tall man, the cobbler's friend, smoothened the last dust of earth with his palms as if he were smoothening a blanket over a child. The priest said three Aves. They all responded hollowly.

They dispersed slowly, as if loath to admit that something final had happened to them all. As each one went down the path he could see the fisherman far away, steadily flogging the water. But they did not go home. They hung around the hotel all the afternoon, the men in the crowded bar, drinking; the women clucking in the back-kitchens. Outside the hotel the heads of the patient horses, growing fewer as the hours went by, drooped lower and lower with the going down of the sun, until only one cart was left and that, at last, ambled slowly away.

It was twilight before the visitors, tired and not in a good temper – they had only been given tea and boiled eggs for lunch – could take possession of the littered bar. They helped themselves to drinks and threw the coins into the pint-glass. Drinking they looked out at the amber light touching the mountain line.

'It's queer,' murmured the priest. 'Why is it, all today and yesterday, I keep on thinking it's the autumn?'

' 'Tis a bit like it all right,' the inspector agreed pleasantly.

'Nonsense,' said the red-haired girl. 'It's a beautiful May day.'

'Thanks be to God,' agreed the inspector.

A frieze of small black cows passed, one by one, along the beach. They watched them go. Then Dinny put his head in from the kitchen.

'Supper, gentlemen.'

'I hope we'll have that salmon that came over the mountains,' smiled the Celt.

Nobody stirred.

'In America, you know, we call it the Fall.'

'The Fall?' said the priest.

'The fall of the leaves,' explained the soldier, thinking he did not understand.

The priest looked out over the dark lake – a stranger would hardly have known there was a lake if it had not been for the dun edge of froth – and, jutting out his lower lip, nodded to himself, very slowly, three times.

'Yes, indeed,' the inspector sighed, watching his face sympathetically.

'Aye,' murmured the priest, and looked at him, and nodded again, knowing that this was a man who understood.

Then he whirled, gave the Celt a mighty slap on the back, and cried, 'Come on and we'll polish off that salmon. Quick march!'

They finished their drinks and strolled into the lamplit dining-room. As they sat around the table and shook out their napkins the soldier said, 'I reckon tomorrow will be another fine day.'

The red-haired girl leaned to the window and shaded her eyes against the pane. She could see how the moon touched the trees on the island with a ghostly tenderness. One clear star above the mountain wall gleamed. Seeing it her eyebrows floated upward softly for sheer joy.

'Yes,' she said quietly. 'It will be another grand day – tomorrow.'

And her eyebrows sank, very slowly, like a falling curtain.

Innocence

All this month the nuns have been preparing my little boy for his first Confession. In a few days he will go in a crocodile from the school to the parish church; enter the strange-looking cabinet in the corner of the aisle and see in the dusk of this secretive box an old priest's face behind a grille. He will acknowledge his wickedness to this pale, criss-crossed face. He will be a little frightened but he will enjoy it too, because he does not really believe any of it – for him it is a kind of game that the nuns and the priest are playing between them.

How could he believe it? The nuns tell him that the Infant Jesus is sad when he is wicked. But he is never wicked, so what can it matter? If they told him instead of the sorrow he causes the Weasel, or Two Toes, or the Robin in the Cow's Ear, all of which live in the fields below our house, he would believe it in just the same way. To be sure he tells lies, he is a terrible liar, and when he plays Rummy with me he cheats as often as he can, and when he is slow and I flurry him he flies into furious rages and his eyes swim with tears and he dashes the cards down and calls me A Pig. For this I love him so much that I hug him, because it is so transparent and innocent; and at night if I remember his tears I want to go into his room and hold his fat, sweaty hand that lies on the coverlet clutching some such treasure as an empty reel. How, then, can he believe that God could be angry with him because he tells lies or calls his daddy A Pig?

Yet, I hate to see him being prepared for his first Confession because one day he will really do something wicked, and I know the fear that will come over him on that day – and I cannot prevent it.

I have never forgotten the first time I knew that I had committed sin. I had been going to Confession for years, ever since I was seven, as he is now, telling the same things time after time just as he will do. 'Father, I told a lie . . . Father, I forgot to say my morning prayers

. . . Father, I was disobedient to my parents . . . And that is all, Father.' It was always quite true: I had done these things; but, as with him, it was only true as a fable or a mock-battle is true since none of these things were any more sinful than his childish lies and rages. Until, one dim, wintry afternoon, not long after Christmas, when I went as usual to Confession in an old, dark, windy church called Saint Augustine's, down a side-lane, away from the city's traffic, a place as cold and damp and smelly as a tomb. It has since been pulled down and if they had not pulled it down it must soon have fallen down. It was the sort of church where there was always a beggar or two sheltering from the weather in the porch or in the dusky part under the back gallery; and always some poor shawled woman sighing her prayers in a corner like the wind fluttering in the slates. The paint was always clean and fresh, but the floor and the benches and the woodwork were battered and worn by the generations. The priests dressed in the usual black Augustinian garment with a cowl and a leather cincture. Altogether, a stranger would have found it a gloomy place. But I was familiar with it ever since my mother brought me there to dedicate me to Saint Monica, the mother of Augustine, and I loved the bright candles before her picture, and the dark nooks under the galleries, and the painted tondos on the ceiling, and the stuffy confessional boxes with their heavy purple curtains underneath which the heels of the penitents stuck out when they knelt to the grille.

There I was, glad to be out of the January cold, kneeling before Saint Monica, brilliant with the candles of her mendicants. I was reading down through the lists of sins in my penny prayer-book, heeding the ones I knew, passing over the ones I didn't know, when I suddenly stopped at the name of a sin that I had hitherto passed by as having nothing to do with me.

As I write down these words I again feel the terror that crept into me like a snake as I realized that I knew that sin. I knew it well. No criminal who feels the sudden grip of a policeman on his arm can have felt more fear than I did as I stared at the horrible words....

I joined the long silent queue of penitents seated against the wall. I went, at last, into the dark confessional. I told my usual innocent litany. I whispered the sin.

Now, the old priest inside the confessional was a very aged man

He was so old and feeble that the community rarely allowed him to do anything but say Mass and hear Confessions. Whenever they let him preach he would ramble on and on for an hour; people would get up and go away; the sacristan would peep out in despair through the sacristy door; and in the end an altar-boy would be sent out to ring the great gong on the altar-steps to make him stop. I have seen the boy come out three times to the gong before the old man could be lured down from the pulpit.

When this old priest heard what I said to him he gave a groan that must have been heard in the farthest corner of the church. He leaned his face against the wire and called me his 'child', as all priests in the confessional call every penitent. Then he began to question me about the details. I had not counted on this. I had thought that I would say my sin and be forgiven: for up to this every priest had merely told me that I was a very good little boy and asked me to pray for him as if I were a little angel whose prayers had a special efficacy, and then I would be dismissed jumping with joy.

To his questions I replied tremulously that it had happened 'more than once' – How soon we begin to evade the truth! – and, I said, 'Yes, Father, it was with another.' At this he let out another groan so that I wanted to beg him to be quiet or the people outside would hear him. Then he asked me a question that made my clasped hands sweat and shake on the ledge of the grille. He asked me if any harm had been done to me. At first I didn't know what he meant. Then horrible shapes of understanding came creeping towards me along the dark road of my ignorance, as, in some indistinct manner, I recognized that he was mistaking me for a girl! I cried out that nothing at all had happened, Father. Nothing! Nothing! Nothing! But he only sighed like the south wind and said:

'Ah, my poor child, you won't know for several months.'

I now had no desire but to escape. I was ready to tell him any story, any lie, if he would only stop his questions. What I did say I don't know but in some fashion I must have made the old man understand that I was a male sinner. For his next question, which utterly broke me, was:

'I see, I see. Well, tell me, my poor child. Was she married or unmarried?'

I need hardly say that as I remember this now I laugh at it for an absurd misadventure, and I have sometimes made my friends laugh at his questions and his groans, and at me with my two skinny heels sticking out under the curtains and knocking like castanets, and the next penitents wondering what on earth was going on inside the box. But, then, I was like a pup caught in a bramble bush, recanting and retracting and trying to get to the point where he would say the blessed words '*Absolve te* . . .' and tell me what my penance would be.

What I said I cannot recall. All I remember distinctly is how I emerged under the eyes of the queue, walked up the aisle, as far away as I could get from the brightness of Saint Monica into the darkest corner under the gallery where the poorest of the poor crowd on Sundays. I saw everything through smoke. The scarlet eye of the sanctuary lamp – the only illumination apart from the candles before the shrine – stared at me. The shawled woman sighed at me. The wind under my bare knees crept away from me. A beggar in a corner, picking his nose and scratching himself, was Purity itself compared to me.

In the streets the building stood dark and wet against the after-Christmas pallor of the sky. High up over the city there was one tiny star. It was as bright and remote as lost innocence. The blank windows that held the winter sky were sullen. The wet cement walls were black. I walked around for hours. When I crept in home my mother demanded angrily where I had been all these hours and I told her lies that *were* lies, because I wanted to deceive her, and I knew that from this on I would always be deceiving everybody because I had something inside me that nobody must ever know. I was afraid of the dark night before me. And I still had to face another Confession when I would have to confess all these fresh lies that I had just told the old priest and my mother.

It's forty years ago, now: something long since put in its unimportant place. Yet, somehow, when I look across at this small kid clutching his penny prayer-book in his sweaty hands and wrinkling up his nose at the hard words – I cannot laugh. It does not even comfort me when I think of that second Confession, after I had carefully examined those lists of sins for the proper name of my sin. For, what I said to the next priest was: 'Father, I committed adultery.' With infinite tenderness he assured me that I was mistaken, and that I would not know anything about that sin for many years to come, indeed, that I would have to be married before I could commit it – and then asked me to pray for him, and said I was a very good little boy and sent me away jumping with joy. When I think of that and look at this small Adam he becomes like that indescribably remote and tender star, and I sigh like that old, dead priest, and it does not help to know that he is playing a fable of – 'Father, I told lies . . . Father, I forgot to say my morning prayers. . . . Father, I called my daddy A Pig.'

The Trout

One of the first places Julia always ran to when they arrived in G—— was The Dark Walk. It is a laurel walk, very old, almost gone wild, a lofty midnight tunnel of smooth, sinewy branches. Underfoot the tough brown leaves are never dry enough to crackle: there is always a suggestion of damp and cool trickle.

She raced right into it. For the first few yards she always had the memory of the sun behind her, then she felt the dusk closing swiftly down on her so that she screamed with pleasure and raced on to reach the light at the far end; and it was always just a little too long in coming so that she emerged gasping, clasping her hands, laughing, drinking in the sun. When she was filled with the heat and glare she would turn and consider the ordeal again.

This year she had the extra joy of showing it to her small brother, and of terrifying him as well as herself. And for him the fear lasted longer because his legs were so short and she had gone out at the far end while he was still screaming and racing.

When they had done this many times they came back to the house to tell everybody that they had done it. He boasted. She mocked. They squabbled.

'Cry babby!'

'You were afraid yourself, so there!'

'I won't take you any more.'

'You're a big pig.'

'I hate you.'

Tears were threatening so somebody said, 'Did you see the well?' She opened her eyes at that and held up her long lovely neck suspiciously and decided to be incredulous. She was twelve and at that age little girls are beginning to suspect most stories: they have already found out too many, from Santa Claus to the Stork. How could there be a well! In The Dark Walk? That she had visited year after year? Haughtily she said, 'Nonsense.'

But she went back, pretending to be going somewhere else, and she found a hole scooped in the rock at the side of the walk, choked with damp leaves, so shrouded by ferns that she only uncovered it after much searching. At the back of this little cavern there was about a quart of water. In the water she suddenly perceived a panting trout. She rushed for Stephen and dragged him to see, and they were both so excited that they were no longer afraid of the darkness as they hunched down and peered in at the fish panting in his tiny prison, his silver stomach going up and down like an engine.

Nobody knew how the trout got there. Even old Martin in the kitchen-garden laughed and refused to believe that it was there, or pretended not to believe, until she forced him to come down and see. Kneeling and pushing back his tattered old cap he peered in.

'Be cripes, you're right. How the divil in hell did that fella get there?'

She stared at him suspiciously.

'You knew?' she accused; but he said, 'The divil a know;' and reached down to lift it out. Convinced she hauled him back. If she had found it then it was her trout.

Her mother suggested that a bird had carried the spawn. Her father thought that in the winter a small streamlet might have carried it down there as a baby, and it had been safe until the summer came and the water began to dry up. She said, 'I see,' and went back to look again and consider the matter in private. Her brother remained behind, wanting to hear the whole story of the trout, not really interested in the actual trout but much interested in the story which his mummy began to make up for him on the lines of, 'So one day Daddy Trout and Mammy Trout . . .' When he retailed it to her she said, 'Pooh.'

It troubled her that the trout was always in the same position; he had no room to turn; all the time the silver belly went up and down; otherwise he was motionless. She wondered what he ate and in between visits to Joey Pony, and the boat and a bathe to get cool, she thought of his hunger. She brought him down bits of dough; once she brought a worm. He ignored the food. He just went on panting. Hunched over him she thought how, all the winter, while she was at school he had been in there. All winter, in The Dark Walk, all day, all night, floating around alone. She drew the leaf of her hat down around her ears and chin and stared. She was still thinking of it as she lay in bed.

It was late June, the longest days of the year. The sun had sat still for a week, burning up the world. Although it was after ten o'clock it was still bright and still hot. She lay on her back under a single sheet, with her long legs spread, trying to keep cool. She could see the D of the moon through the fir-tree – they slept on the ground floor. Before they went to bed her mummy had told Stephen the story of the trout again, and she, in her bed, had resolutely presented her back to them and read her book. But she had kept one ear cocked.

'And so, in the end, this naughty fish who would not stay at home got bigger and bigger and bigger, and the water got smaller and smaller. . . .'

Passionately she had whirled and cried, 'Mummy, don't make it a horrible old moral story!' Her mummy had brought in a Fairy Godmother, then, who sent lots of rain, and filled the well, and a stream poured out and the trout floated away down to the river below. Staring at the moon she knew that there are no such things as Fairy Godmothers and that the trout, down in The Dark Walk, was panting like an engine. She heard somebody unwind a fishing-reel. Would the *beasts* fish him out!

She sat up. Stephen was a hot lump of sleep, lazy thing. The Dark Walk would be full of little scraps of moon. She leaped up and looked out the window, and somehow it was not so lightsome now that she saw the dim mountains far away and the black firs against the breathing land and heard a dog say, bark-bark. Quietly she lifted the ewer of water, and climbed out the window and scuttled along the cool but cruel gravel down to the maw of the tunnel. Her pyjamas were very short so that when she splashed water it wet her ankles. She peered into the tunnel. Something alive rustled inside there. She raced in, and up and down she raced, and flurried, and cried aloud, 'Oh, Gosh, I can't find it,' and then at last she did. Kneeling down in the damp she put her hand into the slimy hole. When the body lashed they were both mad with fright. But she gripped him and shoved him into the ewer and raced, with her teeth ground, out to the other end of the tunnel and down the steep paths to the river's edge.

All the time she could feel him lashing his tail against the side of the ewer. She was afraid he would jump right out. The gravel cut into her soles until she came to the cool ooze of the river's bank where the moon-mice on the water crept into her feet. She poured out watching until he plopped. For a second he was visible in the water. She hoped he was not dizzy. Then all she saw was the glimmer of the moon in the silent-flowing river, the dark firs, the dim mountains, and the radiant pointed face laughing down at her out of the empty sky.

She scuttled up the hill, in the window, plonked down the ewer and flew through the air like a bird into bed. The dog said bark-bark. She heard the fishing-reel whirring. She hugged herself and giggled. Like a river of joy her holiday spread before her.

In the morning Stephen rushed to her, shouting that 'he' was gone, and asking 'where' and 'how'. Lifting her nose in the air she said superciliously, 'Fairy Godmother, I suppose?' and strolled away patting the palms of her hands.

Shades of the Prison House

The village kids said that they fell out with Inch Moran because she had 'levelled' Padna Calla with a stone. That, as far as they knew, was the truth. They had really outlawed Inch because of the things their fathers and mothers were saying about her father. They had turned against him because he was a warder in the jail; because Bantry the tramp was going to be hanged in a week's time for the murder of Boody Bess; and because they were all terrified of everybody and everything connected with the hanging.

Up to the very last day of the trial they had talked only of Bantry and Boody. Did he do it? Would he get off? Would he be certified? Or they would go back and look again into the pond under the alders where she had been found with her red hair spread on the water and her eyes open and her forehead staved in. Or they would stare into the cave where the police found Bantry staring out at them with the starting-handle still clutched in his fist. But on the night of the verdict when they looked out at the jail-tower, and saw the solitary light, somebody said, 'I suppose Moran is in charge of him'; and from that on they began to see Moran locking Bantry into his cell, feeding him his breakfast every morning (for some reason vaguely connected with the idea that condemned men get anything they ask for on the last morning they thought only of his breakfast), and they saw Moran leading Bantry by the arm to the drop, and they even saw Moran holding the greased rope for Pierpoint the hangman. At once, even the man's uniform, that did not have as much as a silver button on it, was connected with death in their minds. They spliced everything he did into their own horror of the hanging. He was a great hand at fretwork, and when they saw his light shining late at night they saw it as a kind of counterpart to the solitary light in the tower. Mrs Calla said it gave her the shivers to see him digging in his garden.

So, for two long weeks, up to the very eve of the hanging, the kids outlawed Inch. It meant imprisonment; for since the murder no child was allowed to go alone outside the village. It meant that she sat, all the livelong day, in the house, or else in the tiny garden high on top of an outdoor stone stairs that climbed for ten steps and stopped in mid-air: the remains of some vanished structure. She was like one of those coloured gnomes that people buy for gardens – fat-legged, rosy, a red row of sausage curls across her forehead, in an old-fashioned coat with many capes like a dwarf highwayman, and her two grey eyes wide and a divilment that had no outlet.

On a level with her lofty throne, staring out through the dormer window, were her two sisters, side by side, two statues with blank eyeballs, facing across the river at the baths where the bodies of the city lads gleamed in the sun. The two mild-faced creatures never spoke to her, or to anyone. When they did speak they spoke to the air, never above a whisper, and never finishing a sentence. One would say, 'We want to.' And the other might reply, 'This is the.' Inch, high among the madder of the valerian, the stonecrop, the budding lobelia, was hardly aware that they were there. The only people who ever spoke to her were the mothers filling their ewers and buckets from the pump below on the pavement. They would say, 'Why don't you go out and play with the childer, Inch? They're all gone out to the quarry.'

She would say, 'I am quite happy where I am, thank you. I have my thoughts to think. They are very interesting thoughts, and very typical.'

At which the women would bend down and pump convulsively.

It was very quiet in the village on the eve of the hanging; Inch, broody on her aerial perch, could hardly hear a sound. The river was at ebb. The turbines in the waterworks, whereby the village lived, were stopped. The only sound was when somebody threw a bucket of slops across the road, or when she heard the voices of the gang ringing in the distance. Always up to now when she fell out with the gang – as, being a little boss, she often did – she won them back after a few days; enticed first one, then another, until she finally had them all with some grand plan they could not resist, such as promise of a marvellous picnic (she was a born organizer), or news of a gorgeous new 'plank', their word for a secret haunt of blackberries, or mushrooms, or wild-crabs. This time not a soul approached her. And there were the wide fields breaking with whitethorn, and celandines, and wild arum. There were the clouds stealing away over the hills, saying, 'Come on, come on.' While she was left there, as she told her father in a fury the night before, like an abandoned female.

Suddenly she saw Rory Baked Beans below her on the road. He was hardly one of the gang, too young to be initiated. At any other time she would have told him to run along and wipe his nose. This time she seized her chance like lightning.

'Hullo, Rory boy!' she greeted, the title the basest flattery.

'Hullo, Inch girl!' said Rory.

'How's yeer cat these days?' asked Inch politely.

He lighted up instantly. 'She have hundreds of kittens. But,' – sadly – 'they're all blind.'

'All kittens is blind,' explained Inch. 'Pups is blind, too. That's because they're born in the dark and aren't used to the light.'

'Gor!' said Rory, in wonder at her vast knowledge. Then, recollecting himself: 'What dark were they born in?'

'In the coal-hole, of course, you fooleen,' said Inch. 'All kittens and pups is born in coal-holes.'

Rory agreed, pondering on the interesting fact. Inch began to tempt him.

'I know,' she whispered, 'where there's a nest of young larks. Larks is never born blind. Will you come out along with me in the morning and we'll see them?'

Rory hesitated but looked fondly up the river at the softening tops of the beechweeds. Inch went on: 'I have a cocoa-tin that we could boil tea in. I have tuppence my Da gave me. We could have a massive picnic. Them too,' pointing to her sisters, 'would come with us, though the Lord knows they're not much use to God or man.'

'Where is it?' asked Rory.

Inch swept out her arm with a gesture worthy of a generalissimo.

'Were you ever out to the tip-top of Pike Hill?' she asked.

'What's there?' he bargained.

'Mrs Calla,' said Inch, and it was a sign of her ruthless genius that she did not even think of the Calla child she had levelled with the stone, but that her eyes dilated instead with the vastness of her indefinable image, 'Mrs Calla says that when you'd get to the top of Pike Hill and look down you'd see *Nothing*! Imagine it, Rory boy – out and out as far we can go, and look down, and see Nothing!'

'Is it out beyond the wood where they caught Bantry?'

'Miles farther,' said Inch, without a tremor.

'Is it out beyond the quarry where they found Boody Bess?' whispered Rory, fearful of giving offence even as he said it.

'Miles beyond that,' laughed Inch. 'Out and out and out!'

That silenced them both, it broke the power of their own imagination. The far cries of the gang sank away. The setting sun caught only the ripples by the gravelled islands of the river. Somebody called Rory's name but he did not stir.

'We'll start in the early morning,' she lured. 'Come up and sit here and we'll plan it.'

He came in and up. The two vacant sisters still gazed away at the slow dusk with the patient eyes of cows. Inch put her arms about him.

'We'll go out and out,' she crooned.

'Out and out?'

'And we'll climb. And look down.'

'Yoy! We'll look down, Inch.'

'And see Nothing.'

'Nothing!'

Again the mother's voice called, despairingly, to Rory. Dark was fallen. The two statues did not budge. The river had become more audible with the fall of night. Beyond the tree-tops, the rounded domes of the sycamores, the sea-weedy elms, the serrated pines, the unrecognizable furry fuzziness of the farthest woods, there rose the hexagonal tower of the jail. The solitary light shone in its tower. Inch smiled down at Rory.

One of the sisters, said, 'Who will put the?' And the other answered, 'Sometimes.'

The next morning the four of them were already approaching the round hill-top before the dew was yet dry on the grassy margins of the roads. She had seen the village kids look with envy after her as she led her opposition down the street. She knew that when she came back she would have such stories that she would have no trouble in leading a larger expedition the following morning. Within three days she would be King of the Castle again. Her thoughts levitated her so that she kept the three of them fast on the march, and before they realized it they had left the village far behind and were looking on unfamiliar country.

The river was now far below them; cattle stood in it, tiny and black. To the west, forty miles away, they saw a neat row of mountains, eight or ten little blue hunchbacks, with white caps on their heads. Hand in hand the four of them left the road and marched up the slope to the globe of green hill, as to a sacrificial altar.

'We'll picnic on the top,' panted Inch, and the grouped trees right and left of the dome of grass invited them.

At last they were on top, sweaty and worn but triumphant. They saw more mountains beyond the hunchbacks. The river crept like a cat through the land. A breath of mist revealed it when the woods hid it. Inch recovered first of all, threw out her hand and said grandly to Rory Baked Beans, 'Well? *There* you are!' If it was not Nothing it was as endless and as bottomless.

It did not occur to the children to turn and look the way they had come until a man and a woman came walking slowly up the hill, and, reaching them, nodded and smiled, and began to look towards the village through a pair of field glasses. Then Inch turned to the familiar spire, the familiar web of smoke, and the hexagonal tower. The four kids listened to the grown-ups.

'*There* you are!' said the man suddenly, with the field glasses stuck to his eyes. 'I see it!'

'Show *me*, darling,' said the young woman, and she took the glasses, focused them, and said, 'Yes. It's quite clear now. I can see it fluttering.'

'It *is* black, isn't it?' said the man.

'It's black all right,' she mumbled, still staring, fascinated.

'If Pierpoint really didn't come,' he said, 'I wonder who they got to do it.'

'Some warder,' she said idly. 'I believe they have to give him ten pounds to do it.'

'May I have another look, dear?' said the man testily.

He looked again. Then she looked. Then they got tired of looking at the flag and began to focus idly this way and that. At last, with another smile for the kids, they wandered away downhill.

Inch, like her two vacant stepsisters, was staring away at the mountains, and at the river that gently turned its white belly like a fish whenever the sun through cloud passed slowly across it. Rory was stitching daisies into a chain. Silently they prepared the picnic. Then they played a game. Then Inch wandered off by herself. The long day leaked away. Rory got tired and wanted to go home, but she would not and would not. He kept saying, 'Why?' She kept saying, 'Just because!'

They quarrelled and she abused him and he cried. At last he said, 'There's nothing to see here,' and sank down and fell asleep under a tree. The hunchbacks became transparent as the sun sank behind them and the sky widened with mackerel backs and pink mare's tails. Rory went off and then came back from some lonely expedition. Inch waked up the two mad sisters who were asleep in one another's arms.

'We must go home, now,' she said, and gave one last long look at the vast West where only the river was bright. They packed up, and dragged their legs home along the dusty road and finally came to the first cottage. Like lambs to the stall the two sisters went into their house. Rory went to Mrs Calla's for his tea. Inch would not go with any of them. She stood in the dark and kicked stones with her boot toe. Mrs Calla came out and made her come into her house for her supper.

The gossips dropped in one by one, but seeing Inch they did not talk. From time to time Mrs Calla kept rubbing Inch's poll and saying, 'Poor child! God help you!' Dadda Calla, whose job it was to scrape the wrack from the waterworks gratings, asked her where she spent the day. She said, lightly, 'Over the hills and far away.'

'Whatdeyeat?' said Dadda, all in one word, which was the way he always talked, as if he had marbles in his mouth and was afraid they'd all fall out.

'Sweets and cakes,' said Inch, very grand in her manner.

'A hake-o'-fish'd-be-betthher,' growled Dadda. 'Hake-o'-fish-and-aloado'spuds!'

'And what'd ye see, childeen bawn?' asked Mrs Calla, stroking the small fat hand.

'Oh, nothing,' said Inch. 'Nothing. But it was quite interesting, thank you,' she added primly. 'It was very typical and interesting to all of us.'

'And will you be going out there now soon again, a grah, with the rest of the children?' asked Mrs Calla, pressing the little hand.

'No thank you,' said Inch, getting up. 'Now I must be going. My father will be expecting me.'

They let her go. At the door she looked up at the sky, and said, 'It's a starry night. A starry night for a ramble.' And fled, choking.

She stayed out as long as she dared. She kicked more stones. Then she got afraid. Tossing her curls she went into her home.

He was by the fire, in a heavy sleep. A piece of fretwork hung dangling from his hand. It had got as far as *God Save Our Gracious Ki*. She smelled him, and said, 'I suppose it's the whiskey.' She went up to bed. The two sisters were awake, staring at the ceiling, side by side. She got into bed beside them. The ripples of the river under the lights of the Waterworks shimmered on the ceiling. The night turbines throbbed softly. At long last she heard him come heavily up the stairs, go to his room, and after a while bed springs creaked. She heard a faint sound of water over the weir, and wondered at it because of the drouth. Then she realized that it was him whimpering in his sleep – like a little dog.

The End of a Good Man

Men who go into competition with the world are broken into fragments by the world, and it is such men we love to analyse. But men who do not go into competition with the world remain intact, and these men we cannot analyse. They are always contented men, with modest ambitions. Larry Dunne was that kind of man. All that there is to say about him, therefore, is that he bred pigeons and was happy.

And yet, this unconditional lump of reality, this unrefracted thought in the mind of God, suddenly did fall into fragments. He fell for the same reason as Adam. For when God was saying, 'Orchards for Adam', and 'Finance for J. P. Morgan', and 'Politics for Teddy Roosevelt', and 'Pigeons for Larry Dunne', He must have added (sotto voce), 'But one pigeon he must never control.' And it was to that one pigeon, that one ambition that Larry Dunne gave his heart. The pigeon's name was Brian Boru. Larry got him on his thirty-fifth birthday from his father.

Any evening that summer you could have met Larry at the pigeon club – it sat every night under the canal bridge on the towpath – and you might have guessed in what direction his heart was already moving by the way he talked endlessly without ever mentioning the fatal bird. You might have heard him, towering over the rest of the club, talking of his runts, tumblers, pouters, homers, racers, without ever mentioning Brian Boru; you might have heard how he had a jacobin, and nearly had a scandaroon; how 'Pigeons, mind you, must never be washed, only sprayed with rain-water. And what's more, pigeons should be sprayed from the shoulders down – never the head, unless you want them to die of meningitis.' What a scoundrel the man in Saint Rita's Terrace was, a low fellow who kept budgerigars and had once actually said that pigeons were mere riff-raff. How his father had stolen a sacred pigeon out of an Indian temple, when he was in Rangoon with the Royal Irish, and how the rajah chased him into the jungle for two miles trying to catch him. 'And what's more, you should never dry a pigeon, unless, to be sure, you wrapped him up in warm flannel – which isn't the same thing.' And anyway, what were budgerigars, only pups off parrots? 'They are not even called budgerigars! They call them budgies – as if anyone would ever dare to call a pigeon a pidgy! Doesn't it show yeh?'

But whatever he spoke of, or whomever he spoke to, you might notice that he never spoke to one little runt of a man who always listened to him with a sly, sneering smile on his face. That was the club-member whose Michael Collins the Second had beaten Larry's Brian Boru in every race since the season began – beaten the bird that had laid its beak on Larry's heart.

Nobody knew the history of this Brian Boru. Larry's father swore he was the great-grandson of the Indian rajah's sacred pigeon, but that, of course, was a tall yarn. Whatever his pedigree, the bird was a marvel. Such speed! Such direction! Such a homer! A bird that had only one flaw! Time and again, when there was a race, Larry had seen that faint speck of joy come into the sky over the flat counties and the chequered market gardens where he lived, each time half an hour, at the very least, ahead of every other bird in the team; and on one occasion as much as fifty-eight minutes ahead of them, and that in the teeth of thirty-mile gale.

For while other birds had to follow the guiding shore line, or the railway line that dodged the hills, Brian came sailing over mountain top and moor like an arrow from the bow. Time and again, after greeting him with an adoring shout, Larry had gone tearing back down the lane to his tumbledown cottage, roaring to his Da to get out the decoys, and to light the primus-stove for some new concoction whose smell was to tempt Brian Boru down to his loft. Back then to the bridge, waving to the sky, calling the bird by name as it came nearer and nearer to the parapet on which stood the club's time-piece – a clock with a glass front on which there was a blue and green painting of a waterfall. (A bird was not officially home until its owner had tipped the waterfall with its beak.)

But . . . time and again the one flaw told. Brian Boru would circle, and Brian Boru would sink, and inevitably Brian Boru would rise again. After about thirty minutes of this he would come down to the telegraph pole over Larry's backyard; and stay there until some slow coach like Michael Collins the Second had walked off with the race. The bird so loved the air that it could not settle down.

'Oh!' Larry had been heard to moan, as he looked up at the telegraph pole. 'Isn't it a sign? Isn't it a symbol? Isn't that poor Ireland all over again? First in the race. Fast as the lightning. But she won't settle down! That bird has too much spirit – he's a high-flyer – and aren't we the same? Always up in the bloody air. Can't come down to earth.' And then he would beseech the bird, as it looked down at him over its prima-donna chest with a bleary eye, rather like an old damp-nosed judge falling asleep on his bench: 'O Brian Boru! Yeh sweet limb o' the divil, will you come down? Look! I've custards for yeh. I have sowanies for yeh. I have yer loft lined with the sweetest straw.' And he would start clucking and chortling at it. 'Coordle-coordle-coordle, Brian Boru-u-u-yu.' Or: 'Tchook, tchuc, thc, thc, thc, thc. Tchook, thc, thc . . . oh, but I'll tchook you if I lay me hands on you, you criminal type from British India! Brian, my *darling,* aren't you *going* to come *down* to me?'

Brian would snuggle his beak on his chest, or make a contemptuous noise like a snore.

Then, that night at the bridge – for on race nights Larry simply had to talk about Brian Boru:

'It's not fair,' Larry would protest. 'The rules should be altered. That bird is not being given his due. That bird is suffering from injustice. Sure, it's only plain, honest reason. The bird is first home in every race – will any member of the club deny it?'

'No, Larry!' they would reply, appeasingly. 'No! He's a grand bird, we all admit it, but a bird who won't settle is no good. And, for another thing, as we're sick and tired of telling you, supposing two birds come into sight at one and the same time, who the blazes is going to tell which one of them is first past the winning post – if there's going to be no winning post?'

'Ah!' Larry would roar, 'But sure this bird is home hours before any of your so-called pigeons – cripples I call them.' And then, true to his happy, light-hearted nature, he could not help laughing and making a joke of it. Six feet two, and as innocent as a child. 'Did I call them cripples? Cripples is too good for them. The one-half of ye must be breeding yeer birds from a cross between penguins and pelicans!'

At which he would recover something of his natural good humour again, and go off chortling – a chortle that would die as he remembered what began it.

As the season approached its end the bird got fat, and Larry got thin; but the bird retained his speed, and Larry became slow-moving and sullen. Those who had always known him for a gay fellow shook their heads sadly over it. He still entered Brian for the races; but each Saturday, now, he would barely stroll to the bridge when the regular two hours were passed since the birds had been released down the country. And when he saw the familiar speck in the sky he would actually turn his back on it.

It was the Easter Monday race that brought things to a head. That day a passing stranger said to him, as Brian Boru came into sight, 'Whose bird is that?'

Larry, leaning with his back and two elbows on the parapet, gave an idle glance over his shoulder at the sky.

'Him? He's my bird. But – eh – he's not in the race, you know. He's what you might call a gentleman pigeon. He's doing it for fun. That bird, sir, could win any race he wanted to. But the way it is with him, he couldn't be bothered. Pride is what's wrong with that bird, sir. Pride! Pride, they say, made the angels fall. Maybe it did. I wish something would make that fellow fall.'

Whereupon, Larry, as if a new understanding of the nature of pigeons had suddenly been vouchsafed to him, turned and gave the circling speck a terrible look. It was the look of a man struck by rejected love. Just at that moment it was that the man who owned Michael Collins the Second said the fatal word, as they all remembered and often recounted long after. He was a shrimp of a creature, a Tom Thumb of a man, who worked as a Boots in a hotel and bred his pigeons out of his tips. Seeing that look of misery in Larry's face he laughed and said, 'Why don't you breed budgerigars, Larry? At least you could take them out of their cage and kiss 'em?' The row of pigeon-fanciers, staring up at the sky, chuckled. They did not see the look of hate in Larry's face, or notice the way he slouched away home to his cabin.

There, as he was at his tea, he suddenly heard the clatter of wings like tearing silk and, looking up through his cabin window, he saw his bird in its loft among the custards and dainties, and now and again it glanced indifferently towards the cabin door. Pushing aside his cup, Larry said to his father – the old man recorded it when there was no use in recording it – 'I wish to God, Da, you never gave me that pigeon. That bird isn't human. He despises me.' And he put his head between his hands.

Later in the night, while the drizzle of rain fell on him, and the red reflections of the city illuminated the sky, he stood outside until his hair was pricked with the dew of the drizzle, talking now to himself, now to Brian; and though his father kept coming to the door, telling him not to be behaving like a child of two, Larry would not stir. He was like a boy hanging about under the window of his beloved.

'Is it the way you're faulting me?' he whispered. 'Is there something you think I ought to do? But what is there I can do? I can't alter the rules, and you won't come down! I know it's a dishonour. It's a dishonour for both of us. I know that, Brian my darling, just as well as you know it. But honest to God, I don't think it's my fault. I brought you up well. I did my best for you. I swear to God above this night I'd lay down my life for you. But, bar flying up in the air myself and bringing you down, what *can* I do?'

From the loft no reply, except the deep breathing of sleep.

Once more he entered the bird. Once more the pigeon scorned the earth. Once more the Boots mentioned budgerigars, and this time he added that canaries can at least sing. Once more, Michael Collins won the race. That finished it. Larry went home, and on the following Monday he sold every bird, box, loft, packet of food, and medicine bottle that he possessed. With the money he bought an old Smith and Wesson, thirty-two bore, and five rounds of ammunition from a former pal of the I.R.A. Then, for the last time, he entered the bird, saw it come, as always, first of the team up against the clouds that floated like bridesmaids over the hedgerows; saw through the veils of the sun how Brian swerved, and circled, and sank . . . and rose again; and did so its usual number of times before making for the inaccessible perch on the telegraph pole. While the dozen heads along the bridge shook their commiseration, Larry gripped his revolver in his pocket, and waited for the Boots to laugh. The Boots laughed. At that Larry's body took on the old fighting slouch; he pulled his hat savagely down over one eye; he buttoned his coat across his chest; he became the old down-looking gunman he had been fifteen years ago when he was in the I.R.A. Then with a roll of his shoulders like a militia man, a trick learned from his soldier Da, he looked at the Boots between the shoulder blades, put on the final bit of the gunman's manner – the ominously casual strolling gait – and walked quietly down the lane. There he found Brian on the pole.

'Brian,' he whispered, but without hope. 'Will you come down to me now?'

The bird rose and flew away, circled and came back again.

'So yeh won't come down?' whispered Larry out of the corner of his mouth. The bird looked haughtily over the lane roofs, as if contemplating another circle of flight. Before it could stir the shot cracked. With one head-sinking tumble it fell with a plop to the ground. Larry stooped, lifted the hot, twitching body in his palms, gave it one agonized look, and pelted back to the bridge, roaring like a maniac.

'By the Lord Almighty!' they said, when they saw him coming, screeching, with the bird in his palms. 'Brian Boru is after winning at last!'

Shouldering their cluster right and left, Larry snapped the beak to the glass of the clock, displayed the celluloid ring on the stiff ankle, and shouted, pale as the clouds, 'Has he won?'

It was only then that they saw the blood oozing down between his trembling fingers; but before they could tell him what they thought of him they saw the mad look in his eyes, and the way his hand stole to his pocket.

'Well?' yelled Larry at the Boots. 'Has he won? Or has he not won? Or maybe you'll say there's a rule that a dead bird can't win a race?'

'He's w-w-won, all right,' trembled the Boots.

'Gimme his prize!' said Larry.

In fear they gave it to him. It was a new dovecot, painted a lovely green. ('Eau-de-canal' the Boots called it afterwards, being the sarcastic brute he was.) Larry took the dovecot, and with the reddening beak hanging from his fist he slouched away. On Monday he sold the dovecot, had the bird stuffed, and put in the window of his lane cabin for the world to see.

You never see Larry Dunne at the canal bridge now. He walks moodily by himself along the towpaths, idly flicking a little twig against the hedges: or he sits with his father at the other side of the fire, learning off bits from his favourite book, *Who's Who*, or he sits gazing into the dancing devils of flame. The sky outside is lurid with the lights of Dublin. And in the little curtained window, the pigeon looks with two glassy eyes out over the damp market gardens, and the heavy, odorous night-fields, at the bloody sky.

Passion

Dearest Love. When will we meet again? It is only a few hours since I left you, and I am already full of melancholy thoughts.

Why on earth did I think tonight, after I had left you, of Conny Hourigan, and of that soft, wet night when the lights of Cork down in the valley were weeping through the haze, and everything as still as before dawn; and not a sound but the jolt of an old tram over the worn points, or the drip of the rain on the old tin shed in the backyard?

I think it was because I went to my window and saw the far away lights of Dublin, and at once I was again listening to that silence of twenty years ago drumming in my ears. I was waiting for my aunt to play the next card, and looking across the cosy eye of the fire in the kitchen-range at Conny breathing contentedly over his evening paper and stroking his Moses beard.

He suddenly lifts his eyes to look over his spectacles at the tiny window, and he says – 'Them bastards of slugs will be out in their marching orders tonight.' And he is just about to heave himself up and go out to his beloved patch of a garden to kill some of them when we hear a ratatatat at the hall-door. With a look over his glasses at my auntie, and a look at the clock, and a 'Who on earth can that be?' he goes shuffling out along the little hall. My aunt suspends her card. We turn our heads when we hear the voices rising sharply and Conny shouting, 'No!' And again, 'I tell you, no!' – and then more loud voices and the slam of the door.

He came back, flushed; gave a hitch to his belly, sat down, growled, 'Bloody cheek!' and tried to resume his reading.

'Who's that, Conny?' said the auntie, still holding up her card.

'Three buckos from Blarney Lane. Asking me to give 'um me six Easter lilies.'

'Oh, law! And why so?'

'Some kid that's dead up in Barrett's Buildings. Name of Delurey.

Molly Delurey. Died up in the Fever Hospital. The best I ever heard. God Almighty! Asking me to cut me six Easter lilies for some wan I never heard of in me life before. Did you ever hear the beat of that?'

His sister, of course, wanted to know all about it. Cork may call itself a city, but it is really a big town made up of a lot of little villages, and in each 'village' everybody wants to know everything about everybody else.

'Delurey?' she says. 'I don't know any wan now of that name. To be sure, we had a little apple-woman used to come here . . . Ah, but she was a Minny Delaney. And how did they come to know that you have the lilies?'

'You may ask. Your brave milkman. Spotted 'um every morning coming in with the milk. I knew that fellow had his eye on me garden. I always said that fellow's too sweet to be wholesome. "Oh, Mister Hourigan, haven't you the grand geraniums! Oh, isn't the verbena massive, Mister Hourigan!" Making a big man out of himself. "Flowers? I'll get ye the flowers. Go up to Mister Hourigan and tell him I sent you. Ask him for his lilies." The cheek of him! The cool, bloody pig's cheek of him!'

My auntie played her card without looking at it. She forgot to take her trick. I suppose she was seeing the little deal coffin, or the child laid out on the bed in the back bedroom. The rain played its harp strings in the yard. The fire purred.

'What they usually do,' she ventured, 'is to make up a collection for to buy the flowers.'

'That's what I said to 'um.' – Over his spectacles. 'They wanted to blind me that there's none in the shops. I don't believe wan word of it. And if there isn't,' his voice kept rising and rising, 'why did they come up to *me* for *my* poor little flowers? How fair they wouldn't go down to Bolster has a glasshouse full of 'um? Oh, no! Up to the foola! Me poor little six Easter lilies that I reared, that I looked after as if they were me own children, that I . . . But these buckos have no consideration. "Go up to Mister Hourigan and tell him I sent you." The . . . But what . . . Me poor little lilies. Who ever . . . God Almighty, I . . .'

He choked off into incoherence.

I said, 'Your trick, auntie?'

She gently swept the cards aside with her hand and breathed

rather than whispered, 'The poor child.'

Down with his paper, off with his specs.

'That's all very fine, woman, but am I going to give me six Easter lilies because . . . And aren't they me own property? Or aren't they? Amn't I entitled to do what I like with 'um? Or amn't I? And if I don't want to give 'um to 'um what right have them cafflers to be coming up to me own hall-door giving me lip?'

'Conny, I hope you didn't have *words*.'

'And am I going to let a pack of Blarney Lane cafflers tell me up to me puss that there won't be luck nor grace about the house if I don't give me flowers to 'um?'

'Conny! Conny! Conny! You refused the dead.'

He dashed down the paper and tore out of the kitchen. We heard the front door opening. I could imagine the dark and the haze and the smudgy lights down in the valley. He shuffled into the bedroom and struck a match. That was for the candle. I saw how the lilies outside the window would be pale against the smudgy lights of the city.

The wind wailed down from the convent grounds behind the backyard. My auntie was slowly putting the cards back into the old cigar-box. The candle clattered against the basin and ewer and then he came shuffling in along the linoleum of the hall. He blew out the candle, took up his paper firmly, and began to read it. The aunt closed the cigar-box and folded her arms about her and turning to the fire was lost in the little fluttering puffs coming out of the coal.

'The loveliest funeral I ever seen was the time of Lord Mayor MacSwiney. All the bands of the city. And the pipers. And the boys marching. And the Dead marching Saul. And the flag on the coffin. And all the flowers. And people in every window crying down salt tears.' Conversationally she inquired of him: 'Isn't Packey Cassidy buried up there with the Lord Mayor?'

'How do I know where he's buried?'

'Sure aren't they all together up in the one plot?'

'I dunno who you're talking about, let me read me paper, woman.'

'Yerrah is it pretending you don't know Packey Cassidy from the Glen worked with you down in the gas-house? Oh then many the night he brought you home when you had a sup taken. Didn't the two of us stand outside there in the garden and the pipers playing him up the Western Road to the Republican Plot?'

Conny pretended to read. The wind brought us the soft broken tolling of the nuns' bell. Conny looked over his specs again at the window and gave a poke to the cosy fire.

'That's a nor'-wester. There'll be a flood in the river tomorrow.'

'Ah, God look down on us. 'Tis no harm to say it – once we're dead we're soon forgotten.'

'You'd betther be beatin' your way home, boy, the last tram is gone.'

I hated to leave the warm kitchen. Somehow this talk of processions and bands and floods in the river and the nuns' bell and the squeaks of the last tram had wrapped me into a cosy nest of Time and Memory, and I remembered with pleasure how somebody had said that 'All Cork is out of the wan eggshell', and I understood for the first time what that meant. I wanted desperately that Conny should give the lilies to the dead child, and I felt bitter of him that he wouldn't do it. Timidly I said, 'Wouldn't you give her three of them, Uncle Conny?' He roared at me, 'No, nor wan nor half a wan.' The aunt's face got pale and venomous and miserable and she stabbed at him:

'No nor I don't think you'd give them to meself if it was a thing that I was stretched in the next room!'

After a moment he said, quietly,

'Go home, boy.'

As I left his patch of a garden – it was about as big as a table – I saw the six lilies, calm as sleep, by the pale light of the hall. The dead child's face would be just as pale. Down in its hollow the little city seemed to have locked every door and window against the storm and the rain. There were few lights.

That was twenty years ago. Why did that wet night flash on me when I walked into my bedroom tonight and saw the land under the full moon?

The sky is bleached, the fields are white, the lights of Dublin are bright as youth. They drained me so that I had to lean on the window-sill and let it all pour over me as if I were a stone under a river. It was like hearing an old, old tune on a brass-band; or the sound of church-bells on a wet Sunday morning; or the hoot of a ship's siren on Christmas Day. Frightening shadows under everything – under the gooseberry bushes, under the cabbages, under an old ash-can. And nothing between those shadows and that high moon but those lights of the city, low down, and poised over them, one long narrow cloud stretched from east to west like a scythe about to sweep the sky. It is the sort of night that might make a man ache for love, and I was suffused with you, dear heart, and should have been full of joy and content.

That night, so long ago, was very different to this serene moon. All through that stormy night the drums of the rain beat on the roofs of Cork. In the morning the river was in flood. Rafts of branches and wrack and reeds torn up by the storm sailed on the muddy water through the city. And Conny's lovely white lilies were battered into the mud. When he saw them he just went back to bed and he stayed there for three days. The aunt didn't say one word to him. But outside his window he could hear everybody who came into the little garden – including the milkman – loud in commiseration. After that I no longer envied him his hobby, as I once used to. I began vaguely to understand that his garden was a sort of torment to him.

Or is it, dearest one, that all passion is an unhappiness? Are we always looking forward to our joy, or thinking back on it, or so drunk with it that we cannot realize it?

The night is nearly finished. The moon is going down. The lights of Dublin are still bright. The shadows are long and pale. You are asleep, with your dear red hair spread on your pillow. I hear a little wind creeping up from the north-west.

Dear Love, when will we meet again? Let it be soon, Dear Love, let it be soon!

A Letter

As she cycled out of the village along the bog-road she was aware of the heads popping out over the half-doors. She was not ruffled. She knew that if she had been a native they would have considered where she might be going, and why, the state of her health, the price she paid for her hat, her general character, her prospects of marriage, the condition and fortunes of her father and mother and brothers and sisters and all her known relations. As it was they would look after her down the road, and look up the road, and return to their affairs.

Just beyond the creamery she passed the three bank-clerks. She threw them a gobbet of pity. What on earth had they to talk about, day after day? They were always together in the bank, always taking the same walk, out by the bog-road, back by the New Line, home to tea to their digs. She saw nobody else until she came to Cappagh Cross where she passed the tall young Franciscan with the umbrella, striding along, kicking his brown habit before him. When she turned under the beeches up the dark road to the Commons she saw the sun at the far end of the tunnel gaze at her with a brilliantly vacant eye.

At the top of the long slope she came out into the sun and saw the rocky landscape of the Commons spread out beneath her. It wavered under its own miasma. The little lake in the centre of it glinted all over. She turned off the road down her favourite boreen, wobbling intently between the cart-ruts, avoiding the overhanging briars that trailed lost threads of hay from the rank hedges on each side.

The boreen wound and dropped until it came to an abrupt end at a gap stuffed with furze bushes. There she threw her bicycle into the hedge and drank from the icy well, noticing how the dribbled water dried on the flagstone. She delayed to admire the line of poplars beyond. She looked for the distant spire of the village. It was so pale that it was almost invisible. She clambered over the gap and thrust through the scrub that borders the lake until she came on open water between tall reeds. She crunched forward on the strand, dazzled by the whiteness of its minute crustacea. When she lay down the water glittered level with her eye.

For a while she lay still, her satchel for pillow, enjoying the heat of the strand, sleepy with rest, hearing nothing but the clucking of invisible coots. Then she squirmed about and pulled out a book and paper from her bag. The paper was a New York periodical several months old: the book was Balzac's *Père Goriot* in English. She read reviews of plays that she was never likely to see, and notices of books she was never likely to read. Then she opened her novel and began to read the description of Eugène de Rastignac's first ball.

From time to time, as she read, her eyes wandered, distracted by a coot zig-zagging across the water, or hypnotized by the mirage shimmering above the violet rocks beyond the lake. A trail of steam from a distant train – too far away to be heard – sieved out of Cappagh woods. Her eyes did not return from the vacant sky into which it evaporated until, with a sudden gesture, she pulled out her writing-pad and her pen and began to write:

Dear Ann,

Here I am back again in B—— after the long summer holidays. I am only a month back today and already I am overcome by the feeling that I am all alone and no one writes to me and I am fed up with my eternal state of being a B.A. teaching kids in a convent school. I am in a rebellious state against God and man at finding myself an economic slave while all the rest of the world is going places and doing wonderful things. Oh! For gondolas, lights and music! I have made up my mind definitely and finally to clear out of this place as fast as I can. I have felt like this ever since I returned. The only reason I haven't written sooner is that I cannot without putting myself into my letters and I loathe whining. (If you dare commiserate with me I'll cut your throat.) You are in London and probably having a much better time. But don't dare to pity me! Now I . . .

The ink in her pen gave out. She lay back again, full length on the hot strand, frowning at the bright sky. She tried again to read but gave it up. She walked back to her bicycle and pushed it back along the boreen to the main road and cycled away around the lake, and on and on as if she were chasing the setting sun. By the time she had turned for home this fickle Saint Martin's heat had been followed by an evening chill, and with a pang she noticed the briefness of the day and the watery crackle of the trees.

The first lights had already sprung up in the village pubs. In the window under the tin roof of the cinema the blue glare of the carbons matched the bruised blueness of the flying clouds. She was too exhausted to do more than sit to her tea in the kitchen of her lodgings listening indifferently to the chatter of the landlady and her mother who was now sitting in her cocoon of shawls by the unnecessary fire. The young husband wandered aimlessly in and out of the kitchen and the talk.

The old woman in the corner was over eighty. From her armchair in the corner she was now surveying life as amusedly and ironically as if she were sitting on a cloud in Olympus. She had kept a lodging house for years in the city and had known some of her student friends.

'Miss O,' she suddenly said, 'do you remember a wild divil of a girl in the University by the name of Kitty Cooney? You do – you know her well. She came easht from near Cloyne. Her father was a vet.'

'I seem to remember the name . . .'

'Yerrah, you can't but know her. Gold hair on her. A fine looking girl. I tell you that wan was a hot piece. She had a boy called Looney. Cooney the Looney we used to call her.'

'Of course! I remember her now. She was a lovely girl.'

'Listen to me, child, she had boys after her like autumn crows in a wheat-field. Every night coortin' in the front room with the lights out. Wan night didn't I go in there forgettin' all about her and I turned on the light. Wasn't Looney inside there and his two hands inside her blouse!'

To hide her blushes she stooped for her writing-pad and prepared to write. Her daughter saw her blush and laughed aloud. The old woman gurgled. The young husband tactfully turned away to switch on the wireless. It cut in on a bit of Mozart.

'Wan time didn't she buy a shtatue of the Blessed Virgin to put in her bedroom. It was as big as herself, aroo. Looney had to carry it up from the shop in his two arums. All the way up the stairs he took it for her. Half an hour it took them to settle it, moryah!

"Ambaisthe, you divil you," says I to him, when they came down, "weren't your arums tired enough from carrying it?" He gave me wan look and he ran out of the house near choked with the laughing. He knew what I was up to. But do you think her ladyship minded? Tell me what happened her at all? Did he marry her?'

'She went to America. She married a French count.'

'Glory be to the lamb of God do you mean to say that wan is a countess? Cooney a countess? Minnie, do you hear what Miss O is after saying?'

Hearing the music rather than their talk she wrote:

... These digs are a gift. A bit of our old lives. They are West of Ireland people who kept a lodging-house in the College Road. I am enjoying their yarns about the inner lives of ones we knew at college. They are talking this minute about Kitty Cooney. Do you remember her? She married a farmer in County Cavan and had twins the first go off. I have made up my mind. I am going to live here in Ireland and enjoy it. These people are marvellous. They have a wonderful idiom. Just now the old woman, talking of the cuteness of the local kids, has said, 'They'd herd geese for you at a cross-road.' Isn't that wonderful? Oh, the people who leave Ireland have no sense, yourself included. Life is delightfully intimate in Ireland. I must ...

The old woman in the corner, finding that her lodger was not in the mood for talking rose painfully and assisted by her daughter and son-in-law made for bed. When her groaning had died away up the little stairs the silence of the night enveloped the kitchen. Sometimes when the music sank away she heard kids in the street rolling their iron hoops on the concrete. So as not to disturb the old woman she turned down the music until it became a delicate whisper in the air.

She wrote on:

I must tell you something. I have an overwhelming desire to lose myself in some grand passion. I believe that it will be music. Not just to hear it and listen to it. No, that wouldn't do. It wouldn't be enough. It wouldn't satisfy me. I want to play it myself. I want to lose myself in it. If I want to live outside a convent or an asylum

I must do this. I have nothing else to do that's DEVOURING enough but read and read and read. I am reading Balzac now. He fills me with a great desire to . . .'

The husband came in again and began to poke for something in one of the drawers of the kitchen-dresser.

'I thought I had a bit of rope there somewhere.'

She leaned back.

'You're writing?' he said over his shoulder.

'A note to a friend.'

The one drawback to these lodgings was that the little house had no parlour: the only place where she could be alone was her bedroom and that was tiny – there was not even room for a chair in it and she had to sit on the bed.

' 'Tis a great night outside, thank God,' and he rummaged away. 'The sky is a riddle of stars.'

'That's a good sign.'

'Mind you, there's a touch of autumn in the air. Where the divil did I put that yoke? There's a right frosty look in the stars.' He found the bit of rope and jammed back the drawer. As he went out he said, with a smirk, 'Don't forget to put in the kisses.'

' 'Tis to a girl,' she said bitterly, but he laughed unbelievingly as he latched the door.

She looked at her letter. 'Fills me with a great desire to . . .' She crossed it out roughly. She leaned to the back window, shading her eyes from the light of the room to look out. The sky was white with starlight.

The music danced on gently. She scribbled:

In another week I will be seeing the leaves wafting down silently and the mists lurking in the trees and floating like grey water in the hollows, a time I dread. How lovely it would be then to have a book-lined room of one's own, with a friend, and deep glasses of old red port, a spider-guarded ruby, and talk, and old songs and . . .

Her hand fished for cigarettes and failed to find them. She rose and dragged on her overcoat and went out and down the street towards the stream of light falling from the window of the paper-and-sweets shop. The stars were like snow. A horse and cart stood outside the shop, his breath enveloping his drooping head. As she left the shop and walked around the block the horse and cart were already rattling out of the village, carrying her mind to the white bog-roads radiating from it under the vast indifference of the night. In her circuit she met nobody.

Back in the kitchen the wife and husband were talking in low voices beside the dying fire, their usual nightly chat, the only time when they had the kitchen to themselves. She bade them goodnight, and sat on her bed, smoking and writing:

I'm afraid this letter is all blether, but if I don't blether I'll relax the reins. For the love of God send me something exciting to read. I have made a tremendous plan which is going to ruin my good looks and destroy my adipose. I'm going to get up every morning at seven and go to bed at twelve and have plenty of time for study and reading and thinking and living inside myself. I don't care if I get scraggy and withered with a thin wrinkled neck. It will give me the pleasure of being FREE, of being DIFFERENT to those other females who carefully do their best to preserve their youth and keep up their market value. I object to this and ALL OTHER TYRANNY.

Your friend,

Joan.

She directed the envelope and folded the letter into it. She threw the red cinder of her cigarette out the window, undressed, and climbed into the deep feather-bed. The pair downstairs stole upstairs. She heard them whispering next door. Far down the village street somebody's footsteps faintly grew out of the hum of the silence, became louder, passed metallically underneath the window and faded slowly away. With them she faded into the night and sleep.

About two months later as she lay in bed with a cold she opened the Balzac and found the letter inside it. November rain fell heavily and crookedly past her tiny window. She could hear it gurgling across the pavement from a rainspout, and she imagined it beating the ruffled lake, and the poplars swaying before it, and the woods of Cappagh dripping, and the little steely pools in every field and how all the roads out across the plain must be blank and bitter.

She tried to recall that lovely, burning September afternoon, but it came to her only in disconnected patches and she thought how, in a year's time, it would probably have vanished as completely as if it had never been lived.

'Why,' she wondered, looking at the crooked rain, 'do I remember these scraps? The drops were drying on the hot flagstone of the well. The spire was so dim against the sky that I barely saw it. The steam of the train evaporating.'

And she began to wonder whether there is any special meaning in what we remember, or is it all a mere chance whether we remember or forget. She looked about her and considered what she was likely to remember of that day, or would she remember anything at all except, perhaps, the crooked rain. Contemplating it where she lay curled up to the pillow she began to wonder what might be the significance of the crooked rain.

Vive la France!

It took Alec Forbes nearly twenty years to notice that his pals began to wink at one another whenever he began to talk about his travels. That was why he folded into his beard all the lovely words that started to burst inside him when he heard the French rugby team was coming to Cork – such as Le Havre, Ostende, Marseille, café-au-lait, cognac, monsieur, mam'selle, and à la bonne chance. Instead he let the clodhoppers around him blether away to their heart's content, while he winked into his glass.

But he made it his business to be at the railway station the night the team arrived. He knew there would be an address of welcome from the Mayor and the Aldermen and the Chamber of Commerce, and he knew that if there wasn't somebody present who knew the ropes they would make an unholy mess of the whole thing. He wore his best bowler hat, his best cravat, cuffs and butterfly collar, and his gold links that gleamed in the arclights. He had brushed and combed his mosaic beard a dozen times. He held his walking stick up on his shoulder like a gun. The reception committee scowled at him.

Sure enough, when the train roared in and the team hung out of the windows waving tricolours through the steam Alec began to run up and down the platform and wave his stick and shout, 'Vive la France!' and when the team fell out of the carriages like bags of apples he was right in the middle of them handshaking all round and shouting, 'Vive la France!, que'st que vous dee dong, millo quattro chinko quaranto. Cognac! Cognac!' – at which they all cheered and laughed and shook his hands and kissed one another and shouted, 'Vive l'Irlande!' and 'Cognac! Cognac! Cognac!'

'Gintlemin,' said the Mayor shouldering Alec to one side, to read his address of welcome.

'Messieurs, mesdames,' corrected Alec out of the side of his mouth. His face was glowing with happiness, his hat back on his poll, his stick on his shoulder like a gun.

'Gintlemin,' said the Mayor sternly. 'I have . . .'

'Blasht yeh,' says Alec, giving him a poke in the back, 'can't yeh say messieurs?' And to cover up he shouted, 'Vive la France!' and they all shouted, 'Vive l'Irlande!'

'Gintlemin,' cried the Mayor, 'I have the greatest honour . . .'

'Yerrah, for God's sake,' cried Alec, 'can't we cut out all this ould guff and go and have a drink somewhere? Listen to me, boys!' he shouted at the team, and waved his stick like a serpent and enveloped them with his arms, his voice, his beard. 'Come on and have a drink at the Railway Arms. Follow me every man Jack of ye. Comme ci, comme ça? Drinko? Oui, oui?'

'Gintlemin,' bellowed the Mayor glancing around wildly, 'I have the greatest honour to say to ye tonight . . .'

But Alec had managed to detach four of the team's followers and although three of them came back to hear out the Address of Welcome he succeeded in hauling one young fellow away with him, down the ramp and out of the station, gesticulating so passionately as he pointed onwards that the young man stopped resisting and decided with a shrug that his benevolent-looking guide was probably the town-pimp.

In the Railway Arms, across the tramlines, Alec said, 'Cognac?' and the young man said, 'Cognac.' They had to be satisfied with Irish whiskey. Alec said, 'Vive la France!' and the young man said, 'Vive la France!' Alec said, 'Toujours la politesse.' The young man, already a little bored, agreed philosophically, 'Toujours la politesse.' A deep silence followed. Alec drummed the Marseillaise with his fingers on the counter but he didn't feel equal to singing it. After a while the young man said, 'Cognac?' so they had some more Irish whiskey.

'You from Marseille?' asked Alec, shaping a whole continent with his hands and stabbing southward at the spittoon to indicate Marseille.

'Marseille?' asked the young man.

'Oui? Vous? Non? Oui? Yes? No?'

'Comprends pas.'

'Look,' said Alec.

He laid his bowler-hat on the marble counter. He stooped over it and like a magician he moulded fantastic air about it with his fingers.

'La France. Comprenez-vous?'

'La France,' agreed the young man, picking a dead fly from the rim of the hat.

'Bong,' said Alec. 'Now watch.'

He laid his walking-stick in front of the hat. Swiftly he spread his hands along the stick, east-west, as if he were drawing it out like a telescope.

'La Mediterranean Sea,' he cried, and gazed hopefully into the eyes of his guest, who at once picked up the stick and returned it with a smile and a bow.

'Votre baton.'

Alec put back the stick a little irritably. Once more he embraced the hat. The barmaid was now watching them both suspiciously. Once more he leaned towards the youth. Once again he indicated the hat.

'La France!' he cried. 'Your country. Comprends?'

The young man sighed as who should say, 'Do we have to do this all over again?' However, he nodded to indicate that he was prepared to agree, for the sake of argument, that this peculiar hat was France.

'Bong!' cried Alec.

Once more he laid out the stick. He placed his two palms in the middle of it. He stared fiercely at the youth. He extended his palms slowly and magnificently along the stick and gazing wrapt into the young man's eyes he intoned –

'La Mediterranean Sea!'

At this the youth began to examine Alec's countenance all over, very seriously and minutely. Finding no explanation there he looked at the barmaid who gazed at him with a half-witted expression. At this the young man looked pensively out the door as if contemplating immediate flight.

'No comprends?' implored Alec. 'Look!' he roared. 'La Mediterraneano! The Meditabloodywellranean Sea!'

'Vive l'Irlande!' said the young man and raised his glass.

Alec looked coldly at his guest. He tipped his beard. He put on his hat.

'Cognac?' he said listlessly.

'Cognac,' the young man agreed so they had some more Irish whiskey.

Now and again Alec stirred as if to speak but sank back each time frustrated. Then he gave the youth a slap on the back that nearly knocked him over the counter.

'Well, honest to God,' he assured the barmaid, 'I'm a proper ould gom and there's no harm to say it. The poor noddle,' he explained to his friend, 'is gone to hell. Off the rocker altogether. Listen! Sure I have two daughters at home that's learning French for the last three years until you think 'twould come out through their eyes. Look, boy, you come along with me. And anyway, what you want inside your belly band is a good bit of hot grub. That stuff you're drinking there is no damn good to you. Bilge-water! I have deux daughter. Two! Two filles!'

He held up two fingers. The young man demurred. He held up one finger.

'Two!' insisted Alec. 'Blast it, don't I know meself how many daughters I have!'

One finger. Two fingers. One. Two.

Alec led him aside. He ate aerial food. He carved it. He devoured his moustaches. He rubbed his stomach. He waved his hands. The young man gave it up and Alec marched him off arm in arm.

They boarded a little rattlebox of a tram in which they swayed and rocked away from the city's lights, between crumbling Georgian terraces, into the dusk. The yellow glow of the tram fell on the blue evening haze. Now and again it touched another yellow stream falling from the door of some little shop, and whenever that happened the young Frenchman would look back at the bright window and glance at Alec, talking fifteen to the dozen, and give a little sigh. They passed tiny terraces where only the fanlights were bright – the sort of houses where a sea-captain might live. High on the hills above were the lighted windows of big houses, and above these were the first stars which were not quite so bright.

'That's Montenotte,' said Alec, seeing his upward glance.

'Le Mont de Nuit? C'est charmant.'

'All the nobs of Cork live up there. That's if you want to call 'em nobs. I wouldn't. Johnny-jump-ups I call 'em. Thick in the head and strong in the back. In from the heath. If you take my advice you'll steer clear of them blokes while you're here. A lot of bloody yahoos – never went nowhere – never saw nothing. That's their ticket.'

The river opened before them, wide and sullen. Across this sullen water a noble avenue led its long linden line down and down to a darkening loch where a river-light winked fitfully. A steamer was chugging outward on the high tide, trailing its red and green mast-lights through the stars. Alec waved his stick across the river at the dusky avenue.

'That's the Marina. The next village down there is Tivoli.'

'La Marina? Tivoli? Mont de Nuit?' cried the youth. 'Mais ce n'est pas l'Irlande. C'est l'Italie!'

The tram disgorged them. They leaned on the quay-wall and looked after the diminishing steamer. From here the rumble of the city was faint and its maze of lights were as yellow as wine or candlelight. They suggested friendship, warmth, company. The young foreigner looked at these suggestive lights, looked at the feathery avenue over the river, looked at the little ship which was by now silent in the distance.

Alec suddenly threw one arm around his shoulder.

'Look, monsieur! I want to tell yeh something. Me. Sailor. I've been all over the world. Do you know what my address for forty years was? I'll tell yeh. "Alec Forbes, First Mate, Malta, Gibraltar, Port Said or elsewhere." That's me. Moi. Toujours. Everywhere. Marseille, Ostende, Le Havre, Genoa, up the Black Sea, down the Black Sea, Constanzia, Constantinople, Leghorn, every bloody place. But them blokes,' arm up to the dark hills, 'never saw nothing. Know nothing. Comprends? Ici? Toujours, ici!'

'Vous?' said the young man miserably.

'No, God blast it! Them! All of 'em. Every man Jack of 'em. Little Jackeens that never went farther than th' Isle o' Man for two weeks in the summer. Fellows that wouldn't know the difference between vin blank and vin rooge. They wouldn't even know how to *ask* for cognac! And they don't believe wan word that I tell 'em. Oh,' he groaned, 'will I ever forget the first time I drank cognac. Forty . . . what am I talking about? . . . 'tis forty-three years ago. In a place called Angers. Up the Rhône. Comprends? Were you ever there?'

'Angers? Mais oui. La Loire. Une petite ville ravissante.'

'The café was called "Le Roi René". I remember it as well as . . . And no wan believes me! Not even me own daughters believe me!'

The young man gazed at the yellow lights of the city and sighed deeply.

'Café,' he whispered. 'Le Roi René. Je m'en souviens. Je veux dire

Le Roi René,' he explained. 'Pas le café. Le duc d'Anjou. Sa fille, je crois, est devenue reine d'Angleterre?'

He looked gloomily into the water at the upturned belly of a drowned dog. He looked dejectedly at the stars. He looked at the pin-point of the lighthouse winking at him indifferently. Abruptly he laid his hand on Alec's hand and spoke to him at great length, with considerable feeling, even with passion. He shook him twice by the lapels. Then he gave him a long distasteful look and folding his arms on the quay-wall contemplated the upturned dog again. Behind them the old tram departed for town, crickety-crockety, taking its light with it, leaving them to the dark, the sucking water, the chill wind. They fell silent.

Alec also looked morosely at the drowned dog. Then he glanced across the road at the city's last pub – it is called 'The Cosmopolitan Bar' – and said, 'Cognac?' The young man agreed, so they went across the road and had some more Irish whiskey.

'Constanzia, now,' declared Alec, 'is a grand port!'

But he saw that his guest was rolling his whiskey around in his glass and paying no attention.

'Allons,' Alec sighed. 'C'm on home! Grub.'

In silence they marched across a little wooden railway-bridge up a steep hill, between the damp walls of an alley whose rare gaslamps flickered on the ivy that glistened beneath them. Far behind and beneath, to the turned head, the walls framed the little city's distended glow. They halted at a tiny lodge, an Elizabethan cottage, the rear entrance to the grounds of somebody's suburban mansion. There was a fluttering of trees overhead. There was a smell of damp laurels and woodsmoke.

The door of the cottage opened on a burst of light and an overheated kitchen. Two red-headed girls of about sixteen and seventeen looked up at them. Both were warm, puffy, negligent, and handsome. The elder and slimmer was standing over an ironing board in the strained pose of any girl ironing – the elbow bent, the knee crooked, one shoulder lifted. Her eyes made the young man think at once of green rock-pools. The younger one was curled in a battered basket-chair before the little stove, her red hair tumbled over her book. She had those gently voluptuous lips that rest perpetually apart like a little trumpet, as if she were always whispering, 'Goose, goose, goose.'

Alec waved introductions: 'That's Molly. This is Jenny. This is . . .' He looked at the youth.

He was staring around the little kitchen, at the girls, at Alec. A long, slow blush was mounting to his forehead. It retired swiftly as if a glass were emptying and he became quite pale.

'Je m'appelle Paul Demus.'

'We'll call yeh Paul.'

The young man bowed respectfully to the girls. They grinned so eagerly that he could guess no boy had so far done anything but chase them in the dark until they screamed, probably down that steep hill, under the gaslamps, their red hair flying.

'Sit down, Paul. Grub, girls! Prestissimo!'

The youth watched while they sat their father on the basket chair, unlaced his boots, brought his slippers, handed him his evening paper and his glasses. He gazed restlessly about him, and once he half-rose as if to go. But now they were talking to him in a macaroni of which he recognized one or two English words, bits of French, and a tongue which nobody ever told him was Irish. However, as they glanced at him, tossed back their curls, made him lay the table, passed him the jam or the pickles or refilled his cup, they also spoke a language which occurs in no dictionary but which he found entirely intelligible and which he soon began to speak just as volubly.

He showed them photographs from his wallet, of his mother, his two sisters, his friends in l'équipe. To explain the word he had to borrow their dictionary and that started a game which moved faster and faster as they became adept at flicking the pages and passing the book to and fro across the table.

'Regardez, mesdemoiselles.' He nicked a word. '*Oriflamme*.'

'Quoi?'

'Vos cheveux!' Tipping Jenny's hair.

'Oriflamme? Oh! Oh!'

'What are ye laughing about? What's that? What's he saying?'

'He says the weather is very close tonight, daddy.'

'Then why don't ye open the window?'

'Regardez, monsieur. Vous êtes un *rogue*.'

'Quoi? Coquin? Moi? Non, non! Regardez. *De tout mon cœur*.'

'What does that mean?' seizing the book. 'Oh! Oh! Regardez! *Heartless*.'

'Moi? *Sans cœur?* Non, non! Regardez. *Qui a le cœur navré, brisé, mort.*'

'What's all this about regardez? Is that window to his liking? What the divil are ye all up to?'

But the three paid no attention. They were leaning over the table in a jumble, laughing, pushing, hair tumbling. The girls pointed to the words:

'*Qui a le cœur libre!*'

He replied: '*Si le cœur vous en dit!*'

'Oh! Oh! Look! *Loin des yeux, loin de cœur.*'

'Oh! Mesdemoiselles!'

Alec laughed happily at their laughter, and returned to his paper.

The noise became louder. He shouted:

'Regardez yerself, Paul, is that window all right?'

At once, gleefully, Paul seized the book and nicked, '*Vue, elevation, perspective, scène,*' and for answer to his question Alec beheld Molly and Monsieur Paul go out into the porch with so much laughing that he demanded, 'What on earth is it all about, Jenny?'

'I think he just wants to see the view of the city,' Jenny explained demurely.

'Sure that's what the boy is at all the night with his regardez. Is that all the French ye have? I could have told ye that meself,' and he resumed his reading.

When Molly returned her hair was like heather on fire. Then Jenny showed him the view, and then Molly showed him the view again, and each time they took a little longer at it, and the next time Paul wanted to see the view Alec got up and declared that they did not know how to show him the view at all and went out with the three of them.

There the four of them stood in the dark, in a line, their arms about one another's shoulders, looking at the thousands of little lights, and the occasional lightning flash when, somewhere, a tram-trolley hopped the wire.

'Do you know what it is, Paul? It's a damn nice little city. It reminds me sometimes of the view over Marseille. Comprenez-vous, monsieur?'

The youth did not reply. It seemed at first that he was considering what Alec had said. Then he shook himself and cried abruptly, 'Faut que je file!'

'Go?' Jenny cried. 'Oh, no, no! Paul, not yet!'

And Molly wailed,

'Oh, but not yet?'

Alec cried,

'By no means! Not yet! You and I are going to have a long talk together. Parlez beaucoup. Vous, moi. Lots of things!'

He insisted. He was almost rude about it. They held him. He tore himself away. They gave in. The two girls went with him, down the dark alley, over the city, swinging out of his arms, gabbling about the nuns, and Mother O'Brien who had once been to France, and about the rugby-match, and when they got to the tramstop he refused to part with them unless they first came with him into the Cosmopolitan Bar.

There they sat in a corner and over hot whisky punch – it was their idea; they said they had it every Christmas – he explained to them at great length something which was evidently of great emotional importance to himself. To everything they nodded seriously and said, 'Oui', and 'Non', and kept making beseeching frowns at one another across the table, and lifting their eyebrows behind his back and shaking their heads, but when he finished and shook their hands over and over again and said, 'Vous comprenez maintenant?' they said, 'Parfaitement', and merely shrugged at one another like Frenchwomen.

He rose. They had to help him up, and all three were laughing as they shoved him into the tram. From the step he kissed them both, to the delight of the conductor and under the frowning eyes of a severe looking priest sitting inside. When the tram was jolting away their friend was deep in explanations to the priest who kept staring at him like an image.

All the way up the dark laneway they argued heatedly. Jenny said he was a Count. Molly said he was engaged to be married to a girl whom he did not love. But they did not quarrel over it and when their Da looked up at the two of them, standing side by side in the porch, the eyes that gazed down at him were starry and golden.

His were not, and seeing his melancholy look they drooped a little.

'Didn't he go off a bit early?' he complained. 'I thought we were getting on fine. I hope ye didn't say anything to offend him?'

Jenny hurled her green beret on to the sofa, and leaned her elbows on the windowsill and looked tragically over the diamonded city. Molly slowly lifted her tam-o'-shanter from her red mop, until it was like a chef's hat, and then sank slowly at his knees in a ball and softly said, wrapping her arms about his legs:

'Fa'rer. Why donsh yeh tell ush shomethin' about Marsheille?'

Alec started up, glared at the two of them over his specs and opened his mouth to say something. Just then, far below on the river, a ship, sailing outward on the tide, hooted softly. He leaned back.

'Marseille?' he murmured.

He looked into the fire. Smiling, he began to stroke his moustaches and his beard. What was he remembering?

The Woman Who Married Clark Gable

She should have lived in Moscow. If she had been a Russian she would have said: 'O God, life is passing and I have yet to live. All last Easter when the baby clouds were passing over the birch-woods, and the streams were whispering of the coming of summer, and the bells were dancing and singing in the monastery towers, I sat at home and drank vodka and longed for love. I do not know whether life is angry with me because I do not live it, or whether I am angry with life because it will not let me live. Ivan Ivanovitch, for God's sake, meet me tonight by the frog-pond and tell me what is this pain in my heart.' And Ivan would have met her and told her in very simple terms. Instead of that she lived in Dublin (South Circular Road, small red house, red terrace, small garden, near the Old Woman's Hostel – full – and Kilmainham Jail – disused). She nagged her husband virtuously when she should have got drunk with him and poured her virtue down the drains. She went twice a week to the movies, hoovered the house until she had all the pile sucked off the carpets, bought a new knick-knack for the mantelpiece every week, washed the dog, polished the windows, slept after lunch, read *Chit Chat* and *Winifred's Weekly*, went for a walk, and then sat around waiting for her husband to come back from the job.

Every night the conversation was the same.

'Had a hard day, darling?' – from her.

'Not so bad, dearie' – from him.

'What did you have for lunch?'

'A very nice lunch. Pork chop, spinach, chips, rhubarb pie, coffee. Very tasty.'

'I washed Herbie. Look at him. It was an awful job. But he is a pet. Aren't you, Herbie?'

'Nice old 'Erbie. Like your bathie. Soapy-soapy? Not tired, dearie?'

And she would always say she was, very tired, or that she had a stitch in her side, or a pain in her head, and she would put on a miserable face, and he would tell her she ought not to do it, not really, and she would tilt her eyebrows and ask sadly for the evening paper. He would suggest a stroll, or a movie, or have a pipe, or tell her a dirty story, and so to bed, and *da capo* the next day and the next. Before she got into bed she would always say the Rosary, and then she would curl up next to him and wait for him to snore. She liked him; he was an honourable, hardworking, straightforward, generous man; but she did not love him. It must be added that they had no children and she worried about that. It must also be understood that he was a Methodist and went regularly to the tin chapel along the road, and she worried about that too. She was always praying that he might be converted: that was why she said the Rosary every night, though she never told him that. He was English and was rather stubborn about religious matters.

One morning as she kissed him goodbye at the gate of her little garden she drew back hastily and peered at him.

'Darling, you haven't shaved?'

He grinned fatuously, lifted his bowler-hat, said: 'I'm growing a moustache,' and ran. For weeks after that their nightly conversation had an extra five lines:

'I don't like that moustache, darling.'

'It's coming on. Chaps at the works rag me a lot abaht it. But I don't mind. Jealous, I say.'

'But it tickles, darling.'

'Aain't that nice, dearie?'

One night they went to the movies to see *San Francisco,* with Jeanette MacDonald and Clark Gable. This picture dealt with a rake and a good man and a singing heroine, friends in spite of everything, even the singing and the fact that the good man (Spencer Tracy) was a priest. The rake had a squabble with the priest, and although the priest – he was a Boxing Padre – could have knocked him on the canvas for twenty he merely wiped the blood off the corner of his mouth and looked sadly at the rake. In the end there is an earthquake and the earth opens and all sorts of things fall down into holes and the rake kneels down and is converted. They show Mr Gable's boot soles because nobody looking at his face would believe it. Then they all join hands and march down the hill into the camera and the closing, gauzy iridescent curtains of the cinema, singing the theme-song, 'Sa-a-n Francisco, Open your pearly gates . . .' (etc.), and everybody goes home happy.

She walked home that night in a dreamy silence. She heard none of his remarks about the picture, and when they were back home she kept looking at him in a strange, distant way. She went restlessly in and out of the parlour, threw guilty sidelong glances at him, did not seem to want to go to bed, hardly said a word in answer to his chatter, forgot to pray for his conversion, and lay awake for hours looking out at the tops of the London plane waving faintly against the dull upthrown glow of the city.

She went to the same cinema, alone, the next day; and that night she made him take her to it again; which he was pleased to do because he wanted to know how they got all those things to fall into holes in the ground. All through the picture she held his hand and stole sideward glances at the black line of his Gablesque moustache. That night she put on her pink chiffon nightgown – the one she bought the time she thought she was going to have a baby and only had a miss; and she had worn it again the time she had her gallstones out; and the time she had the appendix; and the time she went to the nursing home when she tumbled down stairs. She put scent behind her ears and looking at herself in the mirror said,

'Darling, did I ever tell you I had rather a good voice when I was . . . I mean before I married you?' And she swayed and began to hum, 'San Francisco, Open your pearly gates!'

'It sounds like hydraulic pressure,' he ruminated. 'You know, like a lift going down.'

When she lay beside him she looked at his profile and whispered.

'Darling, supposing this was San Francisco. You and me? And the earth begins to shake?'

'Lummy,' he cried. 'Like this?' And he began to bounce up and down on the springs.

She gave a frightened scream.

'Why, dearie, what's wrong?'

'You're so rough,' she said adoringly.

'My poor little upsydaisy, isum frightened?'

She put out the light.

For about two weeks they were happier than at any time since their honeymoon, in that little redbrick house on the South Circular Road. She bought a record of *Open your pearly gates*. She asked him questions about earthquakes and he began to read them up. One Saturday she heard the film was at Bray and, under pretence of a day's outing by the sea, made him take her to it again. This he found a bit boring, but being a kind-hearted chap he humoured her. When it moved on up to Malahide and she wanted to follow it he demurred. To his surprise she crumbled at once and said that if he hit her she wouldn't blame him, and that she probably deserved it. He did no more than tease her when he found a picture of Mr Gable garbed for the boxing-ring pinned up in their parlour the next day. But he did begin to get a bit worried when she bought him a cravat, an old-time three-cornered collar, asked him to take up boxing-lessons, and wanted him to meet her priest and become great friends with him. He drew the line at the priest and the boxing but he did wear the cravat and the collar in which he looked like a horse in demi-harness.

She noticed the worried look on his face the first morning he wore this contraption and decided that he was unhappy because he guessed that she was deceiving him with Mr Gable. She went off to consult her priest.

He heard her problem in complete silence and then said, 'It's a very fine point, I think you'd better give me a week to think it over.' So at the end of the week she went again, this time in a black veil, and he explained to her that the chief end of marriage is, of course, the bearing of children and that what we call Love is, naturally, secondary to this great end. And after all, he said, what *is* Love? Indeed, what are all those curious human manifestations which lead to the great end (which he had already defined)? To a mere celibate these things were all very strange. But then, he added quickly, who are we, anyway, to question the devices of Providence which, indeed, as we may see, are frequently not merely puzzling but baffling? At all events, he hurried on, be that as it might, it appeared to him that, theologically speaking, and always provided that she kept that great end in view, and had no other end in view at any time – he stressed the words *at any time* – there could be no objection to her deciding that she was living with this Mr Mark Cable. Indeed, he added testily, for the matter had caused him a great deal of worry, and caused him to read a great many dull Latin volumes, she could (always provided she kept that great end in view) go on believing that she was living with her grandfather; and he dismissed her abruptly. She left him, a little hurt by the reference to her grandfather, but more content with the propriety of her behaviour than she had ever been since her wedding night.

Her joy was brief. It was on her way home that she purchased the film-magazine which reported, with a large portrait of Mr Clark Gable, that there were rumours flying about New York to the effect that 'our Clark' had lately been seen in gay places in the company of a well-known oil millionairess.

That night she saw at once that her George was giving her worried looks; as well he might since she kept looking at him in a very peculiar fashion.

'Tired, dearie?' he asked.

'A fat lot you care,' she cried tragically.

'But I do care, dearie!'

'You,' she charged with passion, 'care nothing whatsoever for me. What did you have for lunch today?'

'Why,' he mumbled, a bit taken aback by this divergence, 'I 'ad a spot of steak-and-kidney, rhubarb and cuss, black coffee, all very tasty too.'

At this she laughed scornfully.

'Alone?' she challenged.

'Wotcher mean, alone?'

'Were – you – alone?'

'Well, not quite alone. A couple of the chaps as usual.'

'Chaps!'

She uttered what she considered to be a strangled cry, gave a broken sob, ended up with a groan of despair and made a fair shot at hurling herself from the room. He, staring at the dog wagging its tail hopefully, began to examine his conscience; and as any man can always find some little thing somewhere in his conscience, even if it is only a pinched bottom, he played a good deal at finger-under-the-collar before he went up to bed. She did not speak one word to him. Once he asked her if she had a cold, because she was sobbing into her pillow; at which she moaned as if her poor little heart would break, causing him to beg her to tell him if she had a toothache. His patience gave out when she refused to get up and cook his breakfast, for an Englishman will stand much but he will not stand for a breakfast of cold milk and dog-biscuits. He drank neat whisky at lunch and he drank neat whisky (several times) on his way home in the evening, and he tore off his horse-collar and dropped it into the canal, and he had a haircut and shave, and he even had the barber shave off his moustache, and when he squeaked open the garden gate he was full of fight.

She was not. She had bought another film-magazine that afternoon which scornfully denied the story about Mr Clark Gable and the millionairess; said that Mr Gable was very cross about it, in fact. In a high state of nerves she awaited his return and she was trembling when she opened the hall-door. She gave one look at the bald face and collarless neck before her, realized simultaneously that she was being confronted by her husband and had been abandoned by Mr Gable, and the next thing she did was to sink in a faint on the mat and give her poll a terrific wallop off the lino.

It took poor George an hour to bring her around and calm her down, and by that time all the fight had gone out of him. Besides he was too relieved to find that she was her old self again – moaning and groaning at him to his heart's content. When she wanted the evening paper she asked for it (to his great joy) quite snappishly. When, as the night was near ending, he ventured to tell her a dirty story and she laughed loudly and then put on a shocked face and said he ought to be ashamed of himself, he almost winked.

They lived unhappily ever after in complete marital satisfaction.

Lady Lucifer

The three friends had rowed very slowly down-river – half-floated, indeed – seeing only the withered thistles in the fields, cows standing to their ankles in still water. There was not a speck in the sky. Not even a bird; as if they had taken shelter from the humming heat in the pine-forest that rose on one side, dark and cool as a cave. The only sound they heard for a mile was the fall of water in the canal-lock; and when they passed through the lock and were lazily poling along the slim perspective of the canal, everything was again sloth and softness and sun. The narrow road of canal was a dreaming slip of water. They were secluded, lost, tucked-away. The world had died.

The doctor was poling. He wore brief cream bathing-trunks: a finely-built, sandy-haired man, serious but not severe. He had studied in Vienna, New York, and London; he was a specialist in mental diseases; he was just back from six years with the British Army in the East; he bore himself with the authority of experience and power. In the stern the priest lay like Velasquez's picture of 'old Silenus lolling in the sunshine', his bare paunch, immensely pink, spilling over his black trousers. On his brow a garland of purple loose-strife lay crookedly. Malachy, the bank-clerk, was stretched jammed in the prow, both hands in the water, head back, eyes closed, gob-open to the sun. It was he who had said that the priest was like old Silenus. To demonstrate, he had torn the garland from the luxuriance of wild-flowers along the edges of the canal. As they rocked gently along, these two jungles of river-plants undulated faintly – balsam, golden flags, willow-herbs, coltsfoot, purple loose-strife: their delicate pungency scented the warm air. Nobody spoke.

Presently the canal rejoined the river. Here it was wide and smooth. Its width was broken by so many eyots into a network of bayous that there was no main channel and the river could barely stir. In front they saw a toy lock-house perched beside a tiny hump-backed bridge; that, and the much-tarred warehouse nearby, meant that another shallows lay ahead and another canal to by-pass it. They moored by one of the smallest eyots, winding the chain around a clump of flags. When they had clambered ashore they found themselves in a plum-orchard and idly they plucked the fruit. A trout leaped with a splash that startled them. The three lay beside a haycock, facing the barely-moving river, and ate the plums. Malachy looked sideways at the lock-house.

'If somebody gave me that house and a job as lock-keeper I'd be happy for ever after.'

The clerk was only a bank-clerk by avocation: his inward life was in his writing; he wrote novels and stories, over the name of Malachy Lucas. The priest agreed with him, rolling over heavily on his belly, pulling a strand of hay to smell it, murmuring, 'Yes – away from everything.'

It is a lost corner, barely coming to life, some dim noise half-heard through sleep, a moth on a window-pane at morning, an occasional barge slowly dud-dudding along the river, disturbing the coots and the wild-flowers with its arrowy wake. The very air of this deep valley seems too heavy to move. Even then a little cloud lay on the tip of the far line of mountains, too exhausted to persist. The doctor threw a plum-stone into the water. A heron rose from the island and flapped away in bored sloth into the woods.

'You'd have to live on your innards. There's nobody to talk to for miles around. I know I couldn't do it. It's a pipe-dream. And think of the winter nights.'

'I can see it at night with my fire and my lamp lighting and not a sound but the rain pocking the canal. A barge nosing the water like an otter. Like an otter. Greasily. Almost silently.'

'It's a pipe-dream. The river rises six feet in winter and turns this place into a lake. You'd go crackers.'

The priest was fingering the hay under his nose.

'There's nothing like the smell of new-mown hay.'

The doctor glanced downwards sharply and said, 'Hm,' in a voice that made them look at him. He laid down the plums and leaned back into the haycock.

'Lucas, you're not much over thirty. Isn't it a bit early to want to renounce the world?'

The priest grinned.

'I renounced the world at twenty-four.'

'I want to write – to work.'

'You could work in the city.' His voice had sharpened a little.

'I do work in the city. I work to exist. I don't want to exist. I want to write.'

The doctor grinned at him and began to bait him, at first amiably.

'Robinson Crusoe! The commonest Irish complex. Hermitage. People wanting all the time to leave the world and live in a convent or a monastery or in a little village at a little job. Sanctuary.'

The priest looked up.

'What about all our emigrants?'

'They're mostly country-people. Peasants don't have complexes. They have the natural, healthy, human urge to seek their fortune. You must have noticed that most folk-tales, things made-up by peasants, are all about men who travel the world to seek their fortune. But I agree you get both types. We Irish are always either the one or t'other. Our saints were all either hermits or adventurers. The sane ones travelled and kicked up holy murder. The daft ones stayed at home and went into the woods and wrote poetry. Take care, Lucas.'

Malachy laughed.

'You are one of the sane ones who travelled and kicked up holy murder?'

'No wonder you fellows write such sleepy books. Why don't you give us books like Balzac, full of guts and vigour?'

Malachy demurred, and mentioned Liam O'Flaherty.

'Now there's a very interesting case. All his characters are slightly mental. He describes the fellows who stay at home and go around the bend. All your stories,' and his voice was not amiable now, 'are about little spurts of passion. Faint gestures. You should call your next book *Faint Gestures*.'

The priest tried to come to the assistance of the clerk who was now blushing with chagrin.

'After all, nothing much happens in Ireland?' He held up the fistful of hay to be smelled. 'Isn't it gorgeous'

The doctor slapped it down irritably. It was plain that something had broken the calm peace of his day.

'I'm sorry, Father,' he apologized instantly. 'You reminded me of somebody.' He jumped up. 'What about a swim?'

Racing down the bank he hurled himself with a great splash into the pool and struck powerfully for mid-river.

'What's biting him?' asked the clerk.

The priest lumbered up and grunted. He dragged off his trousers and tumbled with a crash into the water. The clerk followed diving cleanly. The whole place was suddenly noisy. The sky from water-level was a desert. The tiny cloud had laboured up the sky, dragging a veil after it, too diaphanous to screen the sun. The treetops of the forest seemed to be watching them. A woman at the door of the lock-house. A blue vein of smoke from the chimney.

When the three were drying themselves and feeling the after-water heat the doctor stopped rubbing and looked affectionately at the water. 'I've been dreaming of that swim for five years. In the heart of the jungle I'd think about it. I'll swim in the Barrow, I used to say. Down at the Clashganny Lock, I used to say.' He threw down his towel in sudden annoyance. 'Damn it, why didn't we bring tea? And after it, I used to say, I'll have some damn good Irish tea. I wonder would that lock-house woman give us tea? I'm going to ask her.'

In his flannels and white shirt he strode off across the lock-gate and over the humpty-dumpty bridge, a fine soldierly figure. In five minutes he was back.

'That's all right. She'll do it. By the way, Lucas, you wouldn't really like it there. It's dark and poky.'

The three, glowing and cool, strolled into the lock-house.

The plain, low-ceilinged kitchen was so dim that the usual red lamp before the usual oleograph of the Sacred Heart was a brilliant eye of scarlet. It was cool after the great heat outside. A gun and fishing-rod hung over the mantelpiece; thighboots broken-necked in a corner; a scythe behind the door; over a pannier of plums wasps rose and sank and folded their wide wings to glut. The young woman was friendly, but shy.

'She should get her teeth attended to,' murmured the doctor. 'And what do you do,' he said to her, 'when the floods come?'

He spoke to her in a loud commanding voice as if to wake her up and dominate her.

'Ah, sir, we have to live upstairs.'

'And how do you get out for food and so on?' he shouted.

'We have a boat, sir. We moor it in the garden.'

The doctor smiled in the direction of the clerk.

'Still,' the clerk protested, 'I'm sure they could do something about it. A flood-wall or something.'

'I expect they could, really. Anyway it would be a lovely place for three months of the summer.' He was plainly trying to make up to the clerk for his earlier rudeness. 'But,' he shouted, 'wouldn't you rather live in the town?'

'I dunno, sir.'

He started to carve the bread in disgust, muttering, 'My God, look at that lump of butter. I haven't seen so much butter together for five years. Well, well, perhaps there's something to be said for being a Crusoe after all.'

The priest poured the tea: it was as black as his sleeve. As they ate they heard the muted dud-dudding of a barge and the young woman went out to attend to the gates.

'Travellers visit the desert island,' laughed the priest.

'Pirates,' said the doctor. 'Bold seafaring men.'

'She should come back leading Man Friday?' laughed the clerk.

They were all happy again.

Through the tiny window they saw the barge nose into the lock. One of the crew leaned his back against the beam of the gate and slowly slewed it against the flood. Another, at the other end, worked the winch. It took a long time. Slowly the stovepipe began to sink below the level of the lock-wall.

'How nice to think,' mused the clerk, elbows on the table as he sipped his tea, 'that they've been doing that for a hundred and fifty years. No wonder life gets into a little rut.'

'Aye, to be sure!' the priest agreed contentedly, lighting his pipe. 'Everything here is old. Old and traditional. That turf-fire. The fishing-rod. The scythe. They don't need much to live. A bit of turf, a couple of fish, a wild duck, a bite of hay for the cow. It's an attractive sort of existence, Doc. And isn't it better anyway than a slum in Dublin?'

'I'm not saying that everybody should leave the country and go into the city. That would be absurd. What I'm talking about is people deliberately trying to bury themselves away somewhere.

Lucas here imagines he'd like it. You really wouldn't, you know. Anybody like you with ambition has to live a full life. Anybody with a bit of pride in him. You'd run out of it in a month.'

'Pride,' smiled the priest, 'can be a dangerous thing. It is one of the Seven Deadly Sins.'

'I have to disagree,' said the doctor stiffly.

'I mean, of course,' the priest leaned forward earnestly, 'pride of intellect.'

It was the first time during the whole day that he had stirred himself.

'I still disagree. There isn't enough pride of any sort in this country. There's too much damned humility.'

'Listen to me, now.' The discussion had suddenly become serious. 'I worked for seven years on the English mission. In Liverpool. You're a doctor, I'm a priest, and between us I suppose we could list every known sort of human horror. I saw them all. I came to the conclusion that there are only two mortal sins in this world, the inordinate love of money and pride of intellect. Pride, Covetousness, Lust, Gluttony, Envy, Sloth . . . You notice that they're the first two in the list.'

'And I still disagree. I'll tell you why. Pride and humility aren't opposites. They're two sides of the same thing. I've seen it over and over again. If a man is born proud he must feed his pride. It was something given to him. Once he starts the humility tack he's lost. Lost and damned. Drowned in the opposite of his own pride. Show me your humble man and I'll show you the pride coiled up in his humility devouring it like a worm. Show me your proud man and I'll show you the humility flowering beneath his pride like a crocus under the snow.'

'You are almost suggesting,' cried the clerk, 'that there is no such thing as humility!'

'Nor is there!' said the doctor with arrogant certainty. 'All our emotions are a tension of opposites. It depends from hour to hour which way the balance swings.'

'I do not follow you,' sighed the priest, as if he were suddenly depressed by the feeling that he was talking to an unbeliever. 'Or do you say that even in the saints there was nothing but a random balance of opposites?'

'The most that any man can achieve.'

'Are you saying,' asked the priest, glowering a little under his eyebrows, 'that Christ was not humble?'

'If Christ was a god who came on earth to show men how to live then that was a mortal man who must have suffered everything that we suffer, all the temptations and allurements of the world, a man who had the same pride and passion that we have, who may have sinned as we sin....'

The priest waved his hand in angry dissent.

'Then,' cried the doctor, 'where was the example? If Christ could not sin....'

'Christ as man could sin but, being also God, he did not. God cannot contradict Himself. It is the only thing which He cannot do.'

The doctor shrugged.

'I cannot follow you into these realms. It seems to me that you destroy the simplicity of the Gospel story with metaphysical explanations – and the value of it!'

He fell silent. He took one of the clerk's cigarettes. They could hear the laughter of the woman as she flirted with the bargemen. The wasps hummed over the plums.

'Father! I was rude to you a moment ago. There on the island.'

'Yerrah, what nonsense. Forget it.'

'You reminded me of somebody. A woman I used to know about twenty years ago. I'll tell you about her. It was the new-mown hay reminded me. She was a nurse in the Asylum at M——, the first post I took the summer I returned from Vienna. She was a beautiful girl. Tall as a spear. Dark as night. Her two eyes were two brown jewels set under her forehead. She was one of the most beautiful girls I have ever known.'

He looked at the ash of his cigarette which glowed in the dim kitchen.

'That place was a little village. The Asylum itself was as big as the village, out on the edge of the filthy little place, beyond the doctor's house, beyond the cross-roads, out where the country began at the end of our wall, where the footpath stopped. I won't tell you her name but I'll tell you what they called her in the Asylum. Lady Lucifer. They had names for everybody, always satirical. They never dared call it to her face, but they were cute enough to have their mean little joke just the same. They shortened the nickname to Lucy, then they lengthened it again to Lucy Lockit, then they lopped it again to Lockit, and they called her that to her face. As nurses in these places are practically warders it wasn't a bad name. But the real humour of it, for them, was that she never knew that the other nickname lay behind it. You know, Lucas, I imagine all hermits have bitter jokes like that?

'The first time I saw her she was up in the female recreation-field, behind the buildings, overlooking the whole level country, its woods and demesnes and its white winding roads. The staff called that place Khartoum, another of their jokes.'

'Khartoum?' from the priest.

'You remember? After the British Government refused to relieve it, the Mahdi took it and sacked it? The desert city where Gordon died. She was standing up there, in her nurse's uniform, the billowing apron, the coif flowing about her head in the breeze, the white expanse of bosom, the skirt blowing between her thighs. She was like a goddess dressed in a wave. She was talking to her best friend – I think before I came he was her only friend – a male nurse named Davidson, Larry Davidson, a gentle drooping fellow with a girlish complexion. They met up there because they were protected from all interference by the patients.

'I know what they talked about because after a while I used to join them. I used to enjoy their talk because it was a kind of talk that nobody else in the institution ever talked. It was an extraordinary mixture of mysticism and ambition. They had stock-phrases, mostly hers, like – "Man must conquer the tyranny of material things; The humility of the spirit is the All Powerful; We must turn emotion into spirit before we can get peace"; and tags like "The wide-open spaces; Do or die; Venture and win".

'They were always adding new phrases to the list. One day I heard her fit the theory of evolution into her own gospel by maintaining that "the most highly evolved creatures are the world's outcasts, because they alone have defeated the material world." As she said it she got up – she was a very effective nurse – to quieten, very tenderly, very kindly – she was most kind – an old woman who was striding up and down the gravel with her white hair streaming behind her crying, "The cake is baking, the cake is baking." She came back to us with, "That poor woman sacrificed herself to her family as Christ sacrificed his life for us."

'I thought I would challenge her that day. I said, "What about

Long Bow?" Long Bow was the worst maniac in the place, a poor wretch who had G.P.I.'

'What is that?' from the clerk.

'Not nice. General paralysis of the insane. Its symptoms are usually delusions of grandeur. Of course lots of people have a *folie de grandeur* without being in the least insane. In fact,' he laughed, 'I think I have a touch of it myself! but it is a symptom of disease if it is part of a general condition: they think they are millionaires, or that they have titles, and so on. This poor devil was homicidal. He had been brought into the place in coils of rope. She didn't burk at my question. "Nobody knows," she said, "what evil that man inherited or what good he may have done in the world. It will never be known until the Last Day, when all our secrets are exposed, what his drop of goodness may have done in the whole stream of life. Just as the smile of a child might alter the life of a king and change the history of an empire."

'I remember I laughed, but Davidson took fire from her, as he always did, and supported her excitedly: they could always agree on any idea that derided the meaning of worldly success and exalted what Dostoievsky calls "the insulted and injured". One of the reasons she liked Davidson, for example, was the way he squandered his salary like grain the first day he got it, and was a pauper for the rest of the month, which was very different to the way the rest of them hoarded up their shillings, cautiously, like all peasants.'

'Is this a parable of humility?' smiled the priest.

The doctor ignored the question.

'Mind you, that wasn't the end of their talk. They always ended by switching over to some plan or other for getting away from that sleepy plain, whose roads were always empty, where you never heard anything but the hum of a mowing-machine or the gabble of hens. They said they wanted to conquer their lower nature by facing the hardships of the world. She certainly did. I always felt it was only a matter of months before she would hand in her resignation.

'Well! We were chatting like that one July day – I remember they were just beginning to cut the hay in the grounds – when we saw a well-dressed stranger come in the iron gate at the far end of Khartoum. Davidson went off to meet him.

' "I seem to know that man," she said, and we watched him shake hands with Davidson and slap him on the back and laugh so loud that all the patients stopped their gabble for a moment. Davidson pointed up in our direction and the man came striding up. By his clothes I thought that he was a returned American. "Why," she cried, "it's Jim Motherway. He was a nurse here six years ago." She ran to meet him. "Jim, where the divil have you come from?" He took both her hands and he stood back to approve her. He paid no attention to me. "Straight from 'Frisco. All around and back again. Shanghai, Bombay, Capetown. By Gosh! You're lookin' marvellous, Lockit!" "And you look as if you've been seeing life?" she said enviously. "I've seen it raw," he laughed, "and I've seen it cooked. And you're still stuck in the same old job? Gee, nothing's changed here. Not a blooming thing. No more than if I'd walked out of this place yesterday morning."

'I left them.

'From that day our talks in Khartoum stopped. Every free day she had after that a grand glittering Packard would come hooting up the avenue, triumphant as a cock-crow. She'd run down the steps, her long legs taking them three at a time, and jump into the car and be whirled off, and she wouldn't come back until the last second before the front gates clanged for the night. Several times I saw the headlights pick out Davidson in the lodge-porch – he'd be keeping old Michael the porter in talk in order to give her a last few minutes.'

The barge began to chug heavily out of the lock into the smooth river: they could see it moor by the wooden warehouse on the tiny quay. The crew began to unload barrels of porter for some inland pub. They did it as leisurely as if they had the whole day before them.

'What sort of a chap was this Motherway?' asked the priest.

'He was a powerful looking fellow. He was a Gaelic-speaker, a Kerryman: the adventurous type. But he had waited just a little *too* long before starting on his travels – he was already grey, about fifty. I went with Davidson several times to chat with him – in the village local – it was for Davidson's sake, really, because I hated to see the poor devil hiding away in corners, pretending not to see the winks and smirks all around him. We used to sit in the little front parlour and all the time Davidson would keep drawing him out and drawing him out, as if he was trying to find the secret of this fellow's success. It was pathetic.

'One morning I remember Davidson asking him about Africa, in his soft, drooly voice.

' "And what part of Africa were you in, now, Jim?"

' "Everywhere. All over the place. Jo'burg, Capetown, Durban. I've been up in the interior. But it's no place for a white man, I tell you. There's places in Africa that'd remind you of the end of the world. God, I'll never forget one time I went up to a place called Beira. That's Portuguese East Africa. A fellow I met was trying to interest me in a proposition he had up there. The dregs of India, the dregs of Egypt, the dregs of East Africa meet there. I went on the worst skite I ever went on in all my born days in that hell-hole. Do you know, Doc, what finished that skite? Funk. Sheer funk. I went into a joint one morning for a drink and I started to hang my hat on the wall. The wall was grey. That whole wall came out to meet me. It bulged! It bulged! It bulged with beetles, that's what made it grey. I went out on the seashore with a bottle of brandy. The shore was scarlet. What made it scarlet? Crabs, millions and millions of them. They call them soldier-crabs out there. I took off my hat to wipe the sweat off my forehead and honest to the Lord on high that shore stirred. It stirred, Larry. No, you needn't laugh, it wasn't the drink. Every bleeding crab on that shore took a pace to the right and a pace to the left. I ran for my life. I didn't wait to finish my business. God, will I ever forget it? I can see it now...."

'And by the terror in his eyes I knew he was speaking the truth. Davidson asked him then, very gently, "And how did you get out of that wild place, now, Jim?"

' "How did I get out of it? Ho, that's a story. No train for three days. No boat for a week. I found a couple of half-breeds from Madagascar with a sort of a sailing-boat down at the harbour. Take me up to Aden. Take me down to Durban. Take me to India! Take me anywhere! I offered them ten quid. No! Twenty quid? No! Thirty quid? No! I bought the bloody boat off them and I sailed it myself. It's hanging off a rotting rope somewhere in the docks of Durban this minute. What a voyage! What a voyage!"

'That morning I had to drag Davidson away. I was becoming frightened at the look in his face, all knotted up, and a stare in his eyes like a fellow that's going to die. Damn it, I've cursed myself a hundred times since for being so stupid about it, but it was that queer look on his face that deceived me. I was concentrating on it. Even the other nurses noticed it and mentioned it to me, and anyway a child could have noticed his changing mood.

'He used to have that queer stare when the Packard would come squeaking on the gravel in the morning and she stood laughing on top of the steps and raised her wrist in greeting to Motherway. And when the car whirled, and she waved to us over the back of it, all Davidson would do was take the pipe out of his mouth and tilt it slowly at her. His eyes never lost their fixed stare as they followed the car. As he waited for that car to come back every night he still held that stare. He gave her the same slight greeting with the pipe, as if he had never stirred since morning. "There'll be trouble, yet," the staff began to say, and they stopped mocking Davidson. Afterwards, of course, they said, "Why didn't he speak up? Why didn't he say something and not keep it bottled up inside him?" '

The doctor fell silent for a moment.

Through the window a pale warm evening light had begun to stream into the kitchen from the west. The woods outside had become darker and the river seemed more calm and glassy. The noises of the barrels made little hollow echoes.

'Then, one weekend, she went with Motherway to Killarney. When she came back I was the first person she told what happened. She came into my office and she sat down before my desk, and she pretended she was asking my advice.'

Again the doctor fell silent.

'The two of them had climbed up a headland over the lakes just as the sun was going down. A bad hour. The time of the evening when – Ah, I've often seen it in the East! – there's a sort of toneless residue of the daylight that breaks your heart with the loneliness. "We were sitting there, Doc, with all the lakes spread out for miles and miles below us. It got cold and he spread his coat over my shoulders. There was a stream behind us and all of a sudden it got so loud that we looked back at it, and when we looked at the lakes again I thought somebody had switched out a light. Jim kept looking and looking but he didn't seem to be paying any heed to anything, and then he began to hum a song to himself. It was in Irish. Then he stopped. Doctor," says she, "and I wouldn't tell a soul but you. He began to cry. He said he'd wandered all over the world and he hadn't a friend and he had no home. You see, Doctor, he's only a kid under it all. He was afraid of the night coming on. Just as if he was a kid. And when he put his two arms around me I had to comfort him, Doctor. I couldn't help it. I couldn't refuse him, now could I? Did I do right, Doctor? Tell me I did right. We're to be married next week."

'She was trembling like a racehorse. But she was the racehorse breed. You don't get many like her. I don't remember what I said to her. All I know is I got her back to her quarters, but I can still see a bloody big red star rising in front of us, and the mist over the plain, and I can smell the smell of the new-mown hay, and I can still feel the feel of the ring on her finger when I shook hands with her.

'That was the worst night I ever spent in that Asylum. Whether it was the heat of July that upset the patients, or whether it was that she had set up some sort of restlessness among the staff, I could feel the whole Madhouse raising its bristles. At supper-time the main dining-room was like a nest of wasps. Two of the good patients, as we called them, had to be dragged out, and when their heels squeaked along the parquet that great hall jibbered like the bloody jungle when a moon rises late to waken the animals. Down in the west wing Long Bow was screaming with laughter. I could hear him out in the grounds when I went out for a smoke to keep my own nerves quiet. The moon was full. It made the sky look tiny. And that blanket of mist on the valley. And that sweet smell of the new-mown hay.

'That night we saw nothing of Motherway, but about ten o'clock Davidson came in to me to report for night-duty and he told me he was down in the village standing champagne all round. I stayed up late visiting the wards waiting for the place to quieten down. About midnight somebody came in to tell me that Motherway was sitting outside on the front steps, and they thought he had taken too much liquor. I went out to send him home, he had no business being there, and there he was, singing quietly to himself, in Irish. And sitting beside him was Davidson. They were like two old friends enjoying the night, and the smells, and the whole plain bright before them. I could see he was drunk so I sat down on the other side of him.

The three of us began to smoke. Nobody was saying a thing. After a while he said,

' "You know I'm taking her away, Doctor?"

' "Is that so?" I said. "And where are you taking her to?"

' "I'm going to make a queen of her. I can do it. Who says I can't do it?"

' "Nobody, Jim," says Davidson, "nobody at all."

' "I know I can do it. Did you," turning to me, "did you say I can't do it?"

' "No," I said. "I'm sure you can do it, Motherway, provided you have the cash!"

'He looked at me, and his eyes were two red moons, inspecting me as if he doubted my sanity. Then he threw away his cigarette and he laughed, and,' cried the doctor, 'it was at that laugh that I knew what an idiot I'd been, and when I looked across at Davidson I saw that he knew too, and what is more that he had known all the time. A nurse, a male nurse, knew it, and I, the doctor, a specialist, back from Vienna, back from the Rockefeller Institute, had noticed nothing at all. Motherway got up, we all got up, and he dived his hand into his pocket and hauled out a wallet. He tore out a wad of dollar bills and flicked them under my nose: he might have had a couple of hundred dollars in all.

' "There's a thousand pounds there," he shouted. "I've ten times as much in my trunk. And ten times as much again in the Bank. I'm worth millions," he shouted. "Millions!"

'He fished in his wallet, and he clawed out a printed visiting-card.

' "Read that!" he screamed.

'By the moonlight I read it plainly. It said, *James Hugo Motherway, M.D., Ph.D., D. Litt., D.Sc., Barrister at Law, Long Island, New York.*

'I looked at the man His hat was on his poll, his grey hair was wild, his eyes were dilated and squinting. I threw the card away. He saw it swim through the air and he let out a roar. Davidson jumped on his back. The dollars fluttered about them. They crashed down the long flight of steps, rolling over and over. A knife glinted. They were both yelling. Before I could get at them Motherway had wriggled from under and he was flashing into the shrubberies and Davidson was clutching his bleeding throat. We searched and we searched for him. I had a whole posse of attendants out all night after him. But we couldn't track him – he knew the grounds too well. While they searched I sat in my room and wondered who was going to tell Lucy.

'I decided to tell her just before the dawn broke – we were certain to get him pretty soon after that. I knocked at her door just as the first bird began to sing, and the first light was touching the windows like a fog. She didn't answer. I opened the door. She was standing by the window in her dressing-gown, with her long hair in two black plaits down her back, leaning out on the sill, her face in her hands, staring over the plain. She barely looked at me over her shoulder as I came in and stood by her. Then she went on looking into the distance.

' "Doc," she said, and she was talking as if our conversation the night before had never been interrupted, "do you know that I've been thinking? I've been thinking of one Christmas morning, when I was a kid and I got up specially early to open my presents. I forget now what it was that I had been expecting, but when I opened the package I found something that wasn't at all what I'd been promised. If I was ever asked what was the most unhappy moment of my life I'd say it was that Christmas morning. But," she turned and blazed at me, "I'm not going to cry now. I thought I had a hard, strong, unbreakable man. I thought he was like iron. It never even occurred to me that there was a soft streak in him. But I don't care! I don't care! I'm going to bring out all the strength that's inside in him. The two of us, side by side, Jim and me, we'll conquer or die!"

'A bird sang just then, in the meadow below us. She saw me listening. I was certain I heard his voice, croaking feebly at some cock-eyed tune that might once have been a love-song. Another bird sang. He came out from behind the great rhododendron, dressed in his shirt and trousers, his hair wild, his eyes searching a treetop. In that instant all the birds burst into a hymn of praise and the first rays of the sun lit the sky. He looked around him, caught a glimpse of white in her window and he ran forward, with his hands outstretched.

'She turned. In the corridor she saw the two attendants waiting for me, one of them with a coil of rope. She whirled back and looked down at him. I have never in my life seen any man or woman acknowledge a fact as instantaneously as she did. I have never seen, under my eyes, as if I could touch them, a woman's supports rush bodily to defend her citadel as her courage rushed to her. Oh, she was a woman! She was a real woman! She shoved me on one side. She ran down the corridor, her pigtails flying, her gown floating, and down the big winding stairs, and through the hall. The sun on the great glass doors flashed right and left as she raced out into the grounds. By the time I got there she was leading him in by the hand, up the steps, and he was gurgling at her like a child. . . .'

A curious light had begun to add a cold gleam to the woods; a delicate, glistering light that made the trees look pale and unreal. Later, when they went out, they were astonished to find that it was the rising moon. On the river, the barge had finished its unloading. The men had tied down the tarpaulin on the hatches and were beginning to cast off. The doctor rose and stood looking out the door at the barge.

'Well, that's all. I moved on. Davidson went to an uncle in California. She remained behind. I saw her two weeks ago. She is the Matron now. She will soon be there nearly thirty years. When I shook hands with her I saw that she was still wearing her engagement ring. He stayed there. He is still there.'

'Well, Father?' the doctor turned from the door. 'Which would you say she was? Which is *her* folly? Humility or pride?'

The young woman came in from the lock carrying a newspaper. 'Would ye like to see the paper?' she asked shyly.

The doctor took it, thanking her, and glanced at the headlines; he looked again, puzzled; then he smiled and handed it back to her.

'It's yesterday's.'

'Ah,' said the girl easily, 'sure it's all wan to us.'

He paid her, and they said goodbye to her. The sinking sun dazzled them. In the distance of the canal they saw the barge drawing its arrowy wake after it, and all along the way as it receded the river-plants on either side bowed their heads deep into the water and slowly swung upwards again when the arrows had passed on. The three men unmoored their boat silently and the doctor rowed them into the calm river, where, now, the trout were leaping on all sides. The clerk lay jammed in the prow, looking back at the toy lock-house, the still pools, the humped bridge, and over them all the moon, enormously red, reflected in the water. The priest lay in the stern, his heavy chin on his chest, his eyes fixed heavily on the clerk.

'Life is a divil,' breathed the clerk.

They entered the dim lane of the canal. It was now a long soft smudge – the flowers, the water, the woods. Only the ridge of the woods caught the sun. Their deeps were warmed by the moon. The evening birds were singing like mad. As the doctor poled he let out a deep sigh of joy.

'Dear God,' he gasped. 'This is heaven! Heaven!'